10727090

A STINK IN THE TALE

A STINK IN THE TALE

Evgeny Gridneff

First published in 2014 by
Telos Moonrise: Criminal Pursuits
(An imprint of Telos Publishing)
5A Church Road, Shortlands, Bromley, Kent BR2 0HP

A Stink in the Tale © 2014 Evgeny Gridneff

ISBN: 978-1-84583-892-8

Cover Art © 2014, Bill Tidy MBE
Cover Design: David J Howe

The moral right of the author has been asserted.

British Library Cataloguing in Publication Data. A catalogue record for this book is available from the British Library.

This book is sold subject to the condition that it shall not by way of trade or otherwise, be lent, resold, hired out or otherwise circulated without the publisher's prior written consent in any form of binding or cover other than that in which it is published and without a similar condition including this condition being imposed on the subsequent purchaser.

Prologue

The whole House was in uproar. Not from outrage but from laughter. The Prime Minister had once again brought the House down.

A Government White Paper was being debated, putting forward legislation to regulate the amount of greenhouse gas emissions responsible for global warming. The Prime Minister, in his usual theatrical way, was trying to emphasise how climate change was a far greater threat to the world than international terrorism. 'Let me put it this way, that if the House, as a group, were all to pass wind at exactly the same time – at the very moment a suicide bomber entered the Chamber – he wouldn't stand a chance. He'd be blown away before he could blow us up!'

'Another example of hot air from the Prime Minister!' The Leader of the Opposition shouted.

'Let me put it another way.' The Prime Minister was enjoying this. 'A tin of baked beans consumed by each Member – provided everyone attends of course – is far more powerful than any tin of Semtex.'

The House exploded into roars of laughter, disapproval, outrage and general heckling. The Prime Minister waited a moment, then held up his arms to silence the assembled MPs. 'If the truth be known … We are more of a danger to the community than any group of terrorists!'

'There'd be less danger if the present Government stood down!' the Opposition Leader responded. There were shouts of 'Hear, hear!' from the Opposition benches.

The Prime Minister smiled, then added more seriously, 'A wind of change is certainly needed if we, as a country, are to regulate gas emissions. We need to show the rest of the world how seriously we all regard the whole question of global warming. In the long term, the real enemy is silent, yet more deadly, than any nuclear bomb …' And he continued, without any further jokes, to put forward the Government's plans for regulation.

Little was the Prime Minister aware that the very ill wind of which he had made so much fun, would indirectly cause his eventual downfall, and that of the rest of his Government.

1

The Lord of the Manor focused his high powered binoculars upon a bare, tattooed backside that bounced up and down from behind a bush. The tattoo was of a naked woman, who appeared to wriggle as the bottom moved. When the action got more frantic, with various legs, arms and a large breast appearing in sight, beads of sweat trickled onto the lenses, which in turn blurred and misted the view.

'Fuck, fuck, fuck!' Randolph cursed as he lowered the binoculars to take out his handkerchief.

By the time he had wiped and focused them once more, the sex had finished. Randolph cursed again. Had these young people no stamina? It was in, out, bang and finish. Like fast food, fast sex was becoming the norm with the young.

It was a favourite pastime of his, spying on lovers who came to spend the day on his estate, and who enjoyed the seclusion that this particular corner of the wood afforded them. The servants had aptly nicknamed it Condom Corner, as there were more discarded sheathes than any other rubbish. Since Randolph was too old and too fat to indulge, he gained immense pleasure from seeing others satisfying themselves. He didn't feel in any way guilty. They were, after all, on his property. He had a right to monitor what they got up to. He was seriously considering installing some CCTV cameras in that particular spot. Not only could he observe any action from different angles, but he'd also be able to record it for future enjoyment.

He looked around again. The couple were leaving the wood, arm in arm, bound in the direction of the fairground. Randolph moved the binoculars across the fields, hoping that he might catch sight of some other illicit activity. He did – but not what he expected.

In an open area, where two of the estate's helicopters were parked, Randolph saw a suspicious-looking figure he didn't recognise moving around one of the machines. Randolph watched the dark figure, shaven-headed with a black beard, suddenly climb up, fiddle with the lock, open the door and climb in. What was he doing? Surely he wasn't stealing it …?

Randolph dropped the binoculars and ran out of his study. Within minutes he was dashing across the front garden, out of the gate and through the wood – where he accidentally disturbed a middle-aged couple having sex. 'Disgusting, at your age!' he declared breathlessly as he continued to run as fast as he could across the field toward the helicopters.

The engine had been switched on and the overhead blades started to rotate. Randolph, puce in the face and struggling for breath, was determined to stop the helicopter. No-one was going to steal from him. 'Stop! … Stop!' It was barely audible.

He managed to get within a hundred yards – when he suddenly stopped and fell to the ground. Gasping for air, he raised his hand in a last bid to attract attention.

The dark figure in the helicopter, completely oblivious to Randolph, piloted the machine up and away into the sky.

2

The woman smiled warmly at Henry Drake as they entered the lift. She was so unbelievably attractive that he immediately felt his groin tingle. Henry gave a polite grin. 'Which floor?'

'All the way …' she smiled, looking him up and down.

He first pressed the button to the twenty-fifth floor and then the one to the nineteenth, where he was heading.

She continued to smile, looking unashamedly at him straight between the eyes. She stood with her back firmly pressed against the shiny back wall of the lift, gently rubbing her thighs as she watched him.

Henry, throughout his 32 years, had never had the courage to chat up a woman without a proper introduction first. Ever since he'd asked out a girl he'd fancied at school and she'd crushed his confidence by telling him he was an ugly, boring twat, he hadn't ventured to be so forward again.

However, today was different. He felt it in his bones. He knew it was the beginning of the rest of his life. It was his first job interview for almost a year, and he had a strong, positive feeling that he was going to be successful. Yes, for once he felt confident – and lucky. *Why not?* he thought to himself. *She can only say no.* Today he felt secure enough to accept a refusal. Although, somehow, he sensed it wasn't going to be the case. He would ask for her phone number and then invite her out for a curry or a pizza. She'd come back to his flat for a night-cap … and then …

Fourth floor … fifth … Henry forced his best macho smile and turned both his eyes on the woman. Her smile grew even wider. He was forced to put his hand in his pocket to disguise the stirring inside. The woman's eyes lowered toward his genitals while she gently moved her tongue across her top lip in the most unsubtle, yet erotic manner. He felt like he was going to burst. It was a moment that Henry had often fantasised about. *Do it now,* he thought to himself, as the lift went passed the sixth and seventh floors, *before the moment is lost, and before my courage vanishes.* Yes … now …

Just as he was about to utter the winning chat-up line – the woman farted.

Now let's not be coy. This wasn't a harmless, undistinguished little pop – that you thought you might have heard, but were not quite sure about. This was a full-blown, extremely loud, emission of wind. A very queen amongst farts.

Eighth floor … ninth … Henry didn't know where to look. What was even more unnerving was that the woman's posture and expression hadn't changed. She continued to smile at him as if nothing had happened. If anything, her eyes sparkled even more invitingly, daring Henry to say something. He stood frozen.

Tenth floor … eleventh … then the smell hit him. The odour was rich and penetrating, and it was slowly starting to engulf him.

Henry coughed and glanced at the woman. She continued to smile … twelfth floor … Henry couldn't stand it any more. He quickly pressed 13 and the lift stopped. The doors opened and he hastily darted out toward the stairs, without daring to glance back. He heard the woman say 'Bye!' as the lift doors closed.

He sniffed the sleeve of his jacket and was relieved that the smell hadn't penetrated. After looking at his watch, he took a deep, invigorating breath and started to ascend the stairs toward the nineteenth floor. He was five minutes early. He would arrive cool and confident. This was, after all, an important day. Getting this job would solve all his current problems.

Fourteenth floor. Just as Henry reached the flight to go up to the fifteenth, he heard a noise, closely followed by a scurry of feet coming up toward him.

He looked down to see three figures, all in black, heads covered in balaclavas, racing up toward him. Two were carrying guns while the third clutched a thick folder. They all carried black rucksacks on their backs and were moving like nobody's business. Henry spreadeagled himself against the wall to give them as much room as possible to pass.

The first figure pushed Henry out of the way. The second bumped into him and breathlessly murmured 'Sorry …' The third suddenly stopped, grabbed Henry, and pushed him up the steps.

'You're coming with us,' shouted a female voice.

'Oh, Delia, why?' said a second female voice.

'He'll be useful as a form of security, for one. And for another – you've just told him my name!'

'Sorry, Delia. I didn't think.'

'No, you didn't, did you? Now come on, that exit door's on the twenty-fifth. We've got two minutes!'

Before Henry could protest, he was silenced by two gun barrels pointed at his crotch.

'Don't say a word. You're coming with us. Understand?'

Henry nodded and put his hands up.

'You can put those down for a start. Now move!'

Henry never did get to his interview. Bundled between two armed women, he found himself being forced outside onto a flat roof at the top of the building, where a helicopter had just landed and was waiting to whisk them all away.

3

Richard Montcasse looked up when he heard the distinct rumble of a helicopter moving across the sky high above him. It was a noise he loved, and at that moment he wished he was actually up there, bound for pleasanter places. Anywhere would have been better than where he was right then.

Richard hated canvassing. It was the one aspect of politics that gave him nightmares. He would much rather stand up and deliver a long speech in front of thousands of people, than face the prospect of going down dull suburban streets, knocking on doors, trying to persuade Mr and Mrs Nobody to vote for him. He had nothing in common with these people and he knew it. He would have done anything to have skipped this particular chore – but realised he had to endure it if he was to get anywhere. Richard was determined to succeed as a politician. Well, it was more than that. He really wanted to be Prime Minister. He was 36, and had set himself a personal target of becoming Prime Minister by the time he was 45.

He sighed as he watched the helicopter disappear into the distance and then swore when he stepped on a dog turd. It was the second time that morning. Still, he had to think positively. Whether he had to tread in shit or champagne to achieve his ambitions, at least he was taking the first step by standing as the Liberal Democrat candidate in the local by-election. He was confident that he would win and decided to treat this canvassing as a necessary formality.

Richard was the first Montcasse to ever enter politics. Lord Randolph Montcasse, his father, strongly disapproved of his wish to become a politician. Instead he wanted his eldest son to take charge of managing Montcasse Manor, the ancestral home. It was the last thing Richard wanted to do. He felt that his younger brother, William, was quite capable of managing the family estate on his own. This had led to an argument between Richard and his father and they'd hardly spoken for months. Richard was determined to go his own way. He wasn't content just to earn a lot of money and enjoy a luxurious lifestyle – he wanted to have influence and power, and what better way than become the most important man in the country?

In society circles, Richard, who was still single, was regarded as a prize catch. It wasn't just that he was from a titled family and was heir to a fortune, or that he was classically tall, dark and handsome. All those attributes helped, but the one that beat all the others by a length was the one he kept well hidden. With their invisible nets, scores of well-born young ladies all hoped to bag him with their charms. Many had managed to debag him – but no-one had yet succeeded in dragging him down the aisle. He was too canny to be caught, and besides he hadn't yet met anyone who fitted his criteria as the ideal wife.

Richard was always a complete gentleman when it came to seducing and deflowering these young hopefuls. During any foreplay, he would always tell them that he had no intention of marrying them, and he would quite understand if they wanted him to stop and leave. However, none did. The very sight of his enormous cock always hypnotised them into joyous submission, no longer caring if he might marry them or not.

Richard anxiously knocked at the hundredth door that afternoon. Twenty had been shut in his face; six had told him to get a proper job; there had been two 'sod offs', one 'bollocks', and a gentle 'fuck off' from a wizened old lady. A dog had torn a trouser bottom, while a three year old had smeared chocolate over his jacket. Richard's smile had worn very thin by the time he came to the next house. The door quietly opened and Richard found himself staring into a pair of beautiful dark eyes.

'Hello …'

'Richard Montcasse, your local Liberal Democrat Party candidate. I wonder if I could count on your vote for next Thursday's by-election?'

'Election? What erection is this?' she said teasingly, and opened the door wider to reveal an alluring figure in a tight-fitting leotard. Nothing was left to the imagination. Richard found himself physically stirred.

'Our party is very keen to improve the local community at large. We are standing on many important and crucial issues.'

'Standing is all right, but sitting is much friendlier. Why don't you come in tell me about your party. I love parties. Comeinfuckoffee' She smiled invitingly.

Richard was suddenly feeling somewhat excited. He read the signs quite clearly. There was no subtlety to her body language. It had been such a bloody afternoon that the possibility of a sexual encounter brightened the day no end. 'I hope I'm not disturbing you … or your husband …?'

'Not married. I've just finished my yoga. Tantric. Ever tried it?'

'Don't believe I have.'

'Perhaps I'll show you a few positions – if you're interested. Come in. You do like coffee?'

'Not instant, I hope?' Richard smiled.

'Fresh, strong and wet – and it's just coming to the boil. You could convert me to being very Liberal if your issues are persuasive …' The woman turned to move down the hall. The sight of her bottom retreating so sensually finally clinched it. Just as he was about to step through the door – he heard his name being called. Richard inwardly cursed and turned around to see who wanted him. It was Guy, an associate of his, running toward him looking pale and agitated.

'Hello Guy. Where's the fire, or have you come to tell me the other candidates have stood down and I've won?'

'Richard, I'm sorry. I must have a word with you …' Guy subtly beckoned him away.

'Oh, right …' Richard could see that Guy was upset. He turned to the woman. 'I'm sorry …'

'Not as much as I am …' She smiled and closed the door.

Richard walked out of the front gate with Guy. 'So what's the problem, Guy?' he said rather testily, 'I was securing us a rather nice vote there.'

'I'm sorry, Richard, I don't know how to put this. Apparently the Estate have been trying to trace you for the last couple of hours …'

'I've had my phoned switched off.'

'Yes, I tried as well … The thing is …' Guy looked uncomfortable.

'Come on Guy, don't dawdle – spit it out.'

'Lord Montcasse … your father … is dead … I'm sorry …'

'I see …' Richard's mind raced ahead. It wasn't his father's death that concerned him so much as the consequences that followed it. 'What happened?'

'Heart attack.'

'Where?'

'On the Estate. He was found by a family who were taking a walk. That's all I know, I'm afraid.'

'Okay Guy, thank you. In the circumstances, I'd better get back.'

'Of course. What about …?'

'Just carry on as planned. You take over. There are votes to be won. Once I've sorted things out, I'll rejoin you.'

'Richard, are you quite sure?'

'We've a lot to do.'

'Shall I go back to the woman you were just talking to?'

'Are you happily married, Guy?'

'Very …' Guy smiled.

'Then you'd better give this one a miss. I'm sure she'll vote for us. You continue on from here. I'll talk to you later.' With that, Richard strode off toward his car, feeling more sexually frustrated than shocked over his father's death.

4

Stella Nightingale stood idly staring out of the kitchen window, gazing mindlessly at a helicopter that was flying across her vision. Yet her mind was elsewhere. She had had enough. She was going to give her husband, Jack, one more chance before deciding to finally leave him.

It was a possibility that she had agonised over for months. She loved him, but there were certain elements in his behaviour that she could no longer cope with. Well, one element really – his flatulence.

She continued to gaze out of the window, remembering the strange way she and Jack had met …

It happened at Euston Station four years previously. After a succession of unhappy love affairs in her home town of Ulverston, she had decided to come to London to start a new life and try to make something of herself.

As she walked across the station, pulling her suitcase, a handsome Nordic-looking young man approached her. Was she an actress? Was she interested in film work? He could certainly get her work if she was interested. If she wasn't an actress then she should be. He explained that he was a talent scout for a famous film producer who was casting his new film. She had the look they were after. Stella was completely taken in. The young man was clean, smelt fresh and wore expensive, fashionable clothes. *Could this be fate?*, she wondered.

She was about to throw all caution to the wind and take up his offer of a screen test when two grubby-looking men approached them and got hold of the young man by the arms. He started to struggle, but they overpowered him.

One of those men was Jack Nightingale. He was unshaven, wearing dirty jeans, trainers, T-shirt and an old leather bomber jacket. His hair was long and greasy and his fingernails were filthy, while his teeth looked like they hadn't been cleaned for years. He also smelt of sweat. His whole image repelled Stella.

What were these hooligans doing to this nice young man? She threatened to call the police if they didn't let him go. Jack explained, with a voice that didn't fit his appearance, that they *were* the police – from the vice squad – and that this man was under arrest. He pulled out his identity card to prove to her that he was genuine. It transpired that the man was part of a large, highly efficient network of professional filmmakers specialising in producing hard porn for the internet market.

Stella, feeling a little foolish, wanted to make her own way to Clapham, where she would initially be staying with her aunt and uncle, but Jack insisted on taking her there in a squad car before she got into any further trouble. His gentle, smiling voice reassured her, and she found herself observing him in a different light. On the way, she asked to open the car window to let in some air, under the pretence of feeling a bit car sick, but it was really because Jack's body odour was a bit overpowering for her delicate nose.

A few days later, Stella answered the door to a very decent and pleasant-looking man. It wasn't until he spoke that she recognised Jack. He appeared transformed. He was smartly dressed, had short hair, was clean-shaven and had manicured nails. His teeth were perfectly white when he smiled at her. She could detect some nice aftershave. Stood rather shyly at the door, he simply wondered if she was settling in, and would she like to go out for a drink with a respectable policeman?

At the local pub he explained that he had been working undercover for several months in an attempt to catch those villains in the act. They talked and laughed, and before another week had passed – they were both 'undercover' in Jack's little flat in Putney.

It was the beginning of a wonderful relationship. Throughout the ensuing courtship, never once did Stella suspect that Jack had a real personal problem. How he managed to suppress it is one of the miracles of love.

Stella moved away from the window and made her way to the lounge. The very act of plonking herself down on the settee brought back her feelings of disgust toward Jack. As she sat, the bottom cushion gave off a whiff of stale, ingrained farts. However many times she washed the covers, the smell never totally disappeared.

She looked at the mantelpiece where their wedding photo stood. It was during their honeymoon on the island of Sark that Jack had finally let himself go, so to speak.

'Stella, love. There's something I've got to tell you. I can't hold it back any longer. I've got this little personal problem …'

At the time, Stella had been too much in love to worry about it. She had been sure it could be dealt with and would blow away in time.

But it hadn't. If anything it seemed to have got worse. Apart from that, she also had to prompt and bully him about having regular baths and showers. If it was up to him, he'd only bother about having a bath once a week. He thought all this personal cleanliness was overrated and unnecessary. But because he loved Stella he tried to make the effort.

Stella looked away from the wedding photo. She would give him one more chance. It wasn't just the flatulence – there was something more important on her mind. Today happened to be their third wedding anniversary. As a surprise, Stella had organised a special romantic supper for two at their favourite restaurant in Barnes. They were going to have the works – champagne, lobster, followed by Jack's favourite dessert, chocolate fudge cake and ice cream. After they had wined and dined, a limousine would pick them up and take them to a little houseboat moored by Kew Bridge, which she had rented. There they would spend the night in each other's arms, making love as the water rippled beneath them. Stella had planned it all to the very last detail. She was determined that it was to be a night Jack would never forget.

5

Henry sat crouched in the corner of the helicopter. It was so uncomfortable that he was beginning to feel the onset of cramp. His initial protestations, as he had been forced into the waiting machine, had been met with a series of rather ugly threats, which, as they had taken off, had ended with – 'One more word and we'll throw you out!' They sounded as if they meant it.

What the hell was he doing here? Stuck in a helicopter, flying god knows where, hemmed in by three determined women, two of them brandishing guns. The pilot, of middle eastern appearance, wore dark aviator sunglasses and hardly said anything. He just nodded and made various guttural noises in reply to the women's orders, which were short and to the point. They weren't giving much away.

Henry knew his life was in danger, but that wasn't what was really worrying him at that moment. He was dying for a pee. He couldn't summon up the courage to ask, because he knew what the answer would be. Anyway, where could he have gone? There wasn't a toilet on board, and there was nothing that he could see that could possibly be used as a receptacle. He imagined they would force him to stand by a half open door to enable him to relieve himself. He could just see all the women laughing at him as he tried to negotiate the air currents in order not to splash himself.

No, he would do his best to control himself – he had to – despite the vibration in the helicopter, which wasn't helping his bladder. He was wearing his best suit and couldn't afford to disgrace himself. He decided to just sit there and hope the journey didn't last long.

So Henry just shut his eyes and tried to concentrate his mind on the events leading up to his present predicament ...

He had felt so optimistic when he had got up that morning. Instead of just hiding under the duvet hoping the day would go away, he had leapt out of bed and got ready without going about his usual self-indulgent rituals.

He didn't spend ages in front of the bathroom mirror squeezing his blackheads and applying the Clearasil to the inflamed areas. He didn't linger in the bathtub trying to soak his problems away, and then go and gaze at his reflected body in the wardrobe mirror – wishing he had been born handsomer, taller and with dark, curly hair. He did none of these things that morning.

Instead of the usual 90 minutes it took him to feel confident enough to face the world, he was ready and dressed in less than half an hour. He was very pleased with himself. He had made an effort and had proved he was capable of managing his own life. This was only the beginning.

It was an important day. He was to attend the final of three interviews. In his heart he knew that he had been successful and that that day's interview was just a formality. He was going to wave goodbye to his unsettling past and say hello to a safer, more regulated future. He was going to become a respected member of Her Majesty's Civil Service. This was his dream. But it hadn't always been that way ...

After leaving school with a decent number of A levels, Henry started as a junior with a reputable firm of stockbrokers. Within five years he had distinguished himself and made several successful killings on the Stock Market – which helped him to buy his flat in South Kensington, a second-hand Porsche and a few designer suits. Henry might have looked like a simpleton, but he had the brains of a sharp operator. The world was his for the taking. What could go wrong? Quite a lot.

Henry began to think he had the golden touch. He got complacent. He made one mistake, then two. His bosses gave him a gentle warning. Mistakes lost money. He listened, and trusted to an instinct that had already abandoned him. As a result of several further miscalculations and bad assessments, one of their most valued clients went bankrupt. Henry was well and truly out. Not only had he lost a prestigious position with one of the City's top brokers – but they made sure no-one else made the error of employing him.

He was crestfallen at first, but then managed to pick himself up and go into the property business. He became an independent estate agent. He entered at the boom, and from then on it was downhill all the way. Within six months he was out of business.

Henry flirted with a succession of different careers but nothing seemed to go right. Either he found he hated what he was doing or he was politely given the push. It wasn't a good time for him. Nobody wanted him. He just couldn't do anything right or impress anyone. No-one saw beyond his gormless look and gauche manner. If he'd been born handsome, with less talent, things might have worked out differently. But they hadn't. He made an effort to get back into the world of stocks and shares, but learnt rather quickly that he had been well and truly blacklisted.

First the Porsche went. Then the designer suits wore out. Finally he was forced to sell his flat and rent a smaller one in West Ealing. He was broke and disheartened. He had been out of work for 18 months. His confidence and self-esteem were at their lowest ebb. Henry had no-one to turn to, no family to speak of. His mother had brought him up single-handedly and always refused to discuss anything regarding his father. All he knew was that he had been conceived after a brief affair and that his mother had decided to have nothing more to do with her lover. When she had sadly died of cancer, Henry had hoped he might learn his father's identity from her personal papers – but there was nothing. He was all alone in the world, and realised he had to make the best possible job of it.

There seemed no hope, until he saw a Civil Service ad in the *Guardian*, seeking applicants for their Management Re-Training Scheme. It was the very opportunity that he was looking for.

He got through the written exam and subsequent interview with flying colours. It was a piece of cake to Henry. The scheme was aimed at 30- to 40-year-olds who had reached a certain position in their career, but had either been made redundant or wanted a change of direction. Successful candidates would be put through an intensive six month training course, where all their abilities, strengths and weaknesses would be duly assessed. Once they had successfully completed the course, they would be permanently transferred to a department that most suited their talents. The only stipulation was that they would be contractually bound to spend at least five years in the department to which they had been assigned.

Henry could think of nothing else to do with his life, and considered that this was as good an alternative as any. It was safe. He would get a decent pension when he retired, and he probably wouldn't have to work too hard either. In other words, Henry, at 32, was giving in and taking the easy way out. The fight and ambition that he once had, to make something of himself, had been knocked out of him. He was going to conform and become an even more boring and grey individual. He didn't care anymore.

That's why Henry was feeling so good that afternoon. He had no doubts that he would be successful at that last interview. There would be no more struggles trying to find work. He would have money in the bank and be able to settle his debts. Perhaps he would meet a nice secretary who would marry him, and who wouldn't mind that he was a useless lover. He'd never had any success with women, even when he was doing well.

It was all beginning to happen for him again. There was even a faint detection of a spring in his step as he entered the high-rise Government building in Whitehall, and made his way to the lifts.

If that bloody woman hadn't farted when she did – Henry's life would have taken a completely different course …

A sudden jolt from the helicopter nearly made Henry wet his pants. By now he was really in agony trying to control a bladder that was fit to burst. The cramp had got worse, but that was the least of his worries. He knew that he wasn't going to be able to hold on much longer. He was almost wishing that they would throw him out. It seemed preferable to what he was going through now. He closed his eyes again and clasped his sweaty hands.

6

It was an hour's drive to the Montcasse Manor Estate in Hampshire. Richard drove his Range Rover Sport down the motorway at a steady 70. He usually did at least 90 and took great pleasure in flashing slower drivers in the fast lane, forcing them to move over so that he could pass. He'd already been fined twice for speeding, and lately realised he'd better start behaving himself if he was to be in the public eye as an MP. But did it matter now? Would he even get that far? His father's death changed everything.

He knew his mother, Lady Gertrude Montcasse, wouldn't be too upset. His parents' relationship, after 40 years of marriage, wasn't unhappy, just simply indifferent. It's not that they had grown apart – they had never been really close to start with. Their union had been socially convenient. She would undoubtedly miss him for the first few months, then probably forget all about him.

What did he personally feel about his father's death? He had a grudging respect for the old man, yet he couldn't honestly say that he loved him. There would be an element of regret, but no tears. The main thing that concerned Richard was the bloody timing of it all. His father could have at least waited until *after* the by-election before dying. By then he would have known whether he had a political career ahead of him or not. Now he was not so sure.

Inheriting his father's estate – and thus becoming responsible for running it – would make Richard's political career a non-starter. The thought of having to look after the Manor, the boating lake and the noisy fairground filled him with horror. Of course he could sell the estate – but Richard wouldn't do that. A strong sense of family duty wouldn't allow him even to consider it seriously. It had been in the family for 230 years. He knew he couldn't rely on his two brothers to shoulder any of the responsibility. William was capable but lazy, and much preferred having a good time than working. The youngest, Tom, was incapable of doing anything with any degree of proficiency. Well, it was more than that – Tom was stupid and a bit simpleminded. Many had commented on how completely different the Montcasse brothers were from each other. Richard had nothing at all in common with either Tom or William, and the thought of having to deal with them now depressed him.

His mother and two brothers were already in the spacious drawing room when Richard arrived.

There were no tears, just gloomy faces. Richard kissed his mother and touched both his brothers in affection.

'I'm sorry it took me so long to get here.'

Gertrude was nonchalant. 'That's all right. It was fortunate that William was around. It's your father's own bloody fault! The doctor had warned him, in no uncertain terms, that he should not exert himself. And what does he do, the silly old sod …?'

'What actually happened? I wasn't given any details.'

'From what we can gather,' William stood up, 'Father was seen running out of the house in a state of agitation.'

'Do we know why?'

'Richard,' Gertrude interspersed, 'we all know that your father got agitated at the best of times for the silliest of reasons. It's surprising he didn't have a heart attack years ago!'

'William, you said he was running?'

'That's what the gardener told me. Father went through the wood and disappeared. That's all we really know.'

'So where exactly was he found?'

'Not far from the helicopter pad. We don't know what he was doing there. The odd thing is, one of the choppers is missing. I only noticed it after the ambulance had taken father away. They weren't scheduled to be used today, so there was no-one about. We thought you might have taken one to London.'

'So it hasn't been reported missing?'

'No. We were waiting for you.'

'All right. Will, first find out if the pilots know anything.'

'It's their day off.' William didn't want to exert himself.

'Phone them. If they haven't got an explanation – then get on to the police with all the details.'

'Anything I can do?' Tom didn't want to be left out. 'D'you want me to dig a grave to bury father?'

'That won't be necessary, Tom, thank you. Why don't you go for a little walk?' Richard was doing his best to be tolerant.

'Can I go up in one of the helicopters?' Tom brightened.

'Not today. Please Tom, if you're going to stay, try not to interrupt. Now Will, did you talk to the doctor after father was found?'

'His brief examination revealed classic symptoms of a major heart attack. There'll have to be a post-mortem of course. Do you think it has anything to do with the missing chopper then?'

'I don't know. I'd better go and inform the staff. As a mark of respect, the estate should be closed to the public until after the funeral.'

'Darling,' Gertrude put her hand on Richard's, 'don't you think a day's grace would be sufficient?'

'What do you mean, Mother?' Richard knew she was trying to get round him.

'Randolph wouldn't have wanted any unnecessary fuss to be made. We could close tomorrow and open the day after. That would be much more sensible, don't you agree? The funeral might not be until next week.'

'I think Mother's right, Rich. If one of us died, father wouldn't have wanted to disappoint all our visitors for longer than necessary. People come from all over the country to visit Montcasse Manor. It is our busy period.' William took his mother's side.

'Life must go on. The carousel must keep turning – not forgetting the other rides!'

added Tom.

'Shut up Tom. Show some respect.' Gertrude didn't want to appear too inconsiderate.

'Sorry, Mother …'

'How much do we lose for every day that we remain closed?' Richard put on his business hat.

'Not less than ten thousand, usually much more.' Gertrude knew the figures by heart.

Richard paced the room. They watched him as he looked out of the window. 'Right. Any objections if we open tomorrow morning and close for the afternoon?'

'That sounds appropriate.' Gertrude smiled. 'Boys?'

'Father would have approved.' agreed William.

'The staff will be disappointed at getting only a half day off,' declared Tom.

'Shut up Tom!' Gertrude and William added in unison .

'Agreed then. I'll put that in motion.' Richard kissed his mother and left the room. If nothing else, Richard was practical at the worst of times.

7

Henry crouched in the corner in complete agony. He wanted to die.

'What's the matter with you?' One of the women looked at Henry through the slits in her balaclava.

'Sorry … I … I've got to …' The pain was unbearable.

'Got to what? Come on!'

'I must get to a toilet …'

'Oh god! Did you hear that? Pilot, would you please land this heap by the nearest public conveniences.'

'Eh?' The pilot was suddenly confused.

'Delia, are you serious?' one of the other women asked.

'What do you think? What does he expect us to do?' She turned to Henry. 'Number ones or twos?'

'What …?'

'Can you only understand plain language! Piss or shit?'

'Pee …' Henry found it difficult to say the word.

'Well I'm afraid you're going to have to hang on,' Delia coldly responded.

'I can't …!' Henry was really desperate and no longer embarrassed at holding himself between the legs in an effort to ease the strain.

'He's in agony. Can't we do something …?' Said the third female, who up until then hadn't said much.

Delia quickly looked around the helicopter. Then she had a thought. She bent down to Henry. 'Have you got a condom?'

'What?' Henry looked blank.

'A condom. French letter. Rubber sheath?'

'I don't usually …' Henry was getting confused.

'That's typical of you men.' Delia stood up. 'You expect us to be on the pill or to be conveniently fitted with a cap – as long as it doesn't detract from your pleasure.'

'I'm sorry … but …' Henry was about to explain that he wasn't in the habit of carrying them, and anyway, it was a pee he wanted, not sex – when the pilot interrupted

'You want a rubber johnny?'

'Have you got one?' Delia turned to face him. He smiled.

'Plain or ribbed?' He undid the button on his shirt pocket.

'You mean I have a choice?' She stared at him.

'I usually have different colours, sometimes different flavours.'

'Flavours …?' one of the women questioned.

'Yeah, chocolate, passion fruit, banana … whatever turns you on.' The pilot licked his lips suggestively.

'What's the point …?' she asked innocently.

'Suck it and see, lady,' he laughed

'You men are all the same,' Delia pointed accusingly at the pilot, 'you only care for what's in it for you!'

'As long as it's in you, what d'you care?' he quickly replied, pleased at his own wit.

'Don't you dare be rude to me!' Delia was angry.

'Listen, lady,' the pilot pointed at her now, 'you want a condom or not? Just spare me the shit, eh.'

'Don't you dare —' Delia was about to put the pilot in his place, when one of the other women interrupted.

'Not now, Delia, please. Look, he's in agony. Just give it to him.'

Without another word, Delia held out her hand while the pilot threw her a condom. She handed it to Henry. For a moment he wasn't quite sure what she meant, but then it all suddenly fell into place. He looked up. All three women were staring at him. The pilot was smirking behind his glasses. Henry tore the top off the packet. They continued to watch him.

'Please …' However much he was bursting to go, he drew the line at a floorshow. 'Turn round girls. We're embarrassing him!' They all laughed and gave him the privacy of their backs.

Henry first blew into the condom like a balloon before slipping it onto the end of his penis. He almost wet himself trying to fit it on. The relief that Henry finally experienced was rapturous. What really surprised him was the incredible volume of fluid that the condom was able to hold. He honestly believed it was going to burst, yet it remained intact after he had finished.

'Excuse me. What shall I …?'

'Tie a knot in it and throw it out.' Delia was certainly not squeamish.

Gently, and careful not to spill any, he did as he was told. The pilot then pressed a button for the hatch to open and let Henry eject the bulging, wobbly sheath, as discreetly as possible, out into the sky.

Below on the ground, some moments later, the sheath landed and exploded, splashing its yellow contents on a couple of very surprised hooded youths who were about to rob an Indian newsagent's. They never got that far. The term *golden shower* came into its own.

'Feel better now?' The third female addressed him. There was a gentle concern in her voice, which was a complete contrast to Delia's harsh tones.

'Thank you … Yes.' Henry managed a smile.

'We'll be there in five minutes.' The pilot glanced toward Delia. He was certainly looking forward to getting paid and rid of them all.

'We need something for a blindfold.' Delia looked at the other two.

'What for?'

'For him, of course.'

'Aren't we just going to dump him when we land?'

'We still need him as a security measure. We're not safe yet. Nowhere near it. He mustn't know where we are or where we're going to take him.'

'I promise, I won't say anything.' Henry was trying to be helpful.

'You shut up. Right, anyone got anything?'

'Will this do?' The softly spoken one produced a silk scarf out of her rucksack.

'Blindfold him. Make sure he can't see out of the corners.'

Taking her cue from Delia, she crossed over to Henry, leant down and, as gently as she could, tied the scarf around his eyes. Henry could feel the warmth of her soft skin against his, and could smell her strong, captivating perfume.

'That's not hurting you too much, is it?'

'No. Thank you. I'm Henry. What's your name?' Henry was intrigued.

'Serena …'

'That's pretty.'

'Thanks.' Serena smiled and caught herself blushing beneath her balaclava.

'Well done you!' Delia blurted out. 'Now he knows both our names!' She turned toward the other woman and shouted at her: 'Why don't you tell him yours as well!'

'It's Melissa, actually. All right Delia? Now stop being so bloody neurotic. He might know our first names, but that's all he does know. By the time we get this business sorted out, there'll be nothing to connect us – and by then we'll all be far away. Don't forget, we're all in this together.'

'We can't afford to make any more mistakes, that's all.' Delia wasn't going to let Melissa start taking charge of something that had been her original idea and had taken her months to plan and organise.

8

This anniversary surprise meant a lot to Stella. She had planned it for months. She had even made sure that Jack put in for official leave for three days. Expecting a simple little supper at home to celebrate, he had no idea of the delights that she had conjured up to excite his every sense. Ever since they had spent a precious weekend on a friend's boat, and made love as never before, Stella had wanted to repeat the experience. The movement of water beneath them had seemed to do something to heighten Jack's responses. He had never performed better or for so long.

Oh yes, she had thought of everything. It was going to be the perfect night to conceive their first child.

Their marriage up to then had been fairly happy in spite of Jack's little affliction. Stella, as a freelance, worked mostly as the personal assistant to a very successful independent television producer specialising in current affairs. The producer had already won a couple of prestigious awards and had built up a good reputation in the industry. She was one of his best PAs. She loved the job, which brought her into contact with many well-known personalities. Because she was attractive and friendly, she was always being propositioned by someone or other, yet had managed to remain faithful to Jack.

Jack, in the meantime, had been transferred from the Vice Squad to the Counter-Terrorism Division. He preferred the challenges and excitement of being in this unit to dealing with pimps, prostitutes and numerous perverse individuals. He'd been constantly amazed, shocked and often disgusted at what people got up to, to satisfy their sexual cravings. He was glad to be out of it.

The main problem that his move had brought about was that Jack was away from home more than in the past. It was a bone of contention between them. With the rise of terrorist activities, Jack was spending more time on so-called secret missions than he was with Stella. This often included the weekends and bank holidays. Jack tried to reassure her that it wouldn't be for long. He was earning good money. It was likely that he would soon get promotion and be able to transfer again to something with more sociable hours. It was one of the pitfalls of having a career in the police force. Although Stella accepted this in theory, she couldn't help but worry about what he was doing and how dangerous it was likely to be. She never knew where he was or when she was likely to see him next. Sometimes it would be days before he was able to call her and let her know if he was coming home.

At least he had been home the night before. He had left early that morning to finish some paperwork at his office and had promised to be back by mid afternoon. He hadn't even left a card or a present. Stella wasn't too upset. This was typical of

Jack, but he usually made up for it. Anyway, within a few hours he'd be home again.

Stella had one last job to do to prepare for the evening. She opened a drawer in his bedside table and took out his supply of condoms. She then proceeded to make small, undetectable pinholes in each and every one of them.

'Oh shit!' Jack was at his desk, just finishing filling in his expenses. He suddenly remembered that he'd forgotten to buy Billy Hughes a leaving present. It was Billy's last day with the Counter-Terrorism Unit, and the gang were having a lunchtime drink as a send-off.

Jack looked at his watch – 10.45 – just enough time to dash down to the shops and get something. What's more, he'd kill two birds with one stone – he'd also get Stella a card and little anniversary something while he was at it. However, his main priority was to get Billy a fitting leaving token. After all, Billy had saved Jack's life during a recent skirmish with some armed dissidents. Jack never forgot his real friends.

If he was honest with himself, Jack wasn't looking forward to his break. He'd have preferred to carry on working and be with his mates. But Stella had nagged him so much that he had eventually promised to take leave during their anniversary. Jack had never been a man of many words. In his own way he did love Stella, but sometimes he found it a strain if they spent too much time together. He knew Stella was desperate to have a baby. Although he eventually wanted children, he wasn't quite ready to be a father yet. He was afraid it would tie him down too much and wasn't prepared to sacrifice the little freedom he had.

Jack spent an hour choosing the right present for Billy – an engraved silver cigarette lighter – and all of five minutes grabbing a card and a bottle of perfume for Stella. He'd quite forgotten that he had given her the same perfume at Christmas and for her last birthday, and he'd also forgotten that she'd gone off that particular perfume. He'd never been that imaginative in the present stakes. As he returned to the office, he made a mental note to buy her a dozen roses. Stella would like that.

'These two tramps were walking along the road when they came to a big pile of what looked like dog shit. It was a bit orange and still steaming. They bent down and studied it, and one of them said, "It looks like it …" The other then declared, "It smells like it …" The first one then said, "Umm, it tastes like it …" Both tramps then stepped over it and said, "Lucky we didn't tread in it!"'

The whole corner broke up into ribald laughter. There were six of them, including Jack and Billy, who had told the joke. They'd all been in the pub for nearly three hours. The table was littered with glasses and empty crisp packets. A lot had been drunk and the atmosphere was pretty rowdy.

Roy, who was big, black and fearsome-looking, stood up and held his large, thick hands up for everyone to be quiet. 'Lads and lads. This is a very sad occasion for us all. No fancy speech would do justice to how we all feel about Billy …'

'Hear, hear!' Jack chorused.

Roy continued, '… losing Billy, will be like losing an arm or a leg —'

'Or a cock!' someone else bellowed.

'Indeed. We've all gone through danger and shite together. It will never be the same again. Yes, there'll be the danger – but now the shite will be missing! Good luck, Billy …' Roy sat down, moved by his own eloquence.

'Speech, speech!' a couple banged their glasses.

'I'm no bloody good at giving sodding speeches! You know that you berks!' Billy, who was genuinely touched, felt uncomfortable with words. He'd always been an action man. 'You've been a great bunch to work with. Thanks … My shout, I think.' Billy left the table and made his way to the bar to avoid further embarrassment, and not let them see the tears that had welled up in his eyes.

Jack looked at his watch. It was nearly four. Roy saw the concerned look on his face. 'What's the hurry, Jack? You're on leave, aren't ya?'

'Yeah … promised the wife. You know how it is.'

'She'll have you all to herself for the next few days. Is an extra hour or two going to make any difference?'

'Suppose not …' Jack was weakening.

'Anyway,' Roy continued, 'we all owe a lot to Billy. He deserves the best send off we can give him.'

'I wouldn't be here if it wasn't for him …' Jack remembered.

'There ya go. Your missus has never saved your life now, has she?'

'No …' Jack took the pint that Billy offered, and his concern about the time vanished as he downed it in one go.

9

'Hold tight, we're going down.' The helicopter pilot was in control now.

The pre-arranged landing field was below. There were no buildings within a mile of the site, so it was an ideal place to land without creating any undue local interest. The coast looked clear. Delia could see nothing that was suspicious or out of the ordinary, apart from a car hidden in a corner of the field.

The helicopter pitched down as close as it could to the car. The blades were still rotating as Delia jumped out and ran toward the vehicle. The car door opened easily. The others could see Delia scrambling about inside looking for something. After a minute she came running back and shouted something to the pilot, which he couldn't hear because of the noise of the blades. Delia gestured for him to switch off the engine.

'What's the matter now?' he said with more than a touch of irritation in his voice.

'What kind of a car you call that! It's a bloody wreck! Anyway, where the hell are the car keys!' Delia was starting to panic.

'Listen lady. I don't know what you've done, and I don't want to know. Just give me what you owe me – and I'll fly away into the sunset.'

'You won't see a penny until I get this bloody car started.'

'The longer this 'copter remains here, the more chance you all have of being seen.'

'Your partner arranged this car for us. He should have been here to give us the keys.'

'I told you before, it's his mother's birthday today. It would have broken her old heart not to see him.'

'I'm very touched, but that doesn't solve the problem.'

'Did you look behind the vanity mirror?

'What?' Delia looked confused.

'Inside the car. The sun shield. Have you never hired a car before? That's where they usually tell you to leave the keys.' The pilot hated working for amateurs. It was more trouble than it was worth.

'I'll look.' Melissa, who was out of the helicopter by now, crossed to the car, opened the passenger door and folded down the sun shield. The keys fell out. Melissa waved them like an excited schoolgirl.

'All right now? My part of the contract has been fulfilled. Can I have my money?'

'Okay … Serena, help our friend get out. Make sure we haven't left anything.'

Serena gently took Henry's hand and guided him out onto firm ground. The pilot stood with his hand outstretched.

'What are you going to do with the helicopter?' Delia took a thick brown envelope out of her rucksack.

'Go about a hundred miles west, then dump it.'

'Good. That's for your services. And that's to keep your mouth shut.'

The pilot quickly flicked through the notes. It was more than he'd expected. He smiled for the first time. His partner wasn't going to get a share of the bonus. 'Any time lady. Any time.' He flipped open his top pocket, took out a condom, and pressed it into Delia's hand.

'What's this for?'

'For luck. Or in case he wants to go again during the journey.'

Before she could reply, the pilot had got back into the helicopter, started it up and taken off.

'Right, let's get these awful things off.' Delia threw the condom onto the grass and they all discarded their balaclavas and put them in their rucksacks. Henry stood silently, still wearing the blindfold. He was sure he had stepped in some cow shit.

'Melissa, search our friend here and see if he has a phone or any sharp instruments on him. And we need to switch all our mobiles off and take the sim cards out.'

'Why ...' Melissa was confused; she wasn't good with technology.

'So they can't trace us!' Delia gave her a dirty look. She then took out three identical mobiles from out of her rucksack, and gave one each to Serena and Melissa. 'We will use these from now on – but only as a contact between each other. I've put in our new numbers. For emergencies only!'

'Have they got any games on them? Angry Birds?' Melissa often spent hours playing games on her phone.

'The only angry bird will be me if you don't do as I ask, Melissa. Now please search him.'

Henry then felt a pair of thick hands almost abusing him as Melissa, very unsubtly, searched his pockets and around the crevices of his body. He could feel the warmth of her excited breath. 'One phone, a biro and a metal comb!' Melissa declared.

'Give them to me, I'll dispose of these later.' Delia took the battery and sim card out of Henry's phone and put it in her rucksack. Henry was about to say something ... 'I don't want to hear another word out of you, my friend, or you'll find yourself without any clothes, tied to a tree in the middle of a wood. Understand?'

Henry nodded, wondering what the hell was going on.

'Bloody cheapskates!' Delia brought the car to a halt in a country lane after they had gone only a few miles. She hit the steering wheel in anger.

'What is the matter now?' Melissa was getting fed up with Delia's outbursts.

'Petrol. It wasn't filled up. We're almost empty!'

'Do you think this car's stolen?'

'Of course it's stolen, Melissa. You don't think that they would have hired it especially for us, do you? Mind you, who'd want to steal this old heap? Look, the sooner we get to the house the better. Then I can get rid of it.'

'How far is the house?'

'About 50 miles.'

'Do we have enough petrol to get us there?'

'I shouldn't think so.'

'Can I ask a stupid question?'

'What is it Melissa?'

'Why didn't the helicopter take us right to the house?'

'Because – if you had been listening when we were planning this little escapade – we might just as well have hired the Royal Philharmonic to announce our arrival!'

'Of course … sorry.' Melissa could be dim sometimes.

'Can I suggest something?' Serena piped up from the back. 'Why don't we stop at a petrol station and fill up? Surely that would solve the problem? According to the map we're near a small town.'

'The whole point was that I didn't want any attention drawn to us. Not while we're all dressed like this.' She indicated their black combat gear. 'And especially now that we have a guest. The less we're seen, the more chance we have of remaining undetected.'

'But it appears we have no choice …' Serena sighed.

'No … Look, I'll get changed and stop to get petrol.' Delia opened her rucksack.

'We needn't get out of the car,' replied Serena, who didn't want to get changed in these primitive surroundings. She sat in the back with Henry, who hadn't been allowed to remove his blindfold. Henry was keeping quiet. Every time he said something he got a mouthful of abuse from Delia. He was totally worn out by all the excitement. At that moment he was more than happy just sitting next to Serena. She felt nice whenever he accidentally touched her. He knew she had a gun but had doubts as to whether or not she would use it if he tried to make a bolt for it. Yet escape was the last thing on his mind. He was too tired. He just wanted to sleep.

After quickly changing into a dress, Delia switched the engine on again and drove off. Within five minutes, Henry was asleep, his head resting on Serena's soft breast. She hadn't the heart to move him.

'Wake up. Come on!' Delia was leaning over, shaking Henry's knee.

'What … what …?' He had been dreaming. Three naked women, all wearing balaclavas, were doing wonderful things to him. Unfortunately the dream had given him an erection.

'We're going to stop at a petrol station in a minute. We will take off your blindfold while I'm filling up. If you make one move or draw any attention to us – Serena will shoot your balls off. Understood?'

'Yes …' Henry was in no mood for heroics.

'Serena, place the gun in his pocket.'

'Delia?'

'Do as I say. Keep your finger on the trigger. If he does something silly – shoot. If you're unhappy about that, Melissa will change places with you.'

'I promise, I won't do anything,' Henry pleaded. The thought of Melissa with her hand in his pocket terrified him.

'Serena?'

Serena took the gun and as gently as possible did her best to place it in Henry's right pocket. It seemed a tight fit, until she realised that Henry was having problems with his own shooter.

'Does that hurt?' She was too shy to say more.

'No ... just a bit to the left ...' He was actually embarrassed.

'Come on, we're wasting time!' With that Delia roughly grabbed the blindfold and prised it off. For the first time Henry saw what they all looked like.

As Delia drove into the filling station, Henry studied the faces that belonged to the voices he had been listening to. They weren't as he had imagined. Delia was a classic beauty with fine chiselled features. Her wide eyes and generous mouth didn't go with the aggressiveness. Melissa was plumper than he had visualised. She had a warm, open, matronly face. Henry turned his head to look at Serena. She had a plain, thin countenance with sharp, expressive eyes. She possessed an ethereal quality, which nonetheless was attractive. Henry was not disappointed by Serena. Far from it. He didn't know what these women had done, or were going to do – but he suddenly got it into his head that he would like to marry Serena – despite the wedding ring on her finger.

The blindfold had been replaced as soon as they had left the petrol station. Delia was adamant that Henry should not know where they were, or where they were going. He had tried surreptitiously to discover the name of the small town where they had stopped, but there had been no signs to give him any clue. It was beginning to get dark, and for the rest of the journey nobody spoke. Henry tried to sleep again, but found that his mind had woken up. As well as the events of the whole day going around in his head, he could not stop thinking about Serena.

He heard the car turn off a main road and go along a long, bumpy track. Then it turned into a gravel drive and stopped.

'Stay in the car while I go and get the keys. I hope they have left them where they said or we're in real trouble. Keep that gun pointed at him. We can't afford to lose our friend now. The blindfold comes off when we get inside.' Delia got out of the car and walked out to the house.

Henry shifted in his seat to get more comfortable. The sudden movement forced Serena to stick the barrel of the gun into Henry's ribs.

'Hey! Steady on. I'm not going anywhere.'

'That's perfectly correct. Just making sure.' Serena kept the gun against his chest.

Henry was confused. He thought Serena was on his side. What was going on? This sweet, tender vision of loveliness had become suddenly assertive. Wasn't she aware of his feelings for her? Obviously not.

'All right Serena?' Melissa turned around in her seat.

'Yes, he won't give us any trouble.'

Delia returned after five minutes. 'Okay. Got the keys. We can go in now.'

They all got out of the car. Since the house was not overlooked by any other building, Henry was led down a path and through a door. Then he had to climb some stairs ... and more stairs ... and even more stairs. Round and round. It seemed never ending. Where were they? He stopped briefly to rest, but a sharp poke in the back soon got him going again.

Henry was pushed through a door that was then closed behind him. He heard footsteps retreat down the stairs. Realising he was alone, he carefully took off his blindfold and looked around him. He was in a small attic room with a sloped ceiling. There was a single bed, a chest of drawers and a narrow wardrobe. The one window was only a foot square. To swing a cat in there would be to subject it to instant death.

Henry stretched out his arms, bruising his knuckles in the process. He pulled back the bed cover. At least the sheets were fresh and clean. He then tried the door – it was locked. If he bashed hard enough he was sure he could get it open. He might try that later, but now he was too tired. Everything was quiet. He looked out of the window, but all he could see were a few odd lights scattered about below him. They were obviously in a village not a town.

He sighed and lay on the bed, trying to relax. He no longer felt terrified. For the first time he suddenly realised how hungry and thirsty he was.

'Don't blame me, Melissa! I made a point of asking the lettings company to provide some basic provisions before we arrived.' Delia watched Melissa opening and closing every kitchen cupboard in frustration.

'There's tea, coffee, sugar, milk and a loaf of bread. Some bacon, oh, and half a dozen eggs ... Sorry, five – one's broken. It's more than enough,' said Serena, who never bothered about food at the best of times.

'That might be all right for a piddling breakfast – but what are we going to eat now? I'm ravenous!' Even at the worst of times Melissa couldn't forget her stomach.

'It'll just have to do, won't it.' Delia was too tired to argue.

'What about that chap upstairs – what's his name?'

'Henry,' Serena added.

'Well I'm sure Henry could do with a bite to eat.'

'Sod him. He can go without. We're not here to play nursemaids to some stupid idiot.'

'It's not his fault, Delia. He didn't ask to be dragged all the way here.'

'He shouldn't have got in the way, should he, Serena? Anyway, we can use him in any negotiations. Henry is our insurance. We're in a far better position now.'

'Be that as it may, it doesn't negate the fact that we need some substantial food right now.'

'You mean *you* need food, Melissa. If you're that desperate then go out and get some!' Delia called her bluff, knowing it was an impossible task at this time of night in such a remote area.

'All right, I will. Give me the car keys.'

'You're not serious ...?'

'I think she is, Delia. Remember the last time Melissa went without food?' Serena recalled an incident when they had all gone on holiday to Corfu. They had arrived late at their rented villa to find there were no provisions. Melissa had been so desperate that she had woken up a local shopkeeper and seduced him into giving them some groceries at two o'clock in the morning.

'Melissa, we can't afford to have any attention drawn to us right now.'

'Don't worry, Delia, I won't do anything silly. If I can't find anywhere open locally, I'll have to do without.'

'Melissa, remember, this is a quiet part of Suffolk. There won't be any late night supermarkets open around here.'

'If it's there, I'll find it.' At which Melissa walked out into the night, leaving the other two shrugging their shoulders in acquiescence.

10

Richard ripped apart his rare pepper steak in such an aggressive manner that a drop of pinkish blood spurted across onto Amelia's cheek. She wiped it with her finger and then licked it.

'Darling, you're really brutalising that piece of meat. Will you brutalise me like that later on …?' She finished her third glass of wine.

'Amelia, do you never give up.' Richard put a forkful of steak into his mouth and chewed it forcefully.

'Let's be honest, Dickie, you've only invited me out because you want to shag me.'

'Amelia … please.' Richard quickly looked around to make sure none of the other diners had heard her.

'Well, it's true isn't it? That's the only reason you ever want to see me. I'm not stupid. You only ring me up when you're feeling randy.' Amelia poured the last dregs of wine from the bottle into her glass.

'I like you a lot, Amelia, you're a good …'

'Shag?'

'Sort. I enjoy your company enormously.'

'Nevertheless, Dickie, you can't wait to fuck me. That's the truth of it, isn't it?'

'I'd rather if you didn't call me Dickie. Please.'

'Why? It suits you. Of all my lovers you happen to have the largest penis …' Amelia raised her voice during this last exchange. Several women looked up curiously toward Richard, making their male dining companions feel very inadequate.

Richard was too tired to get angry. He just looked up at Amelia and gave her one of his cold, disarming looks. There was one thing he couldn't stand, and that was a woman being coarse in public.

'Don't you look at me like that! I'm afraid that if you do want to get in my knickers, you're out of luck – I don't happen to be wearing any!' Amelia screeched with laughter. It wasn't the first time she had behaved outrageously. After a few drinks she tended to speak her mind and send Richard up on purpose. But as Amelia was well aware herself – it wasn't her mind that he was interested in. This didn't bother her in the least. They had this unspoken arrangement. Whenever he rang her up, they would go for a meal and then end up in bed. They never saw each other socially. It was a purely sexual liaison, which suited them both. Amelia would have been more than happy to forgo the meal and get down to business straight away, but Richard felt that if he didn't take her out to eat, it was tantamount to using her. He was always a gentleman in this respect and treated his women properly – that is before getting them between the sheets and driving them ecstatic with his voracious lovemaking.

When he had returned to his London flat after driving back from the estate, all he had been able to think of was that woman with the large eyes who had opened the door to him. How he had wanted her then. Should he go back? He had wondered – he could remember where she lived. She probably had a burly, beer-gut boyfriend, who was now at home feeding his face with chips. No, that moment had passed. Yet he had to have somebody that night. That's where Amelia had come in.

'Come on, let's go.' Richard caught the eye of the waiter and mimed that he wanted the bill.

'I thought you were hungry?'

'I've lost my appetite, all right?'

'Richard darling, have I upset you? Just having a little fun. You know little me …'

'No … it's not your fault …'

'Your father's death has upset you more than you think.'

'So bloody inconvenient of him.'

'You know, I'd like to die while making love. On my back looking up at the stars …'

'Is that all you ever think about?'

'Everything else is so boring, darling, isn't it.'

Richard paid the bill and dragged Amelia out of the restaurant before she could say any more. They got into his car and sped off into the night. After about ten minutes he brought the car to a halt.

'Richard, why are we stopping here?'

The car had stopped in an unlit road surrounded by trees. The nearest house was at least two hundred yards away. Richard took off his jacket and started to undo his trouser belt. 'Ever been had in a Range Rover before?'

'A couple a Jags, BMW … er, a very old Bentley – but, no, not a Range Rover.'

'Then it's your lucky day …'

'Are you serious, Richard?'

'Oh yes …' He began to raise her dress. 'You've had a Brazilian!'

'I've had all nationalities, darling.'

'I mean you've had your pubes done. Are those diamonds …?' He looked closely at some glitter adorning her pubic hair, as if examining the engine of a car.

'Crystals. I've been vajazzled too! I've become a member of the clitterati …'

'I beg your pardon …?' Richard was lost.

'Don't worry about it. It won't interfere with entry, if you still want to come in …?'

Richard wasn't in the mood to try to understand. 'Shall we commence …?'

'It's not like you, Richard. I thought you were strictly a bed only person.'

'Are you complaining, young lady?' He wriggled out of his trousers.

'Certainly not … Good lord, Richard … I swear it's got bigger …'

'Don't swear – just enjoy it …' Richard surprised even himself by his impulsive actions. All the angst and frustrations of the day had suddenly reached their peak. He just couldn't hold himself back any longer.

About a hundred miles away in Suffolk, Delia and Serena got a fright when there was a sudden banging on the front door. It sounded as if someone was kicking it in. They looked at each other.

'Delia, what shall we do?'

'Open it?'

'What if it's the police? What if they've caught up with us?'

'I'd better get the gun then.'

More banging. This time there was an urgency behind it. Gun in hand, Delia gingerly opened the door. It was Melissa, holding two plastic carrier bags.

'About bloody time! My arms were starting to drop off.' Melissa barged in and plonked the bags on the nearest table.

'What's that smell …?' Serena crinkled up her nose in disgust.

'Curry,' Melissa piped up in triumph.

'Curry?' Delia repeated.

'As in take-away. I've got some tandoori chicken, pilau rice, lamb vindaloo, mixed veg, dhall, some nans and a dozen poppadoms!'

'Where on earth did you find an Indian restaurant?'

'In a little village, about five miles down the road. I told you I'd find something.'

'But I don't like Indian food, Melissa.' Serena moved away from the bags as if they were contaminated.

'I'm terribly sorry about that. But there weren't any Mexican or Thai restaurants in the area. You like Indian don't you, Delia?'

'I can take it or leave it, I suppose.'

'Don't do me any favours, either of you. It's there. Please yourselves. There's plenty to go round. Serena, if you could bear to carry it on a plate, I'll give you some to take up to our friend upstairs. I'm sure he'll appreciate it.'

Henry had been dozing on and off for the last hour. His hunger, coupled with fatigue, had induced a succession of waking dreams where he was being chased by cooked chickens, pigs and cows wearing balaclavas, who all wanted to eat him. The banging at the front door had brought him back to his cramped surroundings.

While laying there and wondering what was going on below him, he started to become aware of the smell of curry, which seemed as if it was wafting in through the walls. He dismissed this as another hallucination and closed his eyes to try to forget about the hunger pangs already gurgling in his stomach.

Henry then heard footsteps, followed by a light tap on the door. 'Can I come in …?'

'You've got the key. Be my guest.' Henry sat up and watched the door as it opened slowly. In came Serena carrying a tray in one hand and holding the gun in the other.

'We thought you might be hungry … I'm sorry, but it's only curry … and some water.'

Henry's eyes lit up. To him this was manna from heaven brought by the most exquisite of creatures. He looked at the plate piled high with an assortment of his favourites. 'Thank you Serena, I couldn't have asked for a better meal.'

'You like Indian food then …?'

'Love it. Don't you?'

'No …'

'Why's that? Too spicy …?' Henry took in the various aromas.

'Well … to be honest … I've never tried it. The smell's always put me off.' Serena wrinkled her nose.

Henry looked at her while starting to tear a nan in half. 'My mother always used to declare that you must never say that you don't like anything – unless you've tried it first. If then it doesn't appeal, fair enough.' Henry smiled at her and deposited a forkful of lamb into his mouth, savouring every bit.

'Sensible advice, I suppose.' Serena smiled back. Unconsciously she sat on a chair at the side of the bed.

Henry tore off a small piece of tandoori chicken and held it close to Serena's mouth. Serena hesitated, then, while still pointing the gun at him, took the chicken and bit off the tiniest piece possible. She chewed it slowly around her mouth before eating the rest of it.

'It's quite nice … a sort of smoky flavour.'

'Good. Now try the lamb. It's a bit hot, but you'll find it has a different flavour and texture from the chicken. By the way, you don't have to keep pointing that at me.'

Serena still held the gun, but let Henry feed her a piece of lamb. She chewed a bit, then immediately went for Henry's water and took a gulp.

'Sorry, that was a teeny, weenie bit hot,' she apologised.

'But did you like it?'

'Yes … I suppose I did …'

'Then share this with me. There's plenty for both of us.'

'Well …' Serena hesitated. She found she liked his company and was impressed with the way he had introduced her to a food she had always convinced herself she didn't like. She was about to help herself to a piece of nan – when Delia's voice boomed across behind her. She was holding the gun.

'You're not supposed to feed him, Serena! Now come back downstairs, we've a lot to discuss.'

'Sorry …' Serena composed herself, and ignoring Henry, left the room.

'I hope the food is to your satisfaction,' said Delia. 'Because if it isn't …'

'I couldn't have asked for a nicer meal. Thank you. Mind you, a lager would have gone down well too.'

'Don't push it. You're lucky we got you that. Just don't be sick – because you'll have to clear it up yourself.' Delia looked around the room to check all was in order and then locked the door behind her. Henry took no notice; he was enjoying his food too much. This kidnapping escapade maybe wasn't so bad after all …

An hour later his door opened again and all three women were stood there. Delia pointed the gun, while Melissa was holding some rope. Serena looked guilty as she held a flower vase rather awkwardly. What were they going to do to him – hang him?

'Serena, take the food things.'

Serena, putting the vase down while averting her eyes from his gaze, quickly took the tray from off the floor.

'Now, Henry, do you want to empty your bladder?' Delia waved the gun toward his crotch as she said this.

'Why, what are you going to do …?' All the terror was starting to creep back.

'Don't ask questions. Do you want to urinate or not. I won't ask again, but if you take my advice I'd try my best, because it'll be a long time before you'll be able to again. And we don't want to wet our little selves do we?'

'No … I will go to the toilet …'

'Who said anything about a toilet? Serena.' Serena picked up the vase and handed it to him.

'You want me to do it in this?' Henry held the vase as if it was a bomb ready to explode. 'Surely there's a proper toilet in this house …?'

'There is, but they'll be no lifting of seats while we're here. Now shut up and do it!'

Henry glanced at the women. Only Serena was not looking at him. 'If you would kindly turn around please.'

'What, so that you could smash us on the heads with the vase? Now stop being so coy and get on with it!'

Henry realised he had no alternative, so the best he could do, to retain some modicum of decency, was to turn his back on them and urinate into the vase. Having accomplished that, he made himself decent and held out the vase toward Delia.

'Now drink it.' Delia smiled. Melissa and Serena looked at her in horror.

Henry froze. 'You … cannot be … serious …'

Melissa and Serena piped up together 'Delia!'

'In some health regimes drinking your own urine is supposed to be very beneficial.' Delia licked her lips.

'You'll have to kill me first …' Henry held the vase further away.

'All right then.' Delia pointed the gun at Henry's head.

Serena suddenly pushed the gun away from Henry. 'What's got into you Delia?'

Delia smiled. 'Just my little joke. Serena, take the vase please – and try not to spill any. Melissa – tie him up.'

As Serena left, holding the vase as if it were a bomb, Melissa came forward with the rope in both hands. 'Hands behind your back please.'

'What …?' Henry didn't like the sound of this. 'I promise not to escape. You don't have to tie me up. The door will be locked anyway …'

Delia gestured to Melissa, who forced Henry's arms behind him and expertly tied them up to the metal bed head.

'There!' Melissa exclaimed proudly, 'My girl guide days were not a waste of time after all.'

Delia double checked the knot to her satisfaction, and they both exited the room, leaving Henry trussed up like a chicken. He tried to struggle but this only resulted in him straining a muscle. The meal had been good, but he didn't care for this particular dessert.

11

Eight o'clock that anniversary evening, Jack still hadn't come home. The table had been booked for nine. There was still time. Where was he? Stella phoned his office but there was no reply. She tried his mobile but that went straight to voice mail. 'Where the hell are you …?' she screeched. Had he been whisked away on a mission? There was nothing to indicate from the news that there had been any trouble.

Ten o'clock. Stella phoned the restaurant to cancel. If he came home now they could still go to the houseboat …

Midnight … one o'clock … two … three … Stella had demolished all the crockery in the kitchen and was now exhausted and asleep.

Three thirty. Jack finally staggered home. His treading over broken plates and glasses woke Stella from her fitful sleep. She didn't move. She pretended to be asleep when he came into the bedroom.

He had obviously had too much to drink. Stella could see his silhouette swaying in the dark as he fumbled to take his clothes off. He burped, and followed this with a loud, resonant fart.

'God, you're disgusting!' Stella switched on her bedside light.

'Stella love. Did you break a plate in the kitchen?'

'I broke the bloody lot!'

'Oh. Not have a good day? I get days like that. Don't you worry.'

'And where the hell have you been?'

'Well, one of the lads was leaving. Billy Hughes. We all went for a drink at lunchtime … and it sort of carried on from there. I'm sorry love …'

'You're sorry!'

'Billy Hughes saved my life once. I had to give him a good send off.'

'And that's more important to you than your anniversary – then coming home to a wife you hardly ever see?'

'Hey, happy anniversary, love!' Jack spread out his arms and moved to embrace Stella.

'Don't change the subject.' She pushed him away.

'I didn't forget!' Jack pleaded. 'I got you these …' He fumbled in his bag and took out the card and the bottle of perfume that he hadn't wrapped. 'Happy anniversary, love.'

'I told you the last time, I don't like this perfume anymore …' She then ripped open the card from its envelope. 'And I am not your Mother, and neither is this my birthday!' She flung the card across the room.

'I thought it said *Happy Anniversary to a Special Wife*?' Jack was confused, but didn't like to admit that he'd picked the card in a hurry and gone by the flowery picture rather than the sentiment.

'You just don't think sometimes, do you! I don't ask for much!' Stella started to cry.

'Don't cry, love. I'm sorry. It's been a funny day ...' At which point he accidentally farted again.

That did it. It was the worst thing Jack could have done at that point. Had he immediately taken her in his arms and made love to her, it would have defused the situation.

'I'm leaving you Jack. I can't stand it any longer.'

'Come on Stella! I'm sorry. I'll make it up to you. I'm on three days' leave. We'll go away. Please ...'

Stella started wavering, seeing Jack overcome with guilt and remorse. He looked like a lost little boy. He stood there looking at her, begging her with his eyes to change her mind. One more chance, she thought, one more chance. Oh why was she so weak? 'I've had enough, Jack ...' She was playing with him now, squeezing every ounce of guilt out of him before she would finally give in.

'Please, Stella, love ...' Jack was so agitated and distressed that his bottom expressed what his mouth couldn't. Without realising it, Jack had well and truly finally blown away his marriage.

'I'm sorry, Jack, but this really is goodbye. You'd better sleep on the sofa tonight. We'll sort out the divorce and property matters later. Before you leave, please open all the windows in here.'

Jack was about to make a final plea to win her back over – when his mobile rang.

'Nightingale?'

'Sir?'

'Sorry to disturb you so late.'

'That's all right sir. I was awake.'

'We have a little problem. I appreciate that you have three days' leave ...'

'What is it sir?' Jack knew it was important. You didn't get calls in the middle of the night if it wasn't serious.

'A hostage has been abducted by some terrorists. We need to get some men onto it straight away. Now this isn't an order, neither will it go against you if you prefer not sacrifice your long overdue leave ...'

While Jack listened to his superior offering him a fair chance to refuse, he shrugged pleadingly at Stella. It was up to her.

'Go and play the hero, Jack. Use your disgusting habits to overcome the enemy. I've had enough.'

It was a turning point. Stella had given him no alternative. 'I'd be happy to, sir.' Jack was defiant now. 'I'll be right over.' He started to get dressed again.

Not one more word was said between them, as Jack closed the bedroom door and left.

Half an hour later Jack, having sobered up somewhat, was showing his pass to the security guards at the entrance to the headquarters of the Metropolitan Police Counter-Terrorism Branch. One of them made a quick phone call and let him through.

As he wandered down a labyrinth of anonymous corridors, Jack spent a moment reflecting upon his relationship with Stella. He realised he only had himself to blame. She had done her best to make things work out, but his actions had ruined everything. He should have gone home when he'd promised. He'd wait until this mission was over and then talk to her again. Hopefully she would have cooled down by then and be able to listen to reason. He honestly didn't want to lose her.

'Enter. Ah, Nightingale, good of you to come so promptly. I hope I didn't upset any family plans?'

'No sir.'

'Good, good. Now we think you might be able to help us with this kidnapping. Well, actually, it's not the hostage we're worried so much about – but what his kidnappers have stolen.'

'Sir?'

'Some very highly confidential Government papers and photographs. Top, top secret.'

'What's in these papers, sir?'

'I don't know. They won't even tell me. My instruction is to get the best man onto the job – you.'

'Just me, sir?'

'The fewer that know about it, the better.'

'Sorry, sir – but are you honestly telling me that I – alone – have been requisitioned to try to apprehend the kidnappers as well as recover the documents? By myself, sir?'

'No, no, no, silly boy! You'll of course be working against chaps from MI5, MI6, GCHQ and the SAS.'

'*Against*, sir?'

'I don't quite mean against. You see, each department will be assigning one man onto the case. A sort of crack troop. You will all work together to bring this little problem to a satisfactory conclusion. It doesn't matter if the hostage dies, or if the kidnappers – we think there are three – are killed. As long as those papers are recovered intact. Do you understand?'

'Not really, sir.'

'Good man. I don't understand either. All I personally care about is that you distinguish yourself and prove that the Metropolitan Police Counter-Terrorism Branch is the best of the lot of them. We've won only once in the last ten years. Make sure, Nightingale, that we win this year.'

'Is this some sort of competition, sir?'

'Damn right it is. It's a little junket we all have once a year – to see which Government security department is the best of that year.'

'I'm still not sure I fully comprehend what this is all about, sir.'

'Leave the comprehension to us, Nightingale. You just do your job to the best of your ability – but make sure you win.'

'Is the kidnapping a set-up then – for this "junket"?'

'No – it's a real situation alright. It's just that it happens to be the one chosen as this year's little competition problem. The press know nothing about it. As long as it doesn't blow up into a full scale public emergency, I shouldn't worry.'

'How much freedom do I have, sir?'

'To do what?'

Jack's superior looked him up and down. There was an animalistic presence about Jack that he found unnerving and exciting.

'To do it my way, sir. I mean, I don't have to take orders from the others, do I?'

'No, but there will be a Commanding Officer in charge of all of you. He has no allegiance to any department. A purely impartial observer. It will be his job to monitor progress and ascertain who is doing the best job. Does that answer your question?'

'Are we to be governed by any specific rules?'

'The only rule in my book is to win. Understand that, Nightingale? I'm relying on you.'

'Understood, sir.'

'Good. Nightingale … Jack …'

'Sir?'

'Are you by any chance gay? I know you're married, but …'

'No sir.'

'Ah … pity. Never mind. Good show …'

Jack stood motionless while his superior wandered around the room looking under various files and papers. There was an uneasy silence for several moments. Then the man found what he was looking for: a scrappy piece of paper with some notes scribbled on.

'Here it is. You are all to assemble at this address at 06.00 hours to receive a progress report on the situation, and to proceed with the investigation.'

Jack looked at the office clock. It was now 4.30 am. He had only an hour and a half.

'Not worth going home, Nightingale.'

'No sir …'

'I expect you'll want to phone the missus and tell her not to expect you for some time.'

'She knows already, sir.'

'Good show. Nice to be with someone who understands.'

'Yes sir.'

'I nearly got married once. Pretty girl. We didn't quite hit it off in the bedroom stakes … I'm a doggie man, if you know what I mean … Ah well … Jolly good …' Jack sensed that he had been dismissed, and he left the office. He looked at the address on the paper. It was in Whitehall. He decided there wasn't time to sleep, so he would pass the time by walking to his destination. He thought of Stella. She'd probably be fast asleep by now …

Stella was far from asleep. She had put all of Jack's clothes into four black plastic bags and was carrying the last one into the hall. She opened the front door and dragged a couple of the bags down the front pathway and across the road toward a large skip that was being used for building work.

With a little effort, she eventually managed to put all four bags into the skip. Looking around to make sure she wasn't being watched, she got out a can of hairspray and sprayed all the bags. Then, taking out a box of matches, she set light to them.

The fire in the skip developed into a big bonfire. Stella watched with satisfaction from her bedroom window as the Fire Brigade arrived to put it out. It was too late for them to recover anything – all of Jack's clothes had been burnt to a cinder.

12

Try as he might, and as tired as he was, Henry just couldn't get to sleep. Despite being tied up, he was still able to turn from side to side on the bed. But whether he twisted one way or another, he couldn't get comfortable. He tried various mind exercises like counting down from a hundred. He closed his eyes and started to think about Serena and her delicate hands. Soft, gentle hands, exploring and massaging his whole body, relaxing and soothing every muscle … yes, that was beginning to do the trick … imagining her delicately rubbing herbal oil over his neck … his chest … his arms … along the inside of his thighs … her palms rubbing and alleviating all tenseness … her fingers easing and calming. Henry was numb and about to drift off into a delicious sleep – when the bright chirp of a bird broke into song. Then another answered back, followed by a third. The dawn chorus was in full flight.

That was all he needed right then. Henry hated birds. Near his flat, a couple of magpies had built a nest in a tree outside his bedroom window. Every morning around five they would begin their thick screeching. When that happened there were only two ways he could get back to sleep. One was to stick ear plugs in; the other was to think erotic thoughts and masturbate. When he did both he could really crash out and not wake until late. Now, with the chirping gaining momentum, Henry felt frustrated because he could do neither. Because his hands were tied he couldn't cover his ears, nor relieve himself. If only Serena would come in now and do it for him, what utter bliss that would be …

'Come on, wake up little one … Where's my big boy? …' Amelia was gently stroking Richard's limp member as it lay pink and wrinkled. Richard was fast asleep, exhausted after the manic session in the car, which had been followed by several more athletic rounds at his flat, where they were now. Amelia had slept for an hour and woken refreshed and was now ready for another delicious bout. Her appetite was insatiable. While not exactly a nymphomaniac, she had worn many a good man out with her demands.

Amelia gazed at Richard's sleeping face. It wasn't a peaceful countenance but a look of tortured angst, his facial muscles taut and his lips moving as if he was grinding his teeth. She knew he wasn't really himself; understandably, because his father had just died, and because he had taken her with such aggressive force. He hadn't bothered with his usual exquisite and tantalising foreplay. No, he hadn't been considerate at all. Amelia didn't mind; in fact she was rather turned on by his uncharacteristic behaviour.

She continued to stroke his penis, hoping that it would stir under her experienced touch … 'Come on, sausage, it's time to join me in a hot dog …' Nothing. It felt soft and sluggish. 'Well … we are a tired little piglet … I think you need the kiss of life …' Amelia moistened her lips and was just about to administer one of her specialities – when Richard's mobile started to ring.

'Yes?' Amelia grabbed it, annoyed by the interruption. 'I'm afraid he's in a meeting.'

'Who is it …?' Richard snatched the phone off her.

'He said it was the police …' She didn't like the way Richard had pushed her aside.

'Richard Montcasse … Yes … that's right … it does belong to the estate … Where was it found? … Any damage? … Good … When can it be returned? … All right … I'll come up there personally … Yes, I'll fly it back myself … Of course I have a licence … Thank you …' He put the phone down, his mind elsewhere, having forgotten that Amelia was beside him.

'What was that about, at this time in the morning?'

'What …? Oh, one of our helicopters has been found. I've got to go and pick it up.'

'Not right now though …' Amelia kissed his belly button and was about to work her way further down, when Richard got out of bed, almost dislocating her jaw in the process.

'Dickie! That's not very nice.'

'Don't call me that.' He started to put on his towelling robe.

'Your little honeybum is hungry … She wants her breakfast …' Amelia suggestively licked her lips.

'I'm afraid you'll have to get it yourself. I'm having a quick shower and then I must leave.' He hated it when she called herself honeybum. The name had originated from the fact that she liked her lovers to smear clear honey over her bottom and then to lick it off. It was a practice Richard refused to indulge in. There were many things he'd gladly do, but that certainly wasn't one of them. There were limits.

'Honeybum will soap you all over …'

'No you won't. Not today.' Richard walked out of the bedroom.

Amelia banged the pillows in frustration. She realised there was no point in arguing with Richard once he'd made up his mind. She did momentarily consider creeping up on him in the shower and provocatively wiggling her bare backside at him. It had worked once, but somehow she knew that it wouldn't work that day. She'd only feel humiliated.

Amelia picked up her handbag from the side of the bed and took out her mobile, scrolled down the contacts, and keyed in a number. 'Are you alone …? It's honeybum … I know it's early, darling … I just wondered if my favourite frankfurter needed a hot garnish …? Yes, right now … I can be over in 20 minutes … I can't wait … Darling, by the way, have you got any honey in the house …?

When Richard came back from his shower Amelia had already gone. He thought nothing of it. There was never any love lost between them. He knew she would always be there if he wanted her. But his life was changing, and at that moment he instinctively knew that he would never see Amelia again.

Jack's stomach was playing up as he sat on a plastic chair in front of a large rectangular table in a windowless basement room. There was a smell of stale cigarettes and rising damp. He could feel his insides brewing up his own brand of air, but this wasn't quite the place to break wind. Two others were present, each sitting silently at opposite corners of the table. Apart from a couple of acknowledging nods, no-one had said anything.

While constantly changing positions on his chair in a desperate attempt to avoid disgracing himself, Jack surveyed the other men out of the corner of his eye. They both looked tough and able to take care of themselves. One had very close-cropped hair and a number of tattoos on his neck and arms; the other sported a ponytail and wore a diamond earring in one ear. They both looked slightly apprehensive and uncomfortable in this claustrophobic environment. They were both chewing gum.

The door opened and another man was shown in by a security guard, who closed the door behind him. The newcomer had short, dyed blond hair and a black bushy moustache. He wore an ensemble of black leather with boots to match. He possessed a powerful-looking physique and entered the room like a ballet dancer.

'Hello girls, I hope you haven't started without me!' He gave everyone the quick once-over, smiling and showing a set of perfectly-capped white teeth.

Nobody bothered to answer. Jack looked up and gave a brief nod. The blond man stood there with his hands on his hips. 'Well, that's not a very friendly welcome, is it now?'

The airlessness in the room had made Jack feel dry. He started to clear his throat, and in the process had a minor coughing fit. This in turn unfortunately made him fart at the same time. The blond man looked at Jack and smiled. 'I didn't realise you were that pleased to see me!'

'Sorry, some foods don't agree with me ...' Jack tried to make light of it.

'Don't apologise, petal, it's good to clear your throat sometimes.' The blond man turned to one of the others. 'Hey, I like your ponytail. I tried to grow my hair long once, but it got all wispy and full of split ends!'

'Shut it, will ya,' the man with the ponytail sneered in an accent that was very East London.

'I beg your pardon ...?' The blond man's smile disappeared.

'You heard him,' the man with the tattoos joined in, in a broad Irish accent.

Jack could see the blond man straighten up and take a big breath. He looked more closely at his face and could see he used eyeliner to highlight his eyes, which had suddenly become very piercing. The other two stiffened in response. Jack rose from his seat, but the blond man held his arm toward him as if to warn him off. 'Sit down, petal. This is something me and these girls have got to sort out ...'

'Don't call us girls, you bleedin' poofter!' The ponytailed man stood up and kicked his chair behind him.

'What did you call me? I don't quite think I heard that properly?'

'Come on, fellas, we're here to do a job,' Jack tried to reason with them all.

This time the tattooed man stood up and walked toward the ponytailed man in a gesture of support. '*Some* of us are indeed fellas ...'

'Say what you mean,' retorted the blond man. 'The haircut looks pretty butch, but those tattoos, petal, are very passé ...'

'I don't like queers,' Tattoo declared, his body language indicating he was preparing for confrontation.

'I am not queer. I'm gay. That's the correct expression.'

'Queer, gay, bum bandit, shirt-lifter, dung-puncher, nancy boy, homo … What's the bleedin' difference?' Ponytail smiled at Tattoo.

'The difference, you ignorant queens, is I don't have a problem with who I am. *You* seem to have that problem.'

'So what are *you* going to do about it, my fancy friend?' Tattoo flexed his muscles.

'Give us a kiss and I'll tell you!' the blond man screeched.

Jack couldn't help but smile. 'Come on lads. Let's just all cool down …'

'I'm very cool, petal, it's these two who are getting all hot under the collar. They just don't want to admit they secretly fancy me.' The blond man put his hand on his hip and fluttered his eyelashes.

Ponytail looked at Tattoo and nodded. They both jumped up on the table in front of the blond man, who just looked up at them with a condescending expression. 'I'm impressed. What other tricks do you know …?' Almost in unison the two men raised their feet and were about to drop kick the blond man – when, in a very swift move, the blond man grabbed an ankle from each and brought them both crashing down on their backs on the table. Then, just as briskly, he got hold of each of them by the balls. They squealed in agony. 'You like that, don't you? Shall I squeeze harder?' And he did, which really made them scream in utter torment. Jack couldn't watch. Instead, during all the noise, he broke wind again and felt much better.

The door opened and a man in tweed jacket and cords entered, carrying a swagger stick. He surveyed the scene before him, as the blond held firmly onto the others' testicles. 'Ah, I see you're all getting to know each other. Jolly good.'

13

What a difference a day makes, Henry thought as he lay staring at the mottled ceiling. This time the day before he had been snuggled up in his own bed looking forward to the interview and the prospect of a new life. Then had come the incident in the lift. If only he had been a minute earlier or even later he wouldn't be in the predicament he now found himself in. Just one minute to change his destiny. *Why me?*, he thought. All he wanted out of life was a secure job, a bit of money, a good woman to attend to his every need. Was that asking too much? He'd never done anyone any harm. Would the coming day prove to be the last in his short, boring life? The three women would kill him, bury him in some remote place, and that would be the end of that …

Henry's thoughts of death came into sharper focus when he heard footsteps slowly coming to the door. Was this it? How would they do it? A couple of pillows over the head to muffle the sound of the gunshot – which would also stop bits of his brains cascading over the room? That is if they shot him in the head. It would be much cleaner to put one bullet straight into his heart. Less mess … Perhaps they'd give him a last request? How would he wish to be killed? How would he like to die? Death by sex might be a good alternative. They could kill him with their insatiable desire … He would have a massive coronary during a brutal lovemaking session. It would be Serena's turn. Delia and Melissa would have done with him. It would be Serena's task to finish the job … The final climax would send him to the angels with a smile … Now that would be a fitting end … It would almost be worth dying for …

The sharp tap on the door dragged Henry back to bitter reality. This was followed by the key being turned in the lock. The door slowly opened and Henry could see Serena stood there holding a tray. 'Are you all right …?'

'A bit tied up … What do you think?'

'There's no need to be sarcastic. I've brought you some breakfast.' Serena stepped into the room.

'Why did you knock in the first place?'

'Habit, I suppose. I was always taught to knock before entering any room.'

'How very considerate. It's a good job I was dressed. I wouldn't like to embarrass you.' Henry was sorry after he had said it. He didn't want to be horrible to Serena, but his mouth seemed to be getting ahead of his brain.

Serena decided to ignore the remark, and she put the tray down on a chair beside the bed. She was about to leave the room when Henry said, 'Excuse me, I don't wish to be difficult … but how am I supposed to have breakfast?' He pulled on his ropes to make the point.

'Sorry … I'll untie you, of course.' She smiled sheepishly and came toward the bed. He noticed she wasn't carrying the gun.

He watched as her beautiful fingers attempted to untie the knots. Again the smell of her perfume wafted across and had the effect of arousing him. He gazed up at her leaning, lithe body as it strained to get at the rope. If only he could gently bite into that translucent skin …

'And what do you think you're doing?' Came a booming voice from the door. It was Delia, stood there like Annie Oakley brandishing a gun. From her point of view it looked as if Serena was almost on top of Henry and wiggling in the process.

'I'm trying to untie him … but these knots won't give.' Serena was straining without success to loosen the ropes. She was doing her best not to get too close to Henry. The fact was, the smell that was emanating from Henry's body was not very appealing. The cologne that he had applied the day before had long since soured. The experiences of the last 20 hours had taken their toll on his bodily odour. All that nervous angst, sweating, worry and the last night's curry had all got together to produce a unique assault to the senses. It really turned Serena off. She liked nice, fresh smells. She would only agree to make love with her husband, Matthew, after he'd had a bath or shower. It was a grey area in their marriage. Now, while she was struggling with the knots, she forced herself to hold her breath so as not to gag.

'Come on, I'll do it. Take this and move over.' Delia handed Serena the gun, and virtually pushed her aside while she came across to the bed. Her knee accidentally butted Henry in the side, making him groan. Delia had none of Serena's finesse and vigorously picked at the ropes in an effort to untie them. The whole bed shook as she tried to force the knots to loosen. 'Bloody things!'

'Problem?' Serena was pleased to see Delia not having any joy either.

'Give me a moment!' Delia replied irritably. Henry felt as if he were on the rack as she puffed and pulled, almost dislocating his arms in the process.

'Hey, not so hard!' he pleaded.

'And you can shut up for a start!' In frustration Delia purposely kneed him in the side.

'Ouch! That's painful.'

'Not as painful as what's assailing my nose. Do you know how much you stink? God it's disgusting. You should be ashamed of yourself. You reek like a tramp.'

Henry was rather taken aback by this remark. He'd been too preoccupied with his dilemma to be aware of anything else. He moved his head to the side and took in the rich fragrance wafting from the area of his armpits. The smell offended even him.

'I can't undo these bloody knots. You'll just have to stay like that.' Delia moved away and wiped her hands on her skirt.

'We can't leave him like that.' Serena sounded concerned.

'Of course we can.'

'I'd quite like to have my breakfast,' Henry volunteered.

'Would you now? Anything else?' Delia put her hands on her hips, daring him to challenge her.

'Well, yes … I'd like to go for … for a pee …' Henry replied.

'What – again?' Delia roared.

'But I haven't been since last night …' Henry really felt at a disadvantage.

'D'you have problems with your bladder?' Delia was almost accusing him.

Henry had had enough. He started to shout. 'For god's sake – if you're going to kill me, just get on with it and stop making me jump through hoops! It's not my fault if I stink, or if I have to relieve myself! So if you're going to do it – then bloody well do it ...!

Serena and Delia weren't prepared for this outburst. They both looked at him in surprise.

'Do what?' Melissa was now standing at the door, having heard the commotion and run up the stairs.

'He wants us to kill him ...' Serena turned to Melissa.

'Perhaps we should. His whinging is getting on my nerves.' Delia stomped out of the room and down the stairs.

'We couldn't untie him ... and he wants to go to the loo.' Serena was trying to be helpful.

'Serena – go and get the vase, there's a dear. I'll untie him.'

'But ...' Serena was about to object. Melissa gave her one of her don't-argue-dear looks. Serena smiled apologetically at Henry and went downstairs.

Melissa waddled across to the bed and leaned over Henry to get at the ropes. Her large breasts covered his face as she deftly undid the knots without any effort at all. She leant back and sniffed the air as if she were testing out a new wine.

'I'm sorry ...' Henry was flexing his arms, trying to get some circulation back into them.

'What for?' Melissa gave him an odd smile.

'The smell ... I mean, I could do with a bath ...'

'Nonsense. It's a good, manly smell. I quite like it ...' Melissa had started to look at him in a different way. Her breathing had accelerated, and he could see her chest rising and falling. She moved closer to him on the bed. 'Do you like larger women ...?'

'Well ... they're very nice ...' Henry didn't know what else to say. He didn't want to offend her, but at the same time he didn't want to encourage her either. To fancy a woman with large breasts was one thing – but to fancy one whose bottom was also enormous was not one of his fantasies. Come to think of it, perhaps he would rather be killed than ravaged by Melissa.

As Melissa leant closer, savouring Henry's presence, she gently walked her fingers across his thigh. 'Let the fingers do the talking ...'

'You mean – walking. Let the fingers do the walking. Like in the old Yellow Pages ad ...' Henry desperately tried to make light of the situation.

'A touch can say more than a thousand words,' she cooed as her fingers climbed his chest.

'I thought it was a picture was worth more than a thousand words?' he answered nervously.

'You don't want to have a bath ...' Melissa was stroking his face when Serena returned holding a vase. Melissa wasn't at all embarrassed. She chucked Henry under the chin before rising from the bed. 'Your relief has come ...'

As Serena gingerly held out the vase for Henry to take, Melissa withdrew the gun form her pocket and pointed it at him. 'Remember – no tricks now.'

Henry held the vase and just looked at them. 'Am I giving another show?'

Melissa gestured to Serena and they left the room, locking the door behind them. Henry sighed and undid his flies.

Downstairs Delia was getting her bag ready to go out. Melissa and Serena came into the room.

'Where are you off to?' Melissa enquired.

'Norwich.'

Melissa laughed as a thought struck her. 'When Simon and I were first married, I would always ask him where he was going that day. He often said Norwich ...'

'What did he do there then?' Serena asked.

'It was a figure of speech.'

'Sorry?' Serena didn't understand.

'What are you mumbling about, Melissa?' Delia never had much patience with her.

'Norwich – N.O.R.W.I.C.H. – Knickers off ready when I come home!' Melissa smiled at the memory.

'Knickers is spelt with a K,' Delia pointed out.

'Delia, stop being so pedantic! Why are you going to Norwich?'

'To buy another car. It looks like we're going to be here for a few days. We'll need transport and we can't afford to be caught with a stolen car. I'm going to drive our one up to Norwich, dump it in some street without parking restrictions, and then buy a cheap, second-hand car for cash.' Delia liked to plan things in detail.

'All right – but be careful.' Melissa genuinely meant it.

'I will. Now please don't go out, either of you. I'll bring some fresh groceries in. And keep an eye on our friend upstairs. We can't afford to lose him now. He knows too much about us.'

'Delia – he could do with a bath ...' Serena was already dreading going back up to his room to confront that smell.

'Nonsense. A bath is out of the question,' Melissa bellowed. She had plans for Henry.

'That's a good idea, Serena. Just make sure you keep the gun pointed at him at all times, then we won't have any problems. I'll also buy him some clean clothes. Burn his dirty ones. All right, Melissa?'

'Waste of time if you ask me ...' Melissa moodily replied as she saw her plans swiftly sinking down the plughole.

'We'll sort him out, don't you worry.' Serena was going to make sure Melissa didn't get her way this time.

Upstairs, after Henry had gratefully emptied his bladder, he placed the vase on the mantelpiece. He noticed a small pencil and a scrap of paper. It suddenly gave him an idea. He went over to the tiny window and succeeded in opening it a fraction. Then he quickly scribbled a note, folded it up, and threw it out of the window. Someone was bound to pick it up – and then he would be rescued.

Someone did pick it up. It was Delia, on her way out to the car. She unfolded it and read the brief message – *'HELP! I'm being kept as a prisoner on the top floor. These women are dangerous. Call the police.'*

Delia looked up and smiled. 'You'll have to do better than that, Henry ...'

Henry, unaware that his message had already been found, settled down to have his breakfast. It was just toast and coffee, but he tucked into it with a renewed optimism. He was certain he wasn't going to be a prisoner long.

14

The man in the tweed jacket pointed his swagger stick at Jack. 'Don't tell me – you're from the Counter-Terrorism lot. Am I right, or am I right?'

'Right ...' Jack wondered if the briefing had begun.

The tweedy man walked over to the blond man, who had released the others and was now filing his nails. 'Umm ... let's see now ... SAS, by any chance?'

'Got it in one, dear. Savour All Soldiers – that's my motto.' The blond pouted his lips.

'Jolly good. Gay chap, are you?'

'Oh, I'm always happy, lover.' The blond smiled and ran his finger over the swagger stick.

'Damn fine fighters, you gay lot. Keep it up.'

'I do my best, dear. But even *moi* can only keep it up for so long.'

'Quite right.' The tweedy man next pointed his stick at the man with the tattoo, who was still holding his genitals and in pain. 'M15?'

'M16' Tattoo replied.

'Then you must be M15.' He tapped the man with the ponytail.

'Don't you point that bleedin' thing at me, sunshine – whoever you are!'

'Ah, GCHQ then ...' he smiled.

Ponytail, who was feeling sore, grabbed hold of the stick and was about to break it in two when the door opened. In strolled a large black man dressed very informally. He had piercing eyes, a warm white smile and dreadlocks. In a West Indian accent he addressed them all: 'Ah ... a room full of whiteys. Where are my shades, man. Too much white is bad for my eyes ...' The black man took some dark sunglasses from his back pocket and put them on. 'That's better, a hint of brown always makes me feel more comfortable ...'

'Who the fuck are you?' Tattoo pointed at the black man.

'Sambo Nigger,' he smiled.

'Sambo Nigger ...?' Ponytail repeated incredulously.

'I'm also known by my other aliases – Jungle Bunny, Wog and Coon Spade ...' He enjoyed their incredulous expressions.

'Are you serious, petal?' the blond man asked.

'I'm always serious.' The black man had now changed his accent to Oxford English. 'But all those names are strictly classified. They are protected by the Official Racist Secrets Act. If I hear any of you using them – you will be white meat, my friends. Do I make my point?'

'So what do we call you?' the tweedy man asked, having grabbed his stick back from Ponytail.

The black man took off his sunglasses and looked at all of them in turn. 'My real name is of no consequence to you. But for clarity's sake you will call me Terry.'

'As in chocolate?' Ponytail smirked.

Terry smiled pleasantly and went across to Ponytail, who was exchanging grins with the tattooed man. 'That is very witty, my friend. You have a sense of humour. I like that ...' Before Ponytail was aware of what was happening, Terry had whipped a sharp flick-knife from his pocket – and swiftly cut off his ponytail.

'What the fu–?' Ponytail was too open mouthed to say anything more.

Terry, holding the clump of long hair, shoved it into the man's mouth like a gag. He then held the flick-knife to the man's throat. 'That was funny, but unfortunately, we must all be very careful with the kind of connotations we give words.'

Ponytail spat the clump of hair out. 'That took me fuckin' ten years to grow!'

'Look at it this way, dear,' the blond shrieked, 'no more having to stop in because you've got to wash your hair! You can just leave it in to soak!'.

'Which unit are you from? I can't even guess,' the tweedy man asked.

Terry put the flick-knife away. 'It's of no consequence. I am here to see that there is fair play – and that the best man wins.' His attitude was now serious and formal.

'You're ... you're in charge of us ... Jesus ...?' Tattoo couldn't believe it.

'I'm your CO for this little escapade, yes.'

'Why did you cut off my hair ...?' Ponytail childishly bleated, picking strands of hair from his mouth.

'My friend, we all have lessons to learn in this life. To give orders and to take orders. Discipline is of prime importance. When I say something – I mean it. You must respect that. I don't care what you think of me. What matters is that we all work together to sort out this problem with as little fuss as possible. We cannot afford to fail ... Do I make myself clear?'

Ponytail was still confused. The blond man piped up. 'What he means, petal, is that the colour of his skin must not be taken in vain. Am I right, Terry?'

'It's not the colour that matters ...'

'But it's the size that counts!'

'I do sincerely hope,' Terry gazed at the blond man, 'that we were not, in any way, making a reference to the size of my personal equipment?'

'I wouldn't dream of it, dear! I was referring to the enormity of the situation of course.'

'That's all right then. But just as a matter of reference, and for your information, it's true what they say about the endowment of our race.'

'You don't have to tell me, dear! Sometimes I could faint!'

'Don't you ever stop?' Tattoo was fed up with the blond's remarks.

'If I did – there'd be a lot of disappointed sailors!'

Jack put up his hand. 'Seriously, sir, this is a competition, isn't it?'

'Indeed it is. Your departments are looking to each of you to honour them. There is a tradition that must be upheld. I will not tolerate any dirty tricks or unfair behaviour. Yes, you are singularly working to do the best you can – but this is also a group effort – and as a group we have been accredited with the coded name Forces Against Rebellious Terrorists.'

'Is that how they see us, then?' the blond man chuckled.

Terry looked at him. 'What do you mean, my friend?'

'It's got to be a joke, dear. It's an acronym.'

'What's he fucking talking about?' Tattoo turned to Ponytail.

'I don't know, do I!' Ponytail was still mourning the loss of his hair.

'Peasants!' tutted the blond man. 'Forces – F; Against – A; Rebellious – R; Terrorists – T … making up FART. That's what we are – a bunch of farts!' He laughed.

'I'm sure that was not intentional.' Terry was not amused.

'Well, we'll just have to *blow* them all sky high!' the blond man quipped.

'Yes,' Terry continued in a serious vein. 'It could develop into a life or death situation. That also means *your* lives. I'm just reiterating the fact that there must be no mistakes. If we do not succeed – we will all be for the chopping block.'

'Including you?' Tattoo pointed his finger.

'My black arse is as much on the line as all your white ones,' Terry smiled.

'Boys, boys! This is no time to talk of love!' The blond man put his hand to his mouth in a mock gesture. 'Sorry, boss. Terry …'

'What is your name? Just the Christian one. No surnames.' Terry folded his arms and stared at the blond man.

'Rory … Butch, isn't it? Are you going to put my name in a book or something? Detention after school?' Rory looked at Terry.

'I just think it's time we all introduced ourselves. Your name?' Terry pointed at Tattoo.

'Kieran …' answered Tattoo.

'You?' pointing to Ponytail.

'Barry …' Ponytail was still finding odd hairs between his teeth.

'Jack.'

'And I'm Archie … pleased to meet you all.' The man in the tweed jacket held out his hand – but no-one took it.

'Right. Rory … Kieran … Barry … Archie … and Jack …' Terry pointed to each in turn, making a mental note of their names and their appearance. Rory, blond homosexual … Kieran, tattooed Irishman … Barry, East Ender with diamond earring … Archie, public school Englishman … Jack, a regular looking policeman … What a diverse bunch, he thought as he looked them over. 'This is what we know so far. A hostage – white, male – was taken by three hooded terrorists from a Government building and transported in a helicopter. No-one, as yet, has reported anyone missing, so we don't know the identity of this hostage.'

'Why was he taken?' Jack interrupted.

'Either he got in the way, or he recognised the terrorists.'

'Who are these fucking terrorists?' Kieran was getting bored.

'We don't know their identity. No party has declared themselves.'

'But what have they taken, apart from the hostage, that's so important?' Archie fidgeted with his swagger stick.

'Some documents and photographs. Top, top secret.'

'What are in these so-called documents then?' Barry kept patting the back of his head where his ponytail used to be.

'I don't know …' Terry revealed a streak of frustration. 'All I know is that if they get into the wrong hands – the consequences will be disastrous.'

'Is it really quite as serious as that?' Jack watched Terry to see if he could detect the truth behind the response.

'Oh yes ... That's why we've got instructions to kill if necessary. Those papers must be retrieved at all costs ... Gentlemen, they are more important than all our lives put together ...'

Several miles away, in a little room at number 10 Downing Street, the Prime Minister, Chancellor and Home Secretary were in deep and secret discussion.

'Are you sure this room isn't bugged?' Charles Carter, the Chancellor, glanced around nervously at all possible hiding places.

'Charles, this is the safest place in London,' Alex Brook, the Home Secretary assured him. 'I've had it checked myself. No-one, and I mean no-one but the Prime Minister has access. Not even his PS, PPS or his wife is allowed in here. Isn't that correct, Prime Minister?'

Thomas Lane, the Prime Minister, was doodling on the blotter before him. He hated meetings, especially if it had anything to do with politics. He would rather be out there talking to his people than discussing tiresome policies. He was so engrossed in making pretty patterns with his fountain pen that he didn't hear what was being said to him.

'Prime Minister ... there are only two keys to this room? Yours and mine. That is correct, isn't it?' Alex reiterated.

'Correct.' Thomas scrawled a big tick on the blotter.

'I'm still not happy.' Charles felt under Thomas's chair for any devices. 'These bugging chaps have ways and means ...'

'Look, we know the Cabinet Room is bugged. That's why we hold Cabinet meetings in the other reception. That's why we've especially installed our own recording system to pipe out false agendas in the real Cabinet Room while we discuss the important agendas elsewhere. It's perfectly safe in here.'

'We could all be in deep shit ...' Charles had picked up that expression from his son.

'Charlie, you laugh too little and worry too much.' Thomas stopped doodling.

'Deep, deep shit ...' Charles repeated as if in a trance.

'The Prime Minister's right. You're jumping the gun as usual. By this time tomorrow it will all be resolved.' Alex was always the firm optimist.

'Yes ... the Government will be toppled ... You, I and the Prime Minister here will be locked away in prison ... and that'll be that ...' Charles always responded as the true pessimist.

'Can they put a Prime Minister in prison?' Thomas looked at Charles and Alex. 'Would I get my own private cell with all mod cons ...?'

'It will never get that far, Prime Minister,' Alex assured him, but behind that assurance lay many imponderables, which even he didn't want to bring to the surface.

'Have the press got wind of it yet?' Charles asked.

'Thankfully, no ...' Alex took a deep breath. 'And that's how it must stay. We've enough problems without getting the media involved.'

'So what are we doing about it?' asked Thomas, who had decided to take note of what was being said.

'It's all been taken care of, Prime Minister.' Alex gave one of his don't-interfere smiles.

'I am the Prime Minister, after all – I should know what is being done to protect my position. Or imposition – if those papers or photos surface.'

'We've put a highly secretive and trained commando force onto it. They will deal with it swiftly, efficiently and sensitively.'

'Will lives be at risk?' Thomas wondered.

'There is that possibility, Prime Minister.'

'People might get killed …?'

'There may not be any other way.'

'It's either them or us.' Charles stood in front of Thomas. 'What's a few dead nobodies – if it means our necks will be saved?'

'Umm …' Thomas mumbled, not wanting to commit himself. He picked up the fountain pen and started to doodle again.

Terry stood in front of his team and surveyed them all. 'From where I'm standing you all look like a bunch of wankers!'

'That's a relief!' murmured Rory, who was starting to get bored with the whole proceedings.

'Look at you. You're supposed to be the *crème de la crème.*'

Rory was about to make another risqué comment but didn't want to push his luck too far. He looked across at his fighting companions and inwardly agreed with Terry that they did all look a pretty poor lot – apart from him of course.

'You don't appear to realise how important this mission is. Probably the most consequential one you'll ever have to tackle in your whole miserable lives …'

'Wot in 'ell does "consickwential" mean …?' Barry was confused.

'Tell him Kieran.' Terry turned to him.

'I don't fucking know! You're trying to confuse us with long fucking words that we can't fucking understand!' Kieran shouted.

'What does "fucking" mean, Kieran?' Rory couldn't resist it. 'Is it an old Irish word?'

Kieran took a deep breath. 'Listen you bent cunt, don't you start taking the fucking piss out of Ireland or the Irish …!'

'I wouldn't dream of it, petal. My first love was an Irishman. If he hadn't been murdered during the troubles, we'd probably be married by now …' The thought made Rory feel quite tearful.

'Bloody Nora! All this poncy chatter is doin' me 'ead in!' Barry paced to the end of the room.

'Where's the romance in your soul, Barry?' Rory responded quite genuinely. 'Have you never been in love?'

'Leave it out, will ya! What is all this …!' Barry found it difficult coping with any emotion.

'Enough! Enough, all of you!' Terry took control. 'I was informed that I would be in the presence of the best men in the country. I would learn from them. They would inspire me. They would be able to deal with this situation as a matter of routine. Is that what I see before me? Are you really the best this once great nation has to offer? I'm not convinced, my friends.'

'I know how to do my fucking job, mister.' Kieran remarked aggressively. 'You might be fancy with words, but I know how to kill with these bare hands.'

'Let's just get on with what we 'ave to do,' Barry agreed with Kieran.

'Appearances can sometimes be misleading,' added Archie. 'Now, I might look like a regular soldier ...'

'Regular twat more like it!' Barry quipped

'But that doesn't mean to say —' Archie strolled across to where Barry was seated. 'That I can't handle the most complex and troublesome of situations ...' With that, he thwacked Barry hard across the shoulder with his swagger stick, and before Barry could react, had him on the floor in a complicated wrestle hold. Barry couldn't move and was clearly in agony. 'Anything to add, Barry ...?'

'No ... Leave off, will ya!' Barry squealed.

'Then I think we understand each other.' Archie let Barry go and returned to his seat.

'What a dark horse!' Rory exclaimed. 'You can hit me with your rhythm stick any time.'

'I hope that won't be necessary, Rory,' Archie smiled, not quite understanding the inference.

'Okay, okay.' Terry held up his hands to get back their attention. 'Let's not kill each other first. What you do afterwards is your concern. What happens during this mission is my business. Now, the latest information we have is that the helicopter has been found dumped in a remote location in Wales, near Brecon.'

'I've never bin to Wales,' declared Barry.

'And it doesn't look as if you're going to this time. Forensic have identified some soil samples that come from a particular area in Suffolk. That is where we will start from. I'm in direct contact with the investigating authorities, who will update me as and when any information arrives. Any questions?'

'How are we getting there?' Jack asked.

'There will be some unmarked cars at our disposal. You will travel in pairs. Jack, you go with Archie; Kieran with Barry; and Rory will travel with me in a specially-equipped van.' Terry took from his pocket a couple of bunches of car keys. He threw one to Jack and the other to Kieran. 'Registration is on the labels. You'll find them parked in the multi-storey across the road from here. It is now 08.32. Let's synchronise watches ...'

'I don't 'ave a watch.' Barry saw the others hold their wrists and adjust the time.

Terry produced a digital wristwatch from another pocket and threw it to Barry. 'It's already set to the correct time.'

'You're prepared for everything, aren't you?' Rory gave an admiring glance.

'Let's hope so ...' Terry made a final survey of his troops. One of his father's sayings came to mind: *'Before you start any journey, make sure you are fully prepared. Enough petrol in the tank, enough change in your pocket. And most of all – know which direction you are heading in ...'* He sighed and suddenly realised that there was no going back.

15

While our intrepid crack troop were making their travel preparations, another group of men were having a clandestine meeting at a special venue in West London.

They all looked very out of place, dressed in expensive suits, sat squashed around a plastic table in a corner of a McDonald's. It was a strange setting for a trio of Junior Ministers to conduct a power breakfast meeting. A meeting that had been arranged with the utmost secrecy.

Jeremy Hayward, Simon Dodson and Matthew Croome sat furtively, about to discuss a matter of grave urgency. Jeremy looked around to make sure that they wouldn't be overheard. They weren't close friends as such. What bound them together was the fact that they had positions in the present Government, and that their wives saw a lot of each other. Physically, the men were quite different. Simon was slightly overweight; Matthew was tall and thin; while Jeremy was classically handsome, but with the arrogant bearing of someone born into privilege. They might all have had an allegiance to the same political party, but other than that, their personalities couldn't have been more diverse.

Simon bit longingly into a Big Mac and accidentally shot a piece of gherkin with ketchup onto Jeremy's striped shirt.

'Thank you very much, Simon,' Jeremy sighed, and took a serviette to wipe his shirt.

'This is heaven. I can't tell you how long it's been since I had one of these.' Simon took another big bite, and a bit of fat dripped down his chin, which he quickly wiped off.

'Doesn't Melissa cook you hamburgers then?' asked Matthew, who swigged his Coke and pinched one of Simon's french fries.

'They never taste the same. Umm … I just might have another one.' After every mouthful, Simon meticulously wiped his fingers and mouth with one of the dozen serviettes he had grabbed. He was very particular regarding personal cleanliness.

Jeremy impatiently took a sip of coffee and looked suspiciously around him. The place was empty apart from a couple of truant schoolchildren and a very fat woman who was munching her way through two giant meal deals, taking advantage of the buy-one-get-one-free offers. Jeremy had never been into a McDonald's before. He was more used to having breakfast either at his club or at the Savoy. He had originally objected to meeting there, but had been overruled by both Matthew and Simon, who felt that they should not be seen where they were known or might be recognised. It wasn't just the fact that it was a McDonald's that upset Jeremy – it was that it was located in Acton, an area Jeremy just couldn't relate to. But he had finally agreed that it was far enough from Westminster to be safe.

'So Delia never said anything to you?' Matthew directed his question at Jeremy.

'No, she never said a word. But I knew something was up, because she'd been behaving rather oddly the last couple of days.'

'In what way?'

'I can't exactly put my finger on it. A bit touchy, time-of-the-month sort of thing.'

'How do you know it wasn't that?' Simon licked his fingers.

'Wrong time of the month. That was last week. I always know when Delia has something on her mind. When she had that fling with that young actor chap, she acted oddly.'

'Very good pun that, Jeremy. Acted …' Simon guffawed.

Jeremy looked confused, not having understood the joke. It was one of Jeremy's weaknesses, the fact that he possessed no sense of humour.

'Is she having another fling then?' Matthew suddenly went serious.

'I don't know. I wish I knew.' Jeremy felt distinctly uncomfortable.

'Well I think Serena's definitely having an affair.' The very thought made Matthew sigh. 'She's had hurried conversations on her mobile, always switching it off if I came into the room …'

'Come to think of it – Melissa's been the same,' Simon remembered. 'D'you think our wives are all having affairs – all at the same time. Isn't that a bit of a coincidence?'

'The same sort of coincidence that made them all vanish at the same time, for instance? Remember when they all disappeared to Paris together? They never informed any of us, and they switched off their mobiles.' Matthew was trying to work it out.

'Well, they've always got on. Had holidays together, that sort of thing. Perhaps they've met some triplets and run off with them!' Simon found the idea amusing.

'Triplets? Whatever for?' Jeremy didn't get it.

'To have sex with, silly man! Mind you, how could you tell them apart?' Simon began to wonder.

'Look …' Matthew studied everyone who came in. The place was starting to get busy. 'The reason we're all here this morning is to try to discover what has happened to our wives – before the press get a sniff of it. They'd have a field day if they found out. Our careers would be in serious jeopardy.'

'No,' Jeremy corrected Matthew, 'that's merely the tip of it. The real reason we're in this godforsaken hole this morning, is to *further* our careers. The fact that our wives have disappeared only makes it worse. Also, either they've switched off their mobiles or had them taken away for some reason. I sincerely hope this has nothing to do with the discovery I made. Did either of you mention anything to Melissa or Serena about what I stumbled upon? I certainly said nothing to Delia.'

'Melissa finds anything to do with politics a total bore. If there's a garden party and a member of royalty is present, she's happy.' Simon was concentrating on another diner who was biting into a Big Mac. 'That does it! I'm not holding back anymore.' He stood up.

'What's the matter? What have you remembered?' Jeremy was concerned by Simon's sudden outburst.

'I'm going to have another Big Mac. Can I get anyone anything?' Simon licked his lips.

'Another Coke please.' Matthew emptied his paper cup.

'Right oh. Jeremy?'

'No! Can't you think of anything but food?' Jeremy snapped irritably, but Simon was already at the till, placing his order.

'Come to think of it, I might have said *something* to Serena ...' Matthew searched his memory.

'*What* exactly ...?' Jeremy didn't like the sound of this.

'Just that you had come across some papers – and photographs – that were dynamite – to do with the Prime Minister – and that could be quite useful to us ...'

'Oh, my god ...' Jeremy put his hand to his forehead.

'I never went into any details, if that's what's worrying you.' Matthew tried to sound cheerful.

'If she said anything to either Melissa or Delia on the landlines, we have a bit of a problem.' Jeremy was trying to think it through.

'How ...?' Matthew wasn't with him.

'We all know that our home phones are tapped –'

'Do we?' Matthew sounded surprised. Simon had returned with his tray. 'Simon – are our home phones tapped?'

'Of course, old fellow, standard procedure. Only say what you want others to hear. That's the great thing about also having two mobiles. One public, one private. ' Simon grabbed some fingers of chips and deposited them in his mouth.

'I've got only the one mobile. Jeremy, have you got a second one?' Matthew was always the innocent when it came to any sort of subterfuge.

'Of course. Not even Delia knows the number. Simon, it seems Matthew here told Serena about those papers.' Jeremy watched Simon bite into the hamburger as if he hadn't eaten for days.

'Oh dear ... That could be a problem ... This is absolutely delicious!'

Matthew looked sheepish. 'I'm sure Serena didn't say anything ...'

'How sure, Matthew? You didn't also happen to mention *where* these documents were, by any chance?' Jeremy gave Matthew a steely gaze.

'Only the building ... Not the actual floor or office. She didn't seem very interested.'

'No, but Delia would be if Serena told her. She hates being a Junior Minister's wife. She thinks I should be in the Cabinet, even Prime Minister ...'

'Much chance of that happening, dear boy, while Lane's PM.' Simon continued demolishing his second Big Mac. 'As much chance as me being Chancellor, or Matthew being Home Secretary ...'

'But if we got our hands on those documents – we'd be in a much stronger position. We'd have something to bargain with, to elevate ourselves with.' Jeremy was always one for the main chance.

'Isn't that blackmail, Jeremy?' Matthew was unsure.

'Politics is blackmail, Matthew. Any government has always got a gun to its country's head. We wouldn't be doing anything irresponsible. We'd just be exposing a few home truths – or lies – and offering an alternative leadership. Us. There's nothing wrong in that.'

'The question is – oh, this is so scrumptious – how do we get our hands on those documents?' Simon gobbled the last of the bun.

'That's what I want to talk to you both about –' At that point Jeremy's mobile phone rang. He took it out of his pocket and quietly spoke so that no-one would overhear. 'Hello ... Yes ... What? ...When? ... Oh, shit! ... Thanks for telling me ... I'll talk to you later ...' Jeremy looked grim as he returned the phone to his pocket.

'Bad news?' Matthew enquired.

'Bloody bad news ...' Jeremy's expression looked tortured.

'Can we ask?' Simon had momentarily forgotten about food.

'I just can't believe it ... the bloody timing of it all ... That was Gerald, my researcher. He keeps his ear to the ground ... There's been a terrorist attack on one of the Government buildings ... the one we were talking about ... It seems there was a robbery, and some *sensitive* papers were stolen ...' Jeremy struck his clenched fist on the table, spilling some of Matthew's Coke.

'Surely not the ones we've been discussing?' Matthew wiped up the spillage with a serviette.

'Yes ... the ones *you* mentioned to Serena – who no doubt mentioned them to Delia – *on the home phone – which is tapped* – which was overheard – which is why they suddenly disappeared. Got it?'

'I haven't got it.' Simon wiped his mouth for the twentieth time.

'Gerald also told me that not only did the terrorists steal these documents – but they also took a hostage, or hostages ...' Jeremy paused for full effect. 'Undoubtedly our wives!'

'What ...?' Matthew had his mouth open.

'How do you know that?' Simon wasn't convinced.

'Simon, it's obvious. It all adds up. The terrorists must have kidnapped them all yesterday. That's why they didn't come home last night. Weren't they all having morning coffee together? That's when they were abducted. The terrorists have got these papers and in return probably want a lot of money. If they don't get what they want, they'll no doubt kill our wives in retaliation. It's all been carefully planned out.' Jeremy was certain he had got at the truth.

'Who are these terrorists?' Simon was worried now.

'I don't know. An IRA faction, Al Qaeda, some Arab offshoot, Animal Rights? Could even be Friends of the Earth. That's not what matters ...' Jeremy was feeling fervent.

'What matters,' Matthew added, 'is that we get our wives back.'

'No.' Jeremy interrupted. 'What really matters is that we try to get hold of those documents somehow ...'

16

The folder containing the stolen papers and photographs lay on the coffee table in the lounge. Melissa and Serena sat on the sofa having a cup of tea. They were both quiet, lost in their separate thoughts. Serena wondered what Matthew was doing, how he was coping with her not being there. She thought that she would miss him, but was surprised at her own feelings of indifference. Melissa, eating her third biscuit, hoped that Simon wasn't being silly about food. She did her best to try to keep him on a strict and proper diet, but was aware he sometimes cheated. He was the reason she was so fat in the first place. When they had married they had both been slim and energetic, but as soon as Simon had entered politics he had begun to eat as a way of compensating for the stress. Since mealtimes were the only occasions that they saw each other, Melissa had joined him and found herself quickly putting on weight, and that's how it had all started.

'D'you want the last biscuit?' Melissa turned to Serena, who was trying to remember when she and Matthew had last made love.

'No ...'

'We haven't really had a good look at those papers. Shall we see if our efforts have been justified?' Melissa flipped open the folder, after popping the biscuit in her mouth.

'Delia did say that we weren't to touch them until she got back.'

'Delia also said that we're all in this together, Serena. The responsibility is equal. If we get caught we'll all be for the high jump.'

'Melissa, it's Delia's meticulous organisation that has got us this far. It's only fair we respect her wishes. She knows what she's doing.'

'I suppose so. I'm just bored with this waiting. Delia'll be hours.'

'We mustn't rush things. If our plan is to succeed we've got to be patient. It seems to have gone all right so far.'

'I'd be happier if we didn't have the complication of our friend upstairs. He's really put a spoke in the wheel.'

'It wasn't Henry's fault. He just happened to be in the wrong place at the wrong time.' Serena sounded sorry for him.

'Too bloody right. We should've dumped him earlier.'

'He knew our names. He would have told the authorities. Anyway, as Delia said, he's our insurance should anything go wrong. Don't you agree, Melissa?'

'Why couldn't we have kidnapped some gorgeous hunk, that would've made things much more interesting – instead of that nondescript loser we've landed ourselves with.'

'What do you mean, Melissa?'

'Wouldn't you rather keep a prisoner who was nice to look at, rather than Mr Uglymug upstairs?'

'You're being very unfair. I think he's got a nice face.' Serena meant it.

'I think he looks like a twerp. Does nothing for me ...' Yet Melissa was lying to herself. Henry might not have looked like an Adonis, but to her he certainly smelt like one. 'Talking of Henry ...' Melissa closed the folder, no longer interested in its contents. 'Shall I go and get his breakfast things ...?

'I'll get them, don't worry.' Serena was adamant. 'Anyway, he'd better have a shower before he stinks the place out. I'll sort all that out. You can clean the breakfast things.'

Melissa grudgingly acquiesced. Serena was right. Melissa didn't trust herself. She knew that if she went into his room, one whiff of his maleness would probably make her lose control, and then she'd make a fool of herself.

It was a bone of contention in her relationship with Simon, and one that sorely tested her fidelity. Simon was scrupulous about his personal hygiene, showering in the morning and bathing at night. He stocked rows of aftershave and cologne and always liberally splashed them all over, often smelling like a perfume counter. In the toilet, which also had a bidet, he insisted on scented moist wipes in addition to their normal toilet tissue. When Melissa had once suggested that he didn't have a bath one night, he had thought her mad. As far as he was concerned, cleanliness was indeed next to godliness. Melissa wasn't religiously inclined that way. To her a bit of dirt was a wholesome thing.

Delia listened to Classic FM as she drove toward Norwich to dispose of the car. She couldn't believe that they'd actually succeeded; succeeded in pulling off one of the most important robberies of the century. It meant the future of the present Government was now in their hands. She hummed along to the music, proud of what she had personally achieved. Neither Serena nor Melissa had been convinced initially that it could be done. It was her reasoning, her planning, her underworld contacts, that had made everything a conceivable proposition. It wasn't a perverse desire to be able to commit a criminal act that drove her – it was pure and simple hate. Hate for the present Prime Minister, Thomas Lane.

Jeremy Hayward, a Junior Minister at the Treasury, was her husband. She had married him because she had seen in him a future Prime Minister. It wasn't a passionate love match. It was a combination of family, social circle, position and the fact that she wanted to be a Prime Minister's wife that primarily attracted her. Of all the eligible young up-and-coming politicians, Jeremy Hayward had PM written all over him. It wasn't just Delia who recognised it. Influential names in politics had Jeremy down as a potential leader. His star had been in the ascendant when Delia had baited, caught and married him. In her mind, it had then been only a matter of time before she would be redecorating Number Ten.

Within two years Jeremy had been elevated to the Treasury. He had become the Chancellor's right hand man. Charles Carter had started to groom him for a senior government post. It had been on the cards that at the next reshuffle Jeremy would be offered a seat in the Cabinet. At the time, Thomas Lane had thought very highly of him. Jeremy and Delia had enjoyed many evenings at Number Ten. Delia had made a special point of cultivating a useful relationship with

Pamela Lane, the Prime Minister's wife. She had been determined to learn as much as she could, so that when the time came, she would be totally primed for the duties of a Prime Minister's wife.

Then things had started to go wrong. Thomas Lane, who had been so friendly toward Jeremy, had suddenly become very indifferent. Almost overnight his attitude had turned from a professional respect to a detached dismissal. It had not only happened to Jeremy. Two other rising stars, Simon Dodson and Matthew Croome, had also been left out in the cold. It's not as if any of them had done anything to merit this rebuff. The door had been firmly closed with no reason given.

At first Delia had thought the PM was preoccupied with certain national crises, and that he would change his attitude toward them all once these problems had been dealt with. But no, the knife had been firmly put in when Jeremy had been overlooked for a position that should have rightly been his. An inferior colleague, with only a small percentage of Jeremy's talent, had been promoted above him. Jeremy had confronted Charles Carter to find out why he was being ignored after such an encouraging start. Charles had not been drawn on it, simply offering a reason of 'changed priorities.' Jeremy had been angry but, in a way, philosophical about it. Delia had been angry and cursed the very ground Thomas Lane walked upon.

Now it was all going to change, Delia thought to herself. She, not Jeremy, had the upper hand. Their destiny was under *her* control now. What a wonderful feeling that was. Yet what really thrilled and excited her was the knowledge that the papers she had in her possession would completely destroy the Prime Minister, Chancellor and Home Secretary.

Delia was going fast and turned a sharp corner on the country road. She wasn't aware of a car speeding toward her in the opposite direction until it was too late. The other car skidded and hit Delia's on the side – knocking her off the road, through a hedge and into a field. The car toppled over onto its side. Delia, drooped across the steering wheel, saw a bright light before finally passing out.

'Jesus! You'll get us killed!' Barry shouted at Kieran as they continued to speed along the same road.

'It wasn't my fucking fault!' protested Kieran, 'You saw how that fucking car came at us.'

'Shouldn't we go back and see if everyfing's all right?'

'It just skidded off the road. Probably miles away by now. Anyway, we've got orders not to get involved with anyone.' Kieran put his foot on the accelerator and just missed another car as they turned a bend.

'Bloody 'ell, man! What is it with you?' Barry banged the dashboard in anger.

'Lighten up, my friend. I'll get us there in one piece. Don't you want to get to the rendezvous first?'

'Alive I do.'

Kieran smiled enigmatically. He didn't care too much for Barry. Thought there was something weak about him. He could kill him there and then. That would make one less in the contest. Kieran liked a challenge and the pain that often went with it. The tattoos on his neck and arms had been self administered to prove he had control over his own body. He'd even pierced himself in the genital area, and was proud his gold Prince Albert.

He glanced briefly at Barry, who was concentrating on the road – one hand gripped the door handle, the other brushed the back of his head, still mourning the lost ponytail. Kieran saw there was no threat there. Barry was a loser. It was the others he wasn't sure of. Whatever, Kieran was determined come top in this competition, and he'd play every dirty trick in the book to be number one.

'Excuse me, have you backfired?' Archie turned to Jack, who was driving.

Jack listened. 'The car sounds all right to me.'

'No, I mean have you let one go?' Archie twitched his nose.

'Sorry ...?' Jack tried to look confused.

'Farted, dear chap. Have you farted – or is it the country air?'

'Sorry ... difficult to control sometimes ...' Jack opened the window.

'I once knew a chappie who had a similar problem. The men called him Thumper. He could perform reveille from his anus more effectively than the bugler. Decent fellow. Died in Northern Ireland ...'

'IRA?' Jack sympathised.

'No ... Vindaloo. His friends cooked him an especially hot curry as a sort of joke. It was more potent than they thought. His insides couldn't cope with it. Messy business ...'

'What do you think of this whole situation?' Jack changed the subject. 'What have those terrorists stolen to create such a panic?'

'Don't honestly care, if you want my opinion. The fight's the thing.'

'But don't you want to know *why* you're doing it?'

'Not particularly.'

'Don't you ever question anything you are asked to do?'

'I carry out orders to the best of my ability,' Archie replied. 'I'm not interested in issues, causes or reasons. These terrorist chaps have broken the law. It is my job to bring them to heel.'

'Our job ...' Jack emphasised.

'The best man will take the honours.'

'And are you the best man?' Jack teased.

'What do you think?' Archie smiled. 'I believe we should turn left here ...'

'Right, man, right. We should've turned right.' Terry studied the map. They had driven off the main road and were now travelling down a minor country one.

'Keep your hair on, dear. I know this area quite well. Had a friend who owned a weekend cottage near here.' Rory gave one of his *I-know-what-I'm-doing* looks.

'Are you sure now?' Terry wasn't convinced.

'At the next crossroads you will see two signs. One will point right to Diss, the other will point left to Attleborough. If you look at the map there ...' Rory pointed a well-manicured finger, 'you'll see I'm correct.'

They soon reached the crossroads, and the road signs verified what Rory had predicted.

'I apologise for doubting you,' Terry eventually admitted.

'Do I get a brownie point then?' Rory smiled.

'Is that a reference to my colour?'

'Is that a *black* mark against me then?' Rory pushed his luck.

'Okay, okay. Point taken … Brownie point.' Terry wasn't in the mood to take it further. 'But I must remind you, it's not the journey that counts, but how you perform on the field, that I'll be taking note of.'

'Any particular field, petal? I've performed on many … ah, young love,' Rory reminisced.

'Do you have to bring sex into everything?' Terry sighed.

'Does it bother you?' Rory said caustically.

'It's more important you concentrate your energies on the mission in hand. Don't you want to win?'

'Of course I want to win, dear – and I'm going to. But let's not get too stuffy about it. Professionally I've had to kill 23 people. None of them suffered, I have to add. I carry out my orders with the highest integrity. But a job is a job and a poke is a pleasure. A double entendre is worth any serious single remark. Get my drift?'

'Every man to his own …' Terry smiled with a slight grudging admiration.

'A gay motto if ever I heard one!' Rory laughed, as he noticed some distinctly-patterned skid marks going off the road. He didn't notice the gap in the hedge or realise that it had been the scene of a recent accident.

Several cars and lorries had passed that same spot in the last hour, but because of the dense greenery, none of them could see or had been aware that a crashed car lay on the other side with a female body inside it.

17

'How long d'you think Delia's going to be?' Melissa watched Serena as she sprayed her handkerchief with perfume.

'She said she hoped to be back soon after lunch. Why?'

'Not sure what to do with myself. Can't risk going out for a walk, I suppose.' Melissa was fidgety and wanted something to occupy her mind.

'This house has got a big garden. It's quite secluded. No harm going out there. I know – why don't you see if there's somewhere we can burn Henry's clothes. I'm going up to persuade him to have a shower.'

'Want me to do it …?' Melissa offered again.

'I'll be all right. I've got the gun. I'll shout if I have any problems.' Serena was up the stairs before Melissa could respond. She could detect the perfume that Serena had sprayed, and was momentarily jealous of those earthy smells that were about to assail her delicate nose.

Serena stood outside the door, dreading the stench that was awaiting her. She wondered if it would be insensitive if she kept the perfumed handkerchief to her nose while she attended to Henry. No, that would be too obvious. She didn't want to upset him unnecessarily. It wasn't his fault, after all. Before unlocking the door, she breathed in the fragrances from her handkerchief and prayed that she wouldn't be sick.

Henry was stood by the small window when Selena entered. 'Were you thinking of jumping?' she remarked, and was relieved that the smell wasn't as bad as she had expected. The tiny opening in the window had brought in some fresh air.

'If I were an 18 inch midget there might be a remote chance. Even then, at this height, I'd be a bloody stupid midget to even attempt it.'

'Point taken.' Serena felt suddenly silly.

'And you really don't need to keep pointing at me with that gun.'

'Do you want to be tied up then? I'm sure Melissa would oblige.'

'Er … no …' Henry didn't want to go through that again if he could help it. He would try to escape – but only when he was certain that he'd succeed. 'I promise to be a good boy … honest …'

'Would you like a shower?'

'Of what?' Henry was confused.

'Of water. Hot with soap. To freshen up.' Serena wondered if Henry was as dim as he sometimes made out.

'You'll let me have a shower …?' Henry's mind went into overdrive. There might be a bigger window in the bathroom. While he was showering – he could escape. Serena smiled and nodded. 'When?' he asked.

'Now? If that suits you.'

'Great. Thank you. You can lead the way.' Henry gestured with his hand.

'Why don't you lead the way instead. I wouldn't want you to accidentally push me down the stairs, now would I?'

Serena was ahead of him. The thought had occurred to Henry – but it would have created a dilemma. If it had been Melissa or Delia he wouldn't have had any scruples about doing it. Yet Serena was different. He'd never come across anyone like her before. One moment she seemed sympathetic toward him, the next she appeared as if she would actually pull the trigger. He didn't know where he stood. If he did get a chance to escape, he would try to do so without harming her.

'You'll have to tell me where to go.' Henry walked down and round the steep staircase, making sure that he didn't fall or trip himself.

'It's on the ground floor, second door on the right.' Serena gestured with the gun far enough behind him so that he couldn't suddenly lunge back and disarm her. Henry reached the bottom of the stairs and opened the bathroom door. There was a bath, a shower and a sizeable window. Henry was feeling better already.

'Thank you. You can lock the door – I'll sort myself out. I have showered before.' Henry waited for Serena to leave him. Serena just stood there watching him. 'Well …? Something you've forgotten?'

'No …'

'What then?' Henry wanted to start running the water before making his escape.

Serena sat in a bentwood chair and folded her arms, the gun still pointed at him. 'Carry on … You can put your clothes in those carrier bags.' Serena drew his attention to a couple of plastic bags that she had brought in earlier.

'What for?' Henry was momentarily thrown.

'So that we can burn them, of course. Don't worry, Delia's bringing back some fresh clothes for you. We wouldn't expect you to be without.'

'Okay, I'll do that. Now – can I go ahead and shower?'

'That's why you're here …' Serena smiled.

'But … you're still here …'

'Henry, I'm a married woman. You haven't got anything that I haven't seen before.' Serena did her best to sound nonchalant and unconcerned – but inside she was a touch nervous and shy. Matthew had been her first love and the only man she had ever seen naked.

'You're staying …?' Henry didn't like the sound of this.

'I'm afraid so. Can't have you escaping through that window, can we now?'

Damn, he swore to himself, she really was ahead of him. He could refuse to shower, but even he was sick of his own stench. To be clean with fresh clothes would at least make him feel more comfortable. Did he have a choice? What if he suddenly got an erection, how would he explain that? Serena had probably seen hundreds of naked men in her time, all erect no doubt. Why should it bother him if it didn't bother her? He'd already peed into a condom and a vase in front of them. Having a simple shower was no big deal, he finally convinced himself.

'Look, would you rather I went and got Melissa to sit with you? I don't mind.'

'No …' Henry inwardly panicked. 'It makes no difference to me. You might as well stay if you've got to.' The very thought of Melissa ogling him really did petrify him.

She was secretly pleased that he didn't prefer Melissa to her. As soon as Henry slowly started to undress, Serena flushed inside. She wanted to turn away and be polite, but to do so might endanger her if he attacked. She had to keep the gun firmly pointed at him.

'Can't wait to get out of these ...' Henry made light of the affair as he took off his grubby suit. It was his best interview suit, never to be questioned again. After taking out his wallet, pen, comb and half a packet of sweets, which he had forgotten about, he squashed the trousers and jacket into one of the bags. He then took off his shirt and tie, leaving him in his underpants and socks. He was clearly embarrassed about his white briefs; there was a small yellow stain at the front. He quickly took them off, scrunched them with the shirt, and stood there with his palms in front of his genitals.

Throughout, Serena did her best not to stare too hard, keeping her eyes on his face rather than his body. A whiff of stale sweat assaulted her as he deposited the shirt in the other bag. She bravely managed to overcome any feelings of nausea. With his hands still clutching his modesty he started to climb into the bath.

'Haven't you forgotten something?' Serena whispered, looking down at his feet. He still had his socks on.

'Oh, right ...' To take them off, he now had to fully expose himself. There was no other decent way. As he bent down Serena unavoidably caught her first glance of Henry's limp member. As if transfixed, she found it hard to tear her eyes away from it. Henry quickly pulled off the socks, got in the bath and partially hid himself behind the shower curtain. 'I can shower behind this curtain, can't I ...?' He turned on the shower.

'All right.' Serena saw no danger in that, but her mind was elsewhere. She kept on seeing his dangling penis caught as if in a freeze frame of a film. She felt ashamed of herself yet couldn't get the image out of her thoughts. Why was she so fascinated? She'd seen Matthew's, played with Matthew's dozens of times. What was so different about Henry's? She finally had to admit to herself why she was so mesmerised ... It was considerably bigger than Matthew's, and since his was the only one she had ever seen before, she had always imagined, in her naivety, that all men were the same ... Well now she knew they weren't ... Henry's wasn't circumcised and it looked more elegant to her.

The bathroom door opened and Melissa stood there holding a garden spade. 'Everything all right?'

'Fine ...' Serena was dragged back to reality.

'Thought I'd pop up. Things had gone a bit quiet. Just to check.' Melissa eyed the body behind the curtain. Steam was already starting to fill the bathroom.

'As you can see, all is well. Thanks anyway.'

'We can't be too careful ...' Melissa was frustrated, because she couldn't really see anything.

'His clothes are in those bags – if you'd like to take them now?'

'Right oh. There's a metal bin for burning leaves at the bottom of the garden, I'll get rid of them there.' Melissa picked them up and surreptitiously tried to peek behind the curtain without any luck. Henry was aware of Melissa's presence and purposely kept right to the corner of the bath. He relaxed when he heard the door shut and continued to soap himself all over.

Melissa carried the bags into the lounge and sat on the sofa with them. First she looked toward the small hallway to make sure that Serena wouldn't make an unexpected entrance. Then she took Henry's shirt out and started to sniff it. Her eyes closed at the very bliss of it. The odour was even stronger than she had remembered. It was manna to her senses. It wasn't often that she was so turned on. She now took out his underpants and held them in her hands. Should she … shouldn't she …? The temptation was too great. Just as she raised them to her nose, she heard a noise from the bathroom and immediately flung the pants back in the bag. 'Is everything all right, Serena?' She shouted.

'All okay … Henry just dropped the soap,' Serena called back.

Sighing, Melissa forced herself to leave Henry's clothes alone. No point in getting excited if there was no outlet. The punishment was too much. It reminded her of the countless times she had handled Simon's Y-fronts before they went into the washing machine. She would often sniff them in the hope that some of Simon's raw masculinity had finally been trapped. But no, they always smelt so fresh and clinical. She decided, there and then, that when this little escapade was over she was going to leave Simon and find a real man. A man who didn't bathe every day, who didn't use aftershaves, colognes or deodorants.

Having made this sudden, momentous decision, she carried all the clothes out into the garden. Within five minutes they were burning a treat. Melissa stood in front of the fire watching the flames dispatch the clothes to ashes. She looked upon it as a form of religious ceremony. Those flames were the flames of her real passion; the ashes were her old life with Simon; the smoke, cascading away, would fulfil her dreams to find a new man, a new life.

Serena had begun to speculate how long a man's penis could actually be, and wondered if there'd be an entry in the Guinness Book of Records. She giggled to herself at the thought. Under the category 'Smallest Penis in the World', it would probably say 'Matthew Croome, Junior Minister.' She'd been living a lie all these years. No wonder she had never ever had a satisfactory orgasm.

Henry turned off the shower. He stood there for a moment before poking his head round the curtain. 'I've finished …'

'Feel better?' Serena smiled, still pointing the gun.

'Thanks … Is there a towel …?'

'Of course.' Serena threw him the bath towel that was on the rail. Henry retreated back behind the curtain to dry himself. Serena studied his silhouette as he vigorously towelled himself. Quite a nice physique compared with Matthew's. Not so skinny. Matthew was quite hairy, whereas Henry had smoother skin. She found herself wondering if Henry had a wife. Would there be a little woman at home and two broken-hearted children not knowing where their daddy was …? It must be nice to have children, she thought. She and Matthew had been trying for ages without any joy.

Henry appeared from behind the curtain with the towel wrapped around his waist. He folded his arms and looked at her. 'My clothes have been burnt?'

'Melissa's doing that now.'

'And Delia's bringing me some replacements, is that right?'

'She shouldn't be too long … What are you worried about?' Serena could see that he was suddenly agitated.

'Am I supposed to stay like this until she arrives?' Henry unfolded his arms and extended his hands as if to point out his predicament. The gesture made the towel fall down. Henry caught it just in time. Serena was secretly disappointed – she would have liked to have seen his penis again, if only to confirm what she had observed before.

'I'm not sure if there is anything you can put on …'

'I'll catch my death of cold …' Henry replied childishly.

'Not if we kill you first,' Serena joked. She was sorry she had said it when she saw his pained expression. 'I'll see if there's something in the house, but I can't make any promises. You might just have to wait until Delia returns. You can always cover yourself with one of the blankets. Shall we go?' She gestured with the gun and opened the bathroom door.

'Where are we going now?' Henry stopped outside in the hallway.

'Where do you think. Back to your bedroom.' They started to go upstairs.

'Are you going to tie me up …?

'Are you going to behave yourself?'

'I can't very well escape without any clothes, can I?' Henry was already beginning to feel a touch chilly.

'It would be silly to even try.'

They had reached his room. Henry walked in and hoped that Serena might stay and talk to him. As he turned around, she had already locked the door and was on her way downstairs. Henry sat on the bed and shivered. Taking her advice, he pulled the blanket over his shoulders and felt really sorry for himself.

18

Richard had borrowed his mother's car and chauffeur and was being driven to Wales to pick up the estate's helicopter. He was beginning to get very frustrated. The journey was taking longer than anticipated, because the elderly chauffeur kept five miles below the speed limit.

'Partridge … do you think we could go a little faster?'

'I'm doing my best, Master Richard.'

'You're only doing 65 – we could afford to go to 75 at least, you know.'

'Speed limit's 70, Master Richard.' Partridge still regarded Richard as the young boy he used to drive to school.

'I know perfectly well what the speed limit is, Partridge, but a few extra miles per hour is not going to constitute a major offence.'

Partridge tut-tutted to himself, ignoring Richard's request. He'd been driving for longer than Richard had been alive and wasn't about to change his habits. As far as he was concerned, Richard's generation were always in too much of a hurry. In his philosophy the journey was as important as getting there; and you got there in one piece. He'd never had an accident or scratched a car in his life. He was proud of his unblemished record. 'Beautiful countryside, Master Richard …'

'Would you stop for a moment, Partridge – over there at the lay-by.'

Even though there was no traffic in front or behind them, Partridge still signalled in the appropriate way. The car came to a gentle halt. 'Call of nature, sir?'

'Something like that. Partridge – would you get in the back please.'

'Sir …?' Partridge was curious, but did as he was requested. Perhaps there was a tear in the leather seating.

Richard opened and closed the door for him. He then climbed into the driver's seat and started the engine.

'Surely you're not going to drive, Master Richard …?' Partridge had not been in this position before.

'Yes, I am. I have a driving licence. I am insured. And for your information, and my sins, I am no longer Master Richard – but Lord Montcasse. Just relax and enjoy the ride. I take full responsibility.'

Richard put his foot on the accelerator and within minutes was pushing 80. Partridge was so taken aback that he closed his eyes and slumped into the seat. The shock had been too much for him.

Richard felt better now that he was in control. He purposefully avoided taking any notice of Partridge slumped in the back seat. To avoid conversation or argument he switched on the radio and listened to Radio Four. On some stretches he pushed the car to 85. The faster he went, the more he relaxed he became. He made good time. He knew he had reached his destination when he saw a police roadblock ahead.

Richard identified himself and was let through. The bright yellow and red helicopter, with the 'M' monogram on its side, was parked in a field before him. He drove right up to it.

The Scene of Crime Officers had finished their investigations inside the helicopter, and Richard was given permission to fly it back to the estate. He tried to find out if the police had caught the terrorists or had any clues, but either they weren't telling or they didn't know. After walking round the helicopter and checking that there was no damage, he returned to the car to give instructions to Partridge to drive back home. He opened one of the back doors. 'Everything's in order Partridge ...'

Partridge lay there lifeless. At first Richard thought he was asleep, but the closer he got to him, the more anxious he became. 'Oh, shit ...' he muttered. Had he given the old sod a heart attack with his driving? No wonder he had been so quiet throughout the last part of the journey. Why did Partridge have to go to meet his maker now, of all the inconvenient times! This would surely hold things up. There'd have to be an inquiry ... They should've retired Partridge years before. Richard knew that his mother and Partridge had had a thing between them for quite a few years. That was a reason he was still employed by them. Now he was dead, and it would be down to Richard to sort the mess out. First his father, now Partridge ... Who next – didn't death come in threes?

Richard sighed and turned away. He was about to approach one of the police officers, to explain this unfortunate tragedy, when he heard a croaky voice proclaim, 'Master Richard, have we arrived ...?' He looked back into the car to see Partridge stir, half opening his eyes.

'Partridge ... Are you all right ...?'

'Sorry, Master Richard ... I mean my Lord, I must've dropped off to sleep. What can you think of me? It's never happened before ...' Partridge was very apologetic and ashamed, and couldn't understand Richard's expression of sheer happiness at his unprofessional behaviour.

'Are you feeling fit enough to drive back?' Richard didn't want to take any chances now.

'Oh, yes, my Lord, I shall look forward to it. Is there anything else I can do?' Partridge had regained his composure and was now stood outside the vehicle looking more alive.

'It's all yours then, Partridge. I shall see you back at the estate.'

'Very well, my Lord. Have a safe and pleasant journey.' He got back in the front seat of the car where he belonged.

'Thank you, Partridge,' Richard replied gratefully. Those few moments of panic had taken it out of him. Now that the responsibility was off his shoulders it didn't matter if Partridge fell asleep at the wheel during the journey home.

Richard watched Partridge drive the car carefully out of the field. At his pace, it would probably take him the rest of the day to get back. He strolled toward the helicopter and got in. Within minutes he was airborne, surveying several police cars that had congregated below. Richard didn't care about the incident anymore. The helicopter was safely back and that was all that concerned him.

For the first ten minutes he flew south, toward the Montcasse Estate. Then he changed his mind and decided to make a short detour. He started to navigate east in the direction of Norwich. Another old girlfriend, Pippa Craik, lived only 15 minutes away. The manor house had a concreted area where he could conveniently land. Only the week before she had issued an open invitation for him to come and visit her. It had been quite some time since he'd enjoyed her hospitality. She wasn't like Amelia. Pippa had style and enjoyed sex for the simple pleasure it gave. Neither was she after catching Richard as a prospective husband. He knew he could just drop in, have a cup of tea, enjoy a quick one, and then fly off again. It would be a nice day's interlude, and much better than having tea with his mother.

The thought cheered him up considerably. He erased from his mind all the palaver concerning his father's funeral; the management of the estate; his elevation to Lord, and everything else that was troubling him. For the next couple of hours he would forget all that and immerse himself in the pleasures of Pippa. The very thought began to arouse him. He looked below at the passing countryside and felt alive again … until a bright silver glint in one of the fields caught his eye. He gazed down again and saw that the sun was reflecting off a largish metal object. It glistened amongst a small copse of trees. There was something about it that drew Richard's attention. If he had ignored it and flown on, his life would have progressed in a completely different direction. As it was, he was compelled to take a closer look and investigate. It was a decision that was about to alter his destiny quite dramatically.

19

The Prime Minister sat typing on his laptop: '*Laugh, and the world laughs with you. FART, and you fart alone …*' Rory wasn't the only one to have spotted the unfortunate acronym of Forces Against Rebellious Terrorists. When Alex had first informed him of the special name of the troop, Thomas had thought it was a joke; but then he had realised from Alex's expression that it was in all seriousness.

Thomas spent quite a bit of time in front of his laptop, noting down anything that amused him; jokes he had heard; stories that he found funny. He had them all indexed under numerous headings and categories, so that if he was looking for something specific for a particular occasion or speech, that was where he could find inspiration.

He also accessed various internet sites, not only for his own personal interest but also for making secret, coded e-mail contact with a special advisor in moments of uncertainty, and to ask for guidance regarding particular problems. He wrote under the user name 'Jack of Clubs', while his advisor signed himself 'King of Diamonds.'

Earlier on, after Alex had left, he had sent this cryptic note to his mentor: '*Secret documented in papers and photographs. Now stolen by subversive group. Game could be up if put in wrong hands. Comments? Jack of Clubs.*' Thomas now clicked on to see a message waiting for him : '*Always dangerous if anything is on paper. Depends on group and what they want. Game is never up until the whistle blows. Wait and see before acting. King of Diamonds.*'

Thomas switched off his laptop and sat in his chair, willing himself to remain calm. If he panicked now they'd all be on to him. *It will be all right, it will be all right*, he kept repeating to himself. He glanced at his open diary and remembered that he had an official engagement that evening. He sighed. Supper with the Polish Ambassador and his humourless wife. His large repertoire of jokes and amusing stories – which were one of the reasons he was such a popular Prime Minister – would be wasted on those two. He'd let Pamela do the entertaining and pass the time getting pissed on Polish vodka instead. A sense of oblivion, rather than humour, was what he needed now. Anything to stop him worrying about what might happen to him if his secret leaked out.

Alex and Charles were having a discreet lunch at their club. They stopped talking when the waiter brought in their main courses. Charles looked at his plate. 'What's this …?'

'Prawn Provençale, sir. That is what you ordered, sir.' The waiter knew he hadn't made a mistake.

'Five prawns, a dollop of rice, a bit of parsley and a teaspoonful of sauce is not what I call a proper serving.' It was a pretty picture, but not enough to sustain Charles's healthy appetite.

'We have a new chef, sir,' the waiter added.

'Economising, is he? I notice the prices have gone up. We seem to be paying more for less.' Despite being Chancellor of the Exchequer, Charles was the first to complain about a raw deal. 'What happened to the regular chef?'

'He died, sir,' the waiter said coldly.

'What, from starvation,' Charles quipped.

'Unfortunately he locked himself in the walk-in freezer. They didn't find him until the morning. Would you like me to take this back, sir?'

A look from Alex reminded him that they had more important issues to discuss. 'No, there isn't time,' Charles responded irritably. 'Just leave it and leave us. I shall have words with the maître d' later.'

The waiter departed, cursing Charles under his breath. His personal tax code had recently been raised. He admonished himself for not having spat in the sauce beforehand.

'As I was saying, Charles, we must try to keep calm about the whole affair.' Alex stuck his fork into his rack of lamb.

'Easier said than done when you know what the consequences are.' Charles speared three prawns and demolished them all in one go.

'We're doing all we can. The commando force are onto it now. The helicopter's been recovered. There was obviously a car waiting for them. They're studying the tracks now.' Alex tried to sound optimistic.

'Is that all? Have the terrorists made contact yet?' Charles had already finished eating.

'Not yet ...'

'I don't like it, I don't like it at all.' Charles started on another bread roll.

'Neither do I, Charles, but we've got to sit it out and deal with it as and when it happens.'

'As long as the Prime Minister doesn't cock it up for us.'

'Thomas will do as we say,' Alex assured him.

'Look how he responded during that sex-for-questions-in-the-House scandal,' Charles reminded him. 'One of our Ministers was caught red-handed and exposed. Thomas made a bloody joke of it all. What did he say? Any woman who was willing to offer sex for a question in the Commons might do better for one in the Lords. Less effort for a better return.'

'It did bring the House down and defused the whole situation,' Alex smiled, recalling the incident.

'Yes, but it didn't involve him personally. How is he going to cope with this bombshell if it gets out? You tell me that.' Still hungry, Charles reached across to an empty table near them and took the basket of bread rolls.

'That's not what's actually worrying me at the moment, Charles. I'm concerned about *how* anyone knew about the papers. Only *four* people were aware of their existence. You, me, the PM and Sir Freddy Knatchbull. We should have destroyed them all there and then.'

'If you remember,' Charles reminded him, 'I was all for shredding and burning them. But *you* didn't want that. Oh no, you persuaded me and Freddy to deposit them safely away, as a form of insurance – in the event of the PM getting too big for his boots.'

'It seemed like a good idea at the time ...' Alex chewed on a bit of meat.

'You don't think Freddy had anything to do with it?'

'No ... He's not interested in power or money. He's a multimillionaire and has everything he could possibly require. He never wanted to get involved in the first place, but he's a true patriot and only wished to do what was best for the party and his country. I rang him this morning in Geneva.'

'He seems to spend more time in Switzerland than in England these days,' Charles said enviously.

'Can you blame him? He said he had enough work to keep him busy for years.'

'Yes, and a better rate for his millions. So what did he have to say for himself when you told him?'

'Was very sorry, but didn't see what he could do about it. He'd done his job and that was the end of the matter as far as he was concerned. He assured me that he has never told anybody about our little secret. I have to say that I believe him.' Alex poured them both another glass of wine.

'I do too,' Charles admitted. 'Always been a man of his word, has old Freddy. When we were at Oxford together you couldn't have found a more honest chap. Knatchbull the Incorruptible, we called him.'

'So that leaves you, me and Thomas ...' Alex peered at Charles over his wine glass.

'Don't look at me like that! Why would I want to queer the pitch and upset a very amicable arrangement. I don't want to be Prime Minister, I'm quite happy as I am thank you. Wouldn't *you* have more to gain?' Charles threw the question back at Alex.

'Like what – power? We've got all that. Thomas leaves running the country, and all important decisions, to us. You know I don't want to be Prime Minister either, so it's highly unlikely I'd want to upset the applecart. After all, we have the most to lose if our secret is brought out into the open.'

Charles nodded in agreement as he finished his wine. He felt more depressed than ever. 'It still doesn't answer the question how anyone might have come across those papers in the first place ...' He looked at Alex, who had suddenly caught his depression. They ordered another bottle of wine.

Jeremy Hayward sat at his desk at the Treasury gnawing on a soft cheese and pickle sandwich. He picked up his mobile for the fifth time and rang first his home number and then Delia's mobile. He was hoping that Delia would answer and explain where she had been all night. But for the fifth time, both phones went to voicemail. The more he thought about it, the more convinced he was that his abduction theory was correct. Delia *had* been kidnapped by the terrorists, and it was almost certain that Melissa and Serena had been taken as well.

Jeremy threw the rest of the sandwich in the bin. He had already spoken to both Simon and Matthew several times that morning, and both had confirmed, in coded replies, that their wives were still missing. None of them had answered their phones. Matthew wanted to report the disappearance to the police, but Jeremy had dissuaded him. Too much was at stake. Jeremy wasn't sure what to do about it. He began to wonder if he was really responsible for this state of affairs …

About a month previously, Charles Carter had asked Jeremy to personally deliver some folders containing Royal accounts to a building near Whitehall. Often, highly secretive files had to be deposited in other buildings so as to minimise the risk of them being discovered by unauthorised personnel. The office block was quite new and boasted its own helicopter pad. The actual office, on the twelfth floor, where these documents were to be kept was very small and ordinary. Nothing to distinguish it from the others. On the door it said 'Stationery' – and that was what it was, a stationery store. Only a handful of privileged people knew the real significance of the cover. Behind a special row of shelves lay a hidden door. Behind this door, which was of reinforced steel and had a computerised security lock, there was another small room that housed these top secret and highly confidential files.

The Stationery Officer, who was in charge, welcomed Jeremy like an old friend and ushered him in, before locking the main door to allow no-one else to enter.

'And how are you today, Mr Hayward?' he asked, having not spoken to anyone else all morning. It was a lonely existence.

'Fine thanks …' Jeremy had forgotten the man's name. But he wasn't really fine, as he was suffering from a bit of a stomach ache.

'Do those need to be deposited in the usual place?'

'Yes, if you wouldn't mind …' Jeremy wasn't in the mood to chat. He could feel his stomach rumbling.

'Don't mind in the least, sir. That's what I'm here for after all! The hoi polloi might believe I only dispense paperclips and pens, but I'm proud to be of *special* service to *special* people like you sir … If you know what I mean..?'

Yes, and I suppose you'd kiss my arse, you odious little man, if I ordered you to, Jeremy thought. 'I am in a bit of a hurry …' he added, a touch irritated.

'Of course, Mr Hayward, sir …' The Stationery Officer then swung the row of shelves away from the wall and keyed in some numbers to unlock the steel door.

Just as the door was opened, the office phone rang. The Stationery Officer left him to deposit the folders while he went and answered the phone. Jeremy was glad of this interruption – not only because it got rid of the man, but also because he felt a fart brewing and wasn't sure if he'd be able to hold it in. In order not to disgrace himself, still being within earshot of the officer, Jeremy covered the oncoming wind by quickly knocking the nearest folder to the ground to disguise the sound. It crashed simultaneously with his own loud fart, and saved him from any embarrassment.

Jeremy bent down to pick up the folder, the security seal on which had broken, spilling its contents over the floor. Retrieving odd papers and photographs, he stumbled upon something that shocked him. He couldn't believe his eyes. He realised he had accidentally uncovered a terrifying secret. Then, hearing the officer get off the phone, Jeremy quickly stuffed everything back in the folder and replaced it on the shelf just in time.

'Everything alright sir?' the Stationery Officer asked as he returned.

'Yes … fine thanks … all done. You can lock up now.' Jeremy felt relieved.

The Stationery Officer sniffed the air. 'Bit of a stale atmosphere in here sir.

Better requisition some air freshener. That's the trouble when you've got so many old files bunched together in an airless room like this ...'

'Files that have been put together by a load of old civil servant farts ...' Jeremy cracked the one and only joke he was ever going to make. But it was lost on the Stationery Officer, who looked emotionless as he closed the secret room.

It was another half hour before Jeremy returned to the Treasury. He spent the time sat in St James's Park, mulling over in his mind what he had just been privy to. It simply *couldn't* be true ... but he'd seen the evidence with his very own eyes! If it got into the wrong hands it would be the scandal of the century, if not in the whole history of British politics. How could Thomas Lane have been allowed to get away with it all that time? Something had to be done about it – but what?

That's when he got together with his close friends, Matthew and Simon, and told them about his discovery.

'It's too ludicrous to be true!' said Simon.

'But if it *is* true,' responded Matthew, 'we are in possession of some very dangerous knowledge. Men have been killed for less ...'

'So what do we do?' Jeremy had had a disturbed night.

'Forget all about it,' Matthew suggested, not wanting any trouble.

'I can't ...' Jeremy would have liked to have erased it from his mind but knew he couldn't. If he hadn't farted in the first place, he would've stayed blissfully ignorant of the whole thing.

'Go and see the PM himself,' Simon now suggested. 'If there's any substance to it – he'll have to own up.'

'And then three Junior Ministers will mysteriously disappear and never be seen again ...' Matthew pessimistically added.

Okay, point taken,' Jeremy replied. 'Let's all sit on it for a week or so before we make any decisions.'

'I'd be happy to sit on it forever, if you want my opinion,' said Matthew.

'As Jeremy says, let's just wait a while,' Simon concluded.

'Fine, but under *no* circumstances say *anything* to *anyone* ... and that includes Melissa and Serena ...'

Jeremy was always the best at keeping secrets. He took pride in being the very soul of discretion. With him, a confidence shared was a confidence protected. A very private man, in as far as his job was concerned, he would drive Delia mad because he would never discuss work or anything that was politically sensitive. He was often surprised how much Delia actually did know, and could never work out where she got her information from. He didn't realise that he himself gave her the information – albeit subconsciously.

Jeremy's problem was that he talked in his sleep.

He didn't just mumble odd incoherent words, while asleep beside Delia, but whole sentences would come spilling out with perfect clarity. Everything he said always had some significant substance. It was as if the very pressure of consciously keeping these things to himself during the day, had to find a subconscious release at night.

Delia never told him he talked in his sleep, afraid it might stop him and close a useful door of information.

It was a week after Jeremy's extraordinary discovery that he began to talk about the papers in his sleep. At first Delia couldn't believe what she was hearing – yet there was no reason why it *shouldn't* be true. Things he had disclosed in the past had always proved factual. She learnt the location of the building, the actual office and where these files were kept. As the PM had been so beastly to them, Delia saw this as a chance for them to get their own back ...

Jeremy bit into an apple and continued to go over the events of the last few weeks to try to work out if and how Delia might have found out about the documents. Since Matthew had admitted mentioning *something* to Serena, surely that *had* to be the connection? But what he couldn't understand was how they might have got involved with the terrorists, and how the terrorists had known the location of the documents. Was there a major conspiracy going on somewhere? Was the Opposition planning to bring down the Government? All of these questions and theories rattled around his brain until he could stand it no more.

'You think *what*?' Charles Carter moved quickly across to his office door and firmly shut it.

'My wife has been taken hostage by the terrorists ... I mean, our wives, Croome's and Dodson's too ... All three of them.' Jeremy stood before Charles, trying to stay calm and in control.

'Have you any proof of this?' Charles listened carefully.

'Well, no ...' Jeremy stuttered, 'but they've all disappeared, and I am led to believe it is to do with the terrorists ...'

'You are *led* to believe ... And what leads you, may I ask ...?' Charles watched Jeremy mindfully. Anyone else and he would've either have thrown them out of the office or given them a severe bollocking for wasting his time. But this wasn't characteristic of Jeremy Hayward. Charles knew he never said anything that he either didn't believe or couldn't substantiate.

'It's to do with what the terrorists stole – from the Stationery Office.'

'And how do you know about this ...?' Charles's tone was soft.

'It isn't a secret that some sensitive papers were stolen ...' Jeremy answered firmly.

'No ... But what connection do these so-called papers have with your wives?' Charles didn't like the sound of this.

'Charles ... I'd like to explain.'

'Please do, Jeremy. I'm listening ...'

Jeremy told him the whole story about his visit to the Stationery Office and what he'd found there, and about how it had possibly leaked via their wives, adding that he wanted to do all he could to alleviate the situation. Throughout, Charles listened attentively, revealing nothing from his expression as to what he was thinking. If only Jeremy had looked down behind Charles's desk he would have seen him clenching his fists and digging his nails into his palms.

'Do you believe what you saw in those papers?' Charles asked Jeremy after he had finished.

'Well, I only glimpsed at a couple of pages for a few seconds.'

'A few seconds ... Was it a thick file?'

'Quite thick ...' Jeremy couldn't quite see what he was getting at.

'You make this ridiculous, outrageous assumption, based on a couple of pages ...' Charles suddenly towered over him.

'There was a photograph ... I mean there were many, but I saw one of them.' Jeremy was trying to be logical.

'What do we always say about photographs? Especially ones that we've seen for only a few seconds?' Charles switched to his lecture mode.

'Trust nothing until it has been authenticated ...?'

'Correct. And do you assess the contents of a file by some random pages?'

'No, sir ...' Jeremy was starting to wonder if he'd imagined the whole thing. He began to feel very embarrassed.

'I've heard some cock and bull stories in my time, but I never expected it from you, Jeremy. Wait till I tell the PM. He'll piss himself laughing!' Charles had gained the upper hand and was using this to demolish Jeremy's beliefs.

'But the papers that were stolen ...?' Jeremy was determined to follow it through.

'Yes, we believe some papers were taken, but nothing to worry unduly about. Just some budget forecasts for the next decade. If published they might cause a few hours' embarrassment. Does that satisfy you?' Charles was testing him now.

'What about the hostage that was taken? That's no secret ...'

'A single male hostage, yes. We know nothing about him or why he was taken. The whole thing'll probably turn out to be some university rag stunt.'

'But what about our wives ...?'

'Rather a coincidence that all three have gone AWOL, isn't it? Sure they haven't gone off on holiday together?'

'They would've said.'

'Would they? My wife – thank god – often "disappears" for a couple of weeks. Usually I get a postcard from Rio or some such place.' Charles was feeling much better.

'I still can't help being worried about them.'

'Look, give it a few more days. If you haven't heard by the end of the week, come back to me and I'll have a discreet word with my friends at the Met, and we'll put some feelers out. All right?'

'If you say so, sir.' Jeremy knew he didn't have a leg to stand on.

'Good man. Now, if I were you, I'd wouldn't repeat to *anyone* that silly story you made up ...' Charles stopped Jeremy before he could answer. 'Rumours like that have a way of spreading very quickly and doing a lot of damage. And we wouldn't want that, would we? Jeremy, I know that the PM holds you in high regard. I realise that you were overlooked in the last reshuffle. But I've had a little hint from upstairs that your exemplary work and loyalty haven't gone unnoticed, shall we say. Stick at it and you might be pleasantly surprised.'

'Thank you, sir ... What about Simon Dodson and Matthew Coombe? I did tell them ...' Jeremy didn't want to get them into unnecessary trouble.

'It's quite simple. Explain what we discussed and how you made a false assumption. Just make sure they keep their mouths shut.'

'Yes, sir ...'

'You'll probably find, when you get home tonight, your dear wife will already be there, having prepared you a nice meal. There's bound to be a simple explanation as to where she went. There always is.' Charles smiled and indicated that it was the end of the meeting.

'I hope so,' Jeremy sighed as he left Charles's office.

Charles kept up the smile until he was certain Jeremy was far enough away, before he dropped his guard and picked up the telephone. 'Alex … Deep, deep shit. We must meet. Now! Usual place.' Charles put down the phone before Alex could protest.

'Bugger, fuck and bollocks …' Alex whispered uncharacteristically after Charles had repeated his conversation with Jeremy. 'That's all we need.'

'I did my best to convince him that he was imagining things, to steer him in a different direction. I think he bought it.' Charles's top lip was sweating, and he could taste the salt from the droplets that slid into his mouth. The two men stood in the corner of a Government library, which was thankfully empty.

'And what if their wives *have* been kidnapped?' Alex took a book off a shelf and flicked through it.

'We have a major problem …' Charles dropped his voice even lower. He didn't even like to think about it.

'Who could be behind all this? We've still had no indications.'

'What's the latest?'

'Nothing new. I've ordered a progress report on the hour, every hour, and an immediate briefing when something does break. Until either they make contact or we discover their hiding place – there's nothing else we can do, except wait.'

'And the wives …?' Charles hated bringing it up again.

'I'd better warn our special force to take that into consideration. We can't be too careful. If they are being held captive we cannot afford to have their blood on our hands. Think of the adverse publicity.'

'Unless they know too much …?' prompted Charles.

Alex closed his eyes and remained silent for about a minute while he thought about the consequences. Already it sounded like at least nine other people might know the secret. The three wives … the Junior Ministers … the terrorists … The list was beginning to get out of hand. The odds were creeping up against them. How simple it would be to get them all together and accidentally bomb the place. That would solve their problem in one fell swoop. Alex could feel the nervous sweat trickling down the inside of his arms. It made him shiver. 'We can't sacrifice their lives, Charles …'

'We'll sacrifice ours instead, shall we?'

'You know what I mean. We'll just have to see how things go.'

'That might be too late.' Charles was getting impatient. 'In the meantime, what do we do about Hayward, Croome and Dodson?'

'What do you suggest?' Alex asked.

'Kill them …?' Charles smiled.

'Very funny, Charles. I meant a more practical, eco-friendly suggestion.'

'I thought that was. Maybe not eco-friendly, but it would certainly lower the stakes.'

'Charles, you can be a real mercenary bastard sometimes.'

'That's why I've succeeded in getting where I am – the same goes for you.'

Alex didn't want to argue with that. He realised he had stepped on quite a few toes to become Home Secretary. His rise hadn't been without its casualties. 'Can I suggest we deal with them if and when we find out that their wives *have* been taken hostage. Understood?'

Charles grudgingly acquiesced 'What do we tell the PM?'

'Let's be different for a change.' Alex put the book back on the shelf. 'Let's tell him the truth ...'

Thomas Lane gazed out of the window and watched Alex and Charles, like Tweedledum and Tweedledee, walk away from Number Ten and get into a car. They'd just informed him about the possible kidnapping of the wives and all the implications that went with it. It had been a brief, straight-to-the-point meeting. Alex had done all the talking while Charles had paced about like a caged tiger. The gravity of the situation had been spelt out in broad terms. Things weren't looking good. Thomas had said very little throughout, preferring to listen to what they had to say. Alex had wanted to smooth the way as gently as possible. Charles, in his inimitable way, had wanted to kill everyone, so as to leave no room for mistakes. For the first time in their association, Alex and Charles had turned to Thomas for an answer. What should they do? Thomas had been clever enough to remain enigmatic and had told them both that he needed some time to think. A decision of this magnitude had to be pondered carefully ...

As he watched the car disappear from Downing Street, he had a notion that perhaps he should dispose of Alex and Charles instead. He'd come across an organisation on the internet that openly advertised 'Assassins for hire. No questions asked. Reasonable terms.' Maybe he should contact them to do the job for him ...?

20

The helicopter gently descended into the field below, about a hundred metres from the copse of trees where the metal object lay. As he got closer, Richard could clearly see that it was a car lying on its side.

He parked the helicopter and slowly walked toward the car. The air around him was silent except for the chatter of several birds that were hovering above the crashed vehicle like vultures circling their next meal.

About 20 metres from the car, Richard saw there was a body inside. A seemingly lifeless body. He ran the rest of the way until he reached one of the doors. The woman's body was spread across the front of the car, her arms slumped over the steering wheel, her legs dangled down over the passenger seat. There was a ring of blood on her chest and some dried blood down her chin. There was no sign of breathing. She looked very dead.

Richard stood for a minute wondering what to do. He now wished he'd never spotted the car in the first place. Didn't he have enough on his plate? But he couldn't very well leave her there.

He opened the door and took a closer look at her. She had a nice face. A bit county, yet very open. Richard put his hand on her cheek. It still felt warm. He then touched her wrist and tried to discover if there was a pulse. It was difficult to tell. He thought he sensed one, but it was very faint. He couldn't see if she had any broken bones, but none of her limbs looked at an awkward angle. Should he try to phone for help? He could do, but by the time he had got his bearings and summoned the relevant authorities it might be too late. His best bet was to get her out of the car and take her himself to the nearest hospital.

Richard climbed on top of the car with his legs astride the door opening. He bent down and gently put his arms underneath her arms and started to pull her up. Thankfully the woman wasn't as heavy as he had thought, and there were no obstructions to hinder the release. In three movements Richard had managed to get her out and onto the grass beside the car.

She still didn't stir. He looked at her again. It *was* a nice face ... and quite an attractive figure from what he could see. Even the perfume he could detect had a pleasing, expensive aroma. Who was she; where had she come from; where was she going? What a waste if she was dead ... As he gazed down at her, he momentarily thought he saw her chest heave slightly, as if a breath had escaped. He bent down and put his ear to her mouth – but there was nothing.

Richard knelt down and put his fingers round her lips, as he had once seen demonstrated, and lowered his face over hers. Then, taking a deep breath and closing his eyes, he proceeded to give the woman the kiss of life. It was the first time he had ever done it. He detected a faint smell of curry, which he didn't find unpleasant. After half a dozen blows, and leaning back to take a breath himself, Richard was disappointed to see that there was no change at all. He was wasting his time. He'd better just carry her into the helicopter and take her to hospital. He had done all he could; the rest would be up to the authorities. Such a pity, and she had such nice lips ... And then her chest twitched again suddenly. Richard quickly bent down and gave the kiss of life again, this time with more energy and determination.

The woman's body jerked and she slowly began to breathe. Richard watched her for a moment. Her eyes slowly opened and she looked up at him. 'Welcome back ...' he smiled. She tried to say something, but just couldn't get any words out. Richard leant closer to her face to listen. As he did so she drowsily wrapped her arms around his neck and drew him to her lips. She kissed him passionately.

Richard was rather taken aback by this demonstration of affection, and gently pulled himself away.

'No ... don't ...' she pleaded as if still in a trance.

'You don't know what you're doing ...' Richard stared down at her.

'An angel ... you're a divine angel ...' she mumbled.

He could see that she hadn't fully come to. Her eyes gazed up at the blue sky. She smiled dreamily. 'Heaven ... It is beautiful ...' She turned her eyes toward him. 'My angel ... where are your wings ...?'

'The helicopter's just over there. I think I'd better take you to hospital.'

'Hospital ...? There are no hospitals in heaven ...' She looked confused, turned her head sideways and saw the upturned car. 'This isn't heaven ...?'

'I'm afraid not ...' Richard broke the news gently.

'You're ... you're not an angel ...?'

'I cannot tell a lie. Sorry.' He smiled.

'Then ... then I'm not dead ...' she whispered, like a disappointed child who has awoken from a blissful dream to discover reality.

'You're very much alive, I'm pleased to say. I really thought you were a goner at first. How do you feel?'

'What ...?' She was still disorientated.

'Any major aches or pains? Anything broken? Can you move?'

'I don't know ... I feel numb ... nothing hurts.' She turned her head the other way and saw the helicopter. A car, travelling along the road from where she had skidded, sped past, bringing an only too realistic sound to the scene. Delia now knew that she wasn't dead and that this wasn't heaven. But that kiss ... that had felt unreal ... she honestly had thought her guardian angel had come to transport her away ... She turned back to Richard. 'Who are you?'

'Richard Montcasse. I was passing in the helicopter when I saw your car. Do you remember what happened?'

'No ...'

'What's your name?' Richard felt easy with her.

'My name ... I'm ... I'm ...' Delia wracked her brains. Her expression went blank. 'I ... I don't know ...'

'You can't remember who you are?'

'I'm sorry ...' Delia wasn't as much upset as indifferent. She couldn't remember anything. Who she was, what she was doing there. Somehow it didn't seem to matter to her. It didn't feel important. The man who stood before her had a strong, trustworthy face, wasn't threatening and posed no danger to her. She felt light, devoid of any cares or responsibilities. She tried to sit up, but found it difficult.

'Don't overdo it. Let me help you.' Richard put his hands on her back and helped her sit up. His touch made her shiver. She felt dizzy for a few seconds before sitting up straight. 'All right?'

'I think so … Where are we?' She felt a little stiff.

'In Suffolk somewhere. I can't tell you where exactly. I'm not quite sure myself.' Richard started to climb back into the car.

'Suffolk …' It didn't mean a thing to her. 'What are you doing?'

'Seeing if I can find out who you are. You must've had a bag or something …' Richard searched everywhere inside – under the seats, in the glove compartment, in the boot – but it was strangely empty. 'Not a thing, I'm afraid.' Richard climbed out of the car and looked at it. It was a Skoda, about eight years old. Not the kind of car he would associate with a woman of Delia's obvious breeding. He walked around the perimeter of the car to see if there were any clues, or if anything had fallen out during the crash. He could see nothing and decided to stop looking.

'I remain a mystery woman …' Delia quite liked the thought.

'Do you feel fit enough to move?'

'Where are we going?'

'I think we'd better get you to the nearest hospital. Have you checked over and then try to find out who you are.' Richard made a note of the registration number, which he thought should solve the problem.

Delia made an attempt to get up, but felt stiffer than she had thought.

'Take it easy now,' said Richard. 'I'd better carry you.'

Delia didn't protest, and let him sweep her up in his firm arms and carry her across to the helicopter.

They took off smoothly. Fifty metres away from the car, in some dense grass, lay Delia's handbag, its contents scattered about.

21

The crack troop had all arrived at the spot where Delia and the others had originally set down and picked up the getaway car. Luckily a farmer had spotted the helicopter landing in and taking off from one of his fields, and had notified the authorities. The soil samples, taken from the helicopter when it had finally been dumped in Wales, matched those from this particular area. The local police had been ordered to keep away from the scene so as to allow the special force to investigate. So now Barry, Kieran, Jack, Archie and Rory paced about the field in a desperate search for any clues.

Terry stood to one side and watched while the others studied the ground before them. His brief was merely to keep them in check and observe them, rather than aid them in any way. They all had to be individually judged on their performance, and his final decision would eventually determine the winner.

He made specific notes at each stage of the proceedings, careful to scribble them in code in case his notebook somehow got into their hands. Terry wasn't taking any chances. These men were dangerous and unpredictable. His mobile phone was in direct contact with Alex Brook's office and he was under strict orders to report every hour on the hour or when there was exceptional news to convey. His last communication from London had stressed the urgency of the situation, and the fact that there might also be three female hostages to contend with. Terry had decided not to tell the others yet. He now realised that this was more than just an interdepartmental contest – and if anything went wrong, he would be the first in the firing line.

Kieran bent down and picked something up. Rory, who was nearby studying the tyre tracks, sidled up to him. 'What's that ya got there, petal?' Kieran displayed a condom, still in its packet. 'This is no time to talk of love – right place, wrong moment!'

'Fuck off you!' Kieran angrily threw the condom down on the ground.

'Silly boy, there might have been fingerprints on it.' Rory picked it up carefully. He suddenly had a thought and giggled.

'What is it with you?' Kieran was annoyed at his own stupidity.

'Well … if this condom had been used, d'you think we'd have been able to get penis prints from it? Now there's a thought to conjure with!' Rory smiled.

'Why don't you conjure yourself up yer own arse!' Kieran shouted.

'I've done some magic tricks in my time, dear, but I have to admit that one's always eluded me. Got any tips?' Rory watched Kieran walk away in disgust.

'We'd better keep it, just in case.' Terry, who had overheard them, produced a small plastic bag, which he handed to Rory, who dropped the condom in.

'What if we find it's not relevant to proceedings?' Rory asked.

'Then you, Rory, can have the privilege of wearing it at our passing out parade,' Terry quickly responded.

'I shall stand to attention with pride!' Rory gazed down at the tyre marks, and suddenly something appeared familiar. He bent down and took a closer look.

'What is it?' Jack knew Rory well enough by then to know when he was serious.

'See that criss-cross there? It's distinct from the general tread.' Rory pointed to an unusual pattern made by one of the tyres. Every few feet it repeated itself.

Jack bent down and examined the pattern with him. 'Could be a worn part of the tyre … It's certainly unique and could help us identify the car.'

'Eureka!' Rory suddenly screeched, and started to make a dash for the car.

The others, without knowing why and not wanting to be left out, also ran to their cars. Terry, suddenly realising that he was being left on his own, quickly took a photo of the tyre marks. 'Hey … !' he shouted. Rory had already got in the van and was accelerating out of the field. In close pursuit were Barry and Kieran. Terry ran and just managed to jump in the back of Jack and Archie's car. 'The crazy son-of-a-bitch!' Terry cursed. 'What the hell's he playing at?'

'He obviously knows something we don't,' Archie remarked.

'It had better be good … And please don't lose him.' Terry zoomed in on the photo to get a better look at the tyre mark.

Melissa was hungry. Burning Henry's clothes, and the passions that had stirred, had given her an appetite. She desperately looked around for any morsel, but everything had been eaten at breakfast. The emptiness in her stomach was making her irritable. 'Delia should have been back by now with the provisions,' she bleated at Serena, who had laid out her terrorist outfit and was measuring it out with her hands. 'What are you doing? Thinking of making it a permanent addition to your wardrobe?'

'I was just seeing if it might fit Henry. We're about the same size.'

'Delia said she would bring him some clothes.'

'But what if she got held up and didn't have time? He's got to wear something. We can't leave him with just a towel.' Serena didn't like to think that Henry might be cold.

'You don't think anything's gone wrong, do you?' Melissa's stomach was gurgling.

'Delia's only been gone four hours. Remember, she's got to ditch the car, buy another one, go to a supermarket and stock up with food, then get some clothes … It all takes time. Anyway, I'm not hungry.'

Melissa looked across at Serena's skinny frame. 'Sometimes I think you're anorexic …'

'I can't help it if I don't eat as much as you.'

'Are you implying that I'm fat?' Melissa stood with her hands on her waist. Serena looked at her without replying. 'I know I am. I can't help it if I like my food. I'd much rather have sex than a plate of pasta. But since Simon is either too busy, too tired, or simply not in the mood – I stick food in my mouth instead of other delicacies … Know what I mean?'

Serena was clearly embarrassed. She didn't like it when Melissa started going on about sexual matters. When they had first got to know each other, Melissa had often extolled the virtues of oral sex. Serena had initially thought it just meant talking dirty. She had subsequently been very shocked to learn the true meaning of the practice – something she and Matthew had never indulged in. He had once asked her for a blow job, and she had blown on his face as sensually as possible. She wondered why he had never asked her again.

'I can't stand it! I'm going to the local shop. Can I get you anything?' Melissa was already making for the door.

'Delia did say we should stay put until she returned.'

'I won't be ten minutes … Serena, you worry too much. Look, nobody knows or even cares who we are. A lot of the properties around here are holiday lets. They're used to seeing odd faces about. I'm just popping out for some groceries. Now d'you want anything?'

'No … but don't be long.'

'I shall be there and back before you know it.' Melissa had closed the door before Serena could say anything else.

Upstairs, Henry was feeling thoroughly miserable, wrapped up in the blanket, which was starting to make him itch. He heard the door bang and tried to look out of the window. Yet all he saw were trees and other rooftops. He couldn't see what was going on below or who was coming or going. The room was too high up and the window too tiny for him to be able to see more. Perhaps they'd all gone and left him … Perhaps they'd set a timing device that would explode when they were far enough away … Perhaps he'd never see Serena again …

The door suddenly opened and Serena quickly threw in a bundle of clothes, then locked it again. 'Try those on for now,' she called from beyond the door. 'They'll do as a temporary measure,'

'You can come in¹– I promise I won't do anything silly.' Henry just wanted someone to talk to. He was bored with his own company.

'Sorry, it's best this way.' Serena was tempted, but since she was now alone, she couldn't take the chance.

'Could I at least have something to read?' he pleaded.

'I'll see what there is …' Serena made her way down the stairs.

Henry picked up the clothes. Obviously bought in an army surplus store. There was a thick shirt, a pair of fatigues, woollen socks and a black jumper with leather elbow pads. What every fashionable terrorist wore, bar the balaclava. He then realised there were no underpants to go with the ensemble. He suddenly didn't care. He might as well go commando if he was going to be dressed like one. He tried them on and they fitted almost perfectly. The bonus was that they still smelt of Serena. Her perfume permeated the very fibres and gave him an odd sense of security and peace.

'Sorry, this is all I could find …' Serena managed to slide a thin book under the door. It was one of those popular romances, entitled *Night in Shining Amour*, and the cover showed a woman sleepwalking in an almost transparent nightie with the dark, shadowy figure of a man towering over her, brandishing something that looked vaguely like a sword. 'You haven't read it, have you?' Serena genuinely asked.

'No … I haven't read it …' Henry couldn't wait. 'By the way, the clothes —' But

Serena had already gone. She obviously didn't want to talk. Henry went back to the bed and lay down on it. He opened the book and started reading.

About 50 miles away, Rory came to a full stop by a bend in the road. The two cars behind him almost collided into each other when they had to brake quite sharply to pull up behind him. At first Rory had tried to lose them, and during this initial chase had accidentally run over a couple of stray chickens, which had suddenly made him realise that without Terry present, his discovery might be in vain. So they had all ended up in a ridiculous convey, weaving round the small country roads like dogs trying to sniff at each other's bottoms.

Rory stepped out of his car and stood at the side of the road. Terry joined him. 'What was all that about? I could throw you off this mission for what you just did.'

'I knew I was right ... Don't you remember travelling down this particular stretch?' Rory felt confident.

'No. What's the significance ...' Terry was not in the mood for any games. It was nearly time for him to report back to Whitehall, and he didn't want to have to tell them that they were standing by a road on some wild goose chase.

Rory pointed down to the ground. There were black skid marks going off the road. 'So ...?' Terry was still in the dark. Rory crooked his little finger as if to beckon, which really incensed Terry. 'You've got one minute to explain yourself ...'

'Keep your knickers on! Look ...' Rory bent down by the grass verge and made Terry take a closer look at the tyre marks. He could now see the distinct criss-cross pattern that they had first seen in the field.

'Okay,' Terry acknowledged, 'so the car happened to skid here. What does it tell us?'

Barry, Kieran, Jack and Archie watched as Rory followed the tracks until he was out of sight behind a hedge. Neither Barry nor Kieran remembered driving along this road, or realised that they had actually been responsible for causing what they were all about to witness.

'*Voila!*' Rory proudly proclaimed as he revealed the crashed car lying on its side in the field beyond. They all stood there, half surprised, half irked that they hadn't been the one to make the discovery.

'How did you know?' Kieran asked suspiciously.

'Well ...' Rory teasingly expounded, 'one of the terrorists, lovely boy, phoned me this morning and said that they'd probably be crashing at this very spot ...'

'You're taking the fucking piss again.'

'Is that an invitation ...?' Rory smiled. Kieran had had enough, and furiously pulled Rory to the ground. Before he could throw a punch, Rory had taken out a small knife and quickly made a couple of slashes to Kieran's left arm, before getting up and holding the others back. 'It's all right, our little tiff's over. I've just given our friend here another pretty little tattoo. A matching ensemble.'

Kieran took his bloodstained hand away from his arm. The slashes on his arm resembled the criss-cross tyre pattern.

'I'll get you for this!' Kieran threatened Rory with his finger.

'Promises, promises ...' Rory gently scolded.

While this was going on, Archie and Jack had gone over to the car and started walking round it, being careful not to touch anything. Jack peered through the windscreen before calling out: 'It's empty, but I can see some bloodstains inside.'

This had the effect of defusing the situation and bringing the others over to the car. On the way, Terry took Rory aside for a brief word. 'You shouldn't have done that.'

'And given him an open invitation to beat the shit out of me? I've got my looks to consider, you know. Anyway, if it hadn't been for me, you wouldn't have found the car. Some bonus points there, surely?'

'And how *did* you know about it?'

'Call it intuition, call it a lucky fluke. I'm no Sherlock Homo. I just remembered seeing those skid marks on the way here. There was something about the pattern that stayed with me. And talking of skid marks – or touching cloth as it's known in church circles – I once knew someone who could tell your fortune based on the marks inside your pants ...'

'Please, Rory, not now!' Terry admired Rory's detection skills but was not ready to endure another of his coarse anecdotes.

They had all surrounded the car by now and were studying it from every angle. Barry looked closely at the rogue tyre. The marks matched Terry's photograph of the tracks. They were left without any doubt that this was the escape car. 'Can I 'ave a butchers inside, or do we have to wait for forensics?' Barry asked.

'Got any gloves? Don't want you to obliterate any fingerprints.' When Barry shook his head, Terry reached into his bag and produced a pair of transparent plastic gloves that he handed to him. Barry put them on, climbed on the car and opened the driver's door. Like a snake he crawled in head first.

'Is that blood?' Kieran asked, seeing Barry's face up against the seat where there was a red stain.

'It's blood all right,' Barry called out. 'No mistaking that, mate.'

'How can you tell?' Terry was curious.

Barry twisted his head toward the opening. 'It's a little speciality of mine. When I was in the Murder Squad, I trained meself to be able to distinguish blood from any other red substance. I'm not often wrong.'

'Any idea of the blood type?' Archie added sarcastically.

''Fraid not.' Barry disappeared further into the car, leaving the others with a new perspective on their colleague.

While Barry continued his investigations inside the car, Jack had to pee, and so wandered over to the copse of trees to relieve himself. While stood against a tree, trying to drown some ants that were crawling up it, he turned his head and noticed something lying in the grass a few metres away. Zipping up his fly, he walked over to the spot. On the ground lay an open handbag with various objects scattered around it. Set slightly apart was a small piece of paper with a Suffolk address on it. Without thinking, Jack put the piece of paper in his pocket. As he picked up the handbag he noticed Archie making his way toward him.

'Anything interesting ...?' Archie pointed his swagger stick at the bag.

'Dunno, just spotted it.' Jack took out a bulging envelope. Inside was a stack of £50 notes. 'Shit ... there must be about five grand in here ...'

'Any ID?'

'There's a purse here with more money and about half a dozen credit cards ... belonging to a Delia Hayward ... She must be loaded ... There's some door keys ...'

Jack and Archie, too busy rummaging around the contents of the bag, didn't notice Terry creep up on them. 'And what do we have here, gentlemen?'

'Just some bag, Terry, nothing that would interest you ...' Archie tried to slip the envelope behind his back, but wasn't quick enough to deceive Terry's eagle eyes. Terry grabbed the envelope.

'Just a bag, eh? You weren't going to pocket this, by any chance?'

'Certainly not,' Jack replied indignantly.

Archie had his eye on the main chance. 'Over a thousand each if we split it between the three of us, old chap. The others needn't know. I'm sure she has lots more stashed away.'

'She ...?' Terry now took the purse off Jack and looked inside. 'Delia Hayward ... Oh, bugger bollocks – that's all we need ...'

'Do you know the lady? Who is she?' Archie enquired.

'Looks like the wife of a Government Minister ...' Terry suddenly realised how much more serious the situation had become.

'Do we have a problem, Terry?' Jack asked.

'We do. A bloody big problem ... This concerns all of us.' Terry picked up the bag and threw all the contents in, including the envelope of bank notes. 'And as for splitting this, Archie, *old chap*, you can forget it. This is crucial evidence. Now come and join the others. I've got something important to say to you all.' Terry was now walking back toward the car.

'I hope he's not going to pocket that money himself,' Archie remarked suspiciously.

'I'd be surprised if he did,' Jack assured him.

'Nothing surprises me, old man, not even the contents of that piece of paper you slipped in your pocket before I arrived ...' Archie smiled.

'What piece of paper?' Jack tried to act puzzled.

'We'll talk about it later, shall we. I don't want to miss what our friend Terry is going to impart to us.' Archie moved on ahead, leaving Jack to feel in his pocket to make sure the piece of paper was still there. Then he furtively took it out, memorised the address, screwed the paper up and popped it in his mouth – but not before Archie had turned back to catch him chewing the paper. 'I hope that wasn't a piece of crucial evidence, Jack ...' Jack nearly choked, and it took all his powers of control to stop him from throwing up.

Terry gathered everybody together in a circle. 'Right ... I want each of you to scour *every inch* of this area ...'

'What are we looking for?' Kieran interrupted.

'Anything and everything.' Terry continued. 'You must leave no stone unturned —'

'And don't forget to look under the cowpats!' chirped Rory.

'That's right, Rory – all turds will be *your* special task. And I mean it!' Terry wasn't in the mood for jokes. 'We have a potentially critical scenario here. It's more serious than we thought, and could rather change the game plan.'

'So what's so fucking "potentially critical" then?' Kieran was getting bored with all this intellectual gabble. He just wanted some action.

'Is it to do with this bag we just found, which might belong to some Government Minister's wife?' Jack volunteered.

'Until I've reported to Whitehall, and received further instructions, I can't go into any more details. Now search – as if your lives depended on it.'

Without more being said, the group split up and went in separate directions like the five points in a star, each starting to comb the ground before them. Kieran suddenly stopped and shouted across to Rory: 'Hey, there's some shit down here! Isn't it your job to sift through it?'

Rory stopped and turned in Kieran's direction. 'Thanks, petal. I'm a bit busy at the moment. Can I suggest you either put it in your pocket for later, or ask our friend Barry over there, to give it a good lick – he might be able to tell us whether it's human or animal shit. Talk to you later!' With that, Rory minced off toward his own part of the area.

Terry leant back against the car and phoned Alex Brook's office. He wasn't looking forward to this conversation.

'There's no question about it, Prime Minister, I have confirmation that three of our Junior Ministers' wives have been taken hostage by the terrorists ... One of them might even be dead ...' Alex did his best to sound calm about it, but inside he felt a mass of insecurities.

'Yet these terrorists haven't revealed who they are?' Thomas doodled on a piece of letterhead. He wrote '*Down in street.*'

'No ... there's been nothing.'

'So we don't know what they want?'

'Not yet. It's difficult to know how to proceed ...' Alex was doing his best to steer clear of making any important decisions. He looked across at Charles.

'It was Delia Hayward's bag that was found ...' Charles responded.

'Delia Hayward ... Jeremy's wife? I've never liked the man. No sense of humour whatsoever. Can we trust him?' Thomas doodled a balaclava with a skull and crossbones.

'I believe we can,' Charles spoke. 'I think we can persuade him to keep quiet.'

'And what would be the price of his silence?' Thomas believed that there was always a price to pay. Even he had had to pay that price, to become Prime Minister in the first place.

'Until I've talked to him and gauged his reaction, it's difficult to say what he might ask. I've always found him professional, honest and with a deep sense of party loyalty.' Charles was convinced that he'd be able to convince Jeremy to see reason.

'Perhaps, Prime Minister ...' Alex interjected, 'a Cabinet post? Northern Ireland ...? Minister for Health ...? You did overlook him the last time.'

'Do I have to? I repeat – I just don't like the man. The thought of having to deal with him does not please me.' Thomas was starting to sound petulant.

'You won't have to. Charles and I will do all that – as we have done in the past. Besides, it's always better if you remain slightly distant from the rest of the members of the Government.'

'Do we have an alternative? Would he accept money, some property, free life membership to the best knocking shop in town ...?' A little smile passed across Thomas's mouth.

'Jeremy is reasonably well-off. He's got houses in Kensington, Edinburgh, Paris and the South of France ... I doubt he'd want more.'

'Nonsense, Charles, everyone wants more. I do, you do – Alex does. So you think the temptation of a bevy of beauties wouldn't appeal to our friend? Guaranteed tax and clap free.' Thomas smiled to himself again, he'd have to remember to enter that into his joke databank.

'A rise in position, I feel, would be most enticing in Jeremy's case,' Alex maintained.

'That's tantamount to blackmail.' Thomas realised there was no alternative.

'I'm afraid, in the words of our Intelligence department, he knows too much.'

'I suppose an unfortunate accident is probably out of the question?' Thomas was clutching at straws. 'A lethal injection of laughing gas ...?'

'It's too risky, especially as his wife is now involved. We don't want to be implicated in a conspiracy.'

'No more than we are already, eh?' Thomas made Charles and Alex feel very uncomfortable. 'What about the others – Dodson and Croome? Have I got to have them in the Cabinet as well?'

'Dodson, I'm sure, will accept a financial incentive to keep his mouth shut. As for Croome, he's a bit of a weak toad – I'll do my best to scare the living shits out of him.' Charles was confident he knew these men well enough.

'I hope you're right ...' Thomas scratched a big question mark on his paper.

'We are doing our utmost to contain the situation,' Alex reaffirmed. 'No-one, apart from the special force, is remotely aware of what is going on. We are hoping to defuse the controlling factors as expediently as possible.'

'That's a political euphemism, if ever I heard one.' Thomas looked both of them in the eye. 'I suppose until we do learn of any demands, we must continue with the utmost caution and discretion ...'

'Without question, Prime Minister!' both answered at the same time, and then felt foolish for having done so.

'After all, let's look at it this way,' Thomas took a deep breath, 'we're only as safe as the secrets we keep safe. If the media get a sniff of this, we're all well and truly finished ... Or as my father used to say – we'll be fucked up and far from home ...'

Scott Trimble, award-winning journalist and independent news producer, was busy cutting together a documentary he had just completed, exposing the sexual preferences of certain high ranking officials, when his phone rang. 'Yeah? Yeah, how are you? I'm tied up at the moment ... No, working ... Don't be such a bitch! ... Hostages in a helicopter ...? What ...? Wives of government ministers ...? Yeah, I'm interested ... Tell me more ...'

22

Stella had worked meticulously through the flat, sorting out everything that belonged to Jack. Apart from his clothes, which she had set fire to, the rest of his belongings, which didn't amount to much anyway, were put in a number of cardboard boxes.

She wasn't so vindictive as to completely destroy all his possessions. There were books, CDs, odd files, photographs and other bits and pieces he had accumulated over the years. Most of the stuff in the flat belonged to her anyway. The trauma of throwing Jack out had drained her emotionally, and she spent a lot of the time either sobbing uncontrollably or getting very angry. She didn't experience a release as she had expected, but simply a frustrated emptiness at the futility of it all. While part of her didn't want anything more to do with him, another part wanted him to phone her to try to make it up. She felt so torn apart and confused that she didn't want to talk to anyone and had put the landline answerphone on as well as switching her mobile off, to save getting involved.

She was sat down, having a coffee and wondering what she was going to do with the rest of her life, when the land line rang. Would this be Jack? She listened to her own apologetic message, followed by the beeps, and then a raucous voice came over the speaker: *'Stella … If you're there, answer your bloody phone, will you … I've also left a message on your mobile. Why don't you switch the sodding thing on! It's Scott, and I need to talk to you* trés *urgently … I've got a job for you … a lot of spondulicks involved if we get it right … and if you're not there, then call me as soon as you hear this …'*

'Scott? It's Stella. Sorry – I've only just come in.' She had picked up the receiver.

'Baby, I'm glad I caught you! Have you got anything on?'

'I'm not in the nude, if that's what you're implying,' Stella sarcastically replied, knowing how crude Scott could be.

'Pity – but for once that's not what I meant. Are you busy, are you working?'

'What is it?' Stella wasn't sure if she wanted to work.

'Another BAFTA baby, it's another BAFTA.'

'What's it about?' There were certain subjects that Stella didn't want to get involved with, however well she was paid. She was a good PA, and had worked closely with Scott for quite a few years, but even she drew the line at some of the nasty topics he had made his reputation on. She had walked off his documentary exploring the many facets of bestiality, which had put her off eating lamb for life. The last job she had flatly refused to work on had been one following the daily experiences of a proctologist – which had been the bottom line. She was quite surprised that Scott had called to offer her another job after that.

'It's so hot that I can't tell you over the phone. Know what I mean?'

'Really …?' Stella had heard that one before. Scott had made a fine art out of creative bullshitting.

'Look, d'you want to join me or not? I haven't got time for games, Stella.' Scott sounded serious for once.

'I'm not sure … I'd have to know more … it's only fair.'

'Okay, I should know you by now. Why don't you come over to the flat so that I can tell you about it? I can't say fairer than that.'

'You really can't tell me over the phone?'

'No way, José.'

'When …?' Stella suddenly felt she had to get out of the flat and clear her head. Even if the job didn't appeal to her, it would stop her thinking about Jack for the time being.

'Right *now*, baby, there's no time to lose … Stella, I really need you on this one,' Scott dished out the charm.

'I'll be there in half an hour. And this had better be good.'

'You're the best, babe. You won't regret it. I guarantee that. See ya soon.' And Scott hung up. How many times had she heard him use those phrases? *You're the best; you won't regret it; I guarantee that.* At least a dozen times on every job. She knew he didn't mean them. They were usually aimed at people on the brink of making a decision, or earmarked for favours Scott wanted to extort. Now it was her turn to be on the receiving end. For once she didn't actually care. Despite everything, Scott was the best at his job. He sometimes used unconventional methods to get results, but the final product was always exciting and, more often than not, controversial.

Stella got changed and sprayed herself with perfume. She was pleased Scott had called. It gave her something else to think about. Whatever the situation, Scott was always fun to work with. He was a great ladies' man and he wasted no time in seducing anyone if it helped in getting the programme made. However, Scott had never come on to Stella. Their relationship, over the years, had always been on a strictly professional level. Verbally he'd be quite sexually suggestive with his remarks, but apart from a friendly kiss on the cheek and a theatrical hug, that was as far as he'd ever gone with her.

Stella had at one time wondered if he found her unattractive, but had soon realised that Scott was serious about his work and didn't want to prejudice the programme by getting involved with someone who was such an integral part of it. Secretly she did find him attractive and was sometimes curious about how good he was in bed.

'Great, you made it.' Scott opened the door to his flat and ushered Stella in. She could smell the aroma of freshly-made coffee mixed in with the cologne Scott was wearing. 'You're looking nice, really nice.' It sounded like a real compliment.

'Thank you. Now what's the big secret?'

'First things first. Sit down, make yourself at home. Coffee and a Danish?' Scott, wearing a yellow silk shirt and expensive designer jeans, took her over to his large white leather settee.

'Coffee'll be great, thanks.' Stella had been there many times, but somehow that day felt different. In the background she could hear soothing, tranquil sounds coming from his Bang and Olufsen surround sound system. Scott was very into new age music. Pan pipes and haunting flutes; waves rippling into the sea; Gregorian chants.

He often incorporated them into his programmes, giving the subject a more poignant dimension.

'No Danish?'

'I've had two Swedes, a Norwegian and a Finn already today – don't think I could manage a Danish ...' Stella knew it would appeal to Scott's quirky sense of humour.

'That's what I like about you, Stella,' remarked Scott on his way to the kitchen. 'You're a true European ...'

'As long as everyone speaks the same language!' Stella sunk back into the settee and wondered how many women Scott had had on it. It was comfortable, warm and seemed to envelop you in its vastness. The leather was soft and had a sensuous feel to it. The six pastel-coloured scatter cushions, draped in silk covers, added to the opulence of the settee. The combination of comfort and music made Stella feel like a rag doll after the tenseness of the last 24 hours.

Scott returned carrying a cafetiere, two china mugs and a plate of Danish pastries. 'You might not want one, but I do! Now, you like it black without sugar.'

'Thanks ... What is that music?'

'*Dreams of a Crystal Sunset* ... D'you like it?'

'Umm ... it's beautiful ... makes you forget everything ...' Stella took the coffee and automatically found herself reaching for a pastry.

'And have you got a lot to forget ...?' Scott sat down beside her and looked straight at her.

'What do you mean?'

'You've got something on your mind, I can tell.' Scott smiled and bit into his pastry.

'Everything's fine ...' Stella lied, taking a large gulp of coffee.

'The face might be the mask of many secrets – but the eyes can never lie. I've known you a long time, Stella Nightingale ...' Scott was always very good at reading people.

'I'm just a bit run down. You know how it is,' she said dismissively.

'It's more than that, isn't it?'

'It's not important, Scott, just a woman's thing. Now please tell me about this job.' Stella suddenly felt quite vulnerable. Scott sensed it straight away and poured her some more coffee. 'Terrific coffee ... Blue Mountain, isn't it?'

'Don't change the subject.' Scott wasn't budging.

'There is no subject to change.' Stella was battling.

'Bollocks ...' Scott believed in being direct.

'And bollocks to you too!' Stella was losing her composure.

'How's Jack ...?' He knew he'd hit the nail on the head when he saw her lips tighten.

'Quite frankly, I don't care, if you want to know the truth.' She realised she couldn't hide it any longer.

The music had stopped. Scott picked up the remote and pressed some buttons. A different type of sound vibrated from the speakers. The notes, from a classical guitar, were haunting, emotive and permeated the room with a soothing and romantic air. 'Do you want to tell me about it – or would you rather I minded my own business ...?

Stella felt the music go right through her. 'I've had enough. I've thrown Jack out.'

'Not just another row?' Scott looked at her.

'No ...'

'How serious is it? You *don't* have to tell me. I'll shut up right now if you want me to.' Scott knew how to play her.

'The marriage is over ...' At the very moment she said it, the music reached such an emotional pitch that it prompted Stella to burst into tears.

For almost a minute Scott said nothing. He watched Stella, who was sobbing away, take a handkerchief out of her bag and press it to her eyes. He then stood up and left for the kitchen. Stella wasn't aware that he had gone until the sudden pop from the kitchen made her jump and brought her back to reality. A second later, Scott reappeared carrying a bottle of champagne and a couple of long-stemmed glasses. 'I'm out of vintage bubbly, but I hope this will do.'

'Champagne ... isn't that for celebrations?' Stella watched him expertly fill the glasses without spilling any.

'You've got rid of the old fart – isn't that a celebration?' Scott said rather boldly. For a split second he thought he might have gone too far. At first, Stella's face expressed a stunned surprise, but then a small smile came to her lips.

'Old fart ...' she repeated.

'Just a phrase ... I hope you don't think I'm being too insensitive?' Scott handed her a glass of champagne.

'It's truer than you think ...' She took a sip and visibly relaxed.

'Any chance of patching it up?'

Stella thought for a moment. Did she really want Jack back? Her pride would have liked him to beg her to take him back, but her heart knew it wouldn't last long. Jack was Jack. He would never change. She wanted something different out of life – and realised that Jack could never provide it. 'I doubt it very much ...'

'I'm sorry ... I really am.' He topped her glass up.

'I know. Thanks.' Stella believed him.

Scott's mobile rang. ' ... Kirsty, baby, how are you! ... Long time no feel ... How was the holiday? ... You did what! ... And they didn't arrest you?' Stella felt the call of nature and gestured to Scott that she was off to the bathroom. He nodded, then wandered across to the window to continue his conversation. 'You must be joking! How long was it? These snaps I have got to see!'

Stella closed the bathroom door and sat on the toilet. She stared at her reflection in the opposite wall. The whole room had been covered with different coloured mirror tiles. Hues of yellow, green and blue were set in circular patterns, giving it an almost psychedelic feel. The shower curtain had images of laughing naked men and women prancing about in water. The thick, soft carpet looked like the surface of the sea. Two small speakers, set into a lowered sky-blue ceiling, rang out with the soft tones of the music she had heard in the lounge. It was a most relaxing place to have a pee. She felt as if she were flushing away all her troubles and ridding her body of Jack. It was a good feeling.

Coming out of the bathroom, Stella could still hear Scott chattering away on the phone. He had always been a great one for gossip, and judging by the comments and gales of laughter, it wasn't going to be a short conversation.

Stella remained in the hallway and studied all the watercolours and lithographs on the walls. Scott certainly had an eye for a picture. She wandered further down the hall, where there were two doors, both ajar, leading to other rooms. She had been in one of the rooms. It was Scott's study-cum-office-cum-mini-editing suite. She'd spent many hours working with him in there. The other room, his bedroom, she had surprisingly never actually seen. Since Scott was still babbling away in the background, she couldn't resist a nosy peek.

It wasn't quite what she had imagined. There were no mirrors on the ceiling, no black silk sheets, no manacles on the bed head or rope ties at the bottom. No erotic paintings or drawings on the walls. It had none of those things that she expected from someone of Scott's character and reputation. It was the complete opposite, all very simply and tastefully done. An elegant king-size bed dominated the room. It had the quality of something out of a dream-like film set. You felt safe and pampered in there. But that's not all that Stella felt. From the effects of the champagne and the realisation that she didn't want Jack back, she suddenly felt very randy …

It was another ten minutes before Scott finally came off the phone. He turned around expecting to see Stella, but she hadn't returned from the bathroom. He finished off his glass of champagne and thought for a moment. He was beginning to have doubts. Was Stella the right person for this assignment? She was good at her job, but sometimes a bit too strait-laced for his liking. Would she be able to adapt to the situation in hand? It wasn't like any other job they had worked on. This one required a more flexible approach, and he wasn't sure now if she could cope with it. Her present emotional state worried him, and he wondered if she was really up to it. He knew she was a one-man woman and that this split from Jack would not have been easy for her. Would she suddenly go to pieces half-way through and ruin one of the best opportunities of his career? It was hard to tell. She was one of those women who held a lot back. She kept her private and professional lives clearly apart.

The reason he had never tried to get her into bed was that she just wasn't his type. Stella's figure was classically hourglass curvy, full breasts, slim waist and a pear-shaped bottom. Scott preferred women with boyish figures, which was why he was more attracted to thin models with no discernibly shaped tits and arse.

He'd only opened the champagne to help her relax. He didn't want her running out of the flat in tears. It was a difficult decision for him. Since he believed he was on the brink of an exclusive scoop, he couldn't afford to make any mistakes. Would Stella turn out to be that mistake? The fact that he didn't have an alternative put him in a complex position. It was all bad timing. The two other PAs, whom he rated above Stella, were unavailable. Stella was the only one left whom he could trust. It was her or no-one. He poured himself another glass and went in search of her.

The bathroom door was open and she wasn't in his office. He didn't look in his bedroom, because she wouldn't be in there. As he went back toward the kitchen he heard 'Scott …' coming from the direction of his bedroom. It didn't sound like Stella. There was a softness and urgency to her tone that momentarily confused him. He strode back and entered the bedroom. Scott had seen many things in his erratic life, and there wasn't a great deal that surprised him. But what lay before him then *was* a surprise.

Stella, completely naked, smiled at him from the bed.

'Stella …' He couldn't think what else to say.

'You mean you recognised me without my clothes on?' She had her head propped up on a couple of pillows and looked at him without any nervousness or embarrassment. 'This must be a first …'

'I don't quite … understand …' Scott emptied his glass.

'I've never known you so lost for words.' Stella smiled. He looked literally dumbstruck. 'Don't you like what you see?'

'I ... I always thought you were a natural brunette ...' He was starting to regain his composure.

'That's right, the collar and cuffs don't match. One must always have something secret in reserve.' Stella glanced at the front of his jeans. She couldn't detect any stiffness. Was she not turning him on? 'Doesn't my body excite you ...?' she challenged him.

Scott speedily assessed the situation and wondered what to do. He didn't fancy her and he wasn't in the mood to perform on cue. But at the same time he didn't want to upset her by rejecting her. This job meant a lot to him and he realised that if he was to secure her professional services, he would have to make some sacrifices in the line of duty. And if all he had to do was service her, then that's what he would do. Scott never let his feelings get in the way of business. However, there was one little problem ... and that little problem was his penis. It was asleep and didn't want to know. *Come on boy, don't let me down now,* Scott thought, inwardly starting to panic.

Stella had amazed even herself with her bold approach. The combination of the surroundings, music, champagne and her feelings regarding Jack had suddenly unleashed a deeper, more demonstrative self. She now wanted Scott, and she was going to do her damnedest to have him. She sensed he wasn't a tit man, so she rolled over onto her stomach and raised her bare bottom in the air. 'Is this more to your liking ...?' she whispered seductively.

Scott stared at her voluptuous behind as she wiggled it sensuously. He felt an immediate stirring. 'Very nice Stella ... Where have you been hiding it all these years ...?' *That's more like it*, he thought. *Thank you, my friend,* he addressed his rising member. *Let's get down to some serious business ...*

'I'm glad you like it ...' She turned her head and was pleased to see the front of his jeans now bulging. 'Let the poor fellow out ... I can see he wants to play ...'

Scott undid his ornate Mexican belt and pulled his jeans down. He was wearing Mickey Mouse boxer shorts, while his own Mickey Mouse had forced itself through the flap.

Stella turned onto her back to watch him pull his shorts right down. Scott's penis was smaller than Jack's, but she didn't care. It certainly looked ready for action.

'Don't turn round ... I liked it the way you were before.' Scott was undoing his shirt.

'You prefer my arse to my face. Is that it?' she responded good humouredly, and turned back onto her front.

'It's a beautiful arse ...' He was now completely naked and had started to kiss it and run his tongue over it.

'Is this the foreplay before the main feature?' she giggled.

'You want foreplay? That'll be extra!' he joked.

'Actually, that won't be necessary,' she said in all seriousness. 'I'm ready when you are. Let's get on with it.'

'As madam wishes – I'm ready ...' He took a condom out of his bedside drawer and slipped it expertly on. 'Bottoms up, please, let's get this show on the road!' Scott referred to everything as a theatrical event, not being one for the romantic turn of phrase.

'You really are a bottom man,' Stella remarked as she made herself comfortable by placing a pillow under her front.

'Oh yes …' Scott took something else out of the drawer and unscrewed the top.

'What are you doing now …?' Stella wondered, until she felt his fingers massaging some lotion round her anal area. 'Scott, what are you doing …? Is it what I think you're doing …?' The sensation wasn't unpleasant.

'A hole in one …' He continued gently rubbing the lotion round without actually touching the anus. 'I can stop now, baby … just say the word … My friend is just as happy going in the normal way … It's up to you …' He didn't want to force it.

Stella was really enjoying this new sensation. It was an area Jack had never wanted to explore. He was strictly a missionary position man, and didn't care for trying out anything new, despite some encouragement on her part. She had often wondered what it felt like having anal sex. Some of her girlfriends admitted loving it, which had made her very curious about what she felt was a rather taboo aspect of sex. Now she was being offered the opportunity of actually experiencing it.

'Well, baby … what's it to be? We don't want our little friend to lose interest, now do we …?' Scott was beginning to worry that his erection was about to lose its stiffness.

Stella was tempted. And the more his fingers teased around her anal area, the more excited she was getting. *Why not?*, she thought. She was ready for new experiences. This was her new life. *Bugger it – why not!* She opened her mouth and whispered to Scott, 'Maybe next time … Let's go the usual way …' She had finally lost the courage to go through with it.

Scott was disappointed but tried not to show it. 'As the lady requests, I shall park my bike elsewhere …' With that, he grabbed the sides of her hips and entered her doggy style.

It didn't take long before he came, shouting 'Long live the Queen!'

Stella, who was nowhere near reaching an orgasm, lay forward on the bed when he withdrew. 'I didn't know you were a Royalist, Scott' she said, hiding her own disappointment. She now wondered what it would have been like if she'd consented to be buggered.

'The Royal Family are much maligned in my opinion. The least I can do is praise them at the height of ecstasy.' He had already put his shorts and jeans on, and was now buttoning up his shirt. 'Was that okay for you? Sorry it was a quickie, but I could hold back no longer, if you know what I mean.'

'You were great, Scott, thanks …' she lied. No point in telling the truth and going down another road. At least he didn't fart like Jack after ejaculation. Stella relaxed and watched as he neatly tied a knot in the condom before disposing of it in a small plastic food bag that he kept with his supply of condoms. 'Doggie bag …?' She smiled.

'My donation to the local sperm bank. With every pint you get a badge.'

'Sounds like a lot of work for little return,' she grinned.

'I knew a man once who got repetitive strain injury just because he wanted to get a badge. Right wanker, if you ask me.' Scott deposited the plastic bag in a raffia wastepaper basket. 'Not too much of a disappointment, was I …?'

'You've lived up to your reputation,' she lied again. It had at least provided a form of release from her angst. The main thing was that she didn't feel guilty having had sex with Scott. Emotionally she felt no closer to him. At least this little experience didn't initially look like harming their working relationship. 'So … after that very pleasant interlude … what's this project? That is, if you still want to offer it me?'

'This really is the big one!' he declared enthusiastically.

Stella felt a bit chilly and got under the sheets. Scott got onto the bed bedside her. 'I've got a contact – it's best you don't know who it is at the moment – who's involved in a major operation. The Prime Minister is behind it.' He expected some sort of reaction from Stella, but she gave him nothing. 'Some hostages have been abducted by a group of terrorists.'

'Who are these terrorists?' She tried to sound interested, but so far nothing she had heard was so earth-shattering.

'Nobody knows. They haven't declared themselves. But the hostages are believed to be the wives of three of the Government's Junior Ministers ...'

'That's intriguing ...' Stella turned to face him.

'That's just a part of it! Apparently the terrorists stole some highly confidential documents, the contents of which are rumoured to be extremely explosive. The whole affair is so hush-hush and carefully covered up that the press and TV haven't got onto it yet.' Scott sounded very excited.

'But you know about it?'

'And I'm the only one in the media who does. How about that!'

'So we get a crew together and try to do an on-the-spot exposé – is that the plan?'

'Stella, I wish it were that easy. No, if we took a camera crew, no only would it alert our journalist colleagues, it would also probably screw the whole operation.'

'Then how do you intend to do it?'

'It's got to be just you and me, kid. *We've* got to approach this *undercover*. I will work the camera. Although it's got it's own mike, I want you to work a portable audio recorder as and when necessary, so we achieve the best quality ... It's a great challenge!'

'What do you actually mean by "undercover"?' Stella realised there must be a catch. She wasn't being asked to do her normal job.

'No-one is to know who we are. My contact will keep me up to date with any progress. We'll check into the locality as husband and wife on a little holiday. Mrs and Mrs Smith. It's simple.'

'*Mr* and *Mrs* Smith ...?' Stella repeated.

'That can't worry you, surely. Not after what we've just done.' He flashed open the sheet to reveal her naked body to make his point.

'Hey, that's cold!' Stella laughed. 'Where is this locality?'

'Suffolk. Will you come with me?' Scott made a silent prayer.

'We haven't talked rates yet.' She became businesslike. 'This job requires special skills – that'll cost you extra. A lot extra ...'

'Agreed, agreed – within reason of course ...'

'You know I'm always reasonable.'

'When it suits you,' he parried. 'Now, you are absolutely sure, Stella?'

'When do we leave ...?' She smiled.

He gave her a big hug. The first time he had shown any real emotion toward her.

23

'Twenty-five thousand …'

'Fifty thousand …'

'Thirty …'

'Sixty …'

'Forty thousand … We can't be fairer than that, Simon dear man.' Charles tried to sound pleasant.

Alex could see Charles's face starting to go red. 'Let's agree to 50 thousand and call it a day. What do you say?'

'Seventy-five thousand …' Simon smiled. He was enjoying this.

'Be reasonable, man,' Charles spluttered. 'Tax free and paid all in one go.'

'One hundred thousand …' Simon knew he had them over a barrel. He figured that if he could get a quarter of a million he'd be a happy man.

'Fifty thousand is our limit, Simon.' Alex was now beginning to lose his patience.

'One hundred and fifty …' Simon looked out of the window and wondered if the sky was the limit.

'Fifty thousand and we won't leak that story about your personal dealings regarding the importation of contaminated meat.' Alex now smiled as he watched Simon's expression fall.

'I don't know what you're talking about.' Simon had always been taught to deny everything.

'You made a healthy little killing on that consignment. How much was it? A thousand tons of affected Argentinean cattle …?'

'You can't prove anything.' Simon thought Alex was bluffing.

'You are a co-director of Carcass Imports Direct.' Alex had a sheaf of papers before him. 'Which, I have to add, you've never declared …'

'Just a little business venture. Can't exist on salary alone,' Simon replied matter-of-factly. He didn't believe he was breaking any rules.

'This meat led to many deaths …'

'Only a few lions and tigers. The meat wasn't for human consumption, for god's sake!' Simon still didn't feel he had done any wrong.

'Well, perhaps we'll pass this information on to the animal rights lobby or leak it to the Sunday tabloids. They might be interested …' Alex smiled at Charles, who had regained his composure.

'I don't wish to be greedy, after all. Fifty thousand is most generous.' Simon wanted to back out with dignity.

'Forty thousand …' Charles interjected. The ball was in their court now.

'But you said … all right, all right, I'll accept forty …' Simon could see himself paying *them* money if he wasn't careful.

'Forty thousand it is,' Alex agreed, although Charles wanted to decrease it more. They had decided beforehand to go up to a maximum of 60 thousand, so they were still effectively better off. 'Sign this please.'

'What is it …?'

'Just a little insurance for us in case you change your mind and decide to talk about the PM …'

'I would never dream of doing that, you know me.' Simon grudgingly signed. 'And the money …?'

'A cheque will be paid into your Birmingham account.' Charles watched Simon's mouth open in surprise. 'Under the name of Seamus Patel – correct?'

'How did …?' But Simon said no more.

'Give us some credit, Simon.' Alex put away the signed sheet. 'We do our homework.'

'Thank you, Simon,' Charles added. 'We'll keep in close contact regarding news about your wife – Melissa, isn't it? And you did bring a recent photograph of her with you?'

Simon took a postcard portrait of Melissa from his inside jacket pocket and handed to Alex. 'It was taken last year.'

'Charming, charming.' Alex glanced at the photo, finding nothing remotely attractive about her chubby looks. 'Remember … you will please not discuss any of this with anyone – including Jeremy Hayward and Matthew Croome. Understand?'

'Yes, Home Secretary …' Simon stood up, they all shook hands, and he left the office.

Charles broke the silence a minute later. 'One down and two to go.'

The interview with Matthew was short and sweet. They could sense he was a frightened man and so capitalised on his fear. They offered him no incentives and told him that if he wanted to retain his present position he would have to keep his mouth shut. The Prime Minister was counting on his loyalty and would be very grateful if this was all kept under wraps until they had dealt with the situation. Matthew didn't want any trouble. He was more than happy to agree to whatever they asked. His main concern centred around Serena. He wondered if she was strong enough to withstand being held hostage. Alex assured him that everything in their power was being done to rescue his wife. Matthew handed over his photo of Serena before leaving, his head bowed in submission, and closing the door behind him.

Charles admired the snap of Serena standing against a tree. 'I wouldn't mind giving her one.'

'Can't understand what she sees in that turd Croome. Odious little creep. No backbone or guts.' Alex couldn't respect a man who didn't at least show some modicum of character.

'At least we don't have to worry about him saying anything.'

'I'm not worried about either Croome or Dodson – Hayward's the one we've got to be careful with …' Alex wasn't at all looking forward to their meeting with Jeremy. He knew he couldn't pull the wool over his eyes so easily.

The interviews had been well spaced out so that neither of the three Junior Ministers would see each other. To make absolutely sure, each had been told to go to a different place to wait, from where they would be collected and brought to a special room – one of the many inner sanctums within Whitehall.

Jeremy was kept waiting for only five minutes before he was escorted down a maze of corridors and up several flights of stairs. Alex and Charles were having a cup of tea when he was shown in.

'Ah, Jeremy, so kind of you to come. Tea?' Alex gestured for him to take a chair set before a large desk behind which they were both seated.

'No, thanks. Here's a photo of Delia that you asked for.' Jeremy gave Charles a ten-by-eight portrait. 'Has there been any news?' Alex and Charles looked at each other. Jeremy was astute enough to read into their expressions. 'What is it? Please don't hide anything from me.'

'We have been given reason to believe that your wife, together with the other two missing Minister's wives, has been taken hostage … Your wife's bag was found near the getaway car … which was discovered abandoned – having careered off the road …' Alex had decided to play Jeremy truthfully.

'I knew it. I knew it … And the other two – Serena and Melissa?'

'Nothing as yet … I must warn you, Jeremy, that blood was found in the car. We cannot tell you any more. We are doing everything within our power to find them …'

'Are you insinuating that they could be dead …?' Jeremy stared directly at Alex.

'I don't know. The terrorists haven't made contact. You know as much as we do.'

Jeremy believed him. 'Is there anything I can do?'

'The best thing, old chap,' Charles smiled, realising that Jeremy wasn't going to prove difficult after all, 'is to bear with us and trust us … and to keep it to yourself for the time being.'

'And the Prime Minister?' Jeremy added rather enigmatically.

'Is very troubled, of course …' Charles lost the smile.

'I'm sure he is …' Jeremy tested them. He had thought long and hard about what Charles had previously told him with regard to the papers he had stumbled upon. He knew he *hadn't* made a mistake. He wasn't going to be fobbed off so easily. There was something subversive and sinister behind all this. They couldn't disguise their unease.

'I was talking to the PM only an hour ago,' Alex quickly jumped in. 'He wants you to know how grateful he is, that you are being so patient and discreet about the whole matter.'

'Really … and how grateful is he …?' Jeremy was pushing it as far as he could.

'He mentioned something about a possible position in the new reshuffle. He'd really like you on his team, you know.' Alex was hating this.

'I'm flattered. Doesn't the PM usually contact possible candidates personally …? That is – if he is thinking of offering a position?' Jeremy responded rather innocently, but knew this was the official procedure.

Damn, bugger, bollocks, and shit! Alex inwardly cursed. Jeremy had got one over on them. There was no going back now that they had gone this far. Too much was still at stake. 'I'm sure the Prime Minister would be happy to talk to you …'

'Good. Then I shall look forward to his call.' Jeremy stood up, smiled, and left them.

'Jeremy, it's been so nice talking to you, and I'm pleased you've agreed to take on the position of Environment Minister …' Thomas Lane had to stop himself from slamming the receiver down. Alex had managed to put him right in it. It was bad enough having to actually talk to someone he distinctly disliked, without the added abhorrence of having to offer him a job. Thomas was aware he was being expertly manipulated, but, like the victim of a blackmailer, knew he was in no position to argue. Not only had Jeremy cleverly managed to direct the conversation to his own advantage, but he had ingeniously given reasons why he wasn't suited to go to Northern Ireland or to take on the job of Minister for Health. The environment had always interested him … If there was any chance … Thomas had been unable to say no. He'd fallen right into Jeremy's trap. Things were not going well at all.

In the corner of his private study, his laptop screen was presently displaying a screensaver depicting the faces of the 52 British Prime Ministers of the past nearly three hundred years. One by one, in photographic sequence, they appeared on the screen. Lloyd George … Bonar Law … Baldwin … Ramsey MacDonald … Chamberlain … Churchill … right through to Thatcher … Major … Blair … Brown … Cameron … then Thomas Lane himself, and back to the beginning with Walpole. He watched his own image appear and disappear just as swiftly. Was his career going to be just as transient?

He wandered over and sat on the chair in front of the screen. He desperately needed further advice, and there was only one person he could turn to in complete trust. He proceeded to slowly type out his e-mail message: *'Sorry to disturb you again. Situation getting serious. Other players have forced themselves into the game. Possibility of mask being detected. Could you advise? Jack of Clubs.'* He watched the screen for a minute until a message was downloaded to him. It read: *'Keep calm. Do not lose dignity. Do not do anything on impulse. Remember, there are more winning bluffs than losing certainties. The game is never over until all the cards have been played. Wait until situation is clearer. Will advise then. King of Diamonds.'*

Thomas sat there taking in the message. It was sound advice. He would just have to ride it out for the time being. He got up and went across to his desk. Before him lay copies of the photographs of Melissa, Serena and Delia, which Alex had given him. He picked up Delia's picture and wondered if she was still alive …

24

Delia lay on the casualty bed looking up at the ceiling. The doctor was finishing his examination. She knew she was in a hospital and that she had been involved in some sort of car accident – but apart from that she had absolutely no clue about anything. She closed her eyes several times to see if she could remember some moment from her life. There was nothing, not even a blurred image. She wore expensive clothes, spoke with a home counties accent and felt vulnerable whenever she looked at Richard. Other than that it was a blank canvas. It was a curious position to be in. She didn't feel frightened or anxious in any way. If she had any worries she certainly couldn't remember them. She felt a stranger in a strange land, with only one friendly face that she could trust – and that was Richard. He'd gone off to make a few phone calls, and Delia suddenly felt an internal panic – would he return?

'Well, Mrs … X, shall we call you?' The doctor sat in a chair beside the bed.

'Mrs …?' Delia glanced at her left hand and saw a wedding ring and a diamond engagement ring. Was she married to Richard? If only that were true.

'How are you feeling?'

'All right, I suppose. My head's throbbing a little …' Delia felt the small bump at the back of her head.

'Classic cause of amnesia I would think. You still haven't remembered anything?'

'Sorry …'

'Don't apologise, please. At least there are no other injuries or broken bones, as far as I can detect. You split your gum, but that'll heal in no time. Other than that we've no reason to keep you.' The doctor smiled. He looked a nice man, but she didn't have the same feelings toward him as she did toward Richard. Oh, where was he?

'Will I ever get my memory back?'

'I'm afraid I'm not a neurologist. All I know about amnesia is that there are many diverse facets. It affects different people in different ways. You could regain your memory within the next hour or …'

'I might never regain it?' The thought somehow didn't upset her.

'I couldn't possibly say. The positive thing is that you don't appear to have forgotten the basics. Some people not only lose their memory but also the knowledge of how to *do* things. You know – how to speak, move, all those everyday tasks we've learnt from childhood and take for granted. In that respect you're normal, I'm pleased to say.'

'Very boring to be normal, surely?'

The doctor smiled. 'And you haven't lost your sense of humour.'

'I didn't know I had one. So what do I do now?'

'See your local consultant neurologist, who will run a series of initial tests.'

'I don't know where "local" is …'

'Of course, I'm sorry. One easily forgets … Oh, god, a bad pun if ever there was one. Sorry.' The doctor appeared embarrassed and was relieved when a nurse came to take him away to attend to another patient. 'You're free to go. Good luck …'

'Thank you …' The doctor had already gone before she could ask anything else.

Delia lay there for a moment before another wave of panic set in. Richard hadn't returned. What was she to do now? Where should she go? She got off from the bed and started to walk toward reception. She looked eagerly about her in the hope of seeing Richard amongst waiting patients and relatives, but he wasn't there. He had gone and left her. Probably had an adoring wife and large family and didn't want the burden or responsibility of some unknown woman complicating his life. If the worst came to the worst she could always go to the police. They might be able to trace who she was.

'Candice … how are you feeling?' a dark voice spoke softly behind her. Delia turned round to see Richard smiling at her. 'Candice …?'

'Who's Candice?' Delia was confused.

'Candice Hodges … Does that ring any bells?' Richard watched her eyes for any recognition.

'What a ghastly name. Am I supposed to know her?'

'It could be your name. You live in Milton Keynes?'

'Do I? What are you trying to tell me?' Delia's mind was starting to spin.

'I had a contact check the registration owner of the car I found you in. It belongs to a Candice Hodges, who lives in Milton Keynes. It really doesn't mean anything to you?'

'No … and if my name does turn out to be Candice I shall change it. Did you find anything else out?'

'The car was reported stolen three days ago …' Richard watched her reaction.

'Then I can't be Candice Hodges!' She sounded relieved. She looked at Richard, who was eyeing her suspiciously. 'What's the matter? If I'm not Candice, then I must have stolen the car? Is that what you're thinking?'

'Did you …?'

'I don't know! I can't remember anything! Please believe me … You don't, do you?'

'I have an open mind.' Richard wasn't giving anything away.

'What is that supposed to mean? All right … perhaps I did steal it. Perhaps I escaped from prison. Perhaps I'm really a crazed murderess with a hundred dead victims strewn around the country … Do you want to call the police now? Or have you done so already?' Delia ranted on in anger.

'A woman did escape from prison a couple of days ago. It wasn't far from here. Same build and colouring as you … She is a murderess – she'd killed a dozen people – all men …' Richard informed her.

'What …?' Delia's thoughts went into overdrive. Had she made up what she had just told him, or was it really true? 'Oh my god …'

'But your saving grace is that she's 60 years old and was apprehended last night …' Richard smiled for the first time, and showed her the headline of the newspaper he was carrying. Delia sighed with sudden relief. He had bought it in the hope that there might be something in it about a missing woman of Delia's description. There's wasn't, of course.

'Not having a past is quite exciting in its own way,' Delia said, handing him back the paper. 'But not actually knowing *who* you are, or *what* you've done, is the frightening bit. Can you understand that?'

'I'm sure there's nothing sinister about your past. You've got an honest face. I've always been a pretty good judge of character.' In Delia, Richard saw someone who had a genuine warmth, and the more he looked into that face, the more he felt himself drawn to her. Was it because she was a genuine mystery woman, which appealed to his sense of adventure – or was he simply attracted to her?

'I hope I'm not the first to prove you wrong,' she smiled.

'So – what did the doctor say?'

'Nothing amiss apart from my memory. Mrs X has been officially discharged. He suggested I see a specialist.' Delia's attention was drawn to someone munching on a sandwich.

Richard watched her unconsciously lick her lips. They were full, generous lips. 'Are you hungry? I wouldn't mind a coffee and something. There's a hospital canteen.'

'Please … I'm afraid I haven't any money. Well, you know that already.'

'Be my guest.'

'I've already taken up too much of your time. Won't your wife be worried about you?' Delia fished.

'I'm not married. But you are. I'm sure your husband – wherever he is – is wondering where you are.' Richard didn't like the thought.

'I could be divorced, or even widowed. I might have killed my husband and run away.' Delia said this without thinking as she twisted the rings on her finger. She didn't relish the thought of having a husband she didn't know. No, right now she didn't want to know who she was. Right now she just wanted to be in Richard's company. That was all that counted.

'Stop being so pessimistic!' he chided.

'It's difficult not to be.'

'Just think if you've got children. How do you think they'll be feeling now, wondering what's happened to their mother?'

'I haven't got any children,' she answered with utter conviction. 'I just know I've never been pregnant. I know … Come on, I'm starving.' Without thinking, she grabbed his arm and they walked silently down the corridor toward the canteen.

25

The Dog and Duck was one of those small, independent country pubs that didn't really like or welcome outsiders. There wasn't that much passing trade, and its landlord was more than happy to cater just for the locals; the usual bunch of lonely misfits who treated it like a second home.

Wilf, who had the mind of a 12-year-old in a 40-year-old body, bounded into the pub carrying two dead chickens by their necks. He held them up to the face of the barmaid. 'Chickens!'

'I can see that, Wilf. Been poaching again?' She had a soft spot for him.

'No! Found them in the road. Right dead they were!' He shook them wildly.

'What do you expect me to do with them, Wilf?' She was used to him bringing odd things he'd found into the pub. 'Too late for the kiss of life.'

'Will you give me the kiss o' life instead, Beryl?' Wilf leered, showing yellowing teeth and waggling his tongue like the loony he was.

'Not just now, Wilf. Maybe when you're dead. But only maybe …' she humoured him, and sadly wondered if anyone else would offer to give her the kiss of life. 'Tell you what I will do though. Get them cooked. Fancy curried chicken?'

'I fancy a fuck …' Wilf was always trying it on.

'So do I, Wilf, so do I …' she mumbled to herself as she took the chickens to the kitchen, wondering if she was condemned to die an old maid, since Wilf was the only local who ever propositioned her.

The troop were hungry and had persuaded Terry to stop at the nearest pub for a short food break. Terry, who was quite hungry himself, had agreed on condition they stuck to food and had no alcohol. They still had a job to do and he wasn't prepared to lead a bunch of drunks. As luck would have it, the first pub they came across was only a couple of miles from the crashed car.

The vision of six odd-looking men entering the confines of this peaceful village pub was not the real reason why everyone's head turned in the public bar. Neither was it the fact that they all ordered soft drinks that mainly surprised the inmates. No, the real conversation-stopper was Terry himself. Terry was big and black, and not many – in truth not any – big, black men with dreadlocks had ever stepped into The Dog and Duck before. An alien from another planet stepping out of a spaceship wouldn't have created such interest.

Wilf walked right up to Terry and studied him as if he were an extraterrestrial. He rubbed his finger on his face and was surprised the black didn't come off. 'You been right burnt. Been on yer holidays then …?'

Terry grabbed Wilf by the neck and lifted him up. 'What do you mean, my friend

…?'

'He doesn't mean anything!' the barmaid quickly interjected. 'Wilf's a bit … Simple … Please let him go …'

Terry put Wilf down. Wilf, rubbing his neck, made various childish faces and arm movements before retreating quietly into a corner.

Terry took a deep breath. 'Are you serving food?' he addressed the barmaid, who also stared at him in simple amazement. 'Is there a bar menu?' he rephrased the question.

'You want something to eat?' she answered in her dim, surprised way, as if he had asked her for the use of a sun bed.

'If you have anything …' Terry was tempted to be flippant, but knew it would be wasted.

'Curried chicken is on special today,' she said proudly.

'Anything else?' Terry didn't like any ethnic food.

'We only have one special. That's why it's special. You could have sandwiches, of course. We make sandwiches.'

'What kind of fillings?'

'Whatever you like.' The barmaid had to think for a moment. 'Ham and cheese …'

'Or …?'

'Ham and cheese. You can have them together if you like.' She said this as if the very combination was an exotic delicacy.

'Okay – I'll have a round of cheese, with some pickle, on brown.' Terry didn't want to prolong this exchange.

'We only do white bread. No pickle I'm afraid. Got some tomato sauce.'

'Okay, whatever … You can take my friends' orders. Can we sit in the garden?'

'If you like.' She shuffled across to the group with her notebook. She felt more comfortable with them. 'What can I get you?'

'You – between two slices of bread.' Kieran, who didn't really fancy her, couldn't resist the remark for its possible shock value.

'I wouldn't recommend that, sir. I've got the curse at the moment.'

Some of the regulars smirked behind their drinks. It was always a pleasure to see an outsider put down. Kieran didn't know how to respond. 'Er … the chicken curry, please.'

'I'll have that too,' said Rory, 'so long as it's not cursed as well!'

'Don't think it is, sir. The local witch is on holiday. Any more for the curry?' The barmaid took another order of curry from Barry, while Jack and Archie stuck to the sandwiches. Jack would have liked the curry, but didn't want to tempt fate.

The landlord, who had been in the kitchen, came into the bar and stopped when he saw Terry. He was small, round, with a red drinker's face. He had a beard without the moustache. If you had stuck a pointed hat on him he would have looked very much like a gnome. 'Everything all right, Beryl?' He continued to stare at Terry.

'Three curries and three sandwiches. One cheese, two ham.' She smiled at Archie, whom she liked the look of. 'Are you all going in the garden?'

Archie turned to Terry, who nodded. 'Yes, we shall all dine out in your splendid garden,' Archie smiled back. The barmaid turned and bent down to retrieve a bar towel she had accidentally dropped. Archie noticed her generously-proportioned bottom and imagined what it would be like spanking it with his swagger stick. Beryl caught his look and seemed to read his mind. She smiled again.

The landlord unashamedly kept staring at Terry in an enigmatic way.

'Is there a problem?' Terry looked at him.

'You're not from around these parts, are you?' The others watched with interest.

'No – I'm from Kingston.' Terry put his hands on his hips.

'Jamaica …?' the landlord asked.

'No, he came of his own accord!' Rory couldn't resist it. A look from Terry soon shut him up.

'Kingston in Surrey, if you're really interested. Any more questions?'

'Only curious, only curious …' The landlord backed down.

'Not used to seeing a *black* face are you?' Terry couldn't stop himself.

'We're not racist, if that's what you're implying. We provide curries and we've got some reggae music on our jukebox,' the landlord justified.

'Okay …' Terry cooled down. It wasn't worth it. The silence was suddenly broken by a voice from the kitchen bawling out: 'Three chicken curries and a toad in the hole!' The whole bar relaxed when Terry turned away in resignation.

Archie sidled up to the barmaid. 'It's Beryl, isn't it?'

'That's my name …' She pushed herself against the bar.

'I thought you said the special was curried chicken. You didn't mention toad in the hole?'

'Toad in the hole's not special, we have that every day. D'you want that instead of a sandwich then?'

'If it's no trouble. I love a bit of sausage.' Archie looked her in the eye.

'So do I …' she replied as she sashayed toward the kitchen.

Terry's mobile rang and he disappeared outside to take the call.

Jack, Rory, Barry and Kieran had to take their own food out into the garden. Archie was the only one who had his brought out to him by the barmaid. She gave him a special look before returning inside.

'There's a dog if ever I saw one,' Kieran remarked as he took a bite out of the curried chicken leg.

'She can't help being ugly.' Barry picked an uncooked piece of rice out of his teeth. 'Some of those manky birds go like the clappers.'

'Yes, and that's what you'll catch if you're not careful.' Rory chewed a chunk of chicken, which tasted bitter.

'How would you know?' Kieran looked at Rory. 'You only lift shirts, not dresses.'

'That's not strictly true, dear heart. A couple of my butch conquests, who were cross-dressers, got turned on by me lifting their dresses. But I prefer a man to wear trousers, if you know what I mean! Is your curry all right?' Rory sampled a mouthful of rice.

'Tastes okay to me.' Kieran didn't want to let on that he didn't actually have a sense of taste. He had lost that after an accident, when a rather powerful joke cigarette had exploded in his mouth when he was in the army.

'Nothing wrong with this,' said Barry, who couldn't tell a good curry from a bad one, and who also had the constitution of an ox. As long as it filled his stomach he was happy.

Rory ate a few more pieces of chicken before pushing the plate aside. He'd rather go hungry than eat something that didn't stimulate his palette. He took a large swig of tonic water and noticed Terry coming to join them, carrying his phone. Terry looked around to make sure no-one was in earshot. 'I've just been sent photographs of the three women who are being held hostage. When we've eaten I'll brief you all.' He passed the phone round for everyone to see.

Rory suddenly felt a bit queasy and stood up. 'I'm just going for a little walkette. Need a bit of exercise …' He wandered off feeling decidedly peculiar.

Barry and Kieran, who had quickly demolished their curries, finished off their Cokes. 'Want another …?' Kieran gestured conspiratorially to Barry.

'Don't mind if I do. This curry's made me real thirsty. I'll join you.' Barry got up and went off with Kieran toward the bar. What they both wanted was a good pint or two of beer. With Terry occupied in the garden, now was their chance.

'This whole business is getting very complicated.' Terry ate his sandwich without really tasting it. Alex had really put the pressure on and rejected Terry's plea for reinforcements. He had been told that it was up to them – and only them – to cope and bring the mission to a conclusion. Yes, they were all working in the dark, because no demands had been made. Not until they received some communication from the terrorists would they be able to review the situation. 'If only we had more to go on …' Terry was thinking aloud.

Archie, who had really enjoyed his toad in the hole, elbowed Jack and nodded meaningfully for him to accompany him. 'Must have a pee …'

'Yes, I suppose I could do with a slash too.' Jack got up and joined Archie as they sauntered over to the building. Terry was left alone, wondering if they were gay too. That was all he needed, to be in charge of a bunch of gay soldiers.

Jack and Archie stood at the two stained urinals in the rather dingy toilet, which smelt foul. Jack noticed a row of graffitied arrows that ran up the wall and onto the ceiling. Half-way across the ceiling was a brief message: *'If you can read this, you're probably pissing on your shoes …'*. Jack had been snared: there were splashes on both his feet. 'Shit!' he cursed.

'The oldest trick in the book,' Archie laughed.

'And I fell for it!' Jack wiggled his feet to get rid of the drips.

'Well, Jack, dear man … About this address?'

'What address …?' Jack got a paper towel and was wiping his shoes.

'The one you found in that woman's bag – the one you memorised and then ate – remember?'

'Not sure if I do remember …' Jack washed his hands.

'There's hardly any point in keeping it to yourself, Jack. You're not going to be able to deal with the terrorists on your own now, are you?' Archie had decided on the logical rather than the aggressive approach.

Jack thought for a moment. He knew that Archie was right. 'I suppose not …'

'So what did the address say?'

'Just between you and me – although we might have to tell Terry.' Jack didn't feel comfortable. 'Anyway, this address might not mean anything. Could be a maiden aunt, a lover …'

'Or where the terrorists are holding the women?'

'But why would it be in her bag in the first place?' Jack suddenly thought.

'But it *wasn't* in her bag, was it? You picked it up a few yards away. Could've come out of one of the terrorists' pockets. We've got to check it out.'

'I suppose so … Could be a wild goose chase …'

'What was the address, Jack?'

'Cloudsey House, Perdsea, Suffolk.' It hadn't been difficult to memorise.

'Well we're in Suffolk. Got a map in the car – I'll look it up.'

'Do we tell the others?' Jack was beginning to feel guilty that he had kept it to himself in the first place. Not a professional action.

'Terry, if we have to. But as far as the others are concerned, we keep it to ourselves.'

'Terry might tell them. Have you thought of that?' Jack didn't think that they could get away with it.

'Let me ponder that one. I'll go and look Perdsea up on the map, then we'll decide on a plan of campaign. Say nothing until then.'

Jack nodded and left him. Archie washed his hands, wondering how best to go about this. He could get in the car and go there on his own. But he realised that he couldn't deal with it on his own either. As he left the toilet he bumped into the barmaid, who was coming out of the ladies' toilet. 'Beryl, that was a delicious meal, thank you.'

'I'm pleased you enjoyed it. Would you like a dessert …?' she said, making sure no-one was about.

'What have you got?' Archie asked in genuine innocence.

'I'll show you – this way …' Smiling, she opened the door to the ladies' and almost dragged him in. Archie didn't resist, and watched as she locked the door from the inside. 'I've got a couple of house specialities … If you've got the spotted dick – I've got the custard …'

Next door, in the gents' toilet, unbeknown to Jack and Archie, Rory had been sat in one of the cubicles in absolute agony. The walk had only made him feel worse. His stomach had really started to bubble, and he had realised that if he didn't get to the toilet quickly he might possibly embarrass himself. Just as he had sat down, Archie and Jack had come in. Keeping absolutely quiet, he had heard every word of their conversation. So that was their game! He had almost given away his presence, but due to his expertise in controlling the muscles in his buttocks, he had managed to keep his insides on hold. It had been worse than being in combat, and he hadn't known how long he'd be able to keep it up. Thankfully Jack and Archie had left soon after. As soon as he had released the tenseness, the world had fallen out of his bottom.

Now, as he sat there, feeling blissfully better, he had two dilemmas to contend with. The first was what to do about Jack and Archie's subterfuge; the second was the realisation that there was no toilet paper in the cubicle. He then gratefully remembered that there were some paper towels by the sink. As he gingerly opened the cubicle door, he heard a female voice and banging noises coming from the ladies' toilet. *'Yes! Yes! Yes! Harder, harder, harder! Oh yes! All the way! All the way! Keep going … don't come yet!'* And these were followed by a series of moans and groans. Rory felt quite nostalgic. With his pants and trousers down to his knees, he carefully moved across to the sink and grabbed a handful of towels.

The door suddenly opened and in walked Wilf, his flies already undone. He looked at Rory and smiled. 'Nice day for a crap, in't it?'

26

'You certainly enjoy your food.' Richard watched as Delia cleared the last pea off her plate. He noticed how elegantly she had eaten. Even the manner in which she loaded her fork showed a refined upbringing.

'I do, don't I? That was almost delicious. A few herbs and spices would have accentuated the flavour of the chicken.' Delia laid the knife and fork precisely on the plate.

'Are you a good cook?' Richard studied her delicate hands.

'I don't know. I've a feeling I like food, but whether or not I can actually cook is another question … Well, that feels much better, thank you.'

'Something sweet to finish off?' Richard suddenly felt the craving for some chocolate. He was going to buy himself a bar.

'No …' she thought, 'but if there's some fruit or a yoghurt, that would be nice. Oh, and a black coffee – if that's not being too greedy?'

'Don't be silly.' Richard smiled and went over to the food section of the canteen. Delia watched him amble across. She could tell that he wasn't used to eating in such a place. Come to think of it – neither was she. She didn't feel any affinity with the other diners, some of whose table manners left much to be desired. But who was she? Throughout the meal she had tried to scour her mind to see if she could dredge up any sort of memory that might give a clue as to her identity. But there was nothing. Her earliest memory was of Richard giving her the kiss of life. And it certainly had been a kiss of life, for Delia now wanted to spend the rest of her life kissing him.

'Hope that's all right.' Richard plonked an apple, a thick-skinned orange and a raspberry yoghurt in front of her. Also on the tray were two cups of coffee and a chocolate bar. 'That's mine,' he pointed. 'Chocolate is a weakness of mine.'

'Any other weaknesses …?' she teased.

'Too numerous to mention, if I'm to be honest.' He bit off a large chunk of chocolate and savoured the taste.

'I wonder what my bad points and weaknesses are?'

'A voyage of discovery if ever there was one. We shall have to start finding out. Someone, somewhere must be missing you.'

'Yet I don't feel I'm missing them, somehow,' she answered honestly.

'How are you feeling physically?' Richard imagined giving her an all over massage. The desire to touch her was quite strong, and he was surprised at his own physical feelings toward her.

'Apart from a slight throbbing from that bump, and a sore gum – I feel fine. Still a complete blank as far as the memory is concerned.'

'You're going to have to find out sooner or later who you are.'

'I'd rather it was later. I'm quite happy at present.' She looked directly at him.

'Don't you think you're rather deluding yourself? Might you be running away from something?' Richard returned her look.

'I suppose I'm frightened wondering what I'll discover.'

'But at the same time – you might be in for a splendid surprise.'

'I doubt it … Look, Richard … can we just leave it for a day before any enquiries are made, or I see some specialist?' She really meant it.

'So what are you going to do in the meantime?' Richard found himself looking at his watch.

'Can I … can I come with you …?' She had hoped he would suggest it.

'To the estate?' It hadn't occurred to him. He had thought he would probably take her to the police station in Norwich and let them take care of her. But having been with her for the last hour, his feelings had altered. He didn't actually want to let her go. He felt confused and uncertain.

'I'm sorry …' Delia said. 'I've probably messed up your whole day, and now I'm trying to impose myself on you. I know you feel responsible for me. You've been wonderful. You've saved my life, for what it's worth. I can't ask any more of you … Just take me to the police – then you can get on with your own life …' She hated saying it, but knew she had unfairly put him on the spot.

'You can come back with me on one condition,' he decided.

'Of course.' Her heart suddenly felt light.

'At some point tomorrow we will have to make a start on finding out who you are. They'll be no arguments.'

'But not until tomorrow?' she asked.

'If that's what you want.'

'Thank you … You are absolutely sure now?'

'I'm not sure of anything, but one can't stand still. Are you ready to go?' Once Richard had made up his mind that was it. He stood up and brushed off a few chocolate bits that had dropped on his lap. 'There is one question I'd like to ask.'

'Which is?' Delia was now standing.

'What do I call you? Candice is obviously not to your liking.'

'Certainly not! Why not invent a temporary name. Any suggestions?'

'I'd rather you choose.' Richard wasn't in the mood to play name games.

Delia thought carefully but nothing immediately sprang to mind. 'Can I think about it on the journey?'

Richard nodded and they both left the canteen. The helicopter was conveniently parked in a field a quarter of a mile away. It wasn't long before they were airborne again. This time headed for Montcasse Manor.

Melissa sat on the beach and looked out at a ship that was silhouetted against the horizon. She had a very uneasy feeling about Delia. Something wasn't right. After leaving the house, instead of going to the shop, she had found herself heading in the direction of the sea. This had meant meandering through Perdsea – an experience in itself. Caught in a 1930s time warp, the village was mainly made up of mock Tudor houses. Neat, ordered, and possessing its own lifeless atmosphere. Even the village pond appeared artificial against the backdrop of identical houses. Walking round this somewhat strange location, Melissa had been conscious of a deserted feel to the whole place. No heads peering behind curtains; no children screaming in the roads and narrow lanes. It didn't seem real – but neither did the situation she found herself in.

She threw some pebbles into the sea and wondered if the ripples created any long term effects. Would the fact that they had stolen the papers make any waves? Would it end up a wasted exercise with the possibility of them all ending up in prison? Melissa had never broken the law in her life before. How Delia had managed to convince her and Serena to go through with it in the first place was something that still amazed her. Delia could be very persuasive and present a thousand reasons why you should do as she asked. So, because of Delia, here she was, sat on a remote Suffolk beach, a wanted criminal with nowhere else to run.

Seeing an empty crisp packet being blown by the breeze, she felt her feelings of hunger return. She got up and wiped off the bits of sand and seaweed that had clung to her skirt. She was hoping that Delia would be back by the time she returned to the house.

Henry managed to get no further than page 20 of *Night in Shining Amour*. As bored as he was, he couldn't take any more of the droll descriptions of the different ways Sir Galahead wooed the proper and innocently wicked Lady Hymena … *He forced her arms apart and she felt his cold chain-mail against her heaving chest, his metal codpiece brushing against her thighs … He unsheathed his sword from its leather scabbard, revealing a yard of naked steel. With one expert slash of his sword, he freed her from the restraints of the chastity belt that her tyrant husband had imprisoned her maidenhead in. Hymena had never seen such a display of power – until Galahead unsheathed his very manhood … Locked in an eternal embrace, they didn't notice the enemy army surround the castle …* Henry threw the book against the door with such force that Serena ran upstairs, wondering what had happened.

'Are you all right …?' she asked tentatively from behind the door.

'No!' he shouted childishly.

'Have you finished that book? I've found another by the same author.'

'What are you trying to do to me? What *is* going on?'

'I beg your pardon?' Serena hated any sort of confrontation.

'How long are you going to keep me in here?'

'I'm sorry – I don't know …'

'Well, who does?'

'Delia … She won't be long, I'm sure. I realise it must be difficult for you. We don't honestly mean you any harm. You must believe that.' She needed to justify her actions.

'Why can't you let me go then? What use am I to you?'

Serena didn't know the answers. The only thing that crept into her head was the vision of him standing naked in the shower and her being surprised at the size of his penis. She tried to blot it out but couldn't, and felt disgusted with herself because of it. She had never thought of Matthew in that way. She'd always taken his penis for granted – and here she was thinking of someone else's. Were the strain and pressure starting to get to her? 'Henry … please try and be patient.'

'Come in and talk to me … Please …' Henry pleaded.

'I can't …' She wanted to. She was fed up being alone in the house and having to wait first for Delia and now Melissa. Where was Melissa? She said she'd be ten minutes – that was nearly an hour ago. Surely she wouldn't disappear as well? That was all she needed.

'I promise I won't try anything … I'd just like to talk …' Henry said in his most persuasive tone.

'We can talk through the door, if you like.' Serena was willing to compromise.

'It's not the same …'

'Sorry, Henry …' She really was.

He sighed to himself. He heard her starting to make her way downstairs. He had a sudden idea. 'Serena, I … I think I need to go to the loo.'

'You've got the vase …' Serena wasn't going to fall for that one.

'I'm certainly not going to … to …' He was embarrassed to use any of the usual coarse descriptions. 'To poo in the vase,' he said quickly, and then felt stupid.

Serena smiled to herself. How sweet to call it by that name. At least Henry had some modicum of decency. 'Are you sure you need to go?' She wasn't certain whether to believe him or not.

'It's suddenly hit me, I'm afraid,' he lied. 'Last night's curry has finally come to the end of its journey, if you know what I mean.' Henry listened. Had that convinced her?

'Can you hold on for a bit?' She still wasn't sure.

'I can try …' Then he had another idea. With his lips he did a passable impression of a slow fart. 'Sorry …' he whispered, adding a slight groan before blowing another convincing fart, much louder this time.

'Are you all right …?' She didn't like the sound of it.

'Not to worry. I'll do my best to hold on. You go and do what you have to do. I'll be all right.' He finished with another wet raspberry.

Serena heard them quite clearly. She knew she couldn't leave him in that condition. She took the key out of her pocket and unlocked the door. 'It's open …'

Henry would have jumped her had she not been holding the gun at his head the moment he opened the door. 'Thank you.' He painfully smiled and went in front of her and down the stairs, holding his stomach to make it look as realistic as possible. She followed, the gun firmly pointed at his back. She was surprised and pleased not to detect any unpleasant smells.

As he walked into the bathroom, Serena followed him in. 'Are you seriously going to stay …?' He looked at her with incredulity.

Serena had to think twice. Guarding him while he was having a shower was one thing – but being in the same room while he … 'I'll be outside.' She quickly closed and locked the door. Henry smiled and congratulated himself. It was a very clever move on his part. He turned to the bathroom window. There would be no problem breaking out from there. But first he would conduct his *pièce de resistance*. Making undoing belt noises he then proceeded to groan and blow farting sounds until he heard Serena move away from the door, leaving him to carry out his ablutions in peace. He decided to give it another minute before escaping for good.

27

Stella was doing her best to make sense of all the dials and knobs on the latest portable digital recorder with external microphone, which Scott had plonked on her knee once they had got in the car. It was proving to be more complicated than she had imagined. 'I'll never be a soundwoman,' she sighed. 'How can you expect me to operate this and make notes at the same time?'

'You'll be all right. It's quite straightforward,' Scott reassured her, although he wondered if he might have bitten off more than he could chew. They had just bypassed Colchester and were heading toward Ipswich. They were going to base themselves there until he received further instructions.

'Then you operate it …' She switched on Play and Record accidentally.

'Baby, I shall be behind the camera.' Scott did his best to smile.

'Then you operate it …' the recorder repeated.

'I did it at last!' Stella was pleased with herself. 'I think I'm getting a hang of the knobs.'

'That you are, baby, that you are.' Scott still felt tired from his little session with Stella. On a couple of occasions during the journey he had had to gently steer her hand away from his crotch. Her sudden tactile enthusiasm was going beyond reasonable bounds. He prayed that she wasn't going to be difficult or do something silly like fall in love with him.

'That you are, baby, that you are,' she played it back.

'This is fun! Maybe I'll make a soundwoman yet.'

'You've always been sound to me, Stella,' he joked.

'I'm getting a bit peckish …' Stella licked her lips.

Scott momentarily panicked, thinking she meant sex. At the best of times, sex in his Porsche was never the easiest of manoeuvres, even for a blow job. In his experience, those passionate contortions were often followed by a bad attack of cramp.

'A nice ploughman's lunch would go down a treat with a glass of red wine,' she added.

'As long as the ploughman doesn't object,' he quipped with relief.

'A piece if stilton, French bread and pickle … umm …' She could almost taste it.

'Okay, we'll stop soon.' At which point his phone started to ring. ' … Hello you … How are things? Yes, we're on our way … Where? … Perdsea? Never heard of it … On the coast … Okay, I'll find it … Yes, I will … Talk to you later … Bye … Yes, me too, byee.

'No need to go to Ipswich now.' Scott smiled and visibly relaxed.

'Who was that?' Stella asked. Scott's tone over the phone had sounded as if he was talking to one of his girlfriends.

'My special contact. It looks like Perdsea is the place. Could you just look at the map, love?'

As Stella was about to open the road atlas, she saw a pub directly ahead of them. It was called The Dog and Duck. 'Let's stop here for something.'

Scott took one look at it and put his foot on the accelerator. 'I believe we can do better. I don't think I'd trust the food in there ...'

Archie looked up from his own road atlas as the Porsche sped by. He'd always fancied owning a Porsche. Maybe one day, he thought. But then again, did he really need such a car? He was seriously considering early retirement. He'd accumulated a little nest egg from 20 years with the armed forces; and his wife, who had died of cancer a couple of years before, had left him a bit of money. His ideal was to own a small cottage with the proverbial roses round the door, somewhere near the coast. He'd have a quiet life. A life away from the pressures, the subterfuge, the killings. The only orders he would take would be from himself. He took a deep breath of country air. That was for tomorrow – today had to be got through first. There were never any guarantees that he'd be alive to see tomorrow.

Having looked up and charted the way to Perdsea, he put the atlas back in a side compartment. He wiped an itchy nose with the sleeve of his jacket and could smell the barmaid's cheap perfume still on him. The whole experience made him smile. There was a woman with spunk. It had been a most invigorating encounter, and he hadn't enjoyed such frantic and gratifying sex for many years. Beryl might not have looked a beauty, but her soft, well-rounded body and sheer passionate energy had made up for it a hundredfold. He had never imagined the pleasures that could be enjoyed in such a small space. Archie suddenly felt excited and ten years younger.

'Have you checked out where Perdsea is?' Jack tapped Archie on the shoulder, which immediately brought him back to earth.

'About an hour away on the coast.' Archie composed himself.

'Do we let Terry know?' Jack noticed Rory, looking grim faced, moving toward them.

Archie, who also saw him, looked at Jack. 'A difficult one, old chap. Don't think we have much choice. If we just disappear, they'll probably think we've gone AWOL. Let me just cogitate ...' He shut up as Rory approached.

'Mother's meeting is it?' Rory did his best to elicit a smile.

'Are you all right? You look the colour of that curry you had.' Jack was glad he'd had just a sandwich.

'I've had the shits, if you really want to know.' Rory hoped that he wouldn't have to run to the toilet again.

'Thank you for sharing that with us,' Archie remarked.

'And isn't there something you want to share with me, boys?' Rory's lips tightened.

'Like what, Rory?' Jack realised he was up to something.

'Like *Perdsea* ... for instance?' Rory emphasised the word.

'Who's that? Should we know?' Archie was very good at not reacting in any telltale fashion.

'Tut, tut, girls! Not who – but where. *Cloudsey House* mean anything to you? And *no* is not the answer.'

'It depends on the question ...' Archie glanced quickly at Jack, who was beginning to feel very uncomfortable.

'Let's not beat about the bush, as one prick said to the other. While you two were pointing Percy at the porcelain, I was in one of the bogs ...' Jack and Archie tried to look blank. 'You don't believe me? How about, *'But as far as the others are concerned, we keep it to ourselves'*? The game is up, amigos.' Rory could see that he had broken through.

'So now we tell everyone, is that it?' Archie replied after getting a nod from Jack.

'I wouldn't be that ambitious, petal. Agreed that Terry has to be informed – I'm in his van, anyway.'

'And Kieran and Barry? How would you stop them finding out?' Jack didn't think that was possible.

'You leave them to me, sunshine, I'll sort those little turds out ... Talking of turds – do excuse me, I feel a rumble in the bumble.' With that, Rory quickly shot out of the car park and into the pub.

'We could get rid of him, I suppose ...?' Archie wondered.

'No, let Rory deal with the other two. We'll tell Terry when they're out of the way. Agreed?'

'Agreed, old man. This little caper is full of little surprises.' Archie locked the car and made toward the building.

'Not too many more, I hope.' Jack walked beside him.

In the public bar, Kieran and Barry quickly downed their third pint when they saw Terry coming in from the garden. Jack and Archie met him by the door. 'I need to talk to you all in the garden, right now ...' said Terry, glaring at Kieran and Barry.

'Not giving us black looks, is he?' Kieran wiped some froth from his top lip.

Barry couldn't help but giggle. He felt really good after those drinks. 'D'you think if Terry became a postman he'd be a blackmailer?'

Kieran doubled up with laughter. 'Yeh, and his favourite dance would be the black bottom!'

Despite not being able to hear them from where he stood, Terry saw their contorting body movements, which were enough to tell him that they were behaving unprofessionally. His anger started to rise. 'If they're pissed ...'

'I'll round them up and see you in the garden,' Jack intervened. He didn't want to risk a confrontation. Not now.

'Where's Rory?' Terry looked around.

'A touch of the runs, I believe.' Archie turned to look at Beryl, who was wiping out a glass very dreamily. Her indifferent and uncaring countenance had changed to one of gentle shyness. She looked as if she were literally glowing. Archie had satisfied her as no man had ever done before. She smiled and blew him a kiss.

'Well go up and tell him to run to the garden, double quick – and bring the toilet roll if he's that delicate.' Terry stomped back outside into the garden.

'I'll get Rory if you deal with those two,' Archie told Jack. He then caught Beryl's eye, gestured for her to follow him, and went upstairs. She beamed and nodded. A few moments later, she too went upstairs.

Jack went over to Kieran and Barry, who were about to order another couple of pints. 'I wouldn't do that, fellas. Terry wants to brief us in the garden.'

'Tell that black bastard to fuck off. We're happy here, thanks.' Kieran was braver with Terry out of earshot.

'You tell him. It's no skin off my nose.' Jack wasn't in the mood to argue.

'Wot's 'e want now?' Barry asked belligerently.

'Join us and you'll find out.' Jack turned away from them and headed toward the garden door.

'Bollocks – let's have another drink. Where's that slag gone?' Kieran looked around for the barmaid, who had disappeared. 'Where you going?' He saw Barry move away from the bar. Barry just shrugged. He had suddenly lost his nerve. 'Oh, bollocks!' Kieran wasn't going to be left on his own.

Upstairs, Archie had quickly popped into the gents. The smell was overpowering. He heard an awful groan followed by a machine gun splatter. 'Rory, you in there?' Archie held his nose.

'No, it's a troop of boy scouts after a bean feast!' Rory exclaimed.

'Terry needs us all in the garden. Some sort of briefing.'

'Do us a favour, petal, and shove some of those paper towels under the door. I think I'm going to need a forest!'

Archie quickly grabbed a handful and pushed them under the cubicle door before making a speedy exit.

'Thanks, hon. An Australian friend, I used to call him my up'n-down-under, once told me that a shit a day helps to keep the doctor away. The way I'm going, the whole medical profession will be discharged! Archie, you still there …?' It all went quiet, until Rory began to hear those self same grunts and moans coming from next door – *'Yes, harder, harder, harder! That's lovely! Oh, oh, ooooh …!'*, followed by an ecstatic shriek.

Rory realised he should have had the sandwich instead.

Terry gazed at the men stood before him. The very sight of them made him feel sick. Two were swaying slightly; one looked ill and kept holding his stomach; another had a smile and a sweaty face; while the last one simply appeared fed up. These were the country's saviours. The *crème de la crème*. Representatives of Britain's top security organisations. There to fight the good fight and to protect the nation from those who wished to undermine it. Terry suddenly wished he could crawl into a hole and die. Yet it was up to him to inspire them, to inject them with positive affirmation, to see that they performed their duty with skilled professionalism. He brought to mind one of his father's sayings: *'Treat all passengers as your brother – for one day one of them might very well save your life …'*

'Wot if they've done in those three women already?' Barry asked.

'Then we're too late, aren't we? Any more *bright* questions?' Terry dared them.

'Since the terrorists haven't declared themselves or disclosed their demands, what's the situation with HQ?' Archie took out a handkerchief and wiped his forehead.

'We know who the women are – you've seen the photos – and that they must have been kidnapped before the Whitehall robbery. This is no small-time amateur group. We're dealing with a highly organised, professional body with a lot of experience. They're obviously biding their time.'

'So we continue to wait?' Jack looked at Archie and then Rory.

'There's nothing to go on,' said Terry. 'The stolen car's been checked out. We know about the helicopter. But nothing else to give us a lead. The hostages have to be somewhere in Suffolk … Our present, meagre efforts are proving to be a big embarrassment to the Home Secretary, but they won't give us any further support. We are in shit street …'

'You can say that again …' Rory was still feeling awful, but thankfully the runs had stopped.

'Wot about the competition. Is that still on?' Barry burped.

'That depends on our next move – if there is one. No-one's making any promises anymore. All the goal posts have been shifted.' Terry felt tired.

'We just need some balls to score a few goals,' Kieran joked.

'We'd use yours, petal, only you haven't got any,' Rory deliberately provoked him.

'Say that again, you fucking Nancy!' Kieran was a real glutton for punishment.

Barry came and stood next to Kieran. The drink had made them both defiant. 'If you're such a clever dickhead,' he taunted Rory, 'where are *your* balls?'

'If you step over into my bijou office, I'll show you.' Rory smiled, wiggled his bottom deliberately and walked across to a corner of the garden, beckoning them to follow.

'Come on, guys, let's keep the peace.' Terry took a deep breath.

'We're just going to have a friendly chatette. Just sort out this little misunderstanding. Aren't we boys?'

'Clear the air …' Kieran agreed.

'Get to know each other …' Barry added.

'All right, Terry?' Rory confirmed.

Terry closed his eyes in desperation. Perhaps if they knocked the shit out of each other, it would keep them quiet for a bit. It might also sober Barry and Kieran up. Terry turned his back on them, indicating he wasn't getting involved.

'Terry … Archie and I would like a little word.' Jack beckoned Terry over. 'We think we might have stumbled on something …'

While Jack and Archie took Terry to the opposite end of the garden to tell him about finding the address, Rory confronted Barry and Kieran at the other end. They both had their fists poised, ready to fight him.

'Put those down, you silly queens!' Rory spoke quietly. 'You want to win this competition or not? I've got some information that will give us a head start over the others.'

'Are you winding us up because you're too fuckin' chicken to fight?' Kieran clenched his fists.

'Please don't mention chicken again! Look … you have one of two choices. One, I tell you what I know. Two, we fight it out, and you'll be none the wiser. What's it to be?'

'You're bluffing …' Barry remembered their first encounter.

'Why should I bluff, now? I can't do this on my own. I don't pretend to be the Lone Arranger. I need your help …' Rory did his best to sound convincing.

'Why have you come to us, rather than them over there?' Kieran pointed to the group at the other end, who were deep in discussion.

'Because it will take some *real* men to handle the situation. Jack and Archie are too limp-wristed to be able to cope.' Rory hoped he didn't sound too ridiculous.

'That's a point …' Barry agreed. 'Are you counting yerself as a *real* man?'

'That's for me to know and you to find out, petal.'

'What if we don't agree?' Kieran asked.

'I'm not proud – I'll do a deal with the others instead. As I said, it's your choice, boys.' Rory folded his arms and smiled.

Barry looked to Kieran, who looked back. 'Wot about the black one?'

'Terry? He obviously doesn't know what he's doing. Better we keep him in the dark, so to speak … Are you with me?'

Neither Kieran nor Barry had much time for Terry, so it wasn't a difficult decision for them to make. They realised they had nothing to lose and everything to gain. And there were two of them. They believed they could handle Rory if he got out of hand or double-crossed them.

While Rory started to outline his little plan, across the garden, Jack and Archie were trying to convince Terry to come in with them. 'I should've been informed of the address at the time you found it,' Terry berated Jack. 'I've been made to look like a real incompetent schmuck with Whitehall. They think we don't know what we're doing out here.'

'We don't – do we?' Archie put the knife gently in. 'But we can soon remedy the whole situation.'

Jack realised that he could only convince Terry if he applied a logical argument. 'This was, first and foremost, an interdepartmental competition, where the most resourceful individual would win. That's right, isn't it?'

'Sure, but that's all rather gone out of the window since we learnt that the women had been taken hostage. My original role was as supervising CO – now I will carry the can whatever the outcome …' Terry cracked his knuckles.

Archie poured oil on Terry's predicament. 'It's what's known as a scapegoat in diplomatic terms.'

'And don't I know it!' Terry felt vulnerable for the first time.

'But it needn't be.' Jack sounded positive. 'If that Perdsea address does happen to house both the terrorists and the hostages, between us we can swiftly deal with it and bring it to a satisfactory conclusion. Then who will be the star? You of course! We've got nothing to lose by checking it out.'

Terry let it sink in. 'And the others? This is supposed to be a team effort.'

'Barry and Kieran have done nothing but bad mouth you – behind your back – ever since we got together. They're more likely to screw up the whole operation than help it. Isn't that so, Archie?'

'They don't respect orders either. *Vis-à-vis* the drink,' Archie made his point.

'We don't need them, Terry. What we need is a successful result. That's all that really matters, isn't it? That's what this is really about, isn't it? Not a boys' own competition …'

Terry looked across at Barry and Kieran, still swaying while they listened to Rory, who was expressively waving his arms about as he talked. What was going on? He thought they were about to fight each other? Terry didn't like them, and they had disobeyed his orders. That was enough for a dismissive reprimand. 'And our gay friend?'

'Rory's with us. He's mounting a counter-offensive. Creating a little diversion to get them off our backs—'

'I don't want to know,' Terry stopped Jack from continuing. 'I didn't hear that. If they get lost, that's their problem …'

They were suddenly interrupted by a helicopter flying overhead. They all looked up automatically and watched it disappear into the distance – unaware that one of the women in the photographs, Delia, was looking down at the pub and the cluster of little figures and thinking how dinky it all looked.

28

'What's the matter …?' Richard turned to Delia, who had momentarily frozen.

'I don't know … It's just this extraordinary feeling that I've travelled in a helicopter before …'

'Anything else spring to mind?' Richard wondered if her memory was starting to return.

'No, that was it. It's gone now …' Delia carried on looking out of the cockpit window at the passing countryside below her. It looked like the Garden of Eden. Delia bit into the apple she had taken with her from the canteen. 'I know what!' She suddenly had an idea.

'What's that?' Richard glanced at the fuel gauge and saw that it was very low. Hopefully just enough to get them to the estate. He decided not to say anything to her for the time being.

'Call me Eve.'

'Sorry …?' His concentration had lapsed for a second.

'You have to call me something – then why not Eve?'

'As long as you don't call me Adam or offer me a bite of your apple.' He smiled at her.

'Would that be such a wicked thing?' she teased, brandishing the half eaten apple.

Richard politely declined by nodding his head. He had surprised himself by offering to bring her along in the first place. He was divided in his feelings and was having an internal battle with himself. One part of him shied away from becoming too involved in this woman's life, a responsibility he could really do without, while the other part was strangely attracted and didn't want to let her go. No-one had ever affected him so strongly as Delia.

'Penny for them …?' she broke the silence.

'Show me your penny and I'll tell you … Eve.'

'That's not fair. You know I haven't any money.'

'It wouldn't have been worth it anyway.'

'How do I know unless you tell me?' Delia wanted to know everything about Richard, but was being careful to try not to alienate him. She deduced he was a very private man, and in his defence had erected numerous barriers to protect himself. If only she could melt those barriers and get to the heart of the real man, the man she was finding herself inadvertently falling in love with.

'We'll be there in five minutes.' Without making it obvious, he tapped the window of the fuel gauge, and felt apprehension when the needle dropped down to E. He prayed that it would get them home. Suddenly the motor hiccupped and jerked for a few seconds, before continuing on as before.

'Is everything all right?' Delia wasn't in any way frightened.

'The engine was just clearing its throat,' Richard tried to make a joke of it. His mind raced into overdrive. What if the motor suddenly stopped and plunged them both crashing to the ground? Should he land now and not take a chance? The only problem was that they were flying over a large village that didn't have adequate landing space below. Richard closed his eyes for a moment and said a quick prayer. It was the first time in his life that the prayer came right from his heart rather than his head.

'Oh, Richard ... look ... it's a funfair!' Delia pointed like an excited child.

Richard opened his eyes and said a silent thank you. The funfair was part of the estate, which was spreading out before them. He began the gentle descent down. About a hundred metres from the landing pad, the helicopter gave another blustery jerk, and for a split second the engine cut right out. Richard promptly banged something on the control panel and the motor revived again, finally bringing them down to earth safe and sound, near to the other helicopter.

Delia wiped the sweat off Richard's forehead with a handkerchief as they both sat there after the engine had been switched off. 'Was there a problem?'

'You could say that ... A little difficult to fly when the fuel's run out ... Sorry.'

'This is the second time you've saved my life. You can't go unrewarded.' With that she leant across and gave him a warm, loving kiss on the lips.

'I'm not sure I deserved that ...' Richard had to control himself from taking her in his arms. If it had been anywhere else he might have lost all inhibition, but the sight of one of the estate's pilots running up to meet them quashed his ardour.

'I know no better way of saying thank you.'

'And that's something else you haven't forgotten.'

'What's that?' Delia looked curiously at him.

'How to kiss ... Well, Eve, shall we go and meet my family?'

29

Melissa came out of the local grocery shop with a bag full of things to eat, plus a couple of newspapers. She had tried to engage in friendly conversation with the shopkeeper, but he had just replied to her banter with uninterested monosyllabic utterances. The only sentence she had been able to get out of him had been to inform her that nothing much exciting ever happened in Perdsea. She had been almost tempted to say, 'Show us your willy for sixpence,' but realised it might have drawn unnecessary attention to her.

As she made her way toward the house with the shopping, a sleek car came screeching round the corner and braked right beside her. A window wound down and a woman stuck her head out. 'Excuse me, is this Perdsea?'

'In all its glory.' Melissa bent down and saw the driver combing his hair in the rear-view mirror. He was dressed like an Italian ponce.

'Is there a hotel nearby?' The woman, who looked quite hard, gave a false smile.

'You've got me there!' Melissa put down her bag. 'But I did see a big pub about half a mile toward the beach. The Albatross, I think it was called. You might be able to get a room there. Or they'll tell you where to go …'

Without another word, the window wound itself back up, and the Porsche quickly accelerated down the road.

'Thank you and goodbye …' Melissa muttered as she picked up the shopping and resumed her journey.

'Bloody fat locals! Not very helpful. Probably only thinking about gorging on all those pies that she's probably just bought.' Stella didn't like the look of Perdsea, even though she'd only been there a minute.

'Who's a fattist, then!' Scott was quite surprised to hear Stella being so derogatory.

'Well she *was* fat! Probably sent us in the wrong direction as well.' Stella had a thing about overweight women.

'Let's just see where the road leads.' Scott was quite intrigued by the surroundings. The place had a unique quality that appealed to his sense of theatre.

'I could never live in a place like this,' said Stella. 'It doesn't look … natural.' She took out her compact and spread a layer of lipstick on her mouth. One of the wheels crossed a small hole in the road, making the whole car bump. Stella's hand jerked and a line of lipstick went up from her lip and across her cheek. 'Bloody place!' Already she was beginning to feel a sense of unease.

'This looks like it … Just as that "large" lady said …' Scott stopped the car in front of a big timber and brick building with a huge oak tree shadowing it. A signboard perched on a long pole announced that this was The Albatross. Most of the faded picture, depicting an albatross in flight, was obliterated by years of bird droppings that had built up to give it a somewhat three dimensional effect. The whole place looked ravaged and was badly in need of a coat or six of paint.

Stella wiped away the lipstick smear with a tissue before looking out of the window. 'We are not stopping here ...' She noticed a sign in one of the windows that said 'VACANCIES'.

'It looks great to me. It'll make a change from all those identikit corporate hotels we're always staying in.' Scott started to get out of the car. He didn't care what Stella thought. He was employing her and paying the bills, and the decision would be his.

'But Scott ...'

He banged his door shut, not giving her time to protest. He saw from the stickers plastered underneath a menu case outside that the place accepted credit cards. It couldn't be that bad. Anyway, he sometimes fancied being in places he wouldn't usually frequent. He strolled into the poky reception area and banged on a desk bell, which fell apart.

'Can I help you, sir?' A figure emerged out of the shadows carrying an empty beer crate. He was quite tall and thin, and his clothes fitted where they touched. He was in his fifties, with thinning grey hair and a bulbous nose. His voice, contrary to his whole appearance, was that of a well-educated butler.

'Do you have any rooms available?' Scott noticed a row of keys along the wall.

'That we do, sir. A single ...?' Stella entered at that point. The look on her face as she took in the ambience couldn't have been more damning.

'A double – with bathroom, please.' Scott smiled at Stella and dared her to say anything.

'And how long would that be for, sir?' The manager gave Stella the once-over, which made her skin literally creep.

'A couple of years, maybe ten,' Scott joked. The man did not react to his quip. 'Just for tonight, as a start anyway,' he quickly added.

'Mr and Mrs ...?' The manager opened the visitors' book.

'Trimble ...' Scott decided not to bother using an alias. He'd be paying by credit card and didn't want to complicate matters unnecessarily. 'Stella, could you get the bags out of the boot while I sign us in?' he said without looking at her.

'Yes, dear ...' She walked out, cursing under her breath. He was beginning to treat her like a wife. She had a terrible feeling about this whole place, and wondering if she'd made a mistake in agreeing to take on this job.

When the manager showed them up to their room, it wasn't quite as they had imagined. Stella had had a vision of damp patches, worn carpets, dark oak furniture and torn, faded sheets. He had wondered if it would be something out of the '30s; solid and reliable but without the frills. It was neither. A four-poster bed dominated the centre of the room, with Liberty print cover and matching curtains. Tasteful, co-ordinated wallpaper accentuated good-quality modern furniture, all positioned on a Berber-type carpet. The bathroom was clean and functional, with a good supply of soft towels.

'Will you be having dinner?' the manager asked, as he stood by the door about to exit.

'Not sure yet. Do we have to book, or is it all right if we just turn up?' Scott put the bags on the bed.

'As you wish, sir. We shall be serving from seven until nine. By the way, sir ...' he added, 'can I suggest you park your car away from the tree? It is a great favourite with the seagulls, if you know what I mean. Wouldn't like to see that nice paintwork damaged in any way ... Thank you, sir ... madam.' And he disappeared into the dark, grubby hallway.

'Well ...' Scott surveyed all before him.

'At least it's clean,' Stella had to concur after checking the crisp bed linen.

'As they say, appearances can often be deceptive. My mother used to say that a well-dressed person, who looked nice and clean on the outside, didn't necessarily have clean underwear. Never take anything for granted.'

'Is that your motto?' Stella sat on the bed. It felt soft and inviting. She was starting to feel more relaxed.

'It's like the business we're in. We manufacture images and illusions and guide our viewer to see what we want them to see.' Scott felt passionate about his work.

'We con them, you mean.' Stella was now lying on the bed, looking up at the netted canopy.

'But we also educate and inform, expose and denounce, move and anger. It's not just a gossamer of half-edited lies, its an honest search for truth ...'

'I hope you brought a supply of gossamers. We could be in for a long wait.' Stella bent her knees, which made her dress ride up to her thighs, letting Scott see that she was wearing suspenders. When they had gone back to her flat to collect some clothes, she had changed into them. It was the first time she had ever worn suspenders. They had originally been intended as a surprise for Jack. Since Jack was now out of the frame, she didn't want to waste them.

'We're not on holiday, you know,' Scott tried to be as diplomatic as possible.

'Don't you like them ...?' Stella teasingly revealed a bit more. Lying on strange beds seemed to do something to her.

If Scott was to be honest, he didn't like them. They did absolutely nothing for his libido. Should he tell Stella outright and risk the likelihood of her walking out in a fit of female pique? Or should he pretend and go along with her? He thought he's already given her what she wanted. 'They're very nice. Fancy a stroll on the beach?'

'You know what I fancy ... Haven't gone off me all of a sudden, have you?' Stella tested him.

'Baby, how can you think that?' Scott knew this was going to be difficult.

'I've never made love in a four poster before ... Have you?'

Scott didn't want to admit that he had, several times. It would only result in a barrage of questions that he didn't want to prompt. 'No ...'

Stella slipped off her blouse, revealing a see-through bra. Another surprise for Jack that he would now never enjoy. 'I know you're not a breast man – but they're not too big, are they?' Stella cupped her hand over one and gently massaged it, making herself start to feel quite aroused.

'They're just perfect, babe.' Scott didn't like where this was going. 'Hey, why don't we do a recce round the village? See what the visual possibilities are.'

'Wouldn't you prefer to do a recce of me ...? Lots of visual possibilities there ...' Stella had taken off her skirt and was being as sensuous as she could be.

'Why don't we do *that* later ... after we've had something to eat ...' Scott was finding this really difficult and aggravating.

Stella wasn't giving up. She whipped off her briefs and turned on her front, exposing her bare bottom to him. 'What was it you wanted to do before …? Got any of that cream with you …?'

It was the straw that made the camel stiff. Scott sighed, but knew there was no turning back now.

Cloudsey House was such a distinct towering landmark in the village that you could see it from quite a distance all round. Melissa, who had taken a wrong turning after giving directions to Stella and Scott in the Porsche, soon found her way back to the house. She was then annoyed to discover that there wasn't a car in the drive, which meant that Delia had still not returned. Unless she had decided not to buy a car as planned, and had come by other means.

It felt unusually quiet when she entered the front room. No sign of Serena. She went and plonked the groceries in the kitchen and found that empty too. Melissa stepped out into the garden, but no sign of her there either. She had an eerie feeling in the pit of her stomach.

She went back inside and ran upstairs to where Henry was being kept. The door was wide open and there was nobody inside. Oh god, she thought, has he managed to escape and take Serena with him? Or could she be laying, raped and dead, in one of the other bedrooms? Melissa stopped herself from calling out. Henry might be furtively lurking in some corner ready to pounce on her. *Oh, why was I so stupid as to go out and leave them?* she admonished herself.

She returned downstairs to the front room and went to the drawer where they kept the two guns – they had gone. She then went back into the kitchen and grabbed a meat cleaver.

She searched cautiously in the other bedrooms one by one, looking behind every door and in every nook and cranny, dreading that she was going to be confronted by some horrible sight. But there was no sign of anything untoward. The only place she hadn't tried was the bathroom. She was perplexed to see that a chair had been wedged under the door knob, from the outside. She gingerly unhooked the chair and put her hand on the knob to try to open it. It was locked. She jiggled the knob, but it was firmly shut.

'Who's that?' a male voice spoke from inside.

'Is that … is that you, Henry …?' Melissa asked.

'No, it's King bloody Kong! Who the hell d'you think it is?' Henry sounded really annoyed.

'What are you doing in there?' A sense of relief was returning to her.

'What does one usually do on the lavatory?' Henry was quite disgruntled.

'Serena, are you in there?'

'No, she is not! Would you like me watching you if you were in the toilet?'

'Wouldn't bother me … So, where is Serena?'

'I don't know! She might be outside somewhere …' Henry said rather prudently.

'Outside? What do you mean?'

'Go and bloody well find out for yourself and leave me in peace.'

Melissa couldn't understand what was going on. Still holding the cleaver, she went outside and walked round the house. Underneath the bathroom window sat Serena, her back against the wall, looking thoroughly fed up. The two guns lay on her lap. 'Serena …?'

'I didn't hear you come in … I was getting worried.' Serena looked like a little girl who had been abandoned by everyone.

'What are you doing there, may I ask?'

'Henry said he had to go to the toilet – you know. So I put the chair against the door and came out here …'

'Why … I don't get it?' Melissa was beginning to wonder if Serena had suddenly flipped.

'Henry made an attempt to escape – from out of the bathroom window. I think he was most surprised to find me out here.' Serena brandished both guns.

'Clever you. That was very naughty of our Henry. What's he still doing in there?'

'Sulking, I think. I just decided to leave him to stew, until you came back. Why were you so long?'

'Sorry. Went for a stroll on the beach. The time just whizzed by. Got some food in though … Any news of Delia?'

Serena glanced at the cleaver Melissa was holding and decided not to mention it. 'Nothing. Something's happened, hasn't it? It's not like Delia. She's never been so late before.'

'No, it isn't like Delia to keep us waiting … Something *has* gone wrong, I just feel it … I'm going to ring her mobile …' Melissa started to take hers out of her bag.

'Delia told us, before she left, not to phone her – for security reasons.' Serena did not like disobeying instructions.

'I don't care. This has got silly.' Melissa punched in the number. 'It's ringing …'

In a field, not far from The Dog and Duck, the distant ringtone of a mobile phone could be heard playing the opening bars of Wagner's 'Die Valkyrie'. The phone lay beneath a clump of grass, and had not been found by the men during their search.

It continued to ring until a grubby hand picked it up and pressed the answer button. 'Ello …' It belonged to a male voice with a Suffolk accent. 'Ello … Who's that?'

'Who are you? Where's Delia? Put her on at once!' Melissa demanded.

'It's Wilf … Don't know Delia … but will you talk dirty to me …?'

'I beg your pardon! What have you done to Delia?' Melissa was starting to lose her composure.

'Ave you got nothin on? Are you playing with yourself?'

'What's going on? Who are you?' Melissa was really starting to get wound up.

'I told you, it's Wilf, and I've got my willy in my hand. Would you like to talk to him?'

'I would prefer to talk to Delia! Now where is she? I shall call the police if you don't tell me!'

'Ave you got big tits and a hairy minge? I like big tits … My willy likes big tits …'

'For one last time – I want to know what's happened to Delia, you pervert!' Melissa shouted.

'You're no fun.' Upon which Wilf, who'd just left The Dog and Duck, switched off the phone, which he later threw into a river on his way home.

'What is it, Melissa? What's happened? You've gone pale.' Serena could see Melissa visibly shaking.

'I think Delia's been abducted by some sex fiends … Oh my god, I can't bear to think what she going through right now …'

30

'Mother, this is Eve.' Richard introduced Delia to Gertrude, who was reading Randolph's obituary in *The Times*. 'She was helping me with the by-election. I said I'd show her round the estate. We can put her up for the night, can't we?' He and Delia had agreed beforehand not to mention the accident or the loss of memory, since it would only confuse and complicate matters.

'I'm pleased to meet you, Lady Montcasse.' Delia played the part as if she was born to it. 'This is a wonderful room!'

'Needs redecorating,' Gertrude said rather brusquely, eyeing Delia up and down through her half-moon glasses. 'Eve who?'

'Eve …' Delia looked down at the floor. 'Carpet … Carpetiere.'

'French?' Gertrude put the paper down.

'On my great grandfather's side.' Delia really was thinking on her feet. Richard looked on quite impressed and amused.

'Any relation to the Normandy Karpetieres?'

'I don't think so. Great grandfather came from … Gascony.' Even Delia surprised herself. She might have lost her memory as to her identity, but somehow she seemed to possess a fund of general knowledge.

'Karpetiere …?' Gertrude wondered. 'That was your husband's name as well? Most unusual …'

Delia saw Gertrude notice her wedding ring. Of course, how stupid, she'd forgotten about that. 'My husband … Alexander … died last year … I reverted back to my maiden name.' Delia glanced at Richard, who was looking out of the window.

'What was your married name, my dear?' Gertrude sat like a judge about to pronounce sentence.

Delia looked Gertrude in the eye. 'Irisovitch … His family were Russian. They lived in Paris …' She really thought she had now gone too far.

Gertrude rose and crossed over to one of the large bookcases. She took out a copy of Debrett's and leafed through it. 'Irisovitch … No, they're not in here. What did your late husband do?'

'He … he was in public relations … for a toy manufacturer …'

'Then he certainly wouldn't be in here!' Gertrude slammed the book shut and returned it to the bookcase. Her interest in Delia quickly evaporated.

'Eve, would you like the grand tour?' Richard decided to intervene.

'Oh, yes please …' Delia felt like she had run a race.

'Is that all right, Mother?' He saw that she had picked up *The Times* once more and was carefully scrutinising it. 'Mother …?'

'Why ask me? You've always done as you pleased,' she replied rather petulantly, without raising her eyes from the paper.

Richard nodded to Delia and they left the drawing room. 'Don't mind Mother, she's a colossal snob. If you're not in Debrett's you're no-one. I must say, you handled her very well.'

Delia took in her magnificent surroundings as they strolled down the long corridor filled with numerous art treasures. She stopped to admire a painting. 'It looks like a Canaletto …'

'It is.' Richard looked around to make sure no-one was about. He then pointed to some miniature figures in the corner of the picture. 'See that?'

Delia had to move right up close to the painting to make out what he was pointing at. Amidst a group of courtiers gathered at the side of a church, Delia noticed that the head of one of them had a silly grin and didn't look like it belonged. 'Canaletto must've had a bad day, or he forgot to finish that particular gentleman. I'd never have noticed it if you hadn't drawn my attention to it.'

'Good … No-one else, to my knowledge, has ever noticed it either.'

'What's the significance?'

'I drew that on – when I was 15 … You know, you're the only one I've ever told.' Richard realised he had just exposed a personal secret for the first time.

'Really? You naughty boy, defacing a work of art.' Delia couldn't help but smile at the coy way in which Richard had confessed.

'Father had given me a hiding for being too familiar with one of the maids. She lost her position as a result of it. He'd only just purchased the painting. It was my little way of getting back at him. It was pointless really. I never had the courage to tell him – and now he'll never know …' Richard decided to move on.

'Were you very close to your father?'

'Not at all. We had some good moments, but I can't say I loved him in any sense. Do you think that sounds awful?'

'There isn't a law that says you have to love your parents, or your children.' They were descending an ornate staircase, and one of the maids bowed her head as Richard passed. 'What I want to know,' Delia dropped her voice as the maid continued upstairs, 'is how familiar *were* you with the maid?'

Richard grinned nostalgically at the memory. 'Rachel was 35. She taught me everything a Governess couldn't. I was 15 and wanted to marry her.'

'And you've never found anyone to compare to her? Is that why you're still single?' Delia was trying to understand Richard a little.

'Who knows? I've never been one for deep analysis. Let me show you the library.' Richard abruptly brought that area of conversation to a close. Delia sensed another barrier had gone up, but she was nonetheless pleased that he had confided in her about the painting.

The library was a wall-to-wall-to-ceiling collection of antiquarian rarities. In the centre, two young men, acting like schoolboys, were excitedly playing at a card table. They didn't hear or notice Richard and Delia enter.

'Bust! You owe me five pounds.' William was triumphant.

'No, it isn't! That comes to 20!' Tom pointed to his cards.

'That comes to 23, dear brother. Forgotten how to add up? Most cheats don't know how to.'

'I'm not cheating, you tosser!' Tom was really angry.

'Don't you call me a tosser, you stupid wanker. Seven and four and three and nine make 23!' William prodded his finger on each of Tom's cards.

'That's a six, not a nine, you horse's arse!'

'When it's upside down, shit brain. Look!' William took the card and shoved it between Tom's eyes.

'Oh, bollocks, I'm not playing anymore ...' Tom sulked because William had proved him wrong.

'And these are my two brothers, William and Tom.' Richard loudly announced. 'As you can see, they are not only playing friendly pontoon but also practising that ancient and rare art of verbal abuse.'

'Pleased to meet you both.' Delia smiled and melted Tom's simple heart. William just nodded, regarding Delia as another of Richard's many girlfriends.

'This is Eve. She'll be staying with us this evening.' Richard went over to William and extracted a couple of aces from one of his pockets. 'Cheating is only an art if you're never caught. Isn't that right, William?'

'Can't imagine how they got there,' William said in all innocence.

'Because you bloody well put them there, that's how!' shouted Tom. 'You can't bear the thought of me winning sometimes, can you? You ... you ... fu—' He remembered Delia and managed to stop himself from swearing.

'All right, that's enough, both of you.' Richard was bored with always having to come between his brothers. The less he had to be in their company, the happier he was. Now that their father had gone, he dreaded the thought of having to watch over them.

While Delia was browsing along some book spines, William took Richard aside. 'Richard, we need to talk – about the funeral and things.'

'Can't you see I've got a guest?'

'It's about father's will.' William sounded genuinely serious for once.

'What about it? I thought the solicitor wasn't coming until tomorrow.'

'Lawson wants to talk to us all this evening.'

'Can't it wait?' Richard replied irritably. He wanted to spend as much time as possible with Delia. After the next day he might never see her again. He looked at her perfect posture as she leant on tiptoe to look at a book that was on a higher shelf. He also noticed Tom watching her like an admiring fan.

'I received a message for you to ring him as soon as you arrived. I'm just passing on that message.'

'Does Mother know?' Richard could see the rest of the day being ruined.

'No.' William glanced at his watch. 'Well, I'm off for a ride. See you later.' And he disappeared before Richard could say anything.

Richard might not have thought much of his father, but he thought less of his brothers. William was too lazy to lift a finger to do anything and preferred to spend time with the horses, while Tom was just too stupid. Everything had always been left to him to sort out.

'Eve ... I'm sorry, I've got to make a phone call. Will you be all right?'

'I can look after her.' Tom volunteered.

'Haven't you got something else to do?' Richard didn't like the thought of leaving Delia with Tom.

'No.' Tom smiled at Delia.

'Do what you have to do, Richard. I'm quite happy. Tom will keep me company.' She found Tom quite endearing in an amusing sort of way.

'I'll be as quick as possible. Don't do anything silly, Tom.' Richard gave him one of his big brother looks to warn him not to misbehave, before leaving the room.

'Have you read many of these?' Delia asked him.

'I only like Westerns and crime thrillers. Most of those are so boring. I expect you've read a lot of them?'

'I don't know, I might have done.' Delia was browsing through a first edition of Dickens' *Oliver Twist*.

'What do you mean, you don't know? Either you have or you haven't.' Tom was confused.

'My memory is not as good as it used to be,' she quickly added to keep him quiet.

'We're two of a kind,' he said proudly. 'I forget things. People think I'm stupid. But I just forget … Do you like funfairs?' he added as an afterthought.

'Who doesn't?' she answered enigmatically.

'Want to go on one – now?' he said rather excitedly.

'The one on the estate? Is it open?'

'No, we're closed this afternoon because father died. Sort of a mark of respect. But I'll open it for you, if you like. Get a couple of rides going?'

'Just to ourselves?' This odd idea appealed to her. 'Won't Richard mind?'

'I know he won't.' Tom lied.

'Why not then.'

'Come on, I'll get the keys!' Tom gently took her by the arm and led her out of the library.

It wasn't a large funfair by normal standards, but adequate enough for the day trippers who came to visit the estate. There was something for everyone. Guided tours around parts of the house and gardens for the culturally discerning; a domestic animal farm for the toddlers; helicopter rides for the more adventurous; and a chairlift ride around the grounds for those less enterprising. And, for those who got hungry, a small fast-food restaurant overlooking a boating lake. It wasn't Disneyworld by any stretch of the imagination, but it attracted enough customers to help pay for the upkeep and maintenance of the house, as well as provide a little profit for the Montcasse coffers.

'Ghost train or dodgems?' Tom was like a little boy at a birthday treat.

'Ghost train … but it's not too scary, I hope?' Delia played along.

'It is a bit – but I'll protect you,' he said chivalrously. While Delia got into one of the carriages, Tom pressed a few buttons in the control box. He then jumped in with Delia once the carriage started moving into the main area.

There were the usual luminous drawings of various ghouls, models of headless corpses, eerie screams and spooky sounds as the carriage travelled through the dark maze of second-rate illusions. Tom made silly noises throughout, grabbing hold of Delia's arm in mock fright. It wasn't until something brushed across her head that she screeched and seized Tom by his arm. Tom put his arms round her and used this as an excuse to deliberately squeeze her breasts. Delia shrugged herself away. 'What *do* you think you are doing, young man?' she said more in surprise than anger as the carriage came to a stop outside.

'You didn't mind, did you?' Tom said, as if somehow it was his right.

'Do you make a habit of groping and fondling women's breasts?' Delia watched his naïve expression.

'Only those I'm in love with,' he said in all sincerity.

'And you're in love with me, is that it?' Delia wasn't sure how far she could humour him.

'I wouldn't have done it otherwise!' he protested. 'You can feel my balls if you like.'

'Er, not at the moment, thank you.' Delia sighed.

Tom climbed out of the carriage and got down on one knee. 'I want you to marry me.'

'But I'm already married.' Delia showed him the ring, which threw him.

'Get a divorce. No-one will ever love you as much as I do.' Tom was now down on both knees.

'I think I'd rather have a go on the dodgems, if you don't mind.' She got out of the carriage and began to walk away.

Tom got off his knees and ran up to her. He put his hand round her waist. 'Will you think about it, Eve? About marrying me? I mean it.'

'Tom, I don't deserve you. You will make someone very happy one day … but until then, if you lay one more finger on me I shall castrate you – with the sharpest razor blade I can get my hands on. Understand?'

'You … you won't tell Richard?' Tom looked doe-eyed.

'No. But from now on, behave yourself!'

'Can we still go on the dodgems?' Tom asked, as if nothing had happened.

'Only in separate cars.'

'Great – we can bump each other!' And he ran like a school kid to the dodgems to get them going. Delia walked slowly, wondering if there was a strain of insanity in the Montcasse family.

The following 20 minutes were enjoyably spent racing round the dodgem track. Delia put all her energies into bumping Tom's car as many times as possible, which resulted in him ending up feeling quite sick. Delia felt they were even then.

Back at the house, Richard wasn't at all happy. He had called the family solicitors and tried to put Andrew Lawson – the senior partner – off from visiting that evening. But Lawson had been forcefully insistent. Apparently the particulars, clauses and conditions in Randolph Montcasse's will – which had been revised only a month previously – held several surprises. It was imperative that the whole family be present for the reading. Try as he might, Richard had been unable to glean any indication as to the will's contents, except that it might not be quite what any of them expected.

31

Henry sat on the toilet seat feeling very sorry for himself. His master plan had failed miserably. If only he'd jumped out of the window the moment he'd locked himself in, he would have been miles away by now. Serena had been far too clever, and had beaten him to it. He couldn't help but admire her foresight. There was more to Serena than met the eye. Beautiful, intelligent, shrewd. All the qualities Henry appreciated in a woman. He realised he'd behaved boorishly in her presence and undoubtedly come across as rather a weak, bad tempered inconvenience. He'd never be able to win her now.

'Henry, are you ready to come out now? You've been in there ages. A whole army would have had time to crap by now.' Melissa's booming voice came from behind the door.

'I'm just washing my hands ...' Henry had had enough, and his backside felt numb from having sat there for so long. He went over to the sink and turned the tap on – and then had another brilliant idea. He tiptoed across to the window and tried to see through the thick, mottled glass. Serena's shadow was no longer there. She was obviously now in the house with Melissa. It seemed the ideal opportunity to jump out of the window. 'Won't be a second ...' Henry added as he climbed up onto the sill. Gently he opened the window.

As he stuck his head out, a gun was pressed to his temple. 'Oh, Henry. You won't give up, will you?' Serena moved into view and looked at him with a sense of compassion.

'It is a prisoner's duty to escape. Especially as the prisoner is innocent.' Henry was crestfallen at having failed yet again.

'Marks for trying, anyway.' Serena secretly admired Henry's perseverance. It was a quality that Matthew didn't possess. Matthew always gave up if something didn't work first time. Perhaps if she had said no the first time he had proposed, he might never have asked her again – and her life would have been very different ... 'Now we're going to unlock the door. You must be hungry. We've got some food.'

Henry gazed sorrowfully into her eyes for a brief moment before nodding and jumping back into the bathroom. He did feel a bit empty, and food at least would be a welcome diversion. As soon as the door opened, he saw Melissa standing there pointing a gun. Everywhere he went, someone was pointing a gun at him. Automatically he raised his arms in a gesture of surrender. 'I won't try anything ...' he said rather feebly.

'Damn right you won't. Not a second time, anyway. What do you take us for?' Melissa let him lead the way upstairs, back to his room.

'Delia not back?' he asked out of interest after he noticed Serena join Melissa on the stairs.

'She's on her way. Won't be long,' Melissa lied. She didn't want to give him the impression anything was amiss. They reached his room. 'Lie on the bed please.'

'What are you going to do now?' Henry didn't like Melissa's tone.

'Just a little precaution in case you have any other bright ideas.' Melissa produced from her skirt pocket some strong cord that she had bought at the shop. She handed Serena her gun. 'On the bed. Hands behind you.'

'Please don't tie me up again. I promise I won't try to escape.' He directed this at Serena, hoping that she might dissuade Melissa. Serena turned away, not being able to look him in the eye.

'Sorry, Henry, you've rather abused our trust. Put your hands behind you please. I don't want to say it again.' Melissa stood there like an executioner, holding the cord between both hands.

'Not behind my back, please. It's agony. If you have to tie them, do it at the front. That's not much to ask, is it?' Henry pleaded.

Melissa thought for a second and turned to Serena, who nodded approval. 'All right. You can't say we're not being reasonable. Serena.' Serena moved closer and directed both guns at Henry while Melissa did her expert knotting. As well as tying both his hands together at the front as if he were handcuffed, she also extended the cord so that she was able to bind his feet at the same time, making it impossible for him to move too freely. It wasn't easy for Henry, but at least he was trussed up in a more comfortable position than before. 'There! Would sir now care for something to eat?'

'Is that supposed to be joke. How do you imagine I'm going to eat?' Henry thought they were starting to play games with him.

'I will feed you, of course. That is, if you want anything. It makes no difference to me whether you do or not.' Melissa wasn't in the mood to be nice anymore.

'I would like something ...' Henry looked at Serena and did his best to smile.

'Right, I shall go and rustle something up. Come on Serena.'

They both left the room and locked it.

Is this never going to end?, Henry thought to himself. He lay there letting the whole experience flash back in scenic images. That job with the Civil Service was well and truly lost. Even if the women released him now, he'd never be able to regain his position. They wouldn't give him another interview, that was for sure. And whose fault was all this? That bloody woman in the lift, the one he'd fancied his chances with, the one who'd so shamelessly farted and as a consequence ruined his life. Where was that woman now? Probably riding up and down in lifts, farting and ruining other innocent lives. What was he going to do with his life now? If he did manage to come out of this alive. He could sell his story to the tabloids for a large amount of money – '*Hostage Kept as Sex Slave to Three Women ... He was stripped and bound, then unashamedly seduced by each in turn. They covered him in ice cream and raspberry jam and proceeded to lick him clean, before having their wicked way again ...*' It was a possibility. He might have to spice it up a bit to get a good deal.

The door was unlocked and Serena entered carrying a plate of food and a glass of Coke. 'I hope you don't mind me helping you with this?'

'You mean feeding me? I thought Melissa was going to do the honours.' Henry was pleased to see her.

'If you'd prefer Melissa to do it, I'm happy to go and ask her ...' Serena had persuaded Melissa to let her feed Henry, and now felt that she was being rejected.

'No … no … please don't misunderstand me. I'm pleased it's you. I really am.' Henry smiled and opened his mouth like a baby bird. It made Serena smile. 'What are you going to treat me with?'

Serena reeled off the list rather apologetically. 'Not very ambitious I'm afraid. A bit of ham, cheese, tomato and a soft roll. Oh, and a chocolate bar if you've got a sweet tooth.'

'Sounds all right to me. Ready when you are …' Henry shuffled himself into a more accessible position while Serena brought a chair to the bedside.

'Would you like me to … to feed you in any particular order? I mean, what would you like first?' Serena found herself getting a bit tongue-tied and nervous. Not because she was in any way scared of him, but she somehow felt a touch shy and embarrassed. There was something about Henry that put her off balance.

'Let's start with the ham and work our way clockwise round the plate. How about that?'

'Okay …' With the knife and fork, which she extracted from her breast pocket, she started by cutting the ham into bite-sized pieces. She placed the first piece lightly into his mouth.

'Umm, nice ham.' He chewed and then swallowed. 'Serena …'

'If you intend to ask me any questions,' she interrupted, 'please don't. I can't tell you anything. What we've done, why we're here, when you'll be allowed to go. If you do, I shall just get up and leave you. Do you understand?'

'Perfectly … Are you going to kill me?' Henry took a chance. He wanted to see her reaction.

'Kill you …?' The thought horrified her. She put down the fork for a moment. 'Is that what you think?'

'I don't know what to think. I'm sorry – I won't ask you anything else. Don't go.' His tactic had worked. Her response had at least alleviated one major fear.

'It's a complicated and involved situation. It was unfortunate that you happened to be around at the time … I'm sorry, that's all I'm prepared to say.' Regaining her composure, she stuck the fork in another piece of ham and fed it to him.

'Well, whatever … You make a lovely captor. You can whisk me away anytime.' Henry meant it and she knew it, but she said nothing.

The next ten minutes were spent in silence while Serena fed and Henry ate, each immersed in their own separate thoughts. 'Thank you …' Henry swallowed the last chunk of chocolate bar and drained the Coke. He felt better, despite being tied up.

'And thank you for trying to understand – even if you don't. I could never kill you …' She was quickly out of the room before he could say anything. The door was duly locked and he heard her walk slowly down the stairs. Henry felt tired and closed his eyes. Within five minutes he was asleep.

'Did he give you any trouble?' Melissa was in the front room, having demolished a large plate of food.

'No, poor man. What *are* we going to do with him?' Serena picked up an apple and started to eat.

'Poor man! It was Delia's idea in the first place to lumber us with him. I'm really worried – she could be dead for all we know, or being subjected to some nasty practices.' Melissa unzipped a banana and ate half of it in one bite.

'Practices …?' Serena could be very naïve at times.

'Sexually abused … raped … murdered … Something awful has happened to her, and we're stranded here not knowing what to do.'

'She might have had her handbag stolen with the phone. It could be something as simple as that.' Serena tried to be logical.

'Then why has she not contacted us on our phones?'

'Perhaps she forgot our new numbers. I can't remember mobile numbers offhand if I haven't written them down elsewhere.'

'Perhaps we're overreacting. She could still turn up at any moment. Nevertheless, we shouldn't have let her take total charge in the first place.' Melissa stuffed the rest of the banana in her mouth.

'But we did agree to let her take over the whole thing. We left all the arrangements to her. She had it all worked out, but unfortunately decided not to inform us. We've only ourselves to blame.'

'Yes, we're in the khazie without any toilet paper.' Melissa couldn't think of a more appropriate description. 'And talking about paper – and I don't want any arguments from you, Serena – I think we should now have a good look at these documents that we've put ourselves on the line for.'

'I'm not going to argue.' Serena opened a drawer and put the files on the coffee table before them. 'Let's see if it was really worth it.'

32

Thomas Lane looked at himself in the mirror as he adjusted his black bow tie. The one thing he hated about being Prime Minister was the never ending breakfast meetings, lunches, dinners and suppers he had to attend, where he often had to be nice to nasty people and nasty to nice ones. It was a rare occasion when he had the opportunity of dining alone with his wife, Pamela. But that was the price he had to pay. He had always wanted to be famous, to be able to make people laugh, to be able to change their lives. That ambition had been fulfilled to a certain extent. The problem now was to maintain it.

'Thomas, there's a mark on the bottom of your trousers,' Pamela noticed as she was putting on her shoes.

'What kind of mark?' Thomas moved away from the mirror and buffed his shoes on his black trousers.

Pamela came across and turned him around. 'Could be anything.' With her hand she started to rub it briskly. 'It seems to be coming off …' While she rubbed hard with one hand, the other hand gently slid its way to the front of his trousers and rubbed gently. 'This is the real seat of power, the head of the nation …'

Thomas looked down and smiled. 'Perhaps we should let John Thomas rule the country. People wouldn't be able to tell one dickhead from another.'

'Don't do yourself down. You're doing a wonderful job and everybody knows it.' Pamela was disappointed, because his member remained limp and unexcited despite her experienced touch.

'And that might not be for long …' Thomas sensitively removed her hand.

'There's something up, isn't there?' Pamela stood up and put her arms round his waist.

'I'm afraid there is.' He wrapped his arms around her shoulders.

'Does someone know?'

'It's possible that quite a few do.' Thomas looked her in the eye.

'Oh dear …' Pamela held him tight. She had never loved anyone as much as him.

'It is a bit of a problem.' He kissed her affectionately on the cheek. Pamela was a wonderful woman, who had stood beside him and guided him throughout. If it hadn't been for her he would never have become Prime Minister. So much had happened during the last year. He still found it hard to believe how he had managed to get away with it for so long. It had been a miraculous kind of journey …

Thomas Lane became Prime Minister purely by chance. Six months before a General Election, the Government tragically lost their leader as a result of a heart attack. There was panic within the party, and Thomas, who was Chancellor at the time, was quickly and unanimously promoted to Party Leader to help fight the coming Election.

He was a brilliant money man and had managed to solve many difficult economic problems. There was no-one else in the Cabinet, with his brain and strategic way of thinking, who could lead them to victory and give them another term in office. However, within a month of him becoming Prime Minister, his Cabinet realised that they had made a fatal mistake in electing him as their figurehead.

Thomas was exceptional with numbers but not with people. Many remarked that his personality had been given a charisma bypass. He was so dull and awkward that he started to become quite an embarrassment. Even the most ingeniously written speech was killed by his monotonous delivery. His voice and deadpan manner turned people off in droves. The media and general public began to treat him as a joke. The Opposition were having a field day, and as a result, building up a stronger support. It was a very worrying situation for the Cabinet.

If this carried on, they would surely lose the forthcoming election. It was too late and inappropriate to replace him with someone else. So, amongst themselves, the Cabinet agreed that Thomas had to be taken in hand and groomed in the months that were left. Rather than trust it to a PR firm, the new Chancellor, Charles Carter, and the Home Secretary, Alex Brook, decided to deal with it themselves.

The grooming and makeover of Thomas Lane was done in secret. Only Alex, Charles and two others were in on it. Every spare moment was utilised to make him the man he eventually became.

During this preparation period, Thomas suffered a fall that bruised his face rather badly. He carried on with his duties despite his head being completely bandaged. He jokingly became the 'invisible' Prime Minister when he appeared in public, his head looking like that of an Egyptian mummy. Yet he took all this in his stride and gradually managed to win over the media and public by a newfound wit and determination. People started to claim that he had become a better, more open PM since his fall! The behind-the-scenes grooming was obviously beginning to work.

Between them Alex and Charles had certainly performed a miracle, because Thomas emerged a completely enlightened person: witty, amenable and someone with whom the man in the street could identify. As a result his party went on to win the Election, actually increasing their majority.

Thomas Lane had become eloquent, magnetic and whimsical. It was the strength of his new personality, not policies, that had won the nation over. It was obvious that Thomas owed a debt of gratitude to Alex and Charles. He demonstrated this by actually letting them run the Government for him, while he took a back seat and was more than happy simply to serve as a figurehead. They were the ones who had the real power. He wouldn't do anything without their say so – and they wouldn't let him take any decisions without him consulting them first. There were a few disgruntled voices in the Cabinet at first – but a reshuffle soon got rid of them. Since neither Alex nor Charles wanted to be Prime Minister, the whole arrangement worked perfectly. They were both happy to be able to control and manipulate the country like supreme puppet masters.

But what was their secret? How had they turned a buffoon into such a strong, magnetic personality? They would have liked to have taken all the credit – but the original inspiration had come from Thomas himself.

After only a month in office, before the transformation, Thomas took Alex and Charles aside one evening and told them that he couldn't carry on as he was. He had to admit that his public appearances and comments were so painfully embarrassing that it was beginning to effect the whole party image. More of this and they would surely lose the Election. Thomas was a true politician who believed in his party and felt they deserved the best. He was only making things worse; turning it from a respected party into one of ridicule. He felt he had no alternative but to resign. They would have to find another leader. Alex, however, realised it was too late. There was no-one in the wings to take his place. Thomas's resignation would have a damaging effect on the party. Perhaps if they got in some better speechwriters and employed the best PR guru – who would be able to train his voice and mannerisms and upgrade his whole image – they could save the day. It had worked with other leaders, so it could surely work for him.

Thomas would have none of it. He knew his strengths and weaknesses. He had no doubt that his financial genius could get the country back on its feet; but he also knew that this was not enough, in this day and age, to win an Election. A leader's personality often counted for more than his actual abilities. He was under no illusions: his personality was his Achilles heel. Whatever they did to him – change his hairstyle, his suits, give him a permanent smile – he would still make gaffes in public and provide the media with enough nails to crucify him ten times over. And as he was a loyal and dedicated politician, he didn't want to see his party suffer because of his own shortcomings.

The suggestion that he came up with surprised even Alex and Charles.

Even though he was regarded as one of the country's foremost brains, with an IQ envied by many, Thomas Lane found high-brow literature tedious. To relax at the end of a hard, stressful day he preferred reading science fiction stories and surfing the internet. He enjoyed being an anonymous figure, using several different online aliases. Always fascinated by role-reversal and switched-identity scenarios, he had inevitably fantasised about being two different people at the same time.

This is what gave him the idea of having someone actually take his place.

At first Alex and Charles thought this a preposterous notion. Alex pointed out that there was one major obstacle to the whole scam, even if it could be pulled off. What was going to happen to Pamela Lane, his wife? Surely she would object? Thomas didn't feel that was such a problem. Pamela really couldn't stand him at the best of times. Their marriage was a disastrous convenience, and because of the job, they were publicly locked into it. Pamela enjoyed being the first lady and would put up with anything to remain in that position. Thomas felt positive that he could persuade her to agree to be a part of the whole masquerade.

Alex and Charles were both sure that it could never work. Thomas convinced them otherwise.

An old school friend of his, Sir Freddy Knatchbull, was a prominent plastic surgeon, and had often boasted to Thomas, during their frequent private lunches, that he could transform one person to look like another – as long as the facial bone structure had basic similarities. Thomas suggested that if they could find someone who was willing to undergo plastic surgery to look like him, their problem might be solved. Alex realised that the obstacle wasn't so much substituting a lookalike as finding someone who possessed all those inherent qualities that Thomas lacked. Who could fit such a bill?

Pete Darney, 51, earned an uncomfortable living as a television extra, warm-up man and pub comedian. Despite being very funny, he had never really made it, and was resigned to the fact that he never would.

Pete was hardly ever out of work, since people enjoyed his charm and amusing performances. He had a natural talent, with a positive quality. Yet somehow fate had decreed that his career would never amount to much, despite his minor popularity. When he had reached 50, Pete had finally accepted this and succeeded in putting aside the frustration and bitterness that had plagued him for years. He had reached a stage in his life where he was content simply to carry on in the same vein until he was forced to retire. He had been married and divorced twice but was not blessed with any children. He vowed he would never marry again, content to sow his oats as long as he was capable. All in all, Pete didn't really have any complaints about the quality of his life. He was making the best of what he had. It was a fair living.

Alex was the one who first spotted Pete, among several others, when he saw his picture in a casting directory of film and TV extras. One by one, a prospective shortlist of possibilities was cut down, and they finally ended with Pete. Alex and Charles both watched him perform at a Camden pub and were impressed with the way he commanded the attention of a very rough crowd. Hecklers never stood a chance faced with Pete's off-the-cuff retorts. The two politicians decided that he was the man for them.

Pete wasn't quite prepared for the offer that came his way. However, he accepted it, much to their surprise, without too much deliberation. He thought it was the funniest thing he'd ever heard. Since he had no real family or relatives, he was more than happy to lose his own identity and assume that of the most powerful man in the country. Pete's only proviso was that a substantial sum of money be deposited for him in a Swiss bank account, as payment and insurance should the whole escapade backfire. He was assured that he would be well taken care of. Pete wasn't so stupid as to take their word on it. He didn't trust politicians, and insisted on making sure their assurances were met to the letter before he fully committed himself. They agreed without argument.

With that, Pete Darney was on his way to becoming Thomas Lane, Prime Minister of Great Britain.

Thomas meanwhile insisted that something similar should happen to him in reverse. He honestly felt that to have both him and Pete at large at the same time would be asking for trouble. Thus he would also undergo minor plastic surgery to alter the shape of his nose and chin. Once he had also grown a beard, he would be unrecognisable. He would move to the country and become totally anonymous, with only the computer as a means of contact and communication, to be used in the event of any problems or to provide financial and policy advice.

Thomas had thought it all out so carefully and fully that neither Alex nor Charles could find a reason why it couldn't work. Besides, there was no other plausible alternative. So the whole plan went into action.

Instrumental in achieving the transformation was Sir Freddy Knatchbull. Sir Freddy was the foremost plastic surgeon in the country. He was paid an extortionate amount of money – fiddled from the Treasury coffers – to remodel Pete Darney to look like Thomas Lane, and to reshape Thomas's own features. He was being well paid for his silence, and he certainly had no thoughts of betraying this, the greatest of all confidences.

Part of Sir Freddy's personal procedure, during every job, was to make copious notes and take numerous photographs at each stage in the process. He had built up a comprehensive dossier that was solely for his own private use. He had no ulterior motive apart from having a personal record of all his subjects. This one was no exception. Since it was one of the most challenging jobs he had ever had to undertake, he made the usual detailed notes and took stage-by-stage photographs.

The operation to transform Pete went without the slightest hitch. Sir Freddy had to work swiftly so that the PM wasn't out of the public eye for too long. Before the operation, a press release informed everyone that Thomas had tripped down the stairs at Chequers and had sustained several bruises and facial injuries. All official duties were cancelled for several days while he recovered. Pete's introduction into public life as the Prime Minister came while he was still bandaged up and waiting for the scars to heal. It was the perfect opportunity for him to practice his new role. He jumped in at the deep end, and not only came up swimming but made everyone laugh in the process.

He used the accident and his bandaged face to send himself up. The press couldn't get a joke in edgeways – Pete was always first to make fun of his position, and was able to turn everything around to his advantage. If someone asked him a question about policy, he could come up with a sensible answer and end it with some wicked quip or other. The public loved it. Although Alex and Charles had briefed him well on policy and other related matters, it was Pete's talented spontaneity that saved the day and warmed everyone to him. If someone did throw a tricky question, that either he wasn't prepared for or simply didn't know the answer to, he would use something within the question as the basis for a joke. It was his own quick-witted political way of not answering. Pete was in his element. This was the role he had be born to play.

When the bandages eventually came off, they all agreed that Sir Freddy had done his best work. Alex and Charles couldn't believe how like Thomas Pete looked. Even Pamela, who was happily going along with the whole subterfuge, couldn't tell the difference.

The real Thomas Lane, after he had had his appearance altered, disappeared to the country, leaving only an e-mail address where he could be contacted. The deceit was complete.

Alex was proud that they had managed to pull it off, but something bothered him. What if Pete – he had to remember to refer to him as Thomas now – what if he got too big for his boots? What if he became such a success that he began to feel he didn't need Alex or Charles to guide him? What if Thomas actually decided to get rid of them both by throwing them out of office? Where would they stand then? Who would believe them if, in attempting to fight back, they tried to make known the truth about Thomas being an impostor? It was a scenario that he didn't want to contemplate – but also one he couldn't ignore. They had to have some form of insurance that would protect them in the event of such an occurrence.

That was where Sir Freddy's notes and photographs came in.

Alex found out about the records that Sir Freddy had and where he kept them. Through some underworld contacts, he found someone who subsequently broke into Sir Freddy's office and made on-the-spot copies of all the relevant documents and photographs. The copies were then delivered secretly to Alex, who paid the criminal off. Of course the criminal was now also privy to this explosive knowledge. But not for long, as he met with an unfortunate accident on his way back from seeing Alex, when a hit-and-run driver killed him.

Later it was Charles who personally deposited the incriminating folder – under a false name and cover – in that special 'stationery' room within the depths of Whitehall. The rest, as they say, is history.

Pamela watched Thomas put on his dinner jacket. He looked like her husband, he talked like her husband, but he made love to her like no man she had known before. From the first day he had assumed her husband's identity, her whole world had turned upside down. She had never imagined the extent to which her feelings would be challenged and pulled apart. She had agreed to go along with the whole deception because she was bored and wanted a bit of excitement in her life. What she had got was more – much more.

Her marriage to the real Thomas had become unbearable. They just didn't have anything remotely in common anymore. He spent all of his free time playing about with his bloody computer, and much preferred touching up his keyboard or stroking his mouse than her. She had been about to leave him when he had been asked to take over as Prime Minister. She had then decided to stay, hoping that it would open up a new kind of life for her. It had, but not in the way she had expected. Thomas had proved to be more of a buffoon in public life than he was in private. As he had become a laughing stock, her credibility and standing had soon gone downhill. To have left him then wouldn't have helped the situation. She had decided it was better to remain where she was and cope with the pressure, rather than exile herself to the cold of nowhere. It was at that point that Thomas had revealed his plan.

On the surface Pamela had thought it was a jolly old jape. If it worked her position would be elevated; if it didn't she'd be no worse off. She felt she had nothing to lose – apart from a husband who was going to hide himself away in the country. There was no love lost between them, so it became a mutually agreeable settlement. The only question that did concern her was, would she take to the new Thomas Lane? What would he be like? There was every possibility that he could turn out to be worse than her husband – and where would she be then? She decided it was a gamble worth taking, since she had no more to lose than she already had. She'd always been a survivor.

She was in fits of laughter when she first met Pete, and was still laughing several days later after he had brazenly seduced her. She never left his bed after that, and they became man and wife in a way that she hadn't experienced with her husband. It started off as a very active sexual relationship and then, like a cliché, turned to love. A love that she hadn't experienced before.

But did he really love her as he said he did? Now that there was a possibility of the whole thing being exposed and turning to dust, she wondered if she would lose him.

'If everything does come out into the open … will you leave me?' It was a question she had dreaded asking, but for her own peace of mind she had to know.

'What do you want me to leave?' he replied. 'There's my butterfly collection, only they've all flown away; a set of library books that are way overdue; or you could have the fluff from my bellybutton – it's my navel reserve …'

'Why do you always have to make a joke of everything?'

'Because everything *is* a joke. *N'est pas*?' Thomas took her in his arms and kissed her. 'That answer your question?'

'Not really. It's a serious question that warrants a serious answer.'

'What answer do you want? I've got a million!' He smiled.

'For god's sake, Thomas, stop it!' Pamela was becoming very agitated, because she believed he was ducking the real issue. 'I know that we're not married and that I have no legal hold over you. I love you and I have a right to know … I simply want to know where I stand …' Tears cascaded down her cheek.

'You stand wherever I stand. Our footsteps will merge as one …'

'And what's that supposed to mean?'

'Where's the poetry in your heart, you silly cow? I'm trying to tell you that I love you too and that we shall be together – whatever happens. All right?'

'Do you mean that?' Pamela needed reassurance.

'Of course I mean it! That why I said it. I realise I might talk a lot of crap out there. That's my job. People expect it of the Prime Minister. But what do I have to say to make *you* believe me, eh?'

'You've said it … Thank you …' Pamela felt ready to face the future.

'Are you sure you wouldn't like me to draw up a Bill and get it through the Commons?'

'That won't be necessary. A big cuddle will suffice … later.'

'I'd better make sure that I don't eat or drink too much this evening then. Who are we entertaining?' Thomas could never keep up with all the engagements.

'We're being entertained. The American Ambassador and his wife with a couple of dozen hangers-on, I suppose. So please, no jokes about Iraq, bowel movement or the Kennedy conspiracy.'

'It'll have to be my tricky-dicky Nixon stories then.' Thomas gave one of his wicked smiles.

'Thomas … what *actually* is being done to try to get those papers back intact? Alex is doing something about it, isn't he?'

'A crack troop of experts are onto it this very moment. I'm assured that if they can't sort it out, no-one can …'

33

Kieran and Barry were sat in the back of the car singing bawdy rugby songs. Rory was at the wheel concentrating on the road in front of him, driving speedily toward the coast. There was no time to waste. Two priorities governed his thoughts. One – to get rid of his passengers as efficiently and as swiftly as possible. Two – to arrive in Perdsea before the others had time to deal with any situation that might present itself. He didn't want to miss out on any of the action. Rory knew he had at least four hours to conclude his business, as no-one would make a positive move until it was dark.

It hadn't been too difficult to persuade Kieran and Barry to go along with him. He had waited until Terry and the others had left the pub before outlining his plan. He had bought them a couple of pints, followed by some whisky chasers, and got them both in a more receptive mood. He had made up a convincing story about finding a piece of paper near the crashed car, giving details of a sailing from Harwich. The terrorists were obviously smuggling the hostages abroad somewhere. If they could get on that boat they'd be the nation's heroes. Neither Barry nor Kieran had asked too many questions, because they had been too busy getting pissed to bother about taking in any details. Before leaving the pub, Rory had purchased a bottle of whisky, which he had handed to them as they drove off.

'Rory, yer not such a bad fella …' Barry took a large swig from the bottle.

'Charmed, I'm sure.' Rory noticed a signpost. They were only a few miles from Harwich.

'For a fucking poof that is!' Kieran added, grabbing the bottle back from Barry.

'You boys should try to be a bit more broadminded. Just because we tend to stick our pricks in different places doesn't make us inferior, does it?'

'An 'ole's an 'ole after all!' Barry burped.

'I'm slightly more fussy than that, petal.' Rory couldn't wait to dispose of these peasants. They had no class at all.

'The way I feel now,' Kieran put his hand on his crotch. 'I could poke anything …'

'If that's an invitation, then I'm afraid I'll have to let you down. We've a little job to do first.' Rory was getting really bored with these two.

'Fuck the job! Let's get us some women! And we'll find you a sailor, if you like.' Kieran took another drink.

'I'll find my own sailors, thank you. Now listen, we'll be in Harwich in a couple of minutes. I'll sort out all the tickets and do the talking; you boys just keep as quiet as possible – we don't want to alert the terrorists, do we now?'

'Can we have a drink when we get on board?' Barry saw Kieran polishing off the bottle.

'As many drinks as you like. So remember, keep shtoom, boys.'

'We'll be as quiet as nuns …' Kieran put his finger to his lips.

'I wonder wot a nun's like to fuck?' Barry dropped the bottle on the floor.

Kieran suddenly grabbed Barry by the throat. 'You bastard, don't you dare say that about our holy sisters! They are wonderful people. One more sacrilegious word and I'll kill you.'

'All right, all right … It was only a joke …' Barry realised that Kieran wasn't joking. 'I didn't know you were religious, like.'

'I'm not. But my aunty was a Catholic nun, and she was the sweetest person in the whole world. I won't have a filthy word said against them, understand?' Kieran released his grip.

'How was I to know …?' Barry relaxed back into the seat. For the next five minutes nobody said a word.

'Right, we're here,' Rory declared, pulling into a car park near the ferry. 'We're not taking the car on board, because we won't need it. Now you two just wait there while I get the authority for us to board as foot passengers.'

'Wot authority?' Barry started to question.

'Since we haven't got our passports, petal, we need to get official clearance to board – without creating a scene that might alert the terrorists. Understand?'

'Get the fuck on with it then!' Kieran mumbled impatiently.

Rory went to Passport Control and produced his certified ID, telling the authorities that he and his colleagues were on secret Government business and needed to board the ferry. He encountered no problems and was granted clearance.

Rory was grateful that Keiran and Barry weren't so drunk as to be unable to board the ferry without drawing attention to themselves. They could certainly take their drink – and the bar was the first place they headed for as soon as they hit the deck.

'What's it to be?' Kieran waved a £20 note in the air.

'This round's on me.' Rory put the note back into Kieran's pocket. 'You and Barry go and sit over there, and I'll bring them over. Whisky, was it?'

'Trebles!' Kieran bumped into a chair.

'Get some nuts and crisps too!' Barry plonked himself down in the corner.

Rory leant on the bar admiring the back view of the barman, who was sorting out some glasses. Rory gave a little gasp when the barman turned around. He was tall, dark and Spanish-looking, and by the knowing glint in his eyes was also gay. 'Yes, sir? What can I get you?' The barman smiled at Rory, whose heart missed a beat.

'Two treble whiskeys and a tonic water, please.' Rory couldn't take his eyes off the man.

'Any particular brand? Bell's, Teacher's, Walker – Johnny, that is?' He spoke slowly, with a slight accent.

'Ding dong Bell's will do, thanks. This boat is going all the way to Denmark, isn't it?'

'All the way. Esbjerg, yes. You haven't sailed with us before, have you sir?'

'It's my first time … Do you have any nuts?'

The barman gave him a very camp look. 'Salted penis all right?'

Rory wasn't quite sure if he'd heard correctly. 'Are they the big ones or the small ones?'

'Oh, we only have the big ones, sir.' The barman very subtly pouted his lip for a moment. He put a couple of packets of peanuts on the bar. 'Anything else I can get you …?' he said suggestively.

'Crisps …' Rory was really enjoying this conversation. They both understood each other perfectly. 'Give me what you've got …'

'That would take *all* night, sir … Cheese and onion, Worcester sauce or Brighton cheek …? Just my little joke, if you know what I mean.'

'A couple of cheese and onion will do, thanks.' Rory lightly touched the barman's hand as he handed over a note. 'Keep the change …'

'Thank you, sir. That's very generous. I wish they were all like you … Well, I finish at two. Might see you around?' He gazed into Rory's eyes.

'Who knows …?' Rory couldn't return the look as he took the tray of drinks and snacks. *Bugger, bugger, bugger – or not so much as a bugger,* he cursed. Just when he had met someone he fancied. The boat would have to sail in half an hour without him. Of all his bloody luck. Instead of being able to enjoy himself with that Adonis, he was lumbered with sorting out these drunken bastards. Sod's bloody law. Then he suddenly remembered – just in time.

Putting the tray down on a nearby table, Rory bent down in the pretence of tying up a shoelace. On rising he slyly put one hand into a top pocket and took out a couple of pills. He was about to drop them into the drinks when he realised that Kieran was watching him. Keeping the pills in the palm of his hand, he picked up the tray again and joined his colleagues.

'Found a boyfriend then?' Kieran had watched their body language at the bar. It hadn't been difficult to guess.

'Is that barman an 'omo?' Barry looked incredulously.

'You're all right for tonight then. Me and Barry just need to find a couple of willing young ladies.'

'You mustn't forget why we're here … Good god, look at the size of the tits on her!' Rory exclaimed.

Kieran and Barry quickly turned their heads, which gave Rory enough time to drop the pills into their drinks without them noticing. 'Where …?' Barry looked all around and could see only a couple of very elderly ladies shuffling along.

'You missed her. She went round the corner. Must have been a 52 double-D at least … She might come back … Anyway, before we settle down, boys, can I suggest we go down into the hold and check out the vehicles. It's got to be a van or a lorry that's transporting the hostages.'

'Can't we do that after we set sail?' Barry was getting comfortable.

'Come on, it won't take long. The bar's open all night … We mustn't forget what our objective is, after all. Think of the kudos when we turn them in.'

Kieran, who wasn't in the mood to argue and wanted to get it over with, downed his drink in one. Barry followed suit, putting the packets of nuts and crisps into his pocket. Rory finished off his tonic water and, after a sad glance at the barman, who was now flirting with someone else, led the way out of the bar.

By the time they had gone down a couple of flights of stairs, both Barry and Kieran were finding it difficult to keep awake. They stumbled along a narrow corridor, too dazed to know where they were going. Thankfully there was no-one about to see them. Rory then opened the door to a gents' toilet and forcibly ushered them in. By now they were really in a bad way and couldn't keep on their feet. They simply slumped to the floor in a dead sleep. Rory put a wedge against the door and quickly proceeded to undress them until they were both completely naked. He then sat them on the two toilet seats, tied their hands and feet with torn strips from their own shirts and gagged their mouths with handkerchiefs. He locked both cubicles from the inside, climbing over the top of the door to get out. Taking the rest of their belongings, he left the toilet. Then, as a final touch, he transferred an 'Out of Order' sticker from another door to that of the gents' toilet. All this was accomplished within the space of ten minutes.

Dumping the rest of their clothes out of a porthole, Rory left the boat just before the gang plank was withdrawn. 'Goodbye boys … Give my love to the Swedes!' The sleeping pills, which he always carried with him, would give them a good eight hours at least. It could be more, with all the drink they had put away. Rory felt quite proud of himself. The only downside was missing out on the possibility of an exciting liaison with that barman. Ah well, he couldn't win them all. But he was consoled by the thought that in Perdsea an ex flame awaited him …

34

Archie stared at the road ahead without seeing anything. His mind was elsewhere, back at The Dog and Duck with Beryl. The very thought of the way she had kissed him, her legs tightly wrapped around his waist, aroused him once more. What a passionate woman she had turned out to be. Their brief, intense intercourse against cold blue tiles had created a lasting impression, least of all the indent on Archie's bottom from a protruding screw. He'd never had such lascivious sex before. He felt like a born again Don Juan.

'Wonderful old hostelry The Dog and Duck …' Archie turned to Jack, who was driving.

'You must be joking! I thought it was a right dump.'

'I must say, I felt it had an old fashioned charm all of its own.'

'Behind the times is more like it. Do I take the left or right fork? Why weren't we given cars with sat-navs!' Jack had stopped at a junction.

'Right.' Archie felt a sneeze coming on. He put his hand in his pocket and sneezed into what he thought was his handkerchief. But the soft feel and subtle smell of talc made him look closer. It was a pair of knickers. Beryl's knickers. He put them to his nose. The heady smell aroused him again.

'I think that barmaid took a bit of a shine to you.' Jack hadn't noticed the knickers.

'What makes you say that?' Archie quickly put them back in his pocket.

'The way she always addressed everything to you, rather than to the rest of us. Funny looker, but a nice body on her.'

'Yes …' Archie remembered the way she had groaned when he had bit her large, dark nipple.

'You think Rory will succeed in dumping the other two?'

'Sorry …?' Archie had been too immersed in Beryl's breasts to hear what Jack had said.

'D'you think we'll see Rory, Barry and Kieran again?'

'Rory?' The sudden thought thankfully deflated Archie's unwanted erection. 'I feel Rory knows what he's doing. He's very determined. Not a great deal passes his attention. Had a similar gay chap in my unit once. I have to admit he was the best of the bunch. Reliable, professional and efficient. I think he knows what he's doing.'

'You reckon he'll kill them …?' Jack wondered.

'I wouldn't put it past him at all. Unless they get to him first.'

'That's a point. I wouldn't trust those bastards an inch. Let's hope he's on top of it.'

'On top of it, yes …' Archie's mind diverted back to Beryl, seeing her sad face at the window when they had left.

Terry, who wasn't at all happy, followed behind Jack and Archie's car. He was also thinking about Rory and apprehensive at the possibility of him literally disposing of Barry and Kieran in some insidious way. They were his responsibility too, after all. He was now wishing that he hadn't turned a blind eye in the first place. But it was no use crying over spilt blood, if that was indeed the case. His father, who had been a bus conductor, had taught him a lot of wise aphorisms. One of these now came to mind: '*Don't worry if you leave a customer behind at a stop. There will always be another bus or two. The customer will always find a way. You must never go back, only forward. Make the best of your journey to come ...*' His father was always right, and the thought gave him some assurance. After all, he was being given no back-up or extra support by HQ. They had left it in his hands. It was up to him to deal with it. Perdsea might prove to be the end of their journey, or it could herald the beginning of a nightmare. A nightmare that could end a promising career. Another of his father's maxims comforted him: '*The bus terminal is not the end of the road. The bus might need servicing and repair, but that doesn't mean it is finished. There are always other routes to travel down ...*'

The two cars came to a halt in a car park in Perdsea.

Terry got out of his car and joined Jack and Archie in the back of theirs. 'It's going to be dark in a few hours. We need to find a base to hole up. What arrangement did you make with our friend Rory?'

'That we'd rendezvous at one of the pubs,' Jack replied.

'Which pub?'

'We didn't specify. He said he'd phone you on your mobile at about seven so that we' could let him know.'

'Let's hope he rings and doesn't decide to abandon the operation.' Terry had misgivings.

'He'll be here.' Archie had no doubts. 'Can I suggest that we find a pub that has rooms? One that we can book into. It might be a long wait.'

'Good idea. Should be somewhere suitable around here. When it's dark we'll have to conduct a recce and size up the situation. This place might look safe enough, but it doesn't make our terrorists any less dangerous.' Terry was starting to feel more hopeful.

It wasn't long before they arrived outside The Albatross. Terry decided to go in first, leaving Jack and Archie to wait in the car. In reception, which was empty, Terry accidentally bumped into Stella, who was taking some sandwiches up to her room. He was stood with his back to one of the doors when she walked through. 'I'm so sorry ...' He managed to steady her tray.

'That's okay, no damage done. Sandwiches all intact.' Stella smiled.

'You don't work here by any chance?' Terry asked.

Since she was feeling in such a good mood, Stella didn't take offence. 'I'm afraid not. The manager's in the bar, if that's who you want.'

'Thanks ...' Terry smiled and watched her go upstairs. Now there was a nice, attractive woman, he thought. Stella was also admiring Terry as she disappeared across the landing.

When he approached the bar, Terry was surprised to encounter a young black man serving drinks. 'Hiya, brother,' the man greeted him with a smile. 'Welcome to the Albatross, the resting place for your weary spirit and thirsty heart.'

Terry hated this 'brother' type of exchange that he frequently encountered. He was at least thankful that he wasn't expected to slap palms in friendly recognition of their black kinship. 'Would you know if there are any rooms available …?'

'You'd better converse with our white brother, here.' He pointed to the manager, who was talking to some locals in the corner. 'Hey, Albert, gentleman here looking for rooms.'

The manager got up and came across to him. 'Yes, sir, can I be of assistance? Albert Ross at your service.'

'The place was named after him!' the barman quipped, then went back to work after the manager gave him a disparaging look.

'Do you have a large room? There's myself and three others.'

'Certainly, sir. The family room should suffice. Would you come this way.' The manager led Terry back to reception to sort out the details.

Upstairs, Scott and Stella were tucking into the sandwiches. Stella had suggested a proper meal in the restaurant, but Scott had felt it better they remain in the room out of sight. Anyway, he needed to wait for instructions from his contact. Stella didn't mind that much as she bit into a delicious prawn and lettuce. She looked at Scott, who was still in bed, and wondered if he might be interested in some more of the kind of sex he preferred. Their last little session had unexpectedly turned her on and made her experience new feelings and sensations. It had been exciting because it was something Jack would never have contemplated. Jack only liked it if he was on top. She felt quite ready for another bout of carnal pleasure, but didn't want to come on too strong in the likelihood of putting him off completely. She'd try and be a bit more subtle this time.

'Stella, what are you doing …?' Scott looked up, after wiping a dribble of pink mayonnaise from his chin. Stella was slowly taking her clothes off to a strange silent dance.

'Watch – don't speak.' She continued imitating a mock dance of the seven veils, running round the room, contorting her body this way and that and trying to be as erotic as possible. Scott watched her and inwardly sighed. Hadn't he done more than his fair share of duty? Surely the bloody woman wasn't asking for it *again* …? What did she look like? 'Better than TV, don't you agree …?'

'Depends on the channel,' Scott murmured to himself. He'd much rather be watching the most banal soap than looking at her making a fool of herself.

She bent her back suggestively. 'Why don't you film me so that I can see it later …?'

'Are you serious?' He wondered what had got into her. Their last little session hadn't been as exciting as he had hoped, and he certainly wasn't in any mood for a repeat performance, even though she seemed to have really enjoyed it.

'Why not? Just for our viewing pleasure, of course …' She started to undo her blouse.

He reluctantly reached for the video camera and started recording. Anything but having to sit there and watch her trying to be sexy. 'It's looking good …' he lied. This would be something to show his friends at the Christmas party.

'Beam me up, Scotty …' she whispered as she ran toward the camera lens and then tiptoed back. By now she was completely naked. She watched for any signs of Scott getting aroused, but couldn't detect any. He just lay on the bed pointing the camera at her and chuckling to himself. She realised her seduction wasn't working.

How could she get out of this without making a total twat of herself? Maybe she could do the whole thing in reverse and put all her clothes back on?

Then she had a more amusing idea – she'd put his clothes on instead. That would be good for a laugh, since she'd given up all hope of arousing him again. First she gently slipped on his boxer shorts.

'What are you doing, Stella?' Scott took his eye away from the viewfinder. By now she had on his socks and shirt. 'Those are mine ...' She got into his jeans and started parading around the room like a tomboy. She scooped up her hair and put it under his leather baseball cap, which he always wore during shooting. 'Stella ...?' His voice had a nervous edge to it.

'Okay, boss, where d'you want the tracks laid? How many set-ups are we going for?' she said, deepening her voice like a man's and strutting around with her hands on her hips, looking as butch as possible.

Scott rose up from the bed. His penis was ahead of him, pointing in her direction. Stella couldn't work out what she had done, but something had obviously excited him. Perhaps her dance had had the desired effect after all. It had just taken a bit longer than she had expected. She started to take off his shirt.

'No, no, don't take it off – yet ...' Scott moved toward her. She swore his penis was bigger than before.

'He's *coming* to get you-oooo!' Scott chanted in a silly voice. His face had gone a deeper red and he was walking on his tiptoes and wiggling his hips. Stella thought it a little odd, but she didn't care. In the end it all came to the same result. She felt him strongly behind her. He was breathing quite heavily, his hands tight on her waist. He was starting to rub himself against her. Stella was about to turn around – when his phone went. 'Oh, shit!' he cursed.

He dropped his hands and crossed to where the phone was lying. 'Yes?' he answered rather irritably. 'Oh ... hello ... Sorry ...' Scott's tone changed again. He sounded softer, more conspiratorial. 'Yes, we're in Perdsea ... The Albatross ... It's near the beach ... What? ... Yes, I can meet you there ... In 20 minutes? ... No, that's no problem ... Look forward to seeing you there ... Byee ...' The irritation had been replaced by a more tender disposition. 'That was my contact. We're meeting in 20 minutes.'

'I'm looking forward to meeting him – or her?' Stella could see Scott's member had visibly shrunk. The moment had naturally been lost.

'It's best you don't come to the meeting, babe. Official secrets act and all that. My contact has to remain anonymous – you understand?'

'So what's this clandestine meeting about, then?'

'I'll hopefully get details about where these hostages are being kept. And anything else that's relevant.'

'In Perdsea?' She still couldn't believe it.

'The stillness can sometimes hide a volcano that is bursting to erupt,' he whispered rather dramatically.

'You mean like your willy about two minutes ago?' Stella said quite pointedly.

'I'm sorry about that. Perhaps later. Who knows?' he answered enigmatically. He had no intention of repeating the incident. It was just going to be work from now on. 'Anyway, I won't be too long,' he added, giving her a peck on the cheek.

'Is this mysterious contact a woman?'

'I really can't divulge, lover. Be patient and trust me.'

'If that's how it's to be,' Stella replied rather sulkily. Not only had she been deprived of sex, but she wasn't even going to be privy to meeting this mysterious contact. She really felt like an insignificant hired hand without any say in the matter. Perhaps she'd go down to the bar and pick up that handsome-looking black man she'd bumped into earlier in reception. That was a thought. That would teach Scott!

'Now if I could have my clothes, please?' Scott stood before her, a false smile on his lips.

Stella took his clothes off and huffily went off to the bathroom for a pee. As she sat there she thought about Jack. She wondered what he was doing now. Poor, smelly old Jack. They'd have to face each other again sooner or later to discuss the divorce. She didn't feel guilty or remorseful about what she had done. As far as she was concerned there was no going back, because she didn't want him back. The last 24 hours had proved that she didn't miss him and could do without him. She was surprised by her own feelings but realised she couldn't deny them. She saw a new life ahead of her. A life full of promise and adventure. A life surrounded by fresh air, not sullied by abhorrent odours. No orgasmic climaxes followed by a cacophony of wind. There'd be no more liaisons or relationships with flatulent men. Stella had decided.

A couple of doors away, Jack was feeling quite pleased with himself. Apart from the minor incident in the car with Archie over six hours earlier, he hadn't broken wind at all. This was a record. Stella would have been proud of him. He lay on the bed with his hands behind his head just thinking. Archie was reading a newspaper, while Terry was staring out of the window at the sea, trying to keep as calm as possible.

Jack went over the events of his last argument with Stella. He couldn't really blame her, in a way. He was more at fault than she was. The spark had disappeared from their marriage, and he honestly couldn't visualise it being patched up. It would be for her own good as much as his. The problem would be breaking the news to her. Would she be strong enough to cope with a divorce?

Terry's mobile rang. 'Yes? … Yes … Where are you? … We're at a pub called The Albatross … What was that shriek for …? What about our friends …? Okay, okay … See you in about an hour … We're in room number six, first floor … Very funny … Goodbye …' Terry sighed as he put the phone down. 'That was our friend Rory. I sincerely hope he's not pissed. He sounded very *gay* …'

'Well he is, isn't he?' Jack stated the obvious.

'Silly, is what I mean. He'll be joining us within the hour.'

'Where is he?' Archie was still looking at the paper.

'Wouldn't say. Just said he was on his way and would see us at about eight.'

'Anything about Barry and Kieran?'

'In his own words – what you don't know, you don't worry about. I assume by that, they're not with him.' Terry suddenly felt tired.

'I could do a recce of the house now, if you like?' Jack was bored waiting.

'No. It has to be dark. We can't take any chances.' Terry was adamant.

Archie put down his paper. 'We don't know for sure if this house, this address, has anything to do with the hostages or terrorists, do we? We could all be wasting our time here.'

'Yes, we could. But we don't have anything else to go on. Until I receive instructions to the contrary, we have to act on whatever we've got. Is that clear?'

'Do HQ know where we are?'

'Yes. I checked back before we left The Dog and Duck. There's been no further news. I will be the first to know if anything breaks. In the meantime we take things slowly and carefully. Understand?' Both Archie and Jack gave lazy, weary nods. Terry looked at his watch. He hated the waiting as much as they did.

Archie got off the bed and stretched. 'I'm feeling a trifle peckish. There's nothing we can do before Rory arrives anyway. All right if I go down to the bar for a snack?'

'I might join you there.' Jack's stomach felt empty.

'Okay, but please keep a low profile – and no alcohol. I'll stay here. Just in case HQ do ring.'

'Can we bring you anything back?' Archie asked.

'Yeah … sandwich, whatever … and a pint of lime and soda.' Terry lay on the bed and picked up Archie's paper as they left the room.

'Now I promise I won't be long. Keep the bed warm for me, lover.' Scott caressed Stella's cheek. He had combed his hair and she could smell a fresh application of cologne on him. It had to be a woman he was meeting.

'I might go down to the bar for a drink.' She challenged him to stop her.

'Good idea. Don't go picking up any strange men now!' He took a final look in the mirror, smiled and left the room.

In the corridor he came across Jack and Archie on their way down. They all nodded to each other as people do in hotel corridors. He followed them down the stairs. They went into the bar while he walked out of the front entrance.

A minute later, Stella came out of the room and made her way downstairs. She stopped at the door of the bar and thought for a second. No, she had a better idea. She was curious to know who this contact was. So, rather than go into the bar, she decided to go out and follow Scott instead. Outside, she was relieved to see him in the distance making toward the beach. Taking a deep breath, she headed in the same direction.

Jack came out of the bar on the way to the toilet. He stopped for a moment and smelt the perfume that was still in the air. It reminded him of Stella – she wore the same one. He wondered what she was doing now …

35

Melissa and Serena finished going through all the documents and photographs. It took them a minute or so to gather their thoughts, to take in the magnitude of the whole thing. The career of the most important man in the country, as well as the future of the present Government, lay in their very hands. It was an awesome responsibility and something that instantly frightened them. 'Delia wasn't exaggerating ...' Melissa whispered.

'This country is being run by a second-rate comedian ...' Serena said slowly, accentuating every word.

'It's always been run by comedians – except this time it happens to be a professional one. My god, this is explosive stuff ...' Melissa dropped one of the photographs as if it was burning. 'We can bring down Lane and the whole Government with this ...' She still found it hard to believe, even though Delia had told them that Lane was an impostor and that their whole mission was to expose him.

'I still can't help but like the man ... He does make politics a little fun.'

'Yes, and he's probably ordered a hit squad to come and assassinate us.'

'He wouldn't do that.'

Melissa raised her eyebrow in response.

Serena continued. 'We publicise these and he's finished.'

'He finds us first – and *we're* finished.'

'Do you ... do you think they've got Delia? Is that why she hasn't returned?' Serena suddenly thought.

'Something's gone wrong and that's for sure.'

'Perhaps they're torturing her right now, trying to find out where we are.' Serena had an image of Delia on an old-fashioned rack being pulled apart centimetre by centimetre. 'Poor Delia ...'

'We don't know that.' Melissa straightened her back.

'How can you be so sure?'

'If that was the case then this place would've been overrun by now. Never underestimate the survival instinct. Someone would knock at the door, throw a bomb in – and that would be that. There'd be a simple cover up and no-one would be any the wiser ...' Melissa was sure.

'Can't we phone her?'

'I've tried several times. No response ...'

'So what are we going to do? Without Delia ...'

'Not a great deal at the moment. As my brother would often say – we're up shit creek without a paddle. We'll just have to sit and wait a bit longer. Let's just pray we don't get that knock at the door ...'

Serena tidied up the papers and put them back in their folder. 'There's still Henry upstairs.'

'He's all right, as long as we keep him tied up. Delia was right, his presence might very well save our skins.'

'How?' Serena wasn't too happy about him being tied up for so long.

'As a hostage, of course! Don't you take anything in?'

'It's not Henry's fault, after all. He's an innocent bystander.' Serena surprised herself by how much she cared about his welfare.

'The whole country's an innocent bystander, when it's got a joker as Prime Minister. We're all hostages to a pretender. Do you think he cares about us? Like hell! He's more concerned about staying right where he is. Thinking up more jokes with which to fool the country. At this very minute, he and his henchmen are probably plotting ways in which to annihilate us—' And at that very moment, someone knocked at the front door.

'Who's that ...?' Serena whispered, frozen to the spot.

'How ... should ... I ... know ...?' Melissa mouthed the words silently. She felt her armpits filling up with sweat.

Someone knocked again, only this time with more determination and force. 'What do we do ...?' There was panic in Serena's eyes. Were they about to be murdered? Would someone throw that deadly bomb and blow them to pieces?

Melissa got herself together and pointed at the two guns, which were near Serena. Serena gingerly picked one up and threw the other to Melissa – who dropped it. Thankfully it fell on the sofa. Melissa picked it up.

'It might be Delia?' Serena wondered.

'I didn't hear a car ...' Melissa whispered. She moved closer to the door, her gun pointed. The letterbox flap suddenly opened and an object was forcefully pushed through it. Both Melissa and Serena took a terrified step back as the object rolled a few feet before coming to a standstill. It was black and in the shape of a small cylinder. A white piece of paper was attached by an elastic band.

'Is ... is it a bomb ...?' Serena stood immobilised.

'Doesn't look like one ...' Melissa directed her gun toward it, wondering if she should fire. Then she heard footsteps walking away from the door. The person had obviously gone. She stared at the object, waiting for something to happen. Would it abruptly burst into flames or explode? Might it even now be releasing an invisible, noxious gas that would immediately paralyse and then kill them? None of those things appeared to be happening. Melissa took a few steps toward it.

'Please be careful ...' Serena began to detect a slight smell coming from her own body. For the first time in her life she realised she was perspiring, and she didn't like it one bit.

'Looks sort of plasticky ...' Melissa got nearer and tried to make out some words on the white paper. 'ISH CHU.' What did that mean? Was it some secret Chinese code? Had Thomas Lane hired a bunch of Chinese triad assassins to kung fu them into oblivion? With the tip of the gun she bravely pushed at the object to make it roll over. The words 'DSEA PAR' stared back at her.

'Melissa ...?' Serena wasn't sure whether she was more concerned about the object or her body odour.

'Oh, bloody hell!' Melissa put down the gun, picked up the object and tore off the elastic.

'What is it … what is it?'

Melissa unwrapped the piece of paper and read what it said: '*PERDSEA PARISH CHURCH FETE. Please donate any good quality bric-a-brac. No car boot junk.*' It was attached to a black plastic waste bag.

'It's not dangerous or threatening …?' Serena sighed with relief.

'Unless you want to stick it over your head and suffocate. God, that had me going for a moment. See how stressed and nervous I am?' Melissa pointed to the dark sweat patches under her arms.

'I wish Delia would come …' Serena couldn't bring herself to admit that she was a little sweaty as well.

'So do I … oh, so do I …'

36

Scott's foot crunched on a crab shell as he stepped onto the beach. The shingle moved beneath him as he strode somewhat nervously away from a group of houses overlooking the sea. His instructions were to meet his contact there, somewhere north of the village. He looked ahead of him. Apart from an old woman taking her dog for a walk and a couple of teenagers sorting through the flotsam and jetsam, the scruffy grey area was empty.

He began to have butterflies in his stomach the further he moved along the seashore. It had been nearly six months since they had last met; last had sex. The memories of their torrid affair came flooding back, like the waves crashing on the shore. This particular relationship had had a profound effect on Scott. He'd never before met anyone so adventurous, so full of life, so passionate as a sexual partner. He had never thought such emotion possible. No woman, either before or since, had been able to provoke such depths of desire. Would they be able to continue where they had left off? Scott wanted to, but was afraid of being rejected. It had been a long time; and, after all, the purpose of their liaison was pure and simple business. He shouldn't expect too much. His personal life might not be fulfilled, yet his professional one had every chance of hitting the heights of spectacular success.

Scott paused for a moment. Was that someone waving to him a few hundred yards away …?

Stella watched Scott as he stood on the beach. She could just make out a dark figure ahead of him raising a hand as if to beckon. She saw Scott raise his hand in return and then start to run toward that person. From her well-covered position west of the beach, she able to observe them both without being seen. Scott ran quite comically across the shingle, which caught his feet several times. The other figure, which she still couldn't make out, walked very confidently toward him. Stella moved forward quickly to get as close as possible, while still trying to remain undetected. What happened next was as she had suspected. The two figures met and embraced passionately. It *was* another woman!

Stella moved in closer to try to get a better look at this bitch. However, the nearer she got, the more dumbfounded she became, as she watched them kiss and touch quite recklessly. It wasn't a bloody woman Scott was kissing – it was a *man* …

'So you are quite pleased to see me, petal.' Rory grabbed Scott by his bottom.

'It must be the sea air …' Scott clung closer to him, able to feel Rory's cock getting harder.

Stella felt so angry that she was tempted to run up to them and give Scott a good piece of her mind. But what would she say? Would there be any point? She wasn't married to him. She didn't have any say in his personal life. The fact that they had had sex didn't give her any rights.

In all the years she had known him, never once had she suspected in any way that Scott might be gay, or even bisexual. Was it her, or did he keep it well hidden? Did it really matter now? A lot of things now made sense to her. The manner in which they had had sex; the excitement he had shown when she had dressed up in his clothes. How could she have been so stupid? Working in the media, she thought she'd seen everything, but this little revelation did surprise her. The bugger was a bugger.

She watched them both untangle their arms, then disappear together off the beach toward some trees. Should she follow them? No, it would only complicate matters, and she didn't want to end up in a threesome. Besides, who would be doing what to whom? Stella took a deep breath and slowly made her way back to The Albatross, cursing herself for having got involved in the first place.

Carrying a drink and a sandwich for Terry, Jack came out of the bar and went upstairs, inadvertently passing wind along the way.

Stella entered several moments later to see some feet disappearing up the stairs, and was immediately overcome by the smell that was left behind. If she didn't know better she would have sworn that there was something of Jack about the stink. Like a mother knowing the smell of her own baby, Stella thought she could distinguish one of Jack's famous farts. She wiped the thought from her mind and went into the bar for a much-needed stiff drink.

'Howdy, ma'am. Kelvin at your service.' The young black barman gave her a genuinely friendly smile.

'Double gin and tonic, please.' Stella sat on the barstool.

'Ice and lemon?' He stuck a glass under the spirit measure with one hand and juggled a bottle of tonic in the other.

'The works.' Stella looked around the bar and was disappointed not to see the other black man she had bumped into earlier on. Apart from a couple of old codgers playing cards, there was only one other person present, and that was a middle-aged man who looked as if he'd been in the services.

Archie forked the last chip from the plate and ate it. He finished off his lemonade and turned to look toward Stella. An attractive woman, nice legs. Was she on her own or was she waiting for someone? His sessions with Beryl had given him a confidence and appetite to conquer fresh pastures. Perhaps she was the local hooker? There was certainly something about her that gave off that air. What did he have to lose?

'Kelvin,' he said, approaching the bar, 'another of your delightful lemonades ... and perhaps the young lady would like to join me in a drink?'

'No, thank you.' Stella smiled, but was not interested.

Archie, who always believed that no meant maybe or even yes, moved across and sat on the stool next to her. 'Are you sure I can't tempt you?' he said, being deliberately provocative.

'Very sure.' Stella took a large gulp of gin.

'They call me Archie.' He smiled, nudging a bit closer.

'I couldn't care less if they called you the dog's bollocks – I'm not interested. Is that clear?'

'Now there's no need to resort to that kind of language. I was only trying to be friendly, after all.' Archie remained calm.

'Friendly as in fuck perhaps?' She couldn't stop herself. Stella's mouth was way ahead of her mind. She didn't seem to care what she said anymore.

'If you like …' he replied, taking it as a blatant invitation.

'Kelvin …?' Stella turned her attention to the barman, who was enjoying this little dialogue. 'Do you sell condoms?'

'Er, there's a machine in the gents'.' Kelvin noticed the two old codgers put down their cards.

Turning back to Archie, Stella gently asked: 'Perhaps you could be a gent and go to the gents' and get some …?'

Archie couldn't believe his luck. He wasn't in the least embarrassed that everyone had overheard. 'Right oh.'

'You'll need some pound coins,' Kelvin helpfully volunteered.

'Got a couple here, thanks. See you shortly,' he said to Stella as he left the bar.

Stella quickly took a piece of paper and pen out of her bag and scribbled a brief note. 'Give this to the gentleman when he returns, please.' She folded it and handed it to the barman. She then finished off her drink and swiftly left the bar, running upstairs to her room.

Archie returned looking as pleased as punch. It really was turning out to be a grand day. His face fell slightly when he couldn't see Stella. 'The young lady …?'

'She asked me to give you this …' The barman smiled as he proffered the note, which he had already taken a peep at.

Archie took it, his spirits rising. He was sure it would be an address or the number of her room. He slowly unfolded it.

'Fill one condom with lemonade and have a drink on me. Stick the other on your head and fuck off.'

'Okay?' Kelvin asked when he saw Archie's expression.

'It's the most unusual brush off I've had in a long time. D'you think I came on a bit strong?' Archie sipped his drink, wondering whether to get annoyed or to laugh it off.

'Man, if you don't mind me saying, you really blew it.'

'Where did I slip up?'

'Just by being born, man, just by being born …'

37

Delia and Tom returned to the house from the funfair in very high spirits. Apart from Tom's brief deviation, Delia had thoroughly enjoyed herself. Richard was there to meet them in the hall. He looked very preoccupied and didn't smile.

'Rich, Eve and I had a super time, didn't we?' Tom's bodily mannerisms were gauche and gangly, like a schoolboy trying to impress a girl.

'Can't *remember* when I last went to a funfair ...' Delia said this for Richard's benefit.

'I'm pleased you enjoyed it. Tom, would you go and see William. He's in father's study.'

'What for?' Tom didn't want to leave Delia.

'Just go please. I'll talk to you later.' Richard watched Tom as he just stood there with a silly grin on his face. 'Tom ... Did you hear what I said?'

Tom's face fell and his shoulders hunched. 'Eve, I could show you our new litter of piglets? They're really funny ...'

'Maybe later. You go off now and attend to your business.' Delia made it sound so important that he didn't argue and went off happily.

'I hope Tom hasn't been too much of a nuisance,' said Richard. 'He can be a bit ... er—'

'Is *simple* the word you're looking for?'

Richard's expression lightened. 'You could say that. He means well.'

'We had a very nice time; he's quite sweet really.' Delia felt it best not to go into any details.

'He didn't ... he didn't sort of touch you, or anything?' Richard had to ask.

'What do you mean?' Delia replied in all innocence.

'Obviously not. I'm sorry. It's just that Tom has an unfortunate way with him. Several members of our female staff have complained about his behaviour.'

'Not much different from most males then.' Delia was sorry she had said it when she saw the hurt look on Richard's face. 'Present company excluded, of course. It's funny, I would never have taken you and Tom for brothers. You're both so very different in many ways.'

'You're not the first to say it ...' Richard's thoughts were elsewhere.

'Is everything okay? I feel I'm intruding in some way and stopping you from doing what you have to do. I'm a bit of a hindrance, aren't I?'

'No, you're not. Actually I'm glad you're here. Why don't I show you to your room ...' Richard headed toward the double staircase.

'Your mother doesn't mind me staying, does she?' Delia followed on behind.

'Mother's bite can sometimes be worse than her bark. She's always been very protective toward her sons. Any female friend is regarded with a sense of suspicion.'

They walked down a small corridor.

'Unless she has an acceptable pedigree?'

'Nothing less than royalty ...' Richard smiled as he opened a door to a bedroom and let her enter first.

'Is that why none of you is married?' Delia walked into the bedroom and immediately felt at home. 'This is lovely ...'

'I took the liberty of finding you a change of clothes. I hope they fit. You'll probably want to take a bath, anyway.' Richard pointed to some things that were neatly laid out on the bed.

'Underwear too ...' Delia picked up a tasteful matching set of silk bra and panties. 'One of your ex-girlfriends?'

'Our manager's assistant, Elaine, who's about your size and build, went into the village and bought them.'

'She's got good taste. That's very kind of you, thank you.'

'If you would now excuse me, I've a meeting with the family solicitor. Please make yourself at home. Dinner will be served at about nine.'

'I hope there isn't a problem.' Delia noticed the concerned look that had returned to his eyes.

'So do I ...' With that, Richard closed the door behind him, leaving Delia alone. After looking out of the window, she went into the *en suite* bathroom to run herself a hot, relaxing bath. There was everything that she needed; luxurious bath oils and soaps, including a selection of expensive perfumes. Richard had thought of everything. Delia suddenly wished that her memory would never return and selfishly prayed that Richard would always have to look after her.

Gertrude, Tom, William and Andrew Lawson were already assembled in Randolph's study when Richard joined them. 'Sorry if I've kept you waiting.'

'Did Eve tell you what a good time we had?' Tom was fidgeting with a brass paperweight.

'Yes, Tom ...'

'How long is that woman staying with us? Are you sleeping with her?' Gertrude didn't believe in ducking the issue.

'I'm not sure – and I'm not.'

'Eve this week, who will it be next week?' William added rather sarcastically. He had always envied Richard's success with women.

'Have you all quite finished?' Richard raised his voice. 'I'm sorry, Andrew, we're wasting your time.' He plonked himself down in his father's favourite leather armchair.

'Not at all. It's good that you're all here. I appreciate that it's a sorrowful time ...' He looked at Gertrude, who didn't appear at all upset. 'I'm sorry to have insisted on this meeting at such short notice, but there are certain matters concerning Lord Montcasse's will that require immediate attention.' Lawson took a folder out of his briefcase and wondered how the family were going to take it.

'But Richard's Lord Montcasse now,' said Tom. 'I didn't know you'd made a will, Rich. What's in it?' He clearly thought he was being very witty.

'Tom, my dear boy, do shut up. You're becoming most tiresome.' Gertrude gave him one of her admonishing looks.

'Yes, Mother … sorry. My lips are sealed with superglue.' Tom clamped his mouth shut.

'If only they were,' William added, and he also got one of his mother's stares.

'You were saying that Father revised his will only a month ago,' Richard said. ;Did something specifically prompt this?'

'He said he wanted to put the record straight …'

'What's that supposed to mean – put the record straight?' Gertrude addressed Lawson like one of her servants.

'I will come to that in a moment, Lady Montcasse.' Lawson realised that he would have to tackle this as delicately as possible.

'I hope he wasn't having one of his aberrations when he made it. Randolph was prone to having fits of irrationality.'

'I assure you he was very mindful of what he was doing.'

'Did he feel he was going to die soon, then?' William wondered.

Gertrude put him straight. 'Your father always swore that he'd see me buried first. Apart from a dickey heart, there was nothing wrong with him.'

Lawson pressed on. 'Lord Montcasse gave no other reason for amending his will except to allay his conscience and be truthful to the family tradition …'

'My dear man, perhaps if you spoke in plain English we might understand what you're talking about.' Gertrude was starting to get impatient.

'Mother, Andrew is doing his best.' Richard shifted uncomfortably in his chair.

'I think it's best if I just read the will. It will be in Lord Montcasse's own words.' Lawson unfolded the document.

'Is it long? Randolph could waffle so.'

'Mother …' Richard's tone was now verging on anger.

'All right, all right … Get on with it then and put us out of our misery.'

Lawson cleared his throat and stood there like a judge reading out the charges:

'This is the last will and testament of I, Lord Randolph Percival Montcasse of the Montcasse Manor estate, Hampshire, and I hereby revoke all former wills and testamentary dispositions made by me …'

'Yes, yes …' Gertrude mumbled.

Lawson paused for a moment before continuing:

'Gertrude, I hope you will forgive me for what I am about to do. I know we discussed this many years ago when Richard, William and Tom were children, and that we said we would carry this secret to our graves …'

'What is this nonsense …?' Gertrude went visibly pale.

'Let Andrew continue, Mother,' Richard said softly. It was the first time he had ever seen his mother physically diminish in stature.

Lawson picked up where he had left off:

'I will leave it to you to tell the boys all the details regarding their adoption …' He deliberately paused there to give it a moment to sink in.

'Adoption …?' William was the first to repeat it.

'Who's adopted?' Tom was confused.

'Is this true, Mother …?' Richard turned directly to her.

Gertrude's hands started fiddling with her necklace of pearls as if it were a rosary. She looked up to see all her sons watching her intently. There was silence for a full 30 seconds before she bleated: 'The old bastard – he promised!'

Lawson could see this going on for hours if he didn't manage it properly. He just wanted to get it over with and go back home. It was wife-swap night with their neighbours and he didn't want to be too late. He took command. 'I know this must come as somewhat as a shock to you all, and that you will have a great deal to discuss – but first please let me finish the reading of the will, then I shall do my best to answer any relevant questions pertaining to it.'

'Carry on Andrew – there'll be no more interruptions – from anybody!' Richard addressed them all.

'There isn't a great deal more.' Lawson started to read again:

'My boys have always been my boys – despite the fact that I did not sire them. Gertrude, you know I never blamed you because you weren't able to conceive. It was as much my fault as yours. I couldn't have children either. We accepted our fate and agreed to adopt instead. We loved them as our own, and you will see that I have left them all, and you, a healthy financial legacy. I am sorry that it might not be quite as you expected, but my conscience would not allow me to break a tradition that has been in the Montcasse bloodline for three centuries. As you know, the family title and deeds to the estate are passed from father to elder son. This family tradition has never been broken, and I cannot be the one to change it. I am sorry, Richard, because I know this affects you more than Tom or William. By rights you would automatically assume my title and everything that goes with it. That is – if you were my real son, if you carried my blood ...'

Lawson paused to take breath. He looked up. The whole family were frozen in silence.

'Why couldn't he have just kept his mouth shut and let things be ...' Gertrude's posture had noticeably slumped. All her confident bearing had disappeared.

Richard nodded to Lawson to continue.

'I am truly sorry, Gertrude. I realise I made a promise and now I am breaking it. The situation might have remained the same – had it not been for the birth of my son. My real son ...'

'What? Randolph said he couldn't have children ...' Gertrude gripped her pearl necklace with such force that it broke and sent all the pearls scattering across the highly-polished parquet floor.

'I'll get them!' Tom volunteered, already on his knees and starting to retrieve the pearls.

'Leave them for now, Tom, please.' Richard put his hand on Tom's shoulder.

'But ...?' Tom was disappointed. He was bored with having to listen to matters that he found confusing.

'Sorry, Andrew. This will be the last interruption.'

'I'm nearly finished ...

'Gertrude, it is no secret that during our marriage both of us indulged in various affairs. It was one of the reasons our marriage lasted for so long. It was during a brief affair with a woman I met in London, some 33 years ago, that a miracle occurred and my son was conceived. I never knew of his existence until a year ago when I received a letter from her, which had been forwarded by her solicitor. She had recently died and simply wanted to inform me that I had a son. There were no demands or requests attached. Even the boy has never been told of my existence, and still does not know I am his father. It has taken me a long time to make this decision. It is now my final wish to bestow upon my son his true inheritance ...

'The rest of the will deals with minor bequests.'

'Is there any proof that the woman's son is really his?' Richard was very calm and thoughtful.

'I have here a lot of papers that go into all that,' nodded Lawson. 'Lord Montcasse carried out his own private investigations first. The proof, as you will see, appears conclusive. The son, as yet, has not been informed. Richard – your father wanted you to deal with that. He thought you would understand.'

'Yes …' In an odd way, Richard did understand. He felt no hate or malice toward his father. He turned to look at Gertrude, who looked as if she was just staring mindlessly at a portrait of Randolph.

'And who the hell is this bloody son?' William still hadn't come to terms with everything he'd just heard.

'Ah, yes …' Lawson flicked through a few papers before coming to the one he was looking for.

'Mother …?' Richard put his hand on Gertrude's arm. 'Are you all right?' She didn't appear to acknowledge his touch.

'Got it. His name is—' But Lawson didn't finish when he saw the look on Richard's face.

'Mother?' Richard shook her lightly. She felt cold and stiff. 'Oh god …'

'What is it, Richard?' Lawson put down the piece of paper that bore the name of the new Lord Montcasse.

'I think she's dead …'

38

Scott felt invigorated and at peace with himself for the first time in years. His clandestine and ardent encounter with Rory had reawakened and brought to the surface all manner of inner ghosts. What had suddenly struck him, as Rory pulled down his trousers, was nothing less than a revelation. What he was doing wasn't perverse or abnormal. It felt natural. He'd been suppressing these feelings all his life. It was the combination of sea air, the crashing waves, the damp grass and Rory's energy and experience that had finally made him see the light. Ejaculation had come not just as a glorious relief, but as a divine manifestation. To him it had been like a second coming. The Scott that strutted assuredly back through the doors of The Albatross was a different Scott than the one that had exited less than an hour earlier. He was a new man in every sense of the word. He had ultimately discovered who he really was. His closet door had been unlocked and he had come out in all his glory.

'Sorry I was so long …' he said cheerfully to Stella, who was lying on the bed reading a magazine. 'My contact had a lot to say.'

'I'm sure he did.' Stella didn't look up from her magazine.

'Well, I think I'll go and have a shower and then fill you in on the plan.'

'Like you were filled in?' she said rather pointedly.

'I'm sorry …?'

'Did you bend over backwards to get this information?'

'What are you saying, Stella dear?'

'Don't you "dear" me! If you come anywhere near me with that prick of yours, I swear I'll cut it off and throw it in the sea.' The anger that had been preoccupying her for the last hour finally erupted.

'And what makes you think I want to?'

'I know exactly where it's been, and you can wear a thousand condoms for all I care, but it's not going to touch me.'

'There's no need for you to worry, babe, your body is safe with me.' Scott started to take his clothes off.

'What do you think you're doing?'

'I'm going to have a shower. Any objections?'

'You don't think I know, do you?'

'Know what?'

'That you're a pervert, a bisexual – that you go with *men* as well as women.' She watched his expression, but he only smiled. 'I saw you at the beach …'

'Naughty girl – you followed me,' he said without anger as he took off his shirt and trousers.

'I'm glad I did.'

'I'm glad you did too. So there are no more secrets between us.' He took his socks off.

'Pants off in the bathroom, please. I don't want to see that thing again. I feel so disgusted about what we did …'

'I'm sorry about that. You gave me the impression that you enjoyed it.'

'Well I didn't,' she lied. 'I didn't want to hurt your feelings. What a mistake that was!'

'For both of us. Never mind. Let me just tell you that there was a time when I didn't quite know which way to turn. I deceived myself as well as others. You don't know how tortuous that can be.'

'You make my heart bleed …' She couldn't stop herself from being bitchy.

'Anyway …' Scott deliberately pulled down his underpants in front of her and pointed to his penis. 'My friend here now knows which direction he wants to go in. Rest assured it won't be near you – or any other woman, come to think of it.'

'You're turning gay …?' Stella was surprised.

'I was half-way there. I'm just turning the complete circle now. I've decided to become a full-time member, so to speak. So please, let's not argue about it. We should celebrate instead.' He smiled and exited into the bathroom.

Stella hadn't anticipated Scott behaving in this way. She had been lying there plotting out a scenario as to how she was going to tackle him and shock him by what she had witnessed. His reaction had been the opposite to what she had expected. She could see the difference in his whole manner and bearing. She was sorry now that she had behaved so childishly and harshly. In a sense she was quite jealous, because he had found something that had made him really happy. Could she profess to being as happy? Her estrangement from Jack had made her think, and had turned her life around in such a short space of time. She didn't want just to drift and possibly sleep with any man she fancied. From now on, her life had to have a purpose – but what?

She was so wrapped up in her thoughts that she didn't notice that Scott was stood by the bathroom door, covered in a towel. He was watching her and smiling. 'So a screw's out of the question, then …?'

'What?' Stella wasn't sure if she'd heard him correctly.

'Just joking. We haven't lost our sense of humour now, have we?'

'No …' Stella managed a smile.

'Okay. Whatever else has happened, I don't think we should forget why we're here. Unless you've had second thoughts and want to leave? I would understand. There'd be no hard feelings.' Scott meant it.

'I'm happy to see it through – unless, of course, you want to get rid of me. Then I'd quite understand, without any hard feelings on my part.'

'Well, at least we understand each other!' He laughed. 'Right, this is the situation as it's been relayed to me. It hasn't yet been confirmed whether or not the hostages and terrorists are in Perdsea. My friend – who is part of the task force – has got to check with his colleagues as to their next move. I'm hoping that they won't do anything until morning.'

'Why?'

'Practical reasons. We haven't got a lighting rig. If any manoeuvre is carried out in the dark we're well and truly stymied. No lights, no film. That's always the problem when you're trying to do things undercover.'

Stella had a thought. 'What about the car?'

'What d'you mean?'

'If we can get the car near the location, and if something does happen while it's still dark, couldn't we turn the headlights on? That would provide enough light to shoot in, surely?'

'Not such a bad idea. I'm glad I brought you along.'

'When will we know what's happening, if it is?'

'I'll get a call.'

'So, what do we do while we wait?' Stella smiled and started teasingly to undo the buttons on her blouse.

'You ... you cannot be serious ...' Scott sounded quite anxious and instinctively crossed his palms in front of his crotch.

'Now *you* haven't lost your sense of humour, have you?' Stella did the buttons back up again. 'Why don't we order a bottle of champagne to celebrate your coming out – and we can enjoy it watching some television while we wait for the green light. How does that sound?'

'Perfect ...' Scott had never felt so happy.

There was a sharp, forceful knock at the door. Terry, Jack and Archie all stiffened. Terry took out his gun. 'Who is it?'

'Give us a kiss and I'll tell you!' Rory's voice giggled from behind the door.

'Give me strength ...' Terry mumbled to himself as he went across to open the door. 'You took your bloody time.'

'Sorry, a bit of unfinished business. Well, this is all very cosy.' Rory looked around the room at one double and one single bed. 'Who am I shacking up with, then? I mean, I'm not fussy.'

'Nobody. It's not the intention that we're going to sleep here.' Terry went back and sat on the single bed.

'Pity ... it would've been such fun.' Rory came and sat on the end of the double bed with Jack and Archie.

'So – what did you do with our two friends?' Archie enquired.

'Who's that then?' Rory wasn't giving anything away.

'Barry and Kieran. What's happened to them?'

'Aren't they here yet? On the way we stopped at a little pub. I went to the loo, and when I came back they had disappeared ... I thought they must have come straight here,' Rory said innocently.

'Don't give us that!' Archie pointed an accusing finger at Rory. 'What really happened?'

'You want the truth? They are both tied up, naked, in a ship bound for Denmark. Satisfied?'

'And my name's Walter Mitty.' Archie lay back on the bed.

'You don't believe me. Do you?' Rory looked at Jack.

'If you hadn't said they were tied up and naked I might have believed you.' Jack tried to be sympathetic.

'I suppose it does sound a bit implausible. Okay, I'll tell you what really happened. Now this is not for the squeamish ...'

'That's enough!' Terry stood up. 'Shut up, Rory. I don't want to know.'

'But I do.' Archie was looking forward to this.

'You button up too. As far as we're all concerned, Barry and Kieran have gone

AWOL. That's not our problem anymore. We've more important matters to deal with. Do we all understand?' Terry looked at them each in turn. They all understood. It wasn't worth arguing about.

'So, what's the next step then?' Rory was glad that he didn't have to make up another story, or go into any further explanations.

Terry looked at his watch. 'In about an hour, when it's completely dark, one of us will do a recce around this Cloudsey House building. We will then act on the findings. All agreed?' They all nodded.

'A whole hour to kill …' mused Rory. 'What shall we do with ourselves? Anyone fancy playing hide the sausage?'

Rory was suddenly bombarded by the other three with papers and other things to hand. 'All right! It was only a suggestion. You can't blame me for trying!'

39

The long, leisurely bath made Delia feel much better. She must have spent over an hour soaking in the fragrant oils. Several times she had drifted off into a kind of semi-sleep, her mind assaulted with dozens of strange multicoloured images, none of which made any sense or triggered off any memories. She wished that Richard might come in and offer to scrub her back. Then she'd persuade him to join her in the bath – there was enough room for two – and they'd just languish in each other's company … The perfect end to a wonderful day.

The clothes all fitted just perfectly. Delia admired herself in the cheval mirror. She felt comfortable and at home in her surroundings, and the thought of being the lady of the house appealed to her. Like the clothes, the role would fit her like a glove. She just knew it instinctively. She glanced at the carriage clock on the mantelpiece. It was eight o'clock. Another hour before dinner. She had an inclination to do a bit of exploring around the house; she was sure that Richard wouldn't mind.

She wandered down a few corridors, taking in the paintings and portraits that lined the walls. Most were very dull, very brown and didn't prompt Delia to stop and make any closer inspection. Eventually she found herself at the top of the double staircase that led down to the main hall. She stopped and stared at the whole expanse before her, and in particular the large, ornate chandelier that hung down in the centre, odd speckles of light bouncing off it. The view was so pleasing to her eye that she opened her arms as if to gather it all in. As she was standing there, breathing in the atmosphere, she heard some noises and footsteps coming from one side of the hall. What she saw next was bizarre in the extreme.

Richard, William and Tom entered the hall carrying Gertrude between them. She looked as stiff as a statue. Her arms and legs were bent. It was as if she had been lifted directly from a chair and had not moved her limbs in the process. Delia could see that her eyes were still open, but other than that, Gertrude could have been a waxwork dummy being carried from one location to another. They gently put her down onto one of the chairs in the hall.

Andrew Lawson came hurrying in. 'The ambulance will be here in a moment. There's nothing else we can honestly do.'

'No …' Richard stretched his shoulder. It had gone rigid from carrying his mother.

Delia came down the stairs. 'Is she all right? What happened?'

'Mother's paralysed. You feel her.' Tom prodded Gertrude to show Delia.

'She's not our mother …' William added in a tone of bitter contempt.

'I'm sorry?' Delia couldn't understand the odd looks they were all giving each other.

'I'll explain later. Sorry you had to see this.' Richard touched Delia very lightly on the arm. 'She's suffered a bit of a shock. She might have had a stroke, we don't really know.'

'Is there anything I can do?' Delia could see how helpless they all looked.

Tom studied Gertrude without any emotion. 'She looks a bit spooky sitting there. Even more scary than some of the dummies we've got on the ghost train.'

'Perhaps we should put her there …' William meant every word.

'All right, you two, now stop it!' Richard wasn't in any mood to get into a family dispute at this moment. He breathed a sigh of relief when he heard the siren of an approaching ambulance.

Lawson went over to the front door and opened both sides just as the ambulance came to a halt outside. Two paramedics came rushing in, and for a second weren't sure who the patient was, until Lawson pointed to the seated Gertrude. 'She simply went stiff … We think she's still alive …'

While one of the paramedics made various routine checks on Gertrude, the other went back into the ambulance and returned with a wheelchair. They lifted her onto it and carried her into the ambulance. Hardly anything was said during this procedure. 'Anyone coming with us?' one of the paramedics asked as they got to the door.

'Yes … I'd better come.' Richard knew it was his duty as the eldest.

'Can I come too?' Tom loved hospitals.

Richard put a restraining arm on Tom, who was already making a move. 'No, Tom, you and William stay here. I'll deal with this.'

'Richard – you don't need me, do you?' Lawson was anxious to leave. He'd already been there longer than anticipated. Wife-swapping evening was one of the highlights of his week, and he didn't want to lose another moment.

'No. Thanks for what you've done, Andrew. I'll call you tomorrow and we can start sorting out this bloody awful mess.'

'Of course.' After that, Lawson was out of the door, had got into his car and had sped out of the estate before the ambulance had even started.

'I'm coming with you.' Delia stepped into the ambulance after Richard, who was so preoccupied that he had temporarily forgotten about her. 'And I don't want any arguments.'

'Thanks.' He was grateful for her company. He couldn't have borne the presence of Tom and William. They would only have argued. Richard looked at Gertrude, who seemed to be staring directly at him. 'So many things now begin to make sense … Oh, Mother …'

The ambulance arrived at the hospital within ten minutes. Richard and Delia said nothing to each other during the journey. Gertrude's eerie and unnatural company put paid to any conversation. She sat there staring straight ahead, her grey, pallid features set in stone, her rigid body jiggling from the vibration of the ambulance. Thankfully her wig and false teeth remained in place, otherwise she would have appeared even more sinister.

Richard and Delia waited in reception while the doctors examined Gertrude. 'A touch of *déjà vu* …' Delia looked around her.

'Have you remembered something?' Richard asked.

'No. But only a few hours ago we were in another hospital. It just seems so familiar. Are our lives bound up by being in hospitals? I hope your mother recovers.'

'Yes, she's got a bit of explaining to do … It appears she is not my real mother …'

'Is that why you had to see your solicitor?'

'It all came out in Father's will – only he's not my father either. I'm afraid it's all a bit complicated and somewhat difficult to start to come to terms with.'

'What about Tom and William?'

'They're not my brothers. We're not related, apparently. In a nutshell, because Gertrude and Randolph thought they couldn't have children, they adopted us all. I don't have any details. If Father hadn't put anything in the will, then none of this would ever have come out. I believe it was the shock of what Father had written that had such a tragic effect on Mother …'

'So you're an orphan …?' Delia's hand touched Richard's.

Richard nodded thoughtfully. 'What's even more surprising is that I won't inherit the title of Lord Montcasse. Father had a bastard son whom he wants as his rightful successor. True Montcasse blood …'

'That's not fair! Who is this mysterious son?' Delia felt suddenly angry on Richard's behalf.

'Andrew's got all the details.'

'We have more in common than you thought.'

'What do you mean by that?' Richard looked up at Delia.

'Both orphans in a way. Neither really knowing our true identity.'

'And if Mother dies, I might never know …' Richard saw one of the doctors approach them. He couldn't judge from his expression what the conclusions were.

'Mr Montcasse? Jeff Brewer, Senior Consultant.'

'How is she?'

'It's difficult to tell until we've done few more tests. Naturally we'll need to keep her in for the time being. We can give her a private room if you so wish?' The consultant didn't want to miss an opportunity to boost the hospital's finances.

'Yes – the best that you've got. Is she conscious?'

'Not at the moment. Her heart is very strong, which is a good sign. We still haven't managed to loosen her limbs. We're afraid that if we exert too much pressure we might break some bones in the process. Your mother's acute paralysis is obviously mentally-based. You said that it was the result of some bad news?'

'Yes, it happened immediately after. What are her chances?'

'Difficult to say at this stage. She could recover within the next few hours, or she could remain in this catatonic state for days. A mental shock of any severity to someone of her age can sometimes have a permanent effect on the body, and it some cases it can, well, lead to …'

'Death? She could die?' Richard wanted to come to the point.

'It's possible. I'm sorry that I can't be more positive. The brain has always been a tricky customer. If it's in control, then all we can do is wait. We will be conducting a brain scan, and will hopefully be able to encourage her muscles to relax through various drugs. Be assured that we will make your mother as comfortable as possible.'

'Thank you. So there really isn't anything else I can do?'

'Go home. I will phone you personally if there is any change in her condition. By the way, would you like us to put her in a small or a large room?'

'The small one would be adequate.'

'The larger one has a smart TV, DVD recorder and wi-fi,' the consultant said rather enthusiastically, thinking of the extra hundred pounds a day it would add to the bill.

'I doubt my … mother will want to watch television or surf the net in her condition, wouldn't you agree?'

'Fair enough,' he said rather disappointedly. 'A small room. She'll still be able to listen to the radio if she so wishes. Well, I'll be in touch, Mr Montcasse … Mrs Montcasse.' He walked away wondering if his sales pitch needed refining.

Richard stood up and stretched. He was feeling really tired now. All the events of the last couple of days had finally caught up with him. He just wanted to go home to bed and drift into oblivion. Still in a bit of a daze, he started to wander off.

'Excuse me … Haven't you forgotten Mrs Montcasse?' Delia still sat there.

'What …?' He turned back. 'Mrs Montcasse … she's …' He pointed to where Gertrude had been taken.

'Me – you silly man. That doctor called *me* Mrs Montcasse. He thought I was your wife.'

'Eve, I'm so sorry … I'll get us a taxi. It's been a long day …'

The journey back to the house took nearly half an hour. The taxi didn't go as fast as the ambulance had. Richard kept nodding off, only temporarily coming to when the taxi gave a jolt or went over a bump. Delia decided to keep quiet and not plague him with any more questions. Instead she took his hand and held it tight. She was pleased when he didn't remove it.

The taxi pulled up at the main entrance. Richard and Delia got out, to see Tom and William playing football on the gravel at the front, which was lit by security lights. Richard sighed despondently when he saw them. 'They're like a couple of bloody kids!'

'Boys will always be boys,' Delia remarked.

Tom saw Richard and kicked the ball toward him. Richard moved out of the way, letting the ball roll toward some shrubs. 'I kicked it to you!' Tom said in a disappointed tone.

'And I'll kick you, if you don't behave yourself. William, what is all this? Not a good example to the staff at this time of the evening.'

'It was Tom's idea …' William didn't want to admit that he had encouraged Tom. It had helped him to get rid of some of his pent-up aggression when he imagined the ball to be Gertrude.

'You're both acting like a couple of street hooligans.' Richard now knew why he had nothing in common with his brothers.

'Because that's probably what we are … born on some council estate,' William replied in all seriousness.

'Stop being so melodramatic, William.' But the idea hadn't escaped Richard's own thoughts. Perhaps they had all initially come from poor families. 'I notice neither of you have asked me how Mother is. She might have died for all you know, or seem to care.'

'Is she dead?' Tom had picked up the ball and was holding it.

'No, but her condition is still serious. It could go either way.'

'I know which way I'd vote for.' William kicked some gravel before stomping off into the house.

'Eve, would you like a game?' Tom eagerly showed her the ball.

'No thank you, Tom. It's a bit late.' Delia smiled, trying not to disappoint him too much.

'I'll go in and play my music then …' he said rather moodily, before a thought suddenly struck him. 'Rich, if Mother does die, will we bury her at the same time as Father? That would save some time and money. You know, killing two birds with one stone.'

'Go in and play your music. I'll let you know if anything happens.' Despite the fact that Tom irritated Richard intensely, he still felt responsible for him in a way. He briefly put his hand on Tom's shoulder and gently nudged him toward the door.

'You're very patient with him.' Delia saw the look of compassion on Richard's face.

'He means well … You must be starving, I am. Shall we get something to eat?' And Richard did his trick of wandering off without waiting for her.

They were the only two in the dining room. Tom and William had already eaten and were holed away in their rooms. Richard was grateful. Their unsettling company wasn't an aid to digestion. He had had enough of them both for the time being. 'I'm sorry if I'm not very good company at the moment.' He took a large sip of claret, aware that he hadn't said much during the meal.

'And I'm sorry that you've been lumbered with me. It's what you call bad timing.' Delia wiped her mouth with a napkin.

'When is the timing ever right?'

'When you saved my life. If you hadn't found me, I might very well be dead by now. It was fate.'

'Fate or coincidence?' Richard went back over the course of events during the last couple of days. One simple incident had changed the fortunes of the whole Montcasse family. If Randolph hadn't chased after the helicopter that had been stolen, he'd still be alive now; the secret of their adoption would have remained buried for the time being and Gertrude wouldn't have suffered her stroke …Yet Richard would never have met Delia if that hadn't happened …

'A lucky coincidence for me.' She gave him a warm smile.

'I'm glad you were here. It's been a help.' Richard drained his glass. 'Well, if you'll excuse me, I'm going to retire. A lot to do tomorrow.'

'Yes … And I need to start trying to find out who I am. I can't say I'm looking forward to it.'

'You might be in for a pleasant surprise.'

'Or an unpleasant one … You go off to bed. I know the way to my room.'

'Goodnight …' Richard wanted to kiss her, but didn't feel it was right. He just smiled apologetically and left the dining room. Delia sat there selfishly wishing he had kissed her, but understood his reticence. She emptied the last dregs of wine from the bottle into her glass, drinking it hurriedly down before leaving the dining room herself.

The main hallway was silent apart from the enormous grandfather clock that loudly ticked away. Half-way up the stairs, Delia's attention was drawn to a couple of maids below, scurrying across like mice toward the dining room. She continued on up, looking at the portraits of various members of the Montcasse dynasty. Richard had none of the pinched, eagle-like features of the family. This was now understandable, since he wasn't a genuine Montcasse. She realised that she would have to prepare herself never to see him again after the next day. He had too much to cope with, and she knew he was too nice a man to completely abandon her. It wasn't fair on him for her to be an added burden. As she walked down one of the corridors, she made up her mind to leave first thing in the morning. She wouldn't tell him. She'd simply go at an opportune moment without causing a fuss. It was a difficult decision, but the right one.

As she was about to turn the corner leading to the corridor down which her bedroom was situated, she saw flashing coloured lights coming from one of the other rooms and heard music accompanied by odd snatches of deep, out-of-tune singing. It sounded so off and weird that Delia couldn't stop herself from finding out what was going on.

She crept gingerly toward the half-open door, being careful not to make a sound, although the music and singing would have drowned out any extraneous noise. At the door she cautiously glimpsed inside, being careful not to be spotted. What confronted her was a most unusual vision. Tom, in his pyjamas, was gyrating around the room, singing into a microphone. The flashing lights came from a bank of tiny coloured bulbs that were flickering on and off in timed sequence to the music. These were attached to a karaoke machine, which also housed a monitor that displayed the lyrics to the songs. Tom was doing his best to sing the words in time to the music, but he seemed to be constantly two or three beats behind. Even his jerky body movements displayed no coordination, and certainly bore no relation to the tempo of the music. What Delia found even funnier was that whenever Tom wiggled his hips, his penis sporadically flopped out of his trouser flap as if it was trying to compete with the rest of his body.

It was while she was trying to get a better look that Tom caught sight of her. Still singing, he ran to the door and managed to drag her in. A couple of seconds later the song finished and the system went quiet. 'I'm sorry, but the door was open.' Delia shrugged her shoulders.

'D'you want to have a go? It's great. You can choose from a hundred different songs! There's bound to be a favourite there.' Tom picked up a list, which he shoved under her nose.

'No thanks.' She didn't even look at the list.

'Oh, go on, please.' Tom was looking at her intently.

'I think I'd better go to my room ... I'm sorry to interrupt.'

She was about to turn away when Tom gently grabbed her arm. 'Then will you stay and listen to me do another one. I'll sing one of my best ... Please.' He looked at her like a sad, lost puppy.

'Just the one then.' She didn't want to hurt his feelings.

'Great!' Tom ran across to the karaoke machine and pushed some buttons to load up the required song. Then, getting into position, with the mike poised in front of his mouth, he waited until the music got under way. The opening bars of a sentimental love ballad started, and Tom proceeded to do his very own unique rendition, slowly swaying his hips in an emotive way. It wasn't because it was so awful that Delia began to feel uncomfortable, but the fact that Tom was singing it directly to her as if he meant it. What became even more disturbing was the growing protuberance that was emerging from his pyjama trousers. Delia tried not to look down – but you couldn't really miss it. It appeared like a snake about to strike, and she now noticed that Tom's eyes had glazed over. It was when he put down the mike and took a pace in her direction that Delia thought it was time to go.

'Eve, where are you going ...' Tom said slowly, seemingly unaware of his own erection.

'I'd better go ...' She started to back away.

'But I love you ...'

'No, you don't. I'll see you in the morning. Go to bed.'

'Come with me. We can play doctors and nurses!' he smirked.

'I've had my share of doctors and nurses for today, thank you. Goodnight Tom.' And she was out of the door.

'I liked you from the first moment I saw you!' Tom followed her out.

'Tom, go back in, please.' Delia turned to face him.

'D'you like it? I call it my Mickey.' He pointed down at his member.

'Mickey will catch his death of cold if you don't put him away. Now, for the last time – goodnight, Tom.' Delia took a deep breath and strode off down the corridor.

Tom started to follow. 'Mickey wants to say goodnight.'

'Goodnight Mickey.' Delia quickened her pace and was dismayed to hear Tom coming after her.

'Mickey wants a goodnight kiss.'

'Oh, god ... Sorry, but I'm a vegetarian.' Delia started to run. Her room was in the opposite direction, so her only option was to run as far from him as possible. She ran down one corridor, then across another one, up a small flight of steps and into yet another corridor. Tom came in pursuit, enjoying every moment of this game. 'Please stop following me, Tom ...' she gently pleaded.

'But Mickey likes you!' He was gaining ground.

Delia suddenly found herself at a dead end. It was dark and she was trapped. She looked about and saw the shadow of a halberd that was hanging on a wall. She grabbed hold of it, grateful that it lifted off easily. It was heavy and she held it in both hands. 'Come another step nearer and I swear I'll chop Mickey's head off. He won't like that, will he?'

Tom stopped a few metres from her. The sight of the halberd and the threat of what she might do with it deflated Mickey's ardour, and he quickly retracted back into his nest. 'But Eve, we do love you ... honest ...'

'Get back to your bloody room now, before I use this!' she shouted, having finally lost all patience.

A door at the side opened and a man's shadowy silhouette appeared. 'What's going on? Tom, is that you ...?'

'Hi, Rich.' Tom waved a friendly hand.

'What are you doing up here?' Richard came out into the corridor. He was wearing a towelling robe. He saw Delia clutching the halberd.

'We were just playing a game, weren't we, Eve?' Tom seemed to have no notion that he had done anything wrong.

'Everything all right, Eve?' Richard could see that she was flustered and breathing heavily, slightly out of breath.

'It is now ...' She felt silly holding the halberd. Richard came across, and she could smell his freshly-showered body as he took it off her and hung it back on the wall.

'Go back to your room now, please, Tom.' Richard said it very gently but authoritatively.

'Goodnight Rich … Goodnight Eve …' Tom answered cheerfully, as if nothing had happened, and happily disappeared out of sight.

'Sorry if we disturbed you. Tom just got a little carried away …'

'In what way?'

'He got a bit excited, that's all …'

'Did he expose himself? Well, did he?' Her tone hadn't convinced him.

Delia nodded and then started to cry. The day had finally caught up with her.

'Come in for a moment.' Richard put his arm around her and brought her into his bedroom. 'Sit down. Would you like a drink?'

Delia nodded and did her best to take control of herself. While Richard poured them both a glass of whiskey, she wiped her eyes and took in the room. It was very functional, without any frills. A small television was positioned where it could be seen from the bed. The picture was still on, but the sound had been turned off. He handed her a glass.

'I'm sorry if Tom upset you. One of these days he'll go too far in the wrong company.'

'I know he didn't mean any harm. It's just a bit disconcerting being chased by an erect penis called Mickey …'

'Mickey …' Richard couldn't help but find it amusing.

'Do all men give them names?'

'I don't know. I certainly haven't christened mine. Are you all right now?'

'Thanks, you've saved me once more.'

'From a fate worse than death?' Richard smiled. The whisky had relaxed him and his manner was less formal.

'Has Tom ever … ever forced himself on a woman? You said something earlier about him interfering with the staff?'

'We lost one maid because he kept on patting her bottom. Another complained because he squeezed her breast while pretending a spider was crawling up it. He has been known to do the occasional streak in the gardens …'

'But nothing serious?' She saw Richard smile to himself. 'What?'

'We had an assistant gardener. Her name was Donna. Australian. Pretty little thing, full of fire and expletives. Tom took quite a shine to her. Hung around the gardens and got quite friendly with her. One afternoon, while she was working in one of the glasshouses, Tom decided to expose himself … give Mickey an airing, so to speak.' Richard stopped momentarily, grinning at the memory.

'Poor girl. What did she do?'

'Something that Tom couldn't cope with. Apparently Donna dragged him to the ground and tried to seduce him. She was willing – but he wasn't able. Ran a mile and never bothered her again.'

'Mickey turned out to be a disappointment then. So I really had nothing to fear.'

'No … at least I wouldn't have thought so. A top up?'

'Please.' Delia held out her glass. He leant across and tilted the bottle to pour. As he did so, his towelling robe parted slightly and she caught a brief glimpse inside. Richard was wearing nothing underneath.

'Say when …' He wasn't aware that she had seen anything – but very surprised when she started to untie the belt and then opened the robe fully. 'Eve, what are you doing?'

'Now I can see that you and Tom aren't related. He should rename his Mickey *Mouse*.' It wasn't so much the whisky that had gone to her head, but Richard's close proximity and a sight that had made her light-headed like so many others before her.

Richard stood there aware that all his control was hastily disappearing. The look in Delia's eyes and the way she eased his robe off his shoulders left him with no alternative. He recognised how much he wanted her, and how he had tried to suppress his feelings all day. Now there was no going back – because what was pointing forward, left neither of them in any doubt as to what was going to happen next.

Delia trembled as he quickly undressed her and lay her back on the bed. He was too impatient for any foreplay. He climbed on top and gently entered her. She gasped as she felt him moving inside of her and was about to close her eyes and drift into ecstasy – when she caught sight of something on the television, which was still on. 'Oh, my god!' she suddenly shouted.

Richard thought she was shrieking with passionate delight until he felt her wriggle underneath him. 'I'm not hurting you …?'

'Oh, shit, shit, shit, shit, shit!' Delia looked distinctly annoyed as her whole body went limp.

'Eve?' Richard rolled over to the side. He couldn't understand what was happening.

'It's not Eve … My name is Delia Hayward … I'm married to a Junior Minister at the Treasury …' Her eyes didn't leave the television screen. Richard followed her gaze and saw a picture of Thomas Lane, the Prime Minister, at some conference.

'It's only the news … What's happened? Has your memory returned?'

'With a bloody vengeance! That man you see up there is an impostor, and the whole reason why I was where I was.'

'I'm sorry, I don't understand.' He saw before him another person. All the gentleness and serenity had been exchanged for anger and despair.

'Seeing his smug face brought it all flooding back to me. God, I wish you'd never found me. I wish I was dead.' Delia started to cry.

Richard instinctively took her in his arms. 'I don't wish you were dead.' He meant it. 'Now what's all this about …?'

'You'll never believe me – but I can prove it. Serena and Melissa, they must wonder where I am. I've got to get to them, I've got to get to them now!' Delia's head was cluttering up and she was beginning to mutter. 'I've got to get to them!' She started to get off the bed.

Richard forcefully restrained her. 'You're not going anywhere until you've told me what this is all about.'

'You won't believe me.'

'Try me …'

40

'Okay, time for some action.' Terry looked at his watch.

'I thought you would never ask.' Rory fluttered his eyelids deliberately.

'For fuck's sake, stop pissing about and let's get on with it.'

'That's exactly what I said to a man in a urinal once.'

Terry was on the verge of really losing his temper, but quickly remembered a saying his father used in moments like this: *'Never argue with a customer whose words are empty. Flip a flippant remark on it's head with a smile.'* 'So, Rory, my friend, is it true your mouth is bigger than your cock?' Terry forced a smile and saw that Jack and Archie were smiling too.

Rory pursed his lips as if he was about to lose his cool, followed by an awkward moment of silence. 'You know what, petal …?' Rory visibly relaxed. 'A blow job's nice – but not if you're going to choke yourself.'

'Thank you for that, Rory.' Terry did his best not to react. 'Talking of jobs – who's it to be for the recce?'

'I'll go.' Archie was the first to volunteer. He was bored lying about in that room.

'I'll come with you.' Jack wanted some fresh air.

'I'll get me handbag and we'll all go.' Rory wasn't going to be left out.

'Your enthusiasm impresses me, but for the time being, so as not to arouse any unnecessary interest, it's best if just one of you does the initial recce of the house. It's only fair to do this democratically. I'm just as keen to get out of this place as the rest of you.' Terry took the newspaper and tore off three different-sized strips. Turning his back on them, he rearranged the strips so that the tops looked equal. 'Short strip does the recce. Who's first?'

Rory took hold of a strip and pulled it out. 'My that's a long one! First time I've ever wished to pull a little one …'

Jack was next and pulled out a much smaller one. Then Archie took the second longest. 'My shout then.' Jack was pleased to be doing something useful.

'Be careful, but be back within the hour.' Terry glanced at his watch again.

'Will do.' Jack was by the door.

'Send us a postcard.' Rory went to the corner of the room and started doing various stretching exercises.

'You take care now.' Jack smiled at Rory and exited.

'What are you doing now?' Terry stood with his hands on his hips.

'I'm limbering up, petal. You'd have a body like mine if you took more exercise.' Rory gestured toward Terry's slight pot belly. Terry looked down and had to agree. He was a bit out of shape. 'I've always looked after myself since I was a kid. Had to. Being camp was one thing, but not having a dad made things specially hard. I had to fight all my own battles.'

'What happened to your father then?' Archie asked.

'No idea. Mum never talked about him. Said she had a brief affair.' Rory stretched forward and back, demonstrating how elegantly supple he was.

'So you never knew who your dad was?' Terry was seeing another side to Rory.

'No. Mum once let out that my dad didn't even know I existed – because she never told him about me,' Rory said without any self pity.

'Do you think your mother will ever tell you who he was, or is?' Archie sympathised.

'She's dead now. I'll never know …' Rory deftly touched his toes a dozen times. 'I always imagined I was the product of a love liaison that was destined never to be happy. My mother, young and single; my father, married to someone else. Probably in high society and couldn't afford a scandal …'

'You think you've got blue blood in you, then?' Terry could see an element of the aristocrat in Rory in spite of his effeminate antics.

'Nothing less than a Lord. Nothing less …' Rory smiled at them both before crouching on the floor to go through a set of press-ups.

Scott and Stella, their relationship on a completely new footing, polished off a bottle of champagne and both got rather giggly. Stella was more at ease, and Scott no longer felt he had to perform either in or out of bed. There were no more expectations of each other. It was an opportunity simply to enjoy each other's company without any strings or hidden pressures. Since the champagne had gone to their heads, Stella suggested a brief stroll round the village to get some air. Scott held his mobile just in case Rory rang with any further developments.

It was while they were on their way back to the pub, down a road that was very dark, that they both heard someone fart in the distance. They couldn't see anyone, but the sound, which seemed to echo in the dull silence, caused them both to start giggling uncontrollably. Another loud pop really got them going and they hurried toward the pub before they wet themselves with laughter.

Jack momentarily froze when he heard the giggles. The very strain of keeping still made him fart again, which turned the far off giggles to laughter. He thought it was probably a courting couple out for a walk. There was something about the giggle that reminded him of Stella. She always giggled like that whenever she'd had too much to drink.

Jack relaxed when he heard them disappear in the other direction. He walked leisurely but steadfastly toward Cloudsey House. The sea air felt fresh and invigorating. He was glad to get out of that room and away from the others. He didn't dislike his companions but felt he had nothing in common with them. This whole mission was turning into a kind of charade where no-one really knew what they were doing. It wasn't the first time he'd been involved in an operation that had no momentum or direction. Those in command hoped that the troops would sort it out, while the troops relied on orders to guide them. Neither wanted to take responsibility and both would accuse the other if anything went wrong. At this stage Jack felt it best to take matters cautiously and rationally. This little recce might very well turn out to be a damp squib and they'd all be back where they started.

There were lights on in the house, but from a distance Jack couldn't detect any movement inside. On the ground floor all the curtains had been drawn. No vehicles appeared to be parked nearby. He crept slowly toward it, making sure he wouldn't be seen if anyone happened to look out of the window. Thankfully, there were no other buildings close to, so Jack was quite invisible in the surrounding darkness. As he got closer he saw some tyre marks on the grass. There was enough light to be able to see the distinctive pattern, which Jack recognised as being identical to that of the Skoda found in the field. He felt elated. There *was* a connection. He stealthily crawled on his stomach toward the building. He had to find out as much as possible before reporting back.

He sat with his back against the wall just below one of the windows, listening for any sounds. He heard nothing, so he crawled across to below another window and put his ear to the glass.

'We're imprisoned in here,' a nervous female voice declared.

'Serena, they're going to kill us, aren't they?' another woman answered, sounding even more frightened.

'They've got rid of Delia, Melissa, and we're going to be next …'

The second woman raised her voice: 'Don't point that gun at me like that!'

Jack then heard a crash before everything went silent again. He had heard enough. The situation was serious, and the quicker he got back to the others, the quicker something could be done about it. He crawled until he was far enough away from the building, then got up and briskly started to jog back to the pub.

Inside the house, Melissa and Serena were having another crisis of confidence. As the hours had gone by, they had become even more nervous and insecure. They just did not know what to do. At the point when Jack was by the window they were nagging at each other.

'They've got rid of Delia, Melissa, and we're going to be next …' Serena was waving the gun about in a nervous gesture, and accidentally directed it toward Melissa.

'Don't point that gun at me like that.!' Melissa protested.

Serena was so tense that she waved her arm away, causing the gun to strike a china ornament, sending it crashing to the floor. For a full minute no-one said anything, as they both sat silently down on the sofa, exhausted. They would have been even more perturbed if they had known that someone had been crawling about outside the house, spying on them.

'I'm sorry, Serena. The nerves are a bit jagged.'

'Me too. The last thing we should be doing is bickering with each other.' Serena put her hand on Melissa's arm. 'So what's the answer?'

'It's too late and too dark to do anything practical. I think all we can do is wait until morning, and then if we haven't heard, do something constructive.'

'But what?' Serena felt they had gone over this several times.

'I don't know. I just don't know. My mother always used to say that if you've got a problem and you don't know what to do about it – sit on it. Don't do anything too impulsive. Then, when some time has passed, either the solution will come to you or it will have resolved itself.'

'Do you think, perhaps, that we should ring Jeremy and see if he's heard from Delia?' Serena wasn't happy simply to do nothing.

'Definitely not.'

'Don't you want to talk to Simon?'

'Not particularly – and neither must you talk to Matthew. We all agreed beforehand that we wouldn't involve our husbands until it was absolutely necessary.' Melissa wondered what she would actually say to Simon when the time came.

'Isn't it necessary now ...?' Serena didn't want to give up.

'I'm going to be honest with you, Serena. This whole escapade has made me think. I've decided to leave Simon once all this is over.'

'What ...?' Serena was genuinely surprised. 'I thought you and he ...'

'All on the surface, I'm afraid. Everything's always been so squeaky clean in our boring marriage. I want to change it for a bit of dirt and excitement. Have I shocked you?'

'I suppose I'm surprised, but not horrified.'

'You and Matthew are very happy, aren't you?' Melissa watched Serena's shoulders twinge.

'We jog along ...'

'Jog along? What kind of an answer's that? Either you're happy or you're not.'

Melissa's remark made Serena think. Was she honestly happy? The events and experiences of the last 48 hours had created a kind of vacuum in her mind. She no longer saw Matthew in a normal light. It was as if he was detached from her in some way. Serena found it difficult to try to classify her feelings toward Matthew and her marriage. 'I don't know. Everything's out of context. Can you understand that?'

'Yes – only too well.' Melissa could see Serena struggling with her conscience. This experience was affecting them all. 'You know what I'd like right now?'

'What?' Serena wondered if Melissa was thinking about food again.

'A man ...'

'A man? In what way?'

'Oh, Serena, you can be so naïve sometimes! A man to give me a good seeing to. Sex, Serena, sex! If only one could pick up a phone, and like ordering a take-away, order a male of your choice. No love, no complications, no worry of catching anything. Just a good honest fuck ... Don't you feel like that sometimes?'

'There's only ever been Matthew.'

'Have you never done it with anyone else?' It was the first time Melissa had asked Serena such a frank question.

'No ... only Matthew.'

'So you can't tell whether he's good or bad. Does he give you orgasms?'

'I suppose so.' Serena imagined that the little pleasure she got from intercourse was an orgasm.

'That feeling when everything is bliss and nothing else matters.' She looked at Serena, who appeared slightly puzzled. She could tell that Serena had never experienced a real one. 'That's what I'd like now, a couple of hefty orgasms to make me forget the bloody mess we're in at the moment. I suppose Henry, upstairs, would be better than nothing.'

Serena really looked shocked now. 'Henry? Surely you wouldn't ...?'

'You've got quite a soft spot for him, haven't you? I've noticed the way you look at each other. I'm sure he would happily oblige. Perhaps you should go up and get that release that we both could do with.' Melissa saw Serena visibly blush. She had obviously hit a nerve somewhere, because Serena looked confused and awkward.

'Melissa, that's not very nice.' She tried to hide the feelings that were stirring up inside her.

'Honesty does bring out the worst in me, I'm afraid. Don't worry, I won't force myself upon poor Henry. He's probably so confused about everything that he wouldn't be able to rise to the occasion anyway. I'll just have to do with the next best thing – food.' And Melissa meandered off to the kitchen to see what was left.

Melissa certainly had struck a chord in Serena's own flustered thoughts. The very idea of seeing Henry naked again, and on top of her, stirred up and brought to the surface complex buried emotions. So disturbed was she by what she felt, both in her mind and in her body, that she followed Melissa to the kitchen to get some food herself.

'That's our target all right,' Jack announced as he entered the room.

'Are you sure?' Terry's relaxed body stiffened.

'No doubts – on two counts. One, car tracks outside the house match the ones we saw in the field. That Skoda broke its journey and took the hostages there. Two, I heard women's voices from inside. There was talk of them being shot, and of one of them having possibly been dispensed with already. The names Delia, Melissa and Serena were mentioned. Someone was holding them at gunpoint, and I think he might have struck one of them.' Jack was thorough in his account.

'Delia Hayward, Melissa Dodson and Serena Croome … those are our ladies.' Terry held up his phone showing the photographs of the women to refresh their memory. 'What about the terrorists?'

'Couldn't tell. But it's a difficult place to try to storm. It's not your ordinary house.'

'What problems did you see?'

'Well, it's a funny, thin building. Very tall, like a windmill but without the sails. There's the front and garden entrance and a number of possibly accessible windows quite high up. I noticed one of the top windows was open.'

'What would you suggest?'

'Have you got any ropes and securing hooks?'

'Sure, in the van. What's on your mind?'

Jack got a piece of paper and pen and started to draw a rough sketch of the house. 'If one of us climbs up the side without making any noise, we could get in that way and surprise them.'

'If you don't mind me saying,' Rory interjected, 'that's like putting all your balls in one pair of briefs. Wouldn't it be better if the offensive was conducted in a two-way manoeuvre? Two of us climb up on each side, while the other two are by the front and back entrances ready to force their way in there?'

'It might work …' Archie wasn't convinced.

'Of course it will work, you silly old queen! Unless you've got a better suggestion?'

Archie couldn't think of one. 'I'll stay on the ground if no-one objects.'

'Don't worry, I'll do the climbing – with Jack here, if he's amenable. Terry, you could take the front door, while our friend Archie takes the back.' Rory looked at Terry, who was eyeing him very seriously. 'Whoops, sorry dear! I've rather dominated the action.'

'It sounds pretty plausible to me.' Terry had been listening intently and was pleased that they were thinking logically and positively. Perhaps there was still a chance for them to redeem themselves. 'All I would add is that we have to attack at precisely the same moment, so as to catch them completely unawares. Strike at them from the top, strike at them from the bottom —'

'Don't get me too excited!' Rory quipped.

'–and we should have it all under control within seconds.' Terry finished. 'Any other *sensible* suggestions before we work out the details?'

Everyone nodded. For the first time that evening the adrenaline had started to flow between them. This was what they were trained for. For the rest of the inhabitants of Perdsea, their day had ended. For our group of Forces Against Rebellious Terrorists – the day was only just beginning.

41

' … I was on my way to get rid of the car when the crash happened. That's when you spotted me …' Delia had come to the end of her story.

'It sounds all so farfetched and ridiculous – that it must be true.' Richard was sat up in bed.

'So you believe me?'

'I have to admit that I was rather surprised at the change in the Prime Minister's character. One moment a dull, blundering oaf; the next, a witty and amusing personality. We all rather accepted it because there was no reason not to. The image-makers had done a top class job.' Richard was trying to get to grips with these revelations.

'The documents and photographs categorically prove that a double took Thomas Lane's place. Alex Brook and Charles Carter masterminded the whole deception.'

'What about the real Prime Minister? What about his wife, Pamela?'

'They must be in on it as well.'

'If this is true – the implications could have catastrophic consequences …' Richard looked at it as a politician, and was thinking of the effect it would have on the Government and the whole country.

'I know, that's why we stole the papers in the first place.' Delia could see his interest intensifying.

'I must see these papers … that is, if you want to involve me.'

'Do you want to be involved?'

'The wrong person is running this country and everyone must be made aware of it.' Richard's sense of justice came to the fore.

'My very sentiments. That is, if it's not too late …'

'How do you mean?'

'Anything could have happened. Once the Prime Minister and his conspirators realise their futures are in jeopardy, they'll do everything in their power to safeguard his secret and position. Poor Melissa and Serena, they might even be dead by now. I got them into this …' Delia flopped back on the bed.

'You mentioned a hostage?'

'Yes. What if he's managed to escape or harm them? Oh, it's all too horrible to contemplate. I don't know what to do … I'm sorry, Richard, I don't want to involve you.'

'I think I'm involved already.'

'You don't have to be.' Delia brushed her hand across his arm.

'But I want to. If you still want me to, that is?'

'Yes … thank you.' She smiled.

'Then our only alternative is to get to Perdsea and see if your friends are still there.'

'What – now?'

'Not *right* now … I think we've got a bit of unfinished business to complete first …' Richard stroked Delia's thigh. 'That is … if regaining your memory hasn't changed everything?'

'Not at all. Where exactly were we …?' Delia lay back on the bed and happily watched Richard climb on top of her.

Pamela Lane gently moved, having been on top of Thomas. She looked at him as he lay there in a contemplative mood, half fulfilled, half still wondering how it would all end.

'You were very restrained tonight.' Pamela stroked his face.

'Didn't you enjoy it? I thought—'

'Not that, silly! John Thomas Lane never disappoints me.' She patted the bulge, still noticeable under the sheet. 'I meant the dinner with the Ambassador.'

'Oh. I'm afraid I just couldn't be bothered. My mind was elsewhere, as you can well imagine. Still, it wasn't a complete waste of time. I've managed to persuade him to ask the President if we might spend some time at Camp David for a little holiday – that is, if I'm still in office and haven't been sent to the Tower for treason …'

'I'm sure it'll sort itself out.'

'One way or the other …' As he took in a deep breath, the bedside phone rang. 'Yes? … Alex, what news? … Where? … Perdsea … Good … Does anyone else know? … Good … We will try to limit any casualties, I hope … Yes, I am fully aware that the documents are vital – but I don't want this to turn into a bloodbath unnecessarily. People come before papers. Do you understand? All right, keep me up to date … Thanks …'

'Developments?'

'It appears the hostages have been located in a house in Perdsea.'

'Where's that?'

'East Anglia, on the coast. There's an assault planned within the next couple of hours. Then we'll know what the damage is …'

'So there's still some hope?'

'A day in politics is a long time … casualties can fall by the hour.'

'Oh dear, there's one casualty already …' Pamela pointed to his limp member. 'We'll have to see if we can quickly revive him.'

'Pamela – I'm sorry.' Thomas gently held her back. 'I do love you, but I need to prepare myself – for any eventuality.' It was the first time he had ever refused her since they had known each other.

'And because I love you too – I do understand.' She wasn't put out.

'I have a feeling it's going to be a long night …' Thomas took her in his arms and they just lay there in a quiet embrace.

Alex sat in his study, having just put the phone down to Thomas Lane. He wasn't happy at all. He'd already talked to Charles about the latest developments. Charles had reiterated that they couldn't afford *any* oversights at this stage. There was too much at stake and they *had* to retrieve those papers – at any cost. He looked at his watch. Should he tell Charles what the PM had said? No, after all, weren't they supposed to be in charge? Thomas was their responsibility, and their livelihoods depended on keeping him in office.

Alex convinced himself that it was for the good of the country, and then picked up the phone again, punching in a number that he had on a piece of paper. He waited for a few seconds. He prayed he wasn't going to be too late. 'Come on … come on … answer! Terry, you haven't left yet … Good … I know I wasn't going to phone you, but I've just spoken to the Prime Minister … Yes … The papers are the *priority* … Yes, that is your primary target, and *nothing*, I repeat, *nothing*, must get in the way of retrieving them, do you understand that? I appreciate that your primary duty was to observe and then judge, but that's all changed. You must now take *complete* control. And as leader it is now your personal responsibility to guide matters to a victorious ending. *No-one* must stop you from seizing them … Yes, even if it does mean there are … losses … Understand? Yes, the hostages must be saved, but let me reiterate – the papers come before anything else. And once you have got them, and I mean just *you*, you hold on to them until I arrive and *personally* relieve you of them. Under no circumstances must you read those documents. They are highly confidential and of no use to you. If you succeed there will be high promotion plus one hundred thousand pounds. If you look at the contents, you might find you have not long to live … I wish you luck, and the PM has every confidence in you …'

Alex put down the phone. His hands were sweating. Suddenly he felt nauseous and had to run to the bathroom to be sick.

42

Terry looked down on his phone, ruminating on what Alex had just told him. This certainly was a high profile operation with everything at risk, including their lives. And now it was up to him to lead his merry men and bring the mission to a satisfactory conclusion – regardless of the lives that might be endangered.

Terry had always been ambitious, a fighter, and had gone by the book. Orders were there to be obeyed. He saw in this mission an opportunity to better himself, to step up another rung of the ladder in a white man's world, to prove that a black boy originally from the streets of Shepherd's Bush could achieve respectable success. He had only ever killed one man in his life. That had been in Belfast during a sniper attack. After that experience he had promised himself that as long as he lived he would never unnecessarily take another person's life. He was determined to abide by that principle, despite what Alex had suggested in between the lines. He wasn't going to kill needlessly just because of some papers. He would do it his way and hopefully achieve the same results with the least amount of fatality. This had been his brief to the others and he was going to stick to it, whatever Alex had implied during their last conversation.

'Was that the big boss?' Rory asked.

'We've got the green light,' Terry answered seriously.

'Pity it's not the red light – then we could let trade commence, as a friend of mine used to say.' Rory had come in during the last part of the conversation. He had pretended to go to the toilet, but had surreptitiously sneaked outside to make his own call to Scott to tell him of the plans for the assault.

'You equate everything with sex, don't you?' Terry looked across at Rory, who had started blackening up his face in preparation.

'The world couldn't turn without it. If we fought with our cocks, instead of guns, there'd be less death and more pleasure.' Rory smiled.

'It would give new meaning to the phrase full frontal assault!' Archie chipped in, his face now looking like a blacked-up minstrel's.

They all laughed. It was a humorous release from the tension they were all feeling. A mission like this, with the possible dangers it involved, created a lot of nervous and expectant energy. They had all gone through it many times, but the emotions generated in preparation always followed one of three patterns. There would be humour, anger or total silence. Anger could spawn fights, while silence produced an atmosphere of fear that no-one wanted to own up to. Humour was always the most healthy sign. It could hide a multitude of personal insecurities. Rory, who had applied his blacking in a subtle and expert way, looked at Jack and Archie, who had overdone their camouflage. 'You two look like refugees from a Brixton ghetto.'

'At least we won't be seen in the dark,' justified Jack.

'As long as you don't flash those white eyes or smile with those pearly white teeth,' Rory mocked, and then noticed Terry looking at him. 'No offence, Terry.'

'None taken. You all look a bloody sight. I don't have that problem.' Terry smiled.

'You're lucky. It's hell for the complexion. I always come out in spots after a night mission.' Rory glanced at his image in the mirror.

'Right, are we all ready?' Terry acknowledged their nods. 'Now remember everything I told you. Don't shoot unless you're being shot at – and then aim to wound, not to kill. Is that clear? Good. Your responsibility will be to disarm and capture the terrorists; my job will be to act as backup and to appropriate the documents. Is that understood? Right, before we go, any questions?'

'Has the contest been aborted?' asked Archie.

'Aren't we still supposed to be competing against each other?' Jack added.

'The prime objective is to succeed as a team,' Terry replied.

'Have I lost all my Brownie points then?' Rory smiled.

'Look, guys, we're all in this together. What started off as a departmental challenge has developed into something more serious. I guarantee that if we triumph tonight we're *all* going to be rewarded – probably by the Prime Minister himself.'

'No less than a knighthood, I hope. Or a couple of young knights would do nicely,' Rory added.

'I suppose it's par for the course,' Archie sighed. 'You're told one thing and it's often superseded by something completely different. We should all be used to it by now.'

'Bullshit, to give its official name,' Jack agreed with Archie.

'I'm with you on that, fellas,' said Terry. 'My arse – and I'll have no comments from you, Rory – is right on the line. I stand to lose more than any of you if we foul up. So let's just forget the reason we were brought into this and make the best, more than the best, of what's in front of us now. Understand?' He gave them all a look challenging them to contradict him. No-one had anything else to say. 'Okay. We'll take my van away from the pub and park it somewhere more discreet – where I'll issue firearms and the rest.'

They all collected their things, since it was unlikely that they'd return to the pub. Terry had paid in advance to cover this eventuality. He was the first out of the room and made sure that no-one was about. He walked to the stairs, and seeing that the coast was clear, motioned to the others to follow him quickly out. Terry was out of the front door, with Rory next. Jack and Archie just reached the door when a voice spoke from behind them. 'Have a pleasant evening, gentlemen.'

'Thank you.' Archie was foolish enough to turn and face the manager, who took in the sight of his blackened face. Jack remained frozen, facing out.

'Off to a fancy dress party then?' the manager enquired.

'Going for a swim actually,' Archie answered quickly. He pointed to his face. 'It's good for the skin, keeps the salt from clogging up the pores.'

'Yes, sir. Do mind the jellyfish – they can give you quite a nasty sting ...' And the manager nonchalantly made his way into the bar. He was so used to seeing odd sights that he didn't give it a second thought.

'Shit – that was a close one,' Archie whispered to Jack.

'The night is still young ...' Jack replied somewhat dubiously.

Stella and Scott were upstairs in their room getting ready. The effects of the champagne had worn off, replaced by an overall feeling of flatness. Scott checked the camera and battery, while Stella struggled with the sound recorder, cursing under her breath. 'Are you all right?' Scott noticed her lips sneering.

'No.' She felt like throwing the recorder out of the window but managed to control herself.

'I'm not happy about going out at this time of night either – but that's how the cookie crumbles. God knows if we'll see anything ...' Scott wasn't as perturbed as he thought he would be. His whole perception of everything had radically changed and he didn't feel as anxious as he normally might in such a make-or-break situation.

'Your friend ... he's not buggering us about is he?' Stella said without thinking.

'Rory knows what he's doing – if that's what you *mean?*' Scott emphasised.

'How dangerous is it likely to be?' She ignored the remark.

'Possibly very dangerous. These terrorists won't surrender easily. They've got guns and are holding at least two women hostage.'

'The Junior Ministers' wives?'

'Yes. As long as we keep our distance we'll be safe. The plan is that when the house is stormed and the terrorists apprehended – we will then go in and record our exclusive. Piece of cake.'

'And if the terrorists kill everyone ...?'

'Then we disappear into the night as fast as bloody possible. Are you ready?' Scott was at the door.

'As ever I'll be ...' Stella looked in the mirror to make sure her make-up was okay, and then realised no-one would see her in the dark anyway.

Clutching the camera, Scott slyly came down the stairs with Stella and her recorder behind him. They looked like fugitives escaping from prison. At the bottom of the stairs the manager caught them as he came out of the bar door. He looked at the camera Scott was pressing to his body like a baby. 'Good evening sir, madam. Going swimming by any chance? Mind the jellyfish, they don't like being filmed ...' It was his little joke.

'Er, no ... Thought we'd try and see if we could get some shots of the moon and stars ... It's a very clear night.' Scott was grateful it was a clear night outside.

'I'd mind the bats if I were you, sir, they don't like having their picture taken either ...' The manager then left with a smirk on his face.

'I hope there aren't any bats out there, they make my flesh creep.' Stella shivered at the thought as she climbed into Scott's car.

'It's the terrorists we need to be wary of, not the bats.'

'I'd rather cope with people than flying monsters ...'

'They'll be a lot of things out in the air tonight. We just need to keep calm, keep alert and pray it goes our way.'

'And if it doesn't ...?' Stella looked at him.

'We could all end up dead,' Scott replied matter-of-factly.

43

A rabbit scurried across the road and then stood mesmerised by the headlights of the Range Rover. Richard braked to a stop and waited until it hopped off into the dark before resuming his journey.

'Jeremy wouldn't have stopped. He would have taken great pleasure in running the poor little thing over.' Delia put her hand on Richard's thigh as a sign of affection.

'Doesn't your husband like animals then?' Richard hated the thought of Delia having a husband who now was very real.

'He has a low regard for them. He loves fox hunting, grouse shooting. He's even attended illegal cockfights.'

'And you …?'

'I've never been a part of all that. It's the one thing Jeremy and I have always disagreed on.'

'Nothing else?'

'What?'

'That you disagree on?' Richard wanted to know as much as possible about her. She had been the first married woman he had ever slept with, breaking one of his own cardinal rules to never get involved with another man's wife. He had always been strong enough to resist the temptation. With Delia that control had evaporated. He couldn't and didn't want to resist, and their brief, hungry and wildly passionate union had only confirmed that Delia was more than just another sexual conquest.

'Lots of niggly things, you know. The usual.' Delia didn't want to talk about her marriage. It wasn't that she felt in any way guilty or disloyal to Jeremy, but she wanted the time that she spent with Richard to be theirs, without any reference to the real world.

'I'm sorry … if you feel I took advantage of you.' Richard's conscience wouldn't let him forget it.

'In what way?' Delia knew what he meant, yet wanted him to spell it out.

'Seducing you …'

'But that was *after* my memory returned,' she gently reminded him. 'It was me who took advantage of *you*. I wanted you.'

'And I wanted you.'

'So there isn't a problem. Is there?'

'Your husband?'

'I'm not worried about him. Jeremy has had affairs behind my back.'

'Delia, I'm not sure if an affair – between us – would be a good idea. I'll be perfectly honest, I've never been involved with anyone married before. It's not that

I don't … Oh, God, I'm not really putting this well.' His conscience, rather than his heart, was speaking.

'I agree. Affairs tend to create more problems than they're worth.' Although Delia was secretly pleased that she was the first, she was doing her best to react sensibly and rationally without allowing the heartache of a possible parting to take over her emotions. As a lover, Richard had excelled her expectations. She knew she would never find anyone like him again.

'I am … very fond of you … You should know that …' Richard found it difficult to find the right words without sounding mawkish.

'And I think you're a wonderful man. You saved my life and I will never forget it. Don't worry; I won't make things complicated for you.' She was desperate to say that she loved him as she had never loved anyone before, but she was afraid she would lose him forever if she told the truth.

'And I'll never forget you …' *Damn, damn, damn*, Richard cursed inwardly. Why couldn't he just tell her that he had fallen in love with her and that if she left her husband he would marry her. But he couldn't.

There was silence as they both desperately struggled with their thoughts and emotions. Neither was sure if their feelings would be reciprocated. They had come to an impasse and let the purpose of this journey dominate their present reflections. That at least would keep them together for the next few hours. Neither dared think further ahead or about the eventuality of having to go their separate ways.

'I'm praying that Serena and Melissa are still there …'

'And the documents, of course,' Richard added. 'If you've lost those it would all have been for nothing.'

'Not completely. I wouldn't have met you …'

'No …' Richard wanted to stop the car and take her in his arms, but his sense of purpose wouldn't allow him. Delia wanted him to turn in the opposite direction and drive them to an idyllic little cottage where they could spend the rest of their lives together. For a second they looked tenderly into each other's eyes – and at that very moment they heard a bang and the car jerked sideways. Richard's reactions were very quick and he managed to stop the car before it careered into the ditch.

'What happened?' Delia was back to hard reality.

'I think a tyre blew.' Richard took a torch from the glove compartment and got out of the car. He stood there shining it at one of the wheels, the tyre on which was visibly flat.

'Is it serious?' Delia got out and joined him.

'Puncture … That's all we need in the middle of bloody nowhere.' Richard was quite put out as he waved his arms to indicate the predicament they were in. They had been travelling on a B road and now found themselves right in the heart of the countryside. No lights could be seen for miles.

'Have you got a spare?' Delia surveyed the wheel.

'Of course, it's at the back.' Instead of going to the back, Richard opened the car door and took out his phone. 'The AA shouldn't be busy at this time of night … Oh, damn!'

'What is it?'

'We have three problems. One, I forgot to recharge the phone – it's dead; two, I don't exactly know where we are; and three, believe it or not – I've never changed a tyre in my life.' Richard did his best to make light of the situation, but was still quite concerned.

'That's what comes of leading a privileged existence. I bet you've never made a bed in your life either, have you?' Delia watched him stood there looking slightly helpless.

'Can't honestly remember ...' He smiled.

'Is there a jack in the car?'

'It's with the spare. Why?'

'We'll need it to change the tyre, that's why.'

'Do you know how?' Richard sounded quite surprised.

'I've managed to acquire dangerous firearms; infiltrate a government building; steal highly confidential papers; kidnap a hostage; and organise an escape by helicopter; and I'm about to bring down the government. Changing a tyre is no great shakes.' Delia was already folding up her sleeves. 'Besides, I once took a short course in car maintenance, and that was one of the first lessons.'

'You took a course? Whatever for?'

'Bloody mindedness, I suppose. I got fed up with garages trying to rip me off and blind me with science. But I shall need your assistance to do the heavy work.'

'I am at your bidding ...' Richard bowed like an obedient servant. He was glad that he'd changed into his ex-army surplus casuals for the trip.

'There isn't a moment to lose then.' There were other things Delia would have preferred to do with Richard, but this wasn't the time for wishful thinking. She was more concerned about getting to Perdsea and finding out if Melissa and Serena were safe.

Within 20 minutes the spare tyre had been successfully fitted. Delia had done all of the work, apart from unscrewing the nuts and lifting the wheel on and off. She had left that to Richard, who had never questioned anything but simply let her get on with it. He was impressed by her businesslike and professional attention to the job. He saw yet another admirable facet to her character, which made him feel even more captivated by her.

'Do you want me to drive?' she asked, wiping her hands on his handkerchief.

'I think I can handle that. Besides, no-one else is insured to drive this.'

'I didn't think of that,' she smiled, getting into the car.

Richard gave her an affectionate wink. He started the engine and they were away into the night.

44

Terry's van was parked down a dark lane about a quarter of a mile from Cloudsey House. He had picked a spot that wasn't near any houses or streetlights. They had all sat quietly for ten minutes to make sure the coast was clear.

'Was that you again, old chap?' Archie sniffed and then turned to Jack.

'Sorry everybody …' Jack smiled uncomfortably. The waiting had made him tense.

'Well we are known as the FART team. Might as well live up to it.' Rory deliberately farted to make his point.

'Rory, that was very crude, if you don't mind me saying.' Terry could do without this now.

'I don't mind you saying at all. Just keeping Jack company.'

Terry flicked a small torch onto his watch to check the time. 'Come on, let's get out of here before we die of asphyxiation. I think I'd rather be shot at than gassed.' He got out of the van and went and opened both back doors. Rory and Jack got out of the back to give Terry room to get at the relevant equipment. They all stood watching as he unlocked the hidden panels. After taking out some heavy-duty rope with the appropriate clasps and hooks, which he handed to Rory, he then put his hands on four small submachine guns and numerous rounds of ammunition.

'Serious stuff, eh …' Archie commented, admiring the feel of the gun that Terry gave him.

Terry then dug out four dark bullet-proof vests, throwing one to each of them.

'It doesn't match my ensemble.' Rory put it against what he was wearing. 'Have you got them in other colours?'

Terry smiled, grabbed hold of his gun and suddenly pointed the barrel at Rory's head. 'It also comes in blood red, my friend. Interested?'

'No, I suppose this'll have to do.' Rory realised that he had overstepped the mark once again.

'Any more clever wisecracks and I will get really angry – and you don't want to see that, my friends. Because when I get angry there are no rules in the book to cover it. You won't know what's hit you. Understand …?' Terry gazed at them all in turn until they each nodded in assent. 'Now I don't want to get heavy. We've enough to deal with, without smart arse comments. And by arse I mean you, Rory my friend. Let's all do the job that's been assigned to us.'

'Sorry, Terry. My mouth's always been two steps ahead of my brain.' Rory gave him his best smile as he put on his bullet-proof vest.

'Well get back in step – or I'll hit you with *my* handbag!' Terry wanted to show that he hadn't lost his sense of humour. He now made a final check to ensure they had everything they needed, then grabbed the binoculars, which he hung round his neck. 'Everyone clear about what they have to do? Good. Let's go and capture us some terrorists ...' Terry locked up the van and gestured for Jack to lead the way.

Once they got into a form of line, each deftly clutching their guns, they began to look and act like a troop of seasoned professionals. Their short journey toward the house was conducted with a series of looks and gestures. Nobody had to say anything. They became alert to every single night noise, and would turn their heads simultaneously if someone from a nearby house switched a light either on or off. They moved like a well-trained unit, each adapting to the other's pace, and they'd all stop at the same time if they heard any rustling, which usually turned out to be a cat or some other night creature. The tenseness had given way to a flow of adrenaline in anticipation of what lay ahead of them.

Inside the house, Melissa and Serena were completely oblivious to the activity that was developing outside. Finally accepting the fact that they wouldn't do anything or make any decisions until the morning, they made preparations to go to bed. Melissa was in the bathroom having a relaxing soak, while Serena was up in one of the bedrooms brushing her hair.

Serena looked at her tired, pale face in the mirror. What she needed was a good night's sleep, with a man beside her as protection. It wasn't Matthew that she immediately thought of, but Henry. She'd feel safe in his presence. No-one had been up to see Henry since he'd fallen asleep all those hours earlier. Melissa felt that they should leave him alone and had warned Serena not to go and disturb him. But the more she brushed her hair and thought of him, the more compelled she felt to see if he was all right.

Unconsciously she applied some lipstick before leaving the bedroom. She could hear Melissa humming to herself in the bathroom, so knew that she could take a peek at Henry without her knowing. Not wanting to act totally recklessly, Serena took one of the guns with her.

She quietly crept up the stairs and stood outside his bedroom. She put her ear to the door and could just hear snoring. Cautiously she put the key in the lock and lightly opened the door with one hand while holding the gun firmly in the other.

Henry was asleep, and his snoring came in fits and starts as if he was experiencing some strange dream. Serena couldn't help but take pity on his tormented expression, wondering what was going on behind his flickering eyelids. At least he didn't look too uncomfortable lying there in a foetal position, his hands and feet still tied. She felt impelled to stay for a moment, so sat on a chair near the bed and simply looked at him. His lank hair was greasy and his chin was stubbly. He had a kind and noble-looking face, with genteel features that made her feel safe as well as protective. Serena cast her eyes across his whole body, taking in every crease and curve, until she spotted a swelling below his waist. She continued to sit there, watching him sleep.

The lights of the house could now be clearly seen as the troop carefully progressed up the drive leading to the front entrance. They were only about a hundred metres away when they heard a distant rumble heading in their direction. As it got progressively louder, they could now see the glare coming from two powerful headlights that were turned on full beam. They all scattered just in time before the lights caught them. Guns vigilantly at the ready, our four soldiers hid behind trees or bushes and watched the Range Rover suddenly switch off its headlights and stop some distance from the house.

'It is an unusual-looking place.' Richard could see the silhouette of the building against the moonlight as they sat in the car.

'Lights are on. That's a good sign.' Delia was feeling nervous.

'Appearances can be deceptive,' he answered cautiously.

'You don't want to drive straight up to the house?'

'Better to do it quietly on foot, so as not to alert them – just in case all is not as it should be.' Richard leant over to the back seat and grabbed a rifle that he'd brought along for protection.

Jack eased himself over to where Terry was hiding and whispered: 'I don't like the look of that ... What d'you think?'

Terry put the binoculars to eyes and focused them on the car, but it was too dark to see anything inside. 'Could be a courting couple ... No, wait, someone's getting out. He's carrying a gun ...'

Richard opened the car door and jumped down, one hand holding the rifle. Delia opened her door, but as she put her foot on the ground it suddenly twisted, making her cry out. 'Ouch!'

'What's the matter?' Richard was at her side.

'I just twisted my ankle a bit. It'll be all right.' She stood for a second, but when she tried her first step, her leg gave way slightly. 'It's just a minor sprain. I can walk,' she announced stubbornly.

'I'll take your arm – don't argue.' Richard firmly grasped her left arm and helped guide her toward the house.

From Terry and Jack's point of view, as Richard and Delia neared the house and the light got better, it looked as if the man was forcing the woman toward the house. Terry looked through his binoculars again and managed to catch a clear enough glimpse of Delia's face, looking pained. 'That's one of the hostages all right,' Terry whispered across to Jack. 'He must have hit her in the car and now he's dragging her toward the house. God knows what he's done to her, the bastard.'

'I could immobilise him from here. Shoot him in the leg.' Jack had Richard in his sights.'

'No ... We've got to wait until they're all inside. If we do anything now, the others will be alerted. We've got to catch them all unaware.' Terry had another look through the binoculars. The man and woman were by the front door. He was still holding her arm with one hand while the other had the rifle poised.

The firm knock that echoed from the front door quickly brought both Melissa and Serena out of their separate revelries.

Melissa stood up from the bath and opened the bathroom door. 'Serena … are you there?' she called quietly.

Serena, who was still watching Henry, shocked herself back to reality when she heard the knock and then Melissa's call. Luckily Henry didn't stir, so she was able to leave the room without disturbing him.

The knock came again. 'Serena … !' There was a panic in Melissa's voice as she draped a towel over her ample body.

'It's all right, I'm here.' Serena had bounded down the stairs, the gun still in her hand.

'Who do you think it is at this time of night? Certainly not a collection for charity this time.'

'I don't know … I'm frightened …' There was another knock, which made them both jump. 'Should we answer it?' Serena didn't want to take the responsibility of making that decision.

'All right – I'll grab the other gun while you take a peep out of the curtains and see who it is.' Melissa, wrapping the towel across her, went with Serena to the front room where the second gun was lying. She picked it up, holding it in one hand while securing the towel in the other. 'Go on …'

Serena warily moved the curtain and looked out. 'It's Delia, it's Delia!' she excitedly exclaimed, and ran to the door. She didn't see Richard, who had decided to go round the back, since there had been no response to his knocks.

She opened the door and then instinctively flung her arms around Delia. 'We were so worried …'

'You were worried …' Delia extricated herself from Serena's grasp and walked toward Melissa, who was just standing there holding the gun. 'Melissa.'

'Where the *hell* have you been?' Melissa angrily waved the gun, and the jerky movement prompted the towel to slip to the floor. She stood there obliviously naked, looking directly at Delia.

'I can explain …' Delia couldn't help but stare at Melissa's plump frame, and thought that if she ever got that fat, she'd kill herself.

'And it had better be good!' Melissa was releasing all her pent-up anxiety.

'What happened?' Serena moved across the room.

'It's a complicated story. I lost my —'

'Hello …?' Richard appeared in the doorway, pointing his rifle. The sight of Melissa standing naked and holding a gun rather perplexed him. He didn't see Serena suddenly creep up from behind and hit the back of his head with the butt of her gun. Richard fell straight to the floor, knocked out.

'Jolly good show, Serena. Where on earth did *he* spring from?' Melissa pointed the gun down at him.

'Richard!' Delia crouched down to him.

'D'you know him?' Serena had surprised herself by her own impulsive and spontaneous action.

'I'll kill you if you've killed him!' Delia cradled his head in her lap, one of her palms already stained with a trickle of blood from the gash. 'Oh, Richard ... please don't die. I love you, I love you so much ...'

Melissa and Serena glanced at each other in a bewildered way. What was going on? Delia's eyes filled with tears and she desperately put her lips to his mouth and proceeded to blow in an awkward, amateur fashion. From their point of view it looked as if she was kissing him. 'Delia ...?'

'Do something, for god's sake! He came to help us. He might die ...' Delia, unable to revive him, pleaded with them in desperation.

'That's not how you do it.' Melissa passed her gun across to Serena, pulled Delia out of the way, and proceeded to give Richard a proper kiss of life in a very energetic way.

It wasn't long before Richard's body twitched. His arms flayed about and unconsciously grabbed Melissa's breasts in an effort to disentangle her lips from his. Instead of breathing life into him she was starting to suffocate him by the sheer force of her exertions. Eventually his strength overcame hers and he pushed her away so that she landed on his chest. He opened his eyes to see a large naked lady straddled on top of him. 'Where am I ...?' Richard couldn't fathom what was going on. Was he in the middle of some orgy, being ravished by this bovine beauty? Yet he still had his clothes on ...

'Get off, Melissa! Can't you see you're stifling him. Richard, are you all right?' Delia pushed Melissa off and knelt down beside him, cupping his face in her hands. 'It's Delia.'

'Delia ...?' Richard looked at her, trying to remember.

'Oh, dear god, I think he's lost his memory,' Delia panicked.

Richard's eyes wandered over to where Melissa was stood. 'Why haven't you got any clothes on?'

'Yes – *why* haven't you?' Delia repeated.

For the first time, Melissa became aware of her bare predicament. Automatically she crossed one arm over her breasts and the other over her pubic hair. She looked like one of Rubens' maidens. 'I ... I was having a bath when you knocked ...' she said apologetically.

'Melissa, you look ridiculous, go and get dressed.' Delia watched Melissa turn and quickly run up the stairs, trying to hide her enormous bottom with her small hands.

Delia turned back to Richard, who was now looking at Serena. 'Was it you who hit me?' He raised his head slightly, the pain still throbbing.

'I'm sorry ... I thought you had come to get us ...'

'Richard, it's Delia. Do you know who I am?' Delia gazed at him lovingly, inwardly praying that he would recognise her.

'How could I ever forget ...' he said with a smile.

'Thank God.' She gave him a hug.

'Delia ...?' Serena asked. 'What's going on? *Where* have you been all this time? I think you have a little bit of explaining to do ...'

45

Scott and Stella sat in the Porsche in the pub car park. For the last ten minutes Scott had been trying to get the car started. It had never let him down before, and since he wasn't mechanically inclined he didn't know what to check or look for. Since his mind was more preoccupied with thoughts of Rory and his own coming out, it was actually Stella who pointed out that the fuel gauge showed empty. Scott felt slightly foolish, but not upset. He discovered that the nearest petrol station was now closed, and no-one in the pub could help.

'There goes our lighting support,' Scott declared, getting out of the car.

'What now? Call it a day.' Stella was hoping he would abandon the whole prospect.

'Not likely, this is too big. Lights or no lights, we've got to get to the location.'

'How ...?'

'By foot, of course. It's not that far.' He strapped the camera over his shoulder. 'Come on, we'll be there in a jiff,' he said optimistically, having forgotten about the car.

'It's very dark out there ...' Stella looked up at the sky and imagined thousands of bats swooping on her.

'Because it's night, darling, that's why it's dark. Now get the recorder and let's toddle off before we miss anything. Okay?'

Stella nodded, still feeling a sense of dire anticipation, and wondering why she had agreed to participate in such a crazy escapade. She blamed Jack, the flatulent bastard – it was all his fault.

Jack was blissfully relieving himself against a tree. He'd been bursting and couldn't hold it in any more. In his professional career Jack had been taught to do many things, to overcome many problems – but controlling his bladder was one he'd never been able to master, particularly during an assignment.

'Hey man, watch where you're splashing!' Terry whispered, moving slightly sideways to avoid getting sprayed. He couldn't move further or he'd be in danger of being seen. They had watched Delia enter, soon followed by Richard, brandishing that rifle. Although they couldn't hear anything, apart from some raised voices, Terry sensed something had happened inside, because it went suddenly quiet.

'Sorry about that ...' Jack apologised, doing up his fly.

'Perhaps if I cut your dick off and shoved it up your arse you wouldn't need to piss or fart.' Terry's sense of decency had left him.

'I couldn't help it. Have I missed anything?' Jack changed the subject.

'Certainly not the tree. No – nothing. Wait a minute …' Terry looked through the binoculars and just caught sight of the front door being closed. 'Looks like that's it for the night. We'll give it five more minutes before you and Rory start scaling the house. Is that all right, or is there something else you need to do, umm?'

'I'm ready,' Jack answered defiantly, trying to ignore the rumbling he was feeling in his stomach.

Delia cleaned Richard's wound, while briefly outlining to Serena and Melissa, who was now dressed, exactly what had happened to her and how she had met Richard. Throughout, Richard remained silent, enjoying Delia's ministrations and watching the mixed expressions on the other women's faces. 'So if Richard hadn't come along when he did – I'd probably be dead by now,' Delia concluded.

'Not necessarily.' Richard felt embarrassed.

'But I know it, and I really believe in angels now,' Delia confirmed. 'He came out from the sky like Gabriel.' She looked at him lovingly.

'So you lost all that money?' Melissa folded her arms, eyeing Richard suspiciously. Who was this supposed saviour who had come from nowhere? Had he taken the money without Delia knowing? Before she'd come to?

'My bag disappeared and everything with it. Thank god the documents weren't in there. You have still got them, haven't you?'

'They're safe,' Melissa declared, not wanting to reveal any more.

'Good. I've been so worried.' Delia felt a sense of relief for the first time since she had set foot in the house.

'Delia was very concerned about both of you,' Richard backed her up.

'I'm sure she was …' Melissa looked at Richard, who was sat in the armchair. She could see how Delia clung on his every word. Was he too good to be true? Not Melissa's type, but nevertheless he appeared sincere enough. She just hoped that he wasn't using Delia for his own selfish ends.

'It's fortunate that her memory returned, or we wouldn't be here now.' Richard felt a twinge from his head as he adjusted his position in the chair.

'I'm really sorry I hit you.' Serena, unlike Melissa, had no doubts about Richard's motivation. She was sensitive to the adoring way he looked at Delia, and generally felt secure in his presence. She could also see that Delia had visibly changed since she'd left them. She appeared softer, as if the strain had been lifted from her face.

'Don't be. I'll live – which, I believe, is thanks to you, Melissa.' Richard smiled sincerely at Melissa, making her feel more confused about him.

'How have things been here?' Delia was starting to get back in control.

'Pretty quiet and uneventful.' Melissa didn't think it worth recounting the story of the charity bag, or her little walk.

'And Henry – I almost forgot. How is Henry?'

'Still asleep, I think. Upstairs and secure. Tried to escape once, but we soon scotched that little plan.'

'He hasn't given us any *real* trouble,' Serena added, defending Henry.

'Is this your hostage?' Richard asked.

Melissa felt enough had already been said. 'Delia, may I have a word, please – in private? Do excuse us.' Melissa surreptitiously took her gun and was already on her way to the kitchen.

'What is it, Melissa?'

Melissa closed the kitchen door and faced Delia. 'Do you trust this man Richard?'

'With my life,' she answered unequivocally.

'I appreciate that he might have saved your life and looked after you when you *lost* your memory …' Melissa was testing Delia.

'I did lose it, you must believe that. I wouldn't just have abandoned you and Serena for any other reason.'

'You're quite besotted with him, aren't you?'

'I love him,' was Delia's immediate answer.

'That's pretty strong, considering you only met him today.' Melissa thought the whole premise of love at first sight a lot of tosh.

'Love has no sense of time,' Delia replied without hesitating.

'And does he love you?'

'I don't know …'

'Have you, by any chance, slept with him?'

Delia knew what Melissa was getting at. 'Yes, and it was at *my* instigation. I've never met a man like him … I really don't care if you believe me or not. All I can say is that he's offered to help us, and I want him to. I've told him everything. Melissa, please, you have to trust him. On my life …'

Melissa thought for a moment. She had been a friend of Delia's for many years, and never once had she known Delia to act impulsively, behave capriciously over another man, or lie intentionally. Her responses to her questions sounded genuinely heartfelt. 'Who am I to argue in the presence of an angel?' Melissa smiled, a little jealous of what Delia had found.

Delia gave Melissa a warm hug. 'But you must promise me one thing.'

'What's that?' Melissa returned the embrace.

'He's mine – so keep your clothes on, there's a dear.'

'He might like the fuller figure …'

'That's what worries me. Come on, we've got a lot to catch up on and sort out.'

Delia opened the kitchen door and saw Richard and Serena in deep conversation. For a second she felt jealous and hoped that Richard wouldn't fall for Serena. That would be the final irony.

Rory crawled snakelike along the ground to where Terry and Jack were waiting. 'What's the hold up, fellas?' he whispered.

'Action stations in another couple of minutes. Archie okay?' Terry responded.

'He's having a discreet slash in the bushes.'

'I'm surrounded by weak bladders. Perhaps we should piss on the enemy instead,' Terry sighed.

'It's what I said before. Pricks out at the ready – and fire!' Rory giggled at the thought. 'Cockfighting would take on another meaning.'

'Thank you, Rory … Go back and tell Archie, if he's finished watering the plants, to stand by. We're off in 60 seconds.'

'Will do.' Rory immediately crawled back toward the bushes.

'You still happy about the climb?' Terry wanted to make a final check that Jack was suitably primed to go for it.

'I won't let you down, Terry,' he said reassuringly, gripping the ropes confidently.

'Okay … Remember, don't break in until you get the signal from me.'

'I understood the first time you said it.' Jack hated to be treated as if he was stupid.

'Well, I'm repeating it a second time – for luck.' Terry's attitude was to treat those under his command as if they were stupid.

Stella held on to Scott's arm as they slowly made their way toward the house. She kept looking up at the sky, searching for bats, imagining that they would swiftly dive and bite her on the neck, turning her into a vampire. 'What was that?' She tightened her grip when she heard some rustling in the undergrowth.

'Probably a snake …' Scott teased.

'You're not serious?' She stood absolutely still.

'No – now calm down, there's nothing to be afraid of. Scotty will look after you.'

'But who will look after Scotty?' Stella asked.

They resumed their journey in the dark, both a little more apprehensive about what they were going to meet around the corner.

With their ropes over their shoulders and their guns braced to their bodies, Jack and Rory silently entered the grounds of the house and nimbly scrambled toward the building, each taking an opposite side. Terry and Archie watched and covered them with their guns as they threw up the ropes and started, literally inch by inch, to scale the walls. Terry was impressed and pleased with the proficient way in which both pairs tackled this manoeuvre without making a sound. Step by careful step they both began their ascent.

'Rather them than me,' Archie whispered, 'Always had a touch of vertigo if ever I had to abseil.'

'Thanks for sharing that with me now.' Terry's brief optimism was flattened by Archie's crass remark. 'You do know how to use this gun, I hope?'

'No bullseye is safe in my sights.' Archie held the gun firmly.

'But what about people – ever shot at them?' Terry sarcastically replied.

'If I aim to kill, I kill. If I aim to wound, that is exactly what will happen. I only miss if I mean to.' Archie said it with such conviction that Terry realised it was best to shut up. Archie would soon be able to prove how good he was.

Like stalking spiders, Jack and Rory moved vigilantly up the wall, stopping every foot or so to listen to any sounds that might be coming from inside. This type of climb couldn't be rushed, since there was a danger of being heard if their feet or the rope clasps made any sound. It was like scaling an upright minefield. One wrong step and that would be it.

'They're good, aren't they?' Archie had to admit.

'Some way to go yet …' Terry knew that being overconfident often led to things going terribly wrong. He remembered another of his father's sayings: *'Just because there is no traffic and you're running ahead of schedule, that doesn't mean that the bus won't break down …*' It had taught Terry never to take things for granted.

'Shush … did you hear something then?' Archie stiffened.

'No.' Terry had heard nothing out of the ordinary.

'Footsteps … someone's coming up the drive …' Archie stood from his crouching position, holding his gun at the ready.

Terry honestly didn't hear a thing and wondered if Archie was starting to get jumpy. It regularly happened to troops during combat. Noises would be exaggerated, and men would often hear things that weren't there. 'Are you sure?'

'Permission to check?'

'Be quick about it.' Terry decided it would be easier to let him investigate than to argue about it. 'Back in two minutes sharp.'

'Yes, sir.' Archie moved away like a lion about to stalk a prey, disappearing into the darkness before Terry's eyes.

'That's the house, over there, behind those trees,' Scott whispered to Stella, who was still hanging on to him. They were on the drive to the house.

'Where …?' She was looking in the wrong direction.

'*There*, not there. See that little light at the top?'

'Oh yes …' Stella was suddenly aware of the deep silence that surrounded them. 'It feels very cold here … Know what I mean?'

'Temperature's gone down, that's all.' Scott also sensed the difference, but didn't want to worry Stella unnecessarily at that point. They took a few steps forward before he unexpectedly felt a metal object press at the back of his head.

'Don't move or say one word – or your head will no longer be attached to your body. That goes for you too, madam.' Archie spoke very quietly, having dug the muzzle of the gun into Scott's neck while grabbing hold of the nape of Stella's neck with the other hand. He had them both expertly under his control, certain that they were a part of the terrorist gang who had abducted the women.

Stella thought she recognised the voice but couldn't place it. She was so taken aback by this unforeseen ambush that she nearly wet herself with fright. Scott saw his life flash by and bemoaned the fact that he might never get to have his own coming out party.

'A camera and a recorder, eh. What's this for – filming women undergoing torture, is that it? Get a kick out of seeing people getting hurt?' Archie dug the muzzle in harder and squeezed Stella's neck tighter.

'I can explain …' Scott protested.

'I told you not to say a word.' Archie banged Scott on the head with the gun. 'Now drop that equipment slowly and move over toward those two trees. And don't turn around. One sound or one false move and you will both be food for the bats.'

As Stella put down the recorder and was pushed toward the trees she felt a warm trickle down her leg. The simple mention of bats had made her lose control. Thankfully it was only a trickle. Scott gently placed the camera on the ground, wanting to explain everything, but believing that this maniac – probably one of the terrorists – would sooner kill them, given any excuse.

'Right, I want you both to put your arms around one of the trees. Hug them tightly.' Archie was right behind them.

The two trees were close together and just thick enough for them both to be able to wrap their arms right round. Scott felt a dampness near his waist as he pushed himself against his tree. Had he known it was the very one Jack had urinated against only ten minutes previously, he would have been even more distressed. Archie now quickly frisked them both for any hidden firearms. He was careful with Stella and made sure he searched her in a decent and professional fashion. Although he didn't fully see her face, there was something about her that rang a bell, but he was too absorbed in what he was doing to make the connection with the woman who had made a fool of him in the bar.

From one of his pockets Archie took out a ball of strong cord, from another a small roll of parcel tape. He always carried such versatile objects on a mission, never knowing when they might come in useful. With his Swiss army knife, a box of matches, polythene bags and a pen torch, he was prepared for any eventuality. Luckily, this happened to be one of them. 'Now, I need a handkerchief …' He felt in Scott's pocket and produced a neatly-folded silk one. He tore it in half. 'Open wide … this won't hurt. Remember, one peep and I will surely kill you both.'

Scott and Stella were so terrified by now that they willingly opened their mouths and let Archie stuff a piece of handkerchief in each. Then he applied a strip of tape over their lips. 'Keeps temptation at bay. What you don't say, no-one will hear …' Archie bound both their hands together in front of them, and as a second measure also tied their legs to the tree. 'There, that should keep you out of mischief until we've sorted the rest of you out.'

'*What* is going on?' Terry was standing there brandishing his gun.

The surprise almost caused Archie to fire at him. He lowered his gun immediately. 'Sorry, a couple of unwelcome visitors. They're part of the gang.'

'I see …' Terry looked at how proficiently Archie had secured them. He wanted to ask more questions, but time was running out. 'They're at the top already. It's time for the assault. Good work; we'll deal with these two later. Now get in position at the back door.'

'Those terrorists won't know what's hit them!' Archie declared.

'Let's hit first before congratulating ourselves.' Terry was ever cautious.

46

Delia, Melissa and Serena all sat on the sofa watching Richard in the armchair going carefully through all the documents and photographs. His expression changed continually as he studied the notes. There were looks of surprise, intrigue and sheer incredulity at what he saw before him. 'Well … well … well …' he finally declared, bundling up the papers in his lap and smiling at the women.

'Well what?' Delia felt a tinge of uncertainty

'This is extraordinary … truly extraordinary. Can I ask you all one question? What did you propose to do with these?'

Melissa and Serena automatically turned to Delia, who responded. 'Expose the Prime Minister, of course.'

'How?'

'How?' Delia was slightly thrown.

'In what way did you plan to do that? How were you going to use this information?'

'Release it to the press – and let them bring it all to light.'

'For a price, of course.' Richard looked at Delia.

'Well, we intended to do it somewhat anonymously. Make sure it got into the right hands and leave it to them to deal with it. Didn't we?' Delia turned to the others for corroboration.

'That's true,' Melissa confirmed. 'Although we hadn't agreed upon which paper to give the exclusive to. I favoured the *Independent*, Delia, *The Times*, while Serena preferred either the *Telegraph* or the *Observer*.'

'We didn't want to implicate our husbands in any way,' Serena added.

'And they, presumably, don't know what you've done?' Richard looked at Delia.

'No.'

'How were you going to explain your sudden disappearance?' Richard was keen to know if they had thought this through.

'We'd say we've all been on a short holiday together. It might sound odd, but our husbands wouldn't question it. Melissa, Serena?'

'They're often too busy with their work to bother if we're around or not. We all went to Paris for the weekend once, and they didn't even realise that we'd left.' Melissa remembered how Simon hadn't noticed her absence.

'You've all gone to a lot of trouble over these,' Richard declared enigmatically, shuffling the documents.

'You're not about to tell us that we've wasted our time, are you?' Delia was still unable to gauge what Richard was thinking.

'Quite the opposite,' he smiled. 'The proof couldn't be *more* conclusive.'

The women all sighed with relief. 'Is it enough to topple Thomas Lane from his position?' Serena wanted reassurance.

'Enough? This will surely bring down the *whole* Government. However, I'm not convinced that releasing these to the press is the best way of going about it. This is potent material and needs to be handled extremely carefully. I don't mean to tell you what to do, but it's worth considering other alternatives that might do a more efficient job. Whatever, I'm afraid that all your husbands will be affected as a result, once the party is out of office and power.' Richard expected to see expressions of worry on their faces, but all he saw was indifference.

'You can't create an omelette without breaking some eggs.' Melissa felt a pang of hunger.

'And you don't need your hostage any longer,' said Richard. 'Poor man, you might as well set him free.'

'But he knows who we are. At least our first names,' Delia interjected.

'Does he know why he was kidnapped?'

'He's a form of insurance.'

'What I mean,' Richard continued, 'is does he know about this business?'

'We haven't told him anything,' Serena volunteered when she saw Melissa looking at her sceptically.

'I'm sure if you explained the situation – without, of course, giving any details – and gave him a generous sum in compensation, he might understand and not take it any further.'

'That's what you think we should do, is it?' Melissa said rather sarcastically.

'Look,' Richard could feel Melissa's antagonism, 'I'm simply suggesting a course of action. I'm not trying to dictate, or take over your operation. I shall happily back away if you don't want me to be involved.' Richard directed this mainly toward Delia.

'I asked Richard to help. I think we would benefit from his assistance,' Delia addressed the other two. 'But if you do feel that strongly about it, then say so. We'll only succeed if we're all together. Serena …?'

'We should listen to what Richard has to say – but it must be a majority decision as to what we actually do.' Serena, who still had no doubts about Richard, didn't want him to impose his ideas without consulting them.

'Melissa …?'

'I agree with Serena. We haven't got this far in order that someone else takes over.'

'I'm sure Richard —' But that was all Delia managed to get out before they were all suddenly stopped in their tracks by a shriek from upstairs.

In the bedroom, Henry had suddenly awoken. He'd been in such a deep, heavy sleep, that waking up in a strange place with his limbs tightly bound had momentarily confused and panicked him. While he had lain there wondering what was going on, he had started to hear a weird clumping noise coming from outside. It was like a muffled thud that appeared to be going up the side wall. Thump … pause … thump … pause … getting nearer and nearer … Then Henry had got back his bearings and remembered where he was. A feeling of stiffness and frustration had overcome him, causing him to shriek out in repressed anger, sounding like a blood-curdling lament.

From outside, Rory heard this wail and wondered if the women were being tortured by the terrorists. He now made an extra effort to ascend more quickly, being less careful to avoid making any noise.

Terry and Archie also heard the cry and prepared themselves for the invasion. They could see that Rory and Jack were almost there.

Downstairs, Richard saw the women hesitate about going to investigate. 'Stay here … I'll check it out.' He grabbed his rifle and started toward the stairs.

'The key to Henry's room.' Serena put it in his hand. 'Third floor, on the left.'.

As soon as Richard had disappeared upstairs, Delia collected up all the papers and photographs, stuck them back in the folder and shoved it under the sofa. Melissa and Serena waited in anticipation.

Richard slowly put the key in the lock and opened the door to the room, pointing the gun at Henry, who was wriggling on the bed, trying to get loose. Seeing Richard, he stopped. 'Who are you …?'

'A friend.' Richard kept the gun pointed.

'Friendly executioner, you mean.' Henry managed to sit up and get a better look. The man didn't look like a villain, but then no murderer did.

'No-one means you any harm.' Richard tried to sound sincere.

'Please don't piss me about. If you're going to shoot me – do it. I've had enough!' Henry meant it. His sleep had made him feel groggy and uncertain. He wanted a release from it all. He felt so low and desperate that he didn't care about dying. No-one would miss him … It was preferable to being strung and cooped up like this.

Richard came nearer and immediately felt a sense of recognition about Henry. He was sure he'd seen him somewhere before. Had they met? There was something about Henry that made Richard wonder. 'Do you know who I am?' he asked.

'A hired assassin?'

'We've never met, have we?'

'I don't go to many killer conventions …'

'I'm being serious.' Richard hated it when no-one believed him.

'I'm not in the mood for a conversation – whoever you are. Just shut up and do it.' Henry closed his eyes to prepare for the end. But he opened them again when he felt the rope that was binding him being loosened. 'What are you doing?'

'Untying you. So stop fidgeting.' Richard's strong hands found no problem getting the rope off.

'Are you taking me outside to do it? Less of a mess, easy to bury?' Henry wasn't even bothered about thinking of escape.

'There – you're free. You can go.' Richard directed the rifle toward the ground to try to prove that he meant no harm.

Henry lay on the bed stretching his arm and legs, getting the circulation back into them. 'Free? Why, what's happened? What have you done to those women …?' His thoughts came back to Serena. If she's been harmed …

'They're downstairs. Come and see for yourself.'

Henry wondered if this was a trap; if he was being lulled into a false sense of security, only to be butchered at an opportune moment. 'How do I know you're telling the truth? They might already be dead.'

'For god's sake,' Richard answered impatiently, going to the door. 'Delia, our friend wants to know if you're all still alive!' he called down.

But before anybody could answer, there was an almighty crash, like a muffled explosion, that hit the house and echoed in four places at once.

Terry broke through the front door; Archie through the back; Jack swung in through one bedroom window; while Rory smashed right into Henry's room, surprising both Richard and Henry. 'I bet you didn't expect us, did you boys?' Rory disarmed Richard with his foot and pointed the submachine gun at them.

47

Terry had always been proficient at breaking and entering silently, without causing any damage. He ran into the lounge before the women could catch their breath. Archie bounded through the kitchen at the same time and stood at the other side brandishing his submachine gun. Automatically the two men searched the room to make sure no-one was hiding anywhere. Delia, Melissa and Serena stood there like statues unable to move.

'Are you all right?' Terry addressed them without lowering his guard.

'Who are you?' Delia tried to get her mind back in gear.

'We've come to save you.'

'From what?' Melissa got up courage to speak. She was half thinking about their own guns that were in a drawer nearby.

'The terrorists, of course,' Archie responded, wondering if they'd already been brainwashed.

Terry went across and called up the stairs. 'Rory, Jack – are you all right?'

'We've apprehended two of the terrorists,' Rory called down. 'Jack's just checking the rest of the house. Be down in a sec.'

The women all looked at each other. What *was* going on? 'Terrorists? Who do you mean?' Delia wondered if her memory was playing tricks on her.

'The ones that took you hostage. Were there more than four?'

'Four?' Melissa was now getting confused.

'We've got two of them upstairs and another two we caught outside. Did they hurt you?' Terry couldn't read their faces. Their reaction wasn't what he had expected. Perhaps the shock and trauma had had more of an effect on them than he had imagined.

'But *who* actually are you?' Serena summoned up the courage to speak.

'We've been sent by the Government. At the request of the Prime Minister himself,' Terry proudly declared. He was looking forward to that look of relief and gratitude from them that would make it all worthwhile.

'The Prime Minister ...' Delia repeated, and turned her eyes toward Melissa and Serena, who now understood the situation.

'Do you know where the documents are?' Terry asked, and was puzzled by the horrified reaction he got from them all. Before he could say anything else, Jack and Rory came down the stairs with Richard and Henry, whose hands they had tied up. Jack pushed them into the room.

Richard faced Terry. 'Excuse me, but what the hell do you think you're doing? You've made a terrible mistake. I'd like to explain—'

But Delia was in there before Richard could say another word. 'These men are from the *Prime Minister*. They've come to *save* us,' she prompted him.

'I see …' Richard suddenly closed his eyes to think.

'I'm glad you do.' Terry butted his gun against Richard's body. 'Who do you represent? Your game's up, you know. Who do you work for?'

'I don't work for anybody. Do you know who I am?' Richard tried to remain calm and on top of the situation.

'Are you now claiming you don't know who you are? The boys back in London will get it out of you. Now where are these documents?'

'I don't know what you're talking about.' Richard's eyes quickly scanned the room, wondering where they actually were.

Terry turned his attention to Henry, who was the most confused of all. 'Where are the documents?'

'What documents?' Henry looked blank.

'We're going to have to make it very hard for you if you don't tell us soon.' Terry pointed the gun in Henry's face.

'Why have you tied me up? I'm nothing to do with them. Why haven't you tied *them* up?' Henry gestured to the women.

'You're nothing to do with them …' Terry smiled, looking at the combat clothes Henry was wearing. 'So what are you doing here then? Popped in to sell some double glazing?' Terry humoured him.

'They took *me* hostage,' Henry declared.

Terry, Rory, Archie and Jack all burst out laughing at the same time. Melissa used this as an excuse to sidle surreptitiously across to where their guns were hidden. From out of the corner of her eye, Delia watched her.

'And I suppose they stripped you of your Yves St Laurent suit and made you wear those clothes?' Rory added.

'These *aren't* my clothes. They belong to …' Henry glanced up at Serena and saw her looking mortified. 'I was made to put these on. I've nothing to do with any of them. You must believe me!' Henry felt he could cry. He had stepped from one nightmare into another.

'Are you wearing their clothes as well?' Terry addressed Richard, looking at his ex-army surplus casuals, which Richard wore whenever he did odd jobs on the estate.

'No … but you are all making a terrible mistake …' Richard directed this at Terry, seeing that he was in charge.

'The only mistake we're making is giving you an easy time at the moment. Now I will ask you both once more – where are the documents that you stole from Whitehall? If you tell me now, I will personally make sure that it goes on record that you were cooperative. It will lighten your sentence.' Terry's face was close to Henry's.

'Sentence? What sentence?' Henry's forehead was perspiring.

'Prison, my dear friend. The stealing of government property; the stealing of vehicles – both road and air; the abduction of three females – wives of Government Ministers … I'm sure we could add to that.'

'But I'm *innocent*. Totally innocent!' Henry pleaded.

'And I'm the Queen!' Rory joked.

'This is a conspiracy! I just happened to be in the building when these three women grabbed me. They'll confirm it.' Henry turned to Serena.

Seeing Serena look tormented, Delia, who had edged closer to Melissa, quickly answered. 'All I can confirm is that this man is *not* one of the terrorists.'

'I'm sorry ...?' Terry looked at the others. The whole room went quiet.

'And neither is this man.' Delia pointed to Richard, and at the same time gave Melissa and Serena a trust-me-and-shut-up look.

'What are you saying, lady?' Terry lowered his gun slightly.

'I'm saying what you haven't given us a chance to say, since you came storming in here like a bunch of schoolboys, acting impulsively before getting your facts in order. I'm saying that these two men came to *help* us – after the terrorists left.'

There was a brief silence. '*After*? You're saying that these *aren't* the men that kidnapped you?' Terry's thoughts were spinning. Jack, Rory and Archie shuffled uneasily.

'The real terrorists are *out there* somewhere right now.' Delia pointed out of one of the windows. The troop all automatically turned toward that window. Melissa used this diverting moment to briskly take the guns from the drawer and hide them behind her back.

'If you say these two are *not* involved, then who are the other two we've got tied up outside?' Terry looked at Archie.

'I don't know,' Delia answered, her control and confidence gaining in strength. 'But your terrorists – Middle Eastern looking, with Arabic accents – left us over an hour ago. They had some folders full of papers and photographs, which they took with them.'

'An hour ago ...?' Terry couldn't believe what he was hearing.

'We honestly thought they were going to kill us. It was a dreadful experience. They were brutes, disgusting brutes ...' Delia was on the verge of tears. 'If these two *wonderful* men —' she gestured toward Richard and Henry '– hadn't arrived when they did and frightened them off, god knows what they would have done to us ... I think you should untie them.'

Terry was so convinced by Delia's performance that he nodded to Archie, who cut their bindings.

Henry didn't know what the hell was happening to him. First he was an innocent bystander taken hostage; then he was tied and locked up; then he was mistaken for a terrorist and apprehended; now he was being untied and called a hero by the very woman who had abducted him. Who were these Middle Eastern terrorists? Had he missed something while he was asleep? He looked helplessly toward Serena in a effort to understand what was going on. Serena looked slightly stunned, but managed to give a pleading look for him not to say anything. He was so gobsmacked and disconcerted that he wouldn't have known what to say anyway. Perhaps he'd wake up and discover it had all been a dream ...

'What about the two outside?' Archie asked Terry.

'Was one of these terrorists a woman?' Terry asked Delia.

'No. You've got the wrong people again. D'you think a woman could have pulled this off?' Delia looked at Terry straight between the eyes.

'That'll be the day,' he said chauvinistically. 'Jack, you and Rory go out and find out who those two are. They're tied up by the trees where we waited. Don't untie them until you've reported back to me. I'm going to ring HQ and see what they want us to do.'

Jack and Rory, relaxing their guard, went out into the darkness.

Delia, who was now beside Melissa, took one of the guns off her and hid it behind her back. 'A bit of a cock up, wouldn't you say? If only you'd come earlier …' She moved closer toward Terry.

'If only … one of life's great phrases.' Terry took his phone out of his back pocket.

While Henry plonked himself down on the sofa, totally exhausted and bewildered, Richard watched Delia getting closer to Terry and wondered what she was doing. A sharp look from her advised him not to interfere.

At the same time, Melissa slithered casually toward Archie, who was admiring a painting on the wall. She turned to Delia and nodded.

Simultaneously, in one quick, precise movement, they held their guns to Terry's and Archie's heads. 'Not a sound, gentlemen. Richard, get their guns. Serena, keep a watch out for the others.' Delia smiled.

'What's going on here …?' Terry felt the hard butt of Delia's gun against his temple. He automatically raised his arms.

'Don't you know who we are?' Archie added, seeing the determination in Melissa's eyes as she dug her gun into the back of his head.

'But *are* you who you say you are?' Richard, acting spontaneously, deprived the men of their submachine guns.

'You're making a mistake here. We've been sent from the Prime Minister's office. This is a genuine Government operation. Here's my ID to prove it.'

Terry was about to put his hand in his pocket when Richard pointed his own gun at him. 'Keep your hands up. Henry, would you search his pockets.'

Henry looked up. 'I'll do no such thing! I don't want to know! I'm not getting involved – whatever your game is.' Henry remained seated on the sofa with his arms firmly folded and his head bent. The whole thing had got too much for him. 'God, to think if that bloody woman hadn't farted, I wouldn't be in this mess now!' he raved more to himself than anyone.

Everyone in the room froze, turning their eyes toward him, trying to make sense of his remark. The silence made him look up to see them glaring at him. 'What's the matter? Want to blame me for everything? Why don't you! I've taken enough shit already, you might as well finish the job! This is a madhouse, a bloody madhouse – and I seem to be the only one not in on the joke!' Henry suddenly ran out of steam.

'Henry … Please …' Serena stared at him compassionately.

'And I really fancied and admired you, and thought you were different from the others. But that's not true, is it? You're just like the rest!' Henry directed his tirade at Serena, but was sorry after he saw the hurt look in her eyes. 'I'm going to the loo.' He felt wretched now. 'Anyone have any objections? Or shall I bring down the vase and you can all watch me pee in it!'

'You go and do what you have to, Henry.' Richard spoke gently. Henry's outburst had reminded him of the times when his father, Randolph, had had such a fit. His face had taken on that same crimson and puffed expression. Now Richard understood why he thought he recognised Henry. He reminded him of a young Randolph.

'Your friend has a bit of a problem,' Terry remarked after Henry left to go to the bathroom, where they heard the lock being firmly bolted.

'I think you're the ones with a problem.' Delia had no qualms about searching through Terry's pockets and emptying them of their contents. She found a laminated card with his photograph and Government Department stamped on it. 'These are so easy to forge nowadays …'

'There's another one here.' Melissa took a card out of Archie's pocket.

'Lady, I must warn you, you are interfering in Government business.' Terry thought he would give her another chance.

'I'm afraid I don't believe you are who you claim to be.' Delia took from Terry the mobile phone that he had been holding all this time.

'I have a direct line to the Home Secretary, Alex Brook. He'll verify my story. Let me phone him.' Terry opened his hand to take back the phone, doing his best to remain cool and on top of the situation.

'And how can we be sure it is Alex Brook, and not someone imitating him at the other end?' Richard took the phone from Delia.

'Come on, you guys, give us a break. What do you think you're playing at? This is a serious business.' Terry's coolness was evaporating rapidly.

'It is a serious business, all right,' replied Delia. 'Now go and sit on the sofa like good boys and we'll see if we can sort out this little *misunderstanding*. Melissa, would you like to do the honours?' Delia pointed to the cords on the ground that Richard and Henry had originally been bound with.

'Certainly ...' Melissa set about tying them both up.

'Everything still clear outside, Serena? We've got to be prepared for when the other two return.'

'Can't see anything ...' Serena looked out into the darkness.

Unaware of the little drama that was being played out inside the house, Jack and Rory made their way toward the trees where Archie had secured Scott and Stella. In the moonlight they could just make out the shadows of the two figures hugging the trees. It was an odd, surreal sight.

'Reminds me of my youth,' Rory exclaimed nostalgically as they got within 20 metres of the figures.

'In what way?' Jack covered the area with his eyes, making sure nothing else was untoward.

'Little games my friends and I used to play. One would hug a tree – well, he'd be tied to it – while the others ... No, you wouldn't understand. Being straight, that is. I don't want to shock your sensibilities.'

'I can imagine.' Jack was glad not to hear the sordid details. As they approached, the figures started to writhe, having heard Jack and Rory talking.

'D'you think they're pleased to see us?' Rory observed, but then as they got closer, he recognised the back of one of them. 'Scott? Is that you?'

Scott's movements accelerated as he did his best to nod his head. 'You know him?' Jack declared.

'Yes ... I do ... Oh, deary me ...' Rory sighed. 'There's been a little bit of a *faux pas* ...' He carefully tore off Scott's tape.

Scott forcefully spat the piece of handkerchief out of his mouth. 'What the fuck's been going on, for Christ's sake!'

'I told you to be careful,' Rory reprimanded him.

'Who did this to us?' Scott was still angry.

'One of our colleagues ... thought you were the enemy. Sorry ...' Rory put his arm affectionately round Scott.

'What's all this about?' Jack looked at Rory.

'Would you please untie me from this bloody tree – and perhaps your friend would do the same for poor Stella here.' Scott turned his head toward Stella, who was mumbling behind her gag.

'Stella?' Jack repeated. Then he caught a whiff of her distinctive perfume. 'Stella – is that *you* …?' He couldn't believe it. This sudden surprise made him fart – and then everything went black for both Jack and Rory.

48

Henry sat in the bathroom, trying to make sense of all that had happened. He purposely hadn't switched the light on. He began to doubt his own sanity when he replayed the whole scenario in his head. Perhaps they'd injected him with some kind of drug while he was asleep – a drug that altered his perception, so that he wasn't able to distinguish what was real and what wasn't? Had Serena put something in the food? Would that vision of loveliness do such a thing to him? Was he kidding himself to believe she *wasn't* a hardened terrorist, who would be the one assigned to snuff him out when it came to it? He didn't know anymore. Were the good guys really the bad guys, and the ones that he thought were the bad guys really the good ones? If angels displayed their wings and devils their horns, then the world would be an easier place to live in, he thought.

He must have been sat there in the dark for nearly an hour. He hadn't actually wanted to use the toilet, it had been just an excuse to get away from them all before he really did go mad. He had felt like grabbing one of those submachine guns and mowing the lot of them down – but knowing his luck, it probably wouldn't have fired. He had also considered jumping out of the bathroom window and running for his life; but, aware that some of them were out there, he didn't relish the thought of giving them a reason to beat him up. He wasn't that much of a hero. At least for the time being he was safe. And if any of them wanted to use the toilet, they could bloody well wait and suffer as he had been made to suffer. As it was, no-one came to the bathroom or tried the door. He vaguely heard dull mumblings and odd noises going on in the background, but couldn't distinguish what was what. Then everything went quiet.

Henry listened to the silence for several minutes, then it occurred to him that it was unusually peaceful. He went to the door and put his ear to the keyhole. There wasn't a sound – nothing. He patted his ears to make sure he hadn't gone deaf, and clapped his hands to reassure himself. Perhaps they had all exhausted themselves and were just sat there without saying a word? He had planned to sit it out in the bathroom until he was forced to leave, but now he was curious about what was happening in the house. He was bored and, having calmed down sufficiently, felt ready to face them again.

Unlocking and opening the door, he saw that it was dark in the hallway. He gingerly peered behind the door just in case, and stood there for a moment listening for any noises or movement. Nothing. The lounge door was closed. Henry bent down and squinted through the keyhole but couldn't see a thing. It was pitch black. Were they all quietly waiting in dark corners ready to pounce on him? No, even to him that sounded improbable. He placed a clammy palm on the handle and carefully opened the door. It creaked in the best horror film tradition. He cautiously moved his fingers until he felt the light switch. The light came on. The room before him was empty.

He stepped right in and turned full circle to make absolutely sure that he wasn't missing anything. Empty ... vacant ... uninhabited. The furnishings were as he had left them. Nothing looked disturbed or out of the ordinary. There simply weren't any people there.

'Hello ...?' Henry called meekly. 'Is anybody there ...?' The silence felt even more oppressive. He saw that the front door was closed. He went to open it – but it was locked. The front door had been *locked* from the outside. What was going on ...?

Henry did a quick inspection of the whole house, both upstairs and down. Everything was dark and empty. The kitchen door out to the back was also locked. As with the front one, the mortise must had been turned from the outside, since there were no keys visible inside. He was locked *inside*! That didn't worry him, because he realised he could easily get out of one of the windows, even if he had to smash it. What did worry him was *why* everyone had gone. What was the explanation for this desertion? There were no signs of any fight or scuffle. No belongings or clothes had been left. It was as if they'd gone in a normal fashion, having locked up after them. By why ... and why had they forgotten about him? Serena wouldn't have left him there deliberately – or would she? Was he imagining things? Had it all been an hallucination?

He went back into the lounge and sat on the sofa. *Now get yourself together, Henry and try and think this through,* he prompted himself, as he sat there rhythmically kicking the heels of his shoes against the bottom of the sofa. The first obvious thing to do was to get out of this place and somehow find his way back to London. Unless ... unless they were waiting outside for him. Waiting to jump him when he was far enough away from the house. That was a horrifying prospect. He unconsciously kicked his heels harder and caught the bottom of his trousers on the end of a loose upholstery tack that was sticking out.

Bending down to loosen the hem of his trousers from the very bottom of the sofa, Henry felt his fingers brush against something underneath. He dug his hand down further and pulled out a folder crammed with papers. He momentarily forgot his predicament as he lifted the folder onto his lap and opened it. The first thing to hit him was a photograph of the Prime Minister. He was about to dump the whole bundle, thinking it a pile of political bumf, when he read something that caught his attention: *'Notes on Thomas Lane, aka Pete Darney.'*

Henry spent the next half hour going through all the papers. *Now* he knew what this was all about! So *that's* what the women had stolen and the men from the Government were after. It all suddenly made sense. He hadn't been dreaming it all.

But why hadn't they taken it with them? Surely that was what they had gone to all the trouble for? What had suddenly happened that made them forget the documents – as well as him? One mystery had made way for another. His life really was in danger if the wrong people caught him with these papers. What should he do now? Tear them up? Flush them down the loo? Burn them? He certainly didn't feel comfortable having them in his possession. Perhaps he should put them back where he found them and forget that he ever saw them. Yet he *had* seen them, and it wasn't something one could easily erase from one's memory. He felt trapped again. This time trapped by his own conscience. It was no use, he had to take them with him. What he was going to do with the papers was a question he would deal with once he got home – if he ever got home.

One of the front room windows opened very easily. Henry switched off the light, climbed out and pushed the window from the outside until it appeared shut. Then, lifting a carrier bag containing the folder, he cautiously left the grounds of the house and eventually found his way onto a main road.

49

A couple of days later, a Mercedes came up the driveway to the house. Two figures stepped out of the car and stood in front of the building, both tentatively looking around to see if anyone else was about. Then one of them took out a set of keys and went across to the front door and unlocked it. Seeing the coast was clear, they both entered.

One of them headed straight for the sofa, crouched down and felt underneath. The first sweep caught nothing, the second one produced the same result. 'Give me a hand to move this sofa …' The first figure tried not to sound too anxious.

Taking an arm each, they dragged it forward about a metre. Both stood there staring at the space where the sofa had been. A couple of toffee wrappers, a burst balloon, a magazine, lots of dust … but not what they were looking for. 'If you lift it forward, I'll check in case it's got wedged underneath …'

The second figure pushed the sofa so that the first one could look under. 'Bugger – it's not there.'

'Has someone else got it?'

'Darling, if I knew that, we bloody well wouldn't be back here in the first place!'

'All right, Delia, don't blame me! It's not my fault that it isn't here.' Melissa angrily dropped the edge of the sofa back on the floor.

'It was there when we left.' Delia continued to stare at the floor.

'But it's not there now …'

'I rented this place out for a week. Nobody else should have been in here.'

'Perhaps it got shoved somewhere else. Let's have a good look round.' Melissa was already looking under the armchair and a couple of the rugs.

'*That* is exactly where I put the folder. I'm not likely to forget it. The sofa hasn't been moved. Look at the dust lines.'

'I believe you, but you can't argue with the fact that it's no longer there. Perhaps one of them came back afterwards …'

'*I* locked up behind me. *I* had the only set of keys, apart from the landlord. It doesn't appear as if anyone else has been here. Check if the back door is still locked.' Delia ordered.

Melissa felt it best not to argue at this point, so she crossed to the kitchen and rattled the door handle. 'Totally secure. You want me to double check the windows?'

'You do kitchen, bathroom and first floor bedrooms, I'll do here and the other floors.'

'Delia …' A thought had struck Melissa. 'We've forgotten about the two top floor windows that those Government men crashed through …'

'Shit … I'd forgotten. They're supposed to foot the bill for that. They obviously didn't buy that story we gave them … They must've come back, searched the place, found the folder and left as they had entered. Well ... that was a great deal of bother for absolutely nothing!' Delia felt like bursting into tears.

'We could still try to expose Thomas Lane.' Melissa was trying to be positive.

'Without any proof? No-one will ever believe us.'

'Wouldn't your friend Richard help us? He saw the proof.'

'Seeing and having are two different things. Richard's got his own problems to sort out ...' Delia's heart felt heavy at the mere mention of his name. She hadn't seen him since they parted, both having returned to bleak reality with a sober bump. Losing her memory and meeting Richard was another lifetime away.

'Nothing else we can do then ... I'm a bit peckish, shall we stop off somewhere?' Melissa had eaten more than usual during the last couple of days and was feeling the added pounds she'd put on. Her reunion with Simon had depressed her. It was as if nothing had changed. The personal vows she had made to leave him had somehow taken a back seat. Perhaps later ... perhaps never ... Losing the documents, with all the effort that had gone into stealing them, had drained both their energies and hopes.

'We were so near ...' Delia glanced round the room, remembering.

'At least we tried, I suppose.' Melissa felt like a sad sack.

'And no-one got hurt,' Delia added. 'Having turned the circle – it's back to square one.'

'And Thomas Lane retains his position. Another joke for his portfolio.'

'Let's get out of here before I get too depressed. Fancy some seaside fish and chips?'

'With saveloys, gherkins and pickled onions!' Melissa's mouth watered at the prospect. She didn't notice Delia's tears as she locked the door for the last time.

Thomas Lane was in secret conference with Alex Brook and Charles Carter in his private study. They were all captivated by the computer screen, which was displaying a series of soft pornographic pictures featuring large-breasted ladies in a number of absurd poses. Thomas had come across them while idly browsing. It didn't titillate as much as make him laugh. The one they were presently studying was of a woman menacingly pointing one of her enormous breasts at a mesmerised man in bowler hat and glasses. The caption underneath read: 'Tit in a Trance.'

'I think there should be a Bill,' Alex finally declared.

'Tits to be taxed according to their size,' Thomas remarked. 'The bigger they are, the more tax they have to pay. And we could add VAT to bra sizes over 36 C. That would give us a bit more revenue,' he smiled.

'I meant, to try to outlaw this kind of filth.' Alex didn't see the joke.

'Filth to some, pleasure to others. Whatever turns you on – or indeed off. Were you breastfed as a baby, Alex?' Thomas enjoyed teasing Alex.

Alex sighed and looked across at Charles, who was more interested in the succeeding picture, showing three well-endowed ladies all bending in a row and cupping their breasts in their hands, while the same man in glasses was holding up a cane behind them. This caption read: 'Six of the Best.' Alex moved away despairingly.

'What's the matter, Alex, not to your taste? I always took you to be a tit man.' Thomas clicked the programme off, much to the disappointment of Charles, who indeed was a tit man.

'I don't know how you can still joke at this critical time.' Alex was deadly serious.

'We're dead without humour ...' Thomas declared.

'We're dead if those papers come to light.'

'Have we checked out all the various international terrorist groups who have any contention with the British Government?'

'Nothing's come to light yet.' Alex had reached a dead end.

'What about the Argies – they've always had a beef since the Falklands. Mind you, their meat's still superior to anyone else's.'

'Why do you always make fun of everything!' Alex's blood pressure was rising.

'Because that's why you picked me, because the people like it, and because it's keeping this party in power. The more they laugh, the more they'll vote for us. We all know that policies, however well-intentioned, don't win votes. Personalities win votes – and that's why I'm here.' Thomas was serious now.

'Those papers are still out there somewhere. Until we retrieve them, we'll never be able to rest,' Charles joined in.

'But until that time we must continue as usual. There's no point in worrying about something that might not even happen. Alex, I know you've done everything that you can.'

'We *still* didn't get the papers ...' Alex bleated.

'Your strategy of flying in a second crack team was a brilliant idea. It prevented a lot of unnecessary bloodshed – and as a result we've managed to save the women and not get the media curious or involved.'

'That's right, Alex,' Charles added. 'It could all have got so out of hand. But we nipped it in the bud. You made the right decision in sending in the SAS. There are no deaths on our conscience.'

'No ...' But Alex still wasn't happy. If only he had thought of that second invasion earlier, they might have caught the terrorists and got the documents ...

Alex had tried to contact Terry several times after their last conversation before the troop set off for the house. He had been wondering if he had taken the right course of action by entrusting this mission to just a handful of men. Secrecy was of prime importance, he had thought, but so was the success of the assignment. Would Terry and his merry men be able to handle it? This was what had concerned him. He had wanted to talk to Terry about bringing in extra men, but Terry must have switched off his phone – either that, or something dire must have happened to him. There had been no way of checking what was going on.

Alex had agonised for about half an hour before deciding to organise auxiliary reinforcements. A battalion of a dozen SAS fighters had been quickly assembled, briefed and flown by army helicopter to the outskirts of Perdsea. From there, the fully-armed soldiers had made their way to the house by foot. The captain of this unit had been ordered to search out and reclaim the documents and present them to Alex personally. His instructions had superseded Terry's – but he had been briefed to take care that they didn't end up shooting each other.

Jack and Rory had been just about to release Scott and Stella when the SAS had struck. Mistaken for terrorists, they had both been simultaneously knocked out from behind.

Then, from all sides, the SAS had stormed the house. The 12 men had bundled into the lounge and circled the rest of those present. No-one had had a chance to even blink before, without having to fire a single shot, the soldiers had proficiently disarmed Richard and the women, who themselves had been holding Terry and Archie prisoner. Serena had been so surprised by this raid that she had fainted on the spot.

At first Terry and Archie had been thought to be terrorists, as had Jack and Rory outside. But Terry had been able to prove to the Captain who they were, avoiding any later embarrassment. Delia had stuck to her story about the women having been taken hostage by some Middle Eastern terrorists and Richard coming to their rescue. She had made a point of emphasising that these terrorists had left *with* the documents. There had been no reason *not* to believe her, so a careful search of the place had been abandoned.

After the Captain had reported back to Alex, who had made sure all airports and ferry routes were alerted, the wind-down of the operation and debriefing had begun. Stella and Scott had been untied and released, having claimed that they were lovers out for an evening walk when they had been ambushed. Still traumatised, they had quickly disappeared back to the pub. Jack and Rory, sporting massive headaches, had joined the other two in preparation for the journey back to London. They hadn't got to see Scott or Stella.

This had left Delia, Melissa and Serena. Richard had offered to take them back in his car, but the Captain had already organised flight transportation for them. The plan had been for the women to be counselled and debriefed back in London. Details of their abduction and their consequent confinement had to be logged. Throughout these preparations, Delia had been unable to find an opportunity to retrieve the folder from underneath the sofa. Serena had looked as if she had suffered a minor breakdown, continuing to shake and cry.

The first to depart had been Terry and his men. They had been followed by Richard, who had been unable to get a moment alone with Delia to say a proper goodbye. The Captain had helped Delia to lock up and turn out all the lights before escorting her to a car that would take them all to the army helicopter.

The whole efficient operation had taken less that 45 minutes. And in all that time, no-one had tried the bathroom or remembered about Henry. Serena might have done if she hadn't taken a turn for the worse, but the rest had been so preoccupied with their own problems and secrets that Henry had never entered their thoughts. That's how he had come to be abandoned.

'Come on Alex, it might never happen.' Thomas tried to offer some comfort. 'If tits aren't to your liking, shall I see if I can find a site that specialises in bottoms? Or have you a more capricious taste?'

'How about Iraqi terrorists? Have you tried contacting any through the web?' Alex answered sarcastically.

'That's not such a silly idea. If you can learn how to make a bomb through one of these sites, why not see if there's a who's who of terrorists?' Thomas started to click with his mouse and went into Google, leaving Alex and Charles to make a silent and frustrated exit.

50

The dramatic events of the last few days – which had had the potential to change a lot of lives – all came to nothing. The theft of the papers, the inconsequential siege of the house, changed nothing. All the aims, promises, ideals and personal desires that had spurred everyone on during those desperate hours fell by the wayside, and life resumed its tedious momentum.

That brief, intense period had transported everyone on a diverting journey, only to bring them back with a bump to where they started.

The only people who became progressively happier as the weeks rolled by were Thomas, Alex and Charles. The threat to their livelihoods and reputations was disappearing by the day. Thomas's jokes during Prime Minister's Question Time got funnier, and the party itself continued to grow in popularity. A crisis had been averted, and as a small token of the Prime Minister's gratitude for their discretion, Jeremy Hayward, Simon Dodson and Matthew Croome all found themselves promoted, with their responsibilities and profiles elevated. The party had to stick together and reward the loyal.

The Junior Ministers were naturally thrilled and honoured – but couldn't understand why their wives weren't happy.

Once the debriefing and endless questions about the terrorists and their ordeal had finished – Delia, as spokeswoman, having made up the whole story as she went along – the three women had gone back to their husbands and their habitual lives. Life had became boringly normal and predictable again. Their husbands hadn't changed – but they had. This was the problem. They had stepped from one prison into another, and none of them could see any means of escape. The men's promotion, which before would have delighted them, now served only as a reminder of the illicit farce that was being played out in Parliament. What was worse was that they were powerless to do anything about it. Nobody would believe them without conclusive proof.

Melissa had decided to give her marriage to Simon another chance. After all, he wasn't such a bad old stick. However, things soon went downhill after his promotion was announced. He proudly showed her all the various expensive colognes he had purchased, and told her about his new regime to change his shirt and underwear at least twice a day, having a shower in between. To Melissa, his fetish for cleanliness had gone beyond a joke. She half expected him to tie a lavender bag to his balls. It couldn't have been a bigger turn off for her.

Serena, having recovered from her slight upset, had been happy to be reunited with Matthew. It had lasted only a couple of days before she became guiltily unsettled. His inability to satisfy her sexually was now a problem. He was no different in bed than before. He usually lasted for about 25 thrusts before he came, rolled over and went to sleep. But she had different expectations after talking to Melissa. Since she had glimpsed Henry's penis, the size of Matthew's seemed to have diminished even more. She hated herself for making the comparison and tried to obliterate the memory of Henry from her mind, but the images from the house just wouldn't go away. She wondered what had happened to him. Delia and Melissa assumed he must have gone back with the rest of them, and that was that. He had departed their lives as quickly as he had entered them.

Delia was the one most affected of the three. She realised she didn't care for Jeremy anymore, but she couldn't find the courage to leave him or end the marriage. There was nowhere else for her to go. The only contact she had had with Richard since the siege had been a short, uneasy phone call. Now that they were both back in their own territories, the faint possibility of them continuing a relationship had become even more remote. Neither of them had dared to say what they really felt, and in the end they had exchanged pleasantries with a promise of perhaps having a coffee sometime. That had been the extent of it. Delia was so unhappy that if she hadn't been such a strong person she might very well have killed herself.

Richard, on the other hand, had other things to think about. Since he wasn't going to become a Lord, he had decided to continue with his ideal of trying to become a politician. The by-election for which he had canvassed for before his father's death gave him the stepping stone he needed. He was duly elected as the Liberal Democrat representative for his constituency. His career as an MP had taken off. It was one of the reasons he felt he couldn't get back in touch with Delia. The fact that she was married to another politician would only complicate the issue – and anyway, he didn't think she would want to compromise her husband's promising career. He cursed the fact that he had fallen for a married woman, and vowed never to get involved with one again. Besides, he knew he'd never meet anyone like Delia again. The only way he could forget about her was to immediately take up with all his old girlfriends. It wasn't difficult, because once word that 'Dick was back in town' got round, he was never short of eager unattached damsels to share his bed. He now became more liberal and less of a democrat in his pursuit of the perfect woman.

Jack felt he owed Stella an explanation, but because she had changed the locks to the flat, he never got to see her. She had even had her telephone numbers changed and had sent all his personal belongings to his mother's, while she herself had moved in with an old girlfriend so that Jack wouldn't be able to find her. She had suffered enough humiliation and just wanted to get away and rethink her life. Jack went and stayed with his mother and was grateful for the cosseting he got at home. It also gave him the time to think things over.

And what of our friend Henry? How did he fare in the days that followed his little ordeal? If anything, he became marginally worse off.

Leaving Perdsea didn't prove too much of a problem. Through walking and hitching a couple of lifts, he eventually managed to get back to his London flat in one piece the next morning. The first thing he found was a letter from the Civil Service: *'In view of your non-attendance at the final interviews, we regret to inform you that you have not been selected for a place on the Management Re-Training Scheme ...'*

This really was the final blow for something that wasn't his fault in the first place. Henry threw down the folder of documents, picked up the phone and dialled. 'Hello, this is Henry Drake … I'm ringing about the final interviews … Yes, I know … I was supposed to be there, but … I know I wasn't there; that's why I'm ringing … Let me explain. The robbery that took place in the building … What d'you mean, "What robbery?"? The one involving the helicopter, that took a hostage – that was me … What d'you mean you know nothing about it? … *I* was taken hostage by these three women – that's why I never got to the interview … I beg your pardon? I am *not* making a ridiculous excuse! That's what happened! … You have to give me another chance. There are extenuating circumstances, you must believe me! Hello, hello! … Oh bugger, bollocks!' Henry slammed down the phone in frustration.

After having a bath and changing into some fresh clothes, Henry went out and bought copies of all the newspapers. He spent the next hour going carefully through them, trying to find even a paragraph relating to the events he had just experienced. There was nothing, absolutely nothing for him to be able to seize on to, to give him a good reason to go to the press with his story. If those in the very building denied the incident, then how could he prove it *had* all happened? How could he make the newspapers believe it in the first place? Maybe it would be better just to forget about it and chalk it all up to bitter experience.

A photograph of the Prime Minister in one of the broadsheets suddenly reminded him of the documents he had found. Would they be proof enough? Henry picked the folder up off the floor and looked at the papers again. They seemed pretty authentic and certainly convinced him. If they were what he believed them to be, then he was sat on a goldmine. A treasure trove that would solve all his financial problems and probably make him a celebrity in the process. *Henry Drake, saviour of the nation. The man who exposed the biggest scam in political history.* He'd write a bestselling book; do guided tours round the house where he was imprisoned; make countless television appearances; sign autographs; seduce worshipping groupies who'd all throw themselves at him; maybe even star in the film version of his kidnapping. He'd be the man of the decade. The man the Civil Service rejected! The name Henry Drake would become synonymous with exposure. To be 'draked' would mean being denounced and unmasked, and it would become the buzzword of the year. The whole idea appealed to Henry very much. The feeling of being one step away from fame and fortune cheered him up considerably. Perhaps this was all a blessing in disguise.

A few days later, after locking the folder of documents in his briefcase, Henry decided to go on a little tour of newspaper offices to offer them the scoop of the century. He'd be looking for the highest bidder for the newspaper rights in the material. He'd show each editor in turn a tantalising titbit, just enough to whet all their appetites, before asking them to submit their bids – to be above £1,000,000 – via his solicitor, when he found one, within 24 hours. After which he'd decide who to give the exclusive to. The same would be done over the television, film and publishing rights.

They won't know what's hit them, Henry happily thought, as he crossed the road in search of a taxi. He was on his way to talk to a solicitor he knew from the old days when he worked in the City.

A pretty girl on a bicycle, similar in looks to Serena, momentarily distracted him – and suddenly he didn't know what had hit *him*, as he was sent crashing to the ground.

The last thing he saw, before he passed out, was his briefcase, containing his fame and fortune, soaring away up into the air.

'You 'it him, you silly bastard! I think we should stop.' Barry looked behind him.

Kieran put his foot on the accelerator. 'Should've been looking where he was going, stupid fucker. Pity it wasn't our friend Rory.' And the car sped away into a side street before anyone noticed them.

Kieran and Barry, the two members of the FART team last seen tied, gagged and naked in a ferry toilet bound for Denmark, had been thrown into a Danish prison for several days. It had done nothing to temper their hate and anger toward Rory, who had got them into that mess. It had taken countless phone calls and e-mails to establish their identities before they were eventually released and sent back to England.

Both Kieran and Barry had only one thought in their heads now that they were back in London – and that was to find Rory and deal out their revenge. Nothing short of murder would satisfy them.

51

At his personal request, the funeral of Lord Randolph Montcasse was a small family affair with just Gertrude, Richard, William and Tom. Nobody else was allowed to attend the burial, which took place on the estate itself, apart from the priest who conducted the brief service. Randolph had always hated the pomp and hypocrisy that went with funerals. Apart from the false eulogies, and people attending only to be seen, he had wanted to avoid the family going to the expense of feeding and watering the mourners. As far as he had been concerned, death was the end, so there was no point in labouring the issue or spending money unnecessarily. Gertrude, who was just as mean as her husband, had carried out his wishes to the letter. There wouldn't have been flowers if Richard hadn't stubbornly insisted, and even then they had been picked from the estate.

Gertrude had made a slow recovery. Her mind was as sharp as ever, but due to the minor stroke she had suffered, her body no longer functioned as well. She was now confined to a wheelchair, and was pushed everywhere by the loyal Partridge. Richard hadn't had the chance to talk to Gertrude properly since hearing the news of their adoption. She had purposely avoided the subject and insisted on waiting until Randolph was six feet under before discussing the topic.

Now, as they left the gravedigger to fill in the hole, Richard dismissed Partridge and took control of the wheelchair. 'So, Mother ... But of course it's not quite correct to call you that,' he said teasingly, knowing that she'd react to it.

'I brought you all up from babies. As far as I'm concerned, I am, and always have been, your mother.'

'We saw more of nanny than you,' William responded petulantly.

'I loved nanny ...' Tom added in all innocence.

She turned to look at them all. 'I've always loved you as my own ...'

'Where did we come from? We've got to know sooner or later.' Richard knew it hurt her.

'Barnardo's ...'

'All of us?' William looked at her.

'Yes. It was all above board. We adopted you fairly and legally.'

'And our *real* parents?' William kept on digging.

'You haven't got any.'

'What do you mean we haven't got any?' Richard hated it when Gertrude threw out such illusive statements. 'Tell us the truth ... please.'

'It is the truth. Your birth mothers were all single and died giving birth to you. You were all sent to Barnardo's as babies because there was no-one to look after you.'

'But what about the fathers?'

'Either the mothers didn't want to say or didn't actually know who the fathers were.'

'That all sounds rather convenient. Are you just saying that to stop us trying to trace our real parents?' William felt angry.

'You are free to check. I'm sure they will still have all the records and papers. Randolph and I made it a condition for adoption: the babies had to be orphans without living relatives. Without natural ties, we knew that there would be no problems in the future. So, as far as everyone was concerned, I gave birth to you all. Apart from Barnardo's and the family doctor, who were always discreet, only Randolph and I knew your true history ... And if that bloody old fool hadn't mentioned it in the will, you would still have been none the wiser.'

'You would never have told us?' Richard looked her in the eye.

'No ... and I don't apologise. None of you had a future until we adopted you. To all intents and purposes we brought you up as our own.'

'I still don't understand. How could you fool the rest of the world – if you didn't even get pregnant?'

Gertrude laughed. 'That was the fun bit. Cushions are not simply for putting on chairs. I got to be quite an expert at padding myself to look the right size at the right time. People will believe what you want them to believe. Even the servants had no idea. You were all "born" on the estate, secretly smuggled in from the orphanage. No hospitals were involved. Just the family doctor who "delivered" you personally.'

'We've been living a lie all this time.' William said through gritted teeth.

'My real father might have been a famous scientist,' Tom wondered.

'Probably the village idiot, judging from the stupid things you come out with.' William had had enough and stormed off toward the house.

'Which village would that be?' Tom went off on another tack and followed William, leaving Richard and Gertrude alone.

'Whatever they think – you'll always be my mother.' Richard uncharacteristically kissed her on the cheek.

A tear appeared in the corner of her eye. 'Thank you, Richard. You've always been my favourite ...'

'So ... what are we going to do about the new Lord?'

'I don't want to do anything. The whole thing is so preposterous and outrageous. The family will become a laughing stock when it comes out in the open. *Do* we have to tell anyone? I'm sure if we gave Andrew Lawson a nice fat bonus he might accidentally mislay Randolph's will ... Nothing has been made public yet.' Gertrude always liked to scheme and use money constructively.

'I don't think we can, Mother. Besides, if I'm to be honest, I'd much rather be a politician than a Lord. Can you understand that?'

'You've always been ambitious.' She managed to squeeze his arm, which was her way of showing affection. 'But I would be grateful if you dealt with the whole matter of sorting the new Lord Montcasse out. I don't feel I could take it ...'

A week later, Lady Gertrude Montcasse died peacefully in her sleep. There were no suspicious circumstances. It was social pride that killed her. With the changes that would soon come to Montcasse Manor, she no longer wanted to live. Once she had made up her mind – that was it. No drugs or pills were needed. She said nothing to anyone and outwardly continued as normal. But inwardly it was Gertrude's own strength of will that sapped the life force out of her. She had had enough there. It was time to move on. And if there was another life, she'd certainly have strong words with Randolph if she caught up with him.

'Your mother made out her will three days ago. She must have known.' Andrew Lawson had come to see Richard.

'She knew all right.' Richard looked tired. 'She always said that she'd die when it suited her, not when the Grim Reaper wanted to take her.'

'Lady Gertrude was a remarkable woman.' Andrew felt particularly buoyant, since it was bondage night with the neighbours. 'The will's pretty straightforward. She's divided her assets equally between the three of you, apart from a small property in Cornwall – she's left that to you.'

'I never knew about that.' Richard sat up.

'It's just a tiny peasant's cottage. One up, one down. I believe it was where she was born.'

'She always told us she was born in Belgravia …'

'This came with the will.' Andrew handed him a small envelope.

Richard opened it and took out a piece of paper with scribbled, spidery writing:

'Dear Richard, look after Primrose Cottage for me. If things ever get too much for you, spend a few days there and you will return refreshed. It's not where you come from, but who you become that is the most important thing in life. I love you.'

Richard was visibly moved. 'Any other surprises …?'

'No. I checked up with Barnardo's, and everything that Lady Gertrude told you about your early circumstances was correct. Your real mothers did die in childbirth, and there are no other traceable relatives.'

'That's something, I suppose. I don't think I could cope with dealing with a new set of parents. It's hit William pretty hard. But he'll bounce back in time. Tom hasn't really taken it in, and I'm quite worried about him. He's always lived on the estate. Not sure if he could look after himself. I don't know what will happen if he has to move. That'll all depend on the new owner, I suppose. Any further news?'

'Nothing concrete as yet. He's moved from the last address we had. I've put a private investigator onto it. As soon as we trace the new Lord I will let you know.'

'When you do find him, I'd like to be the one to tell him.'

'Richard, are you sure? Haven't you enough on your plate with your new duties as a Member of Parliament?'

'I feel he needs to be told the family history so that he understands, from the very beginning, what he is taking on with the legacy that has been left to him. I am still a Montcasse, and I want him to become as proud of the name as I am. I want to make sure that whoever takes my father's place is aware of the obligation that has been bestowed upon him.'

'You'll be the first to know as soon as we trace him.' Andrew had been admiring the old velvet bell pull in the corner of the room. The thought of being tightly bound up gave him a pleasant tingling feeling in anticipation of his evening to come. The neighbours were bringing some velvet bindings.

52

Rory was in bed with Scott. They were laughing about their various exploits in Perdsea. 'And when I saw you tied to that tree, I was very tempted to have you there and then!' Rory patted Scott's thigh, happy that he had been asked to move in with him.

'Not quite the right ambience, I think. I was more worried about those bastards who hit you and your team mates over the head. They could've killed you.' Scott finished off the champagne and waved the glass. 'Fancy a top up?'

'I'd like a drink first!' Rory raised his eyebrows teasingly as he watched Scott get out of bed and go to the kitchen. He looked at a photograph of an old couple that was on the dressing table. Scott returned with another bottle of champagne. 'Is that your mum and dad?'

'Alive and well and living in Worthing.' Scott poured them each a glass.

'I wish I'd had both parents … They say what you've never had, you never miss. But I've always missed having a dad.'

'You never found out who he was?'

'Mum took his identity to the grave.' Rory sighed.

'Your father might have been – or be – someone famous.'

'Or infamous. I don't suppose I'll ever find out …' Rory took a large gulp and changed the subject. 'We'll have to start getting ready soon, or our guests won't have anything to eat or drink.'

'It's no big deal. Just a little party to celebrate my new life, and to introduce you to some of my close friends – and me to some of yours.' Amongst others, Scott had invited Stella along, while Rory had persuaded Jack to join them. Neither was aware that the other was coming. It wasn't some dastardly plot to bring them together, just an odd coincidence.

'Well, I like to be prepared. First impressions are so important in this fickle world. So in a minute I'm going to get me clobber on and do a little shoppette at Sainsbury's. Want to push the trolley?'

'I'll stay here and tidy up. But you're not going just yet, are you?' Scott smiled at Rory.

'Want to suggest something to *fill in* the time?' Rory put down his glass.

'You know what?' Scott took Rory's hand. 'I do love you, you know. I've never said that to anyone else before – and meant it.'

Rory was so genuinely moved that he welled up with tears. 'And I love you, petal …' Just as they both got into a clinch – the front door bell went. Scott looked at his watch. 'It's a bit early for guests …'

'And no nibbles on the table.' The bell went again. 'It's probably for you. Not many people know I'm here.' Rory sat up in bed and watched Scott put on his dressing gown and leave the bedroom. He heard the front door open, followed by a scuffle and the words 'Where is he, that fucking poof?'

Rory was about to get up and investigate, when Scott was forcefully pushed into the bedroom. 'What do you think you're doing? Who are you?' he said before tripping and falling to the floor.

Rory looked up to see Kieran and Barry staring angrily at him. 'Hiya girls, this is a surprise. Where did you both skive off to?' he said as if nothing had happened.

'Why, you fucking cunt …!' Kieran took out a gun and pointed it directly at Rory. 'Say your prayers, because I'm going to enjoy shooting those clever balls off first, before I finish the job.'

'Kieran, 'ang on a sec.' Barry held on to his arm.

'He deserves everything he's going to get.' Kieran shoved Barry aside.

'I think there's been a bit of a misunderstanding here.' Rory kept calm. He looked at Scott and indicated for him to keep silent. 'You are rather overreacting to the situation.'

'I beg your fucking pardon! *We're* overreacting? *You* stitched us both up, right and fucking proper. We could've died!'

'If I had wanted to kill you, you wouldn't be here now. And anyway, how did you find me?' Rory was doing his best to keep fully in control.

'A simple phone call to your base office, who kindly obliged.' Barry thought they had been clever.

'Any last words before it's goodbye cruel world?' Kieran brought the gun closer to Rory's groin.

'I was only following orders …' Rory was waving his hands, but still trying to retain his composure.

'What d'you mean? Whose orders?' Kieran was slightly taken aback.

'HQ. They wanted a decoy.' Rory was thinking quickly.

'What shit is this? Decoys are for fucking ducks!' Kieran gripped the gun tightly. His hand was shaking slightly.

'It was at The Dog and Duck – remember where we all stopped for lunch? It seemed that the terrorists were on to us, so we had to organise a diversion to put them off our trail. While Terry and the others went one way, we went the other.'

'Why didn't you – or that black son-of-a-bitch – tell us?'

'Because *I* wasn't told either – until I got back to base. You know as well as I do that HQ never tell you everything. The less you know, the happier they are.' Rory looked at Barry, trying to win his trust.

'We just carry out orders and do the fighting.' Barry agreed.

'That doesn't excuse you drugging us and taking our fucking clothes.' Kieran's anger rose again.

'Is *that* what happened to you?' Rory looked suitably horrified. 'It wasn't *me*. You remember that I went to the loo while we were still in the bar? When I came back, you'd both disappeared. I searched everywhere! Then I thought you might have got off the ferry – so that's what I did … Where did you end up?'

'In fucking Denmark, that's where!'

'I'm so sorry – and you thought it was *me* all this time? No wonder you were both so angry. I would've been spitting …' Rory acted concerned. 'Can I get you boys a drink? By the way, this is my friend Scott – he's a television producer.'

'Pleased to meet you …' Scott got up off the ground.

'Not so quick. How do we know you're telling the fucking truth? How do we know it's not a lot of clever bullshit? Eh?' Kieran was confused.

'Get in touch with Terry. He'll put you straight,' Rory bluffed.

'Sounds fair to me,' Barry concurred, somehow relieved that there might not be any bloodshed.

'You – get in that bloody bed with your bent friend!' Kieran angrily pointed the gun at Scott. 'Bloody nancies, should all be shot at birth!'

'Kieran, what are you doing …?' Barry saw the murderous look in Kieran's eyes.

'What we came here to do. I've always hated homos and their gay liberation. I'll give 'em gay liberation …'

'But but that's not fair!' Scott was quite frightened by now. 'I've only just come out.'

'You're going to come out, all right …' Kieran smiled dangerously

For the first time since the two men had arrived, Rory was overcome by a strong sense of doom.

Three hours later the doorbell went. It was Jack – the first guest to arrive. He rang the bell several times and, getting no answer, started to wonder if he might have got the time or day wrong. He was on the point of leaving when Stella also arrived. They were surprised to see each other.

'Stella …?'

'Jack – what are you doing here?' She was half thinking of turning tail.

'Friend of Rory's. He was on our team. D'you know him?'

Stella nodded. 'Scott invited me. I used to work for him. I was working for him in Perdsea, when …'

'I'm sorry, I didn't know. You never gave me a chance to explain.' She was about to stomp off when Jack grasped her arm gently. 'Please don't go like this. We can't just ignore the situation. Let's just go in and have a few civil drinks. Then, if it doesn't work out, we'll call it a day. Stella, it's not much to ask …' Jack looked like a lost puppy dog.

'I suppose not,' Stella relented. There was no point being childish about it. They had to sort it out eventually.

Jack rang the bell a couple more times. 'What time did they say?'

'Eight o'clock.'

Jack looked at his watch. 'It's 8.15. Would they have gone out and forgotten, by any chance?'

'Not like Scott, I must say.' Stella still felt uncomfortable.

'Something's not right. I can feel it. I'm going to break in …' After a couple of unsuccessful attempts at slamming his shoulder against the door, Jack stepped right back and kicked it in with both feet. 'Something they don't teach you at business school,' Jack quipped before going into the kitchen, while Stella went toward the bedroom.

'Oh, my god!' she screeched. 'Jack!'

Jack bounded into the bedroom, preparing to see the worst. 'What the hell's been going on here?' He looked at the two bodies on the bed.

'It's so horrible … Are they still alive?' Stella scrunched up her face in distaste.

The sight before them was truly unnatural and peculiar. Scott and Rory were bound together like a couple of Egyptian mummies. Positioned back to back, they had been tied up and then completely wrapped around with thick brown parcel tape. They resembled Siamese twins, joined together from head to foot. Their faces were covered and it was difficult to distinguish between them. Yet the most frightening sight came from their naked genital regions – the one area that didn't have parcel tape sticking to it. Each set of testicles had a piece of cord tied around it with a weight attached to the end. It meant that if they moved, the weight would tighten the cord on their testicles and cause a lot of pain. Staying perfectly still was their only option.

'D'you think we might be interrupting something?' Jack had heard of some strange sex games.

One of the figures moved slightly and then moaned with pain as the weight pulled down.

'I don't think so, Jack. They couldn't have done it to themselves, now could they? Come on, you untie those weights from their thingies, and I'll get some scissors to cut them out of this. I hope we're not too late …' Stella went to the kitchen.

Fifteen minutes later, Scott and Rory were lying on the bed trying to get the circulation back in their bodies, having explained to Jack and Stella what Barry and Kieran had done to them. They were lucky to be alive. The most damage had come from the parcel tape that had stuck to their body hairs. It had been torture slowly ripping it off them. Rory hadn't lost his sense of humour, though, remarking that it had saved him the trouble of going for a body wax.

Jack stayed with Scott and Rory until they were ready and able to face their public, while in the lounge Stella acted as hostess and entertained the other guests who had started to arrive soon after.

The evening, which had started rather shakily, developed into a roaring success as everyone got steadily pissed. Stella and Jack found themselves being drawn even closer as they danced slowly to some romantic music. Their relationship might have stood another chance – had it not been for an unmarked DVD that someone inadvertently slotted into the player when looking for a blue movie.

What appeared on the screen was a soft version of a blue movie. The woman stripping and behaving lewdly seemed familiar to Jack – and suddenly he realised it was Stella who was performing! Everyone present was gazing open-mouthed at the recording that Scott had made of Stella in the bedroom of The Albatross in Perdsea, which he had later transferred, but then forgotten about. Stella tried to explain, but it was too late – Jack had staggered out of the party and into the night. Stella felt so ashamed and agitated that she farted. The tables had turned.

53

Henry opened his eyes to find a big, friendly black face staring down at him. 'Hello dear, would you like a nice cup of tea?' The nurse smiled warmly.

'Where am I …?' He tried to turn his head but found his neck achingly stiff.

'It ain't heaven, but we do our best!' she laughed, adjusting the blanket to make him more comfortable.

'Hospital … this is a hospital?' He looked at her uniform.

'Still thankfully open for business. We'll put you back on the right road – but not the same one you were knocked over on, eh!' she chortled.

'A car … it was a car that hit me?' Henry started to remember.

'One of those nasty hit and runs. You were lucky my dear, very lucky.'

'How bad am I …?' He couldn't feel much. His head felt heavy.

'It's too early to call the priest yet!' The nurse roared with laughter, her ample bosom wobbling in rhythm.

'I'm not going to die …'

'Not *today*, no. But you can go home tomorrow.' Her white teeth sparkled mischievously.

'I'm really okay? No broken bones, internal injuries?'

'The good lord was looking after you, dear. A couple of bruises and a little bump on the head. You'll be able to carry on where you left off. Sugar with your tea?'

'Please …' Henry suddenly remembered. 'My briefcase … I had a briefcase.' He could still see it cascading through the air. Probably lost. Someone would have picked it up – or thrown it away.

The nurse bent down toward the locker next to his bed and withdrew the battered briefcase. 'We tried to open it, but it was locked. Hiding all your love letters?' she joked.

'Actually, the contents will probably bring down the Government, if you want the truth.' Henry clasped the briefcase to his chest.

'You don't say.' She laughed as she wandered off to get his tea. 'We hear some funny things in the ward, but that one goes down as today's special …' She continued to chuckle, grateful to find Henry wasn't one of those moaners she usually had to humour in her daily quest to tend to the sick and needy.

Henry was discharged from hospital a day later as promised. He took a taxi back to his flat. While paying the driver, he noticed a funny little man across the road, seated in a clapped-out Renault scribbling notes. Probably from the social security, keeping tabs on one of the many local residents who worked illicitly while collecting the dole. Henry wondered if that was the kind of job for him. He'd like to see justice done, but didn't favour the snooping bit. No, Henry still had hopes that the documents in his possession were the key to his future success.

Although he felt reasonably well, apart from a couple of minor aches and pains, his energy levels were still very low, and he just didn't feel like doing anything too demanding. When he entered his flat, he threw the briefcase under the bed until such time as he felt ready to involve a solicitor and tackle the newspaper world. Another day or two wouldn't make any difference.

His brief spell in hospital had given him a fresh perspective on things. He'd been fortunate in not sustaining any serious injuries. He could easily have been killed or lost a limb or been turned into a vegetable. There was something to be thankful for. But it would have been even better if he hadn't been knocked down in the first place. If that girl hadn't distracted him ... Which brought his thoughts back to Serena. What was she doing now? Should he try and see her, perhaps? What excuse would he have? What would he say? 'Hello, do you remember me? Henry. You kidnapped me and tied me up. Just dropped round to say hello. Fancy a coffee, talk about old times?'

No, that wouldn't work ... But what if he took the documents and gave them to her as a sort of present? 'Been looking for these, by any chance? Any use to you? Accidentally came across them when you left me for dead in that house. How can you thank me? Well, how about some sex? What do I like? I'm not that fussy, to be honest ...' No, she'd probably pass the folder onto that Delia woman and he'd be fobbed off with some verbal token of their esteem. Why should he give them that satisfaction when all they had given him was a hard time? Well, Serena had been reasonably fair. He couldn't blame her completely ... No, that little episode of his life was best erased. The sooner he forgot about her the better.

Henry felt hungry, but found nothing edible in the fridge or the cupboards. He decided to go to the local shops and get some provisions. The funny man in the Renault was still there when he went out. The walk to the shops proved more tiring than he had thought, and he was quite exhausted by the time he reached them. Deciding to stay in and recuperate for the next couple of days, he bought enough food to keep him going. Leaving the newsagent's after buying some magazines, Henry saw the same Renault parked across the road from where he now stood. It looked empty, so taking no more notice, he slowly shuffled his way back home.

He didn't see the little man bob up from under the seat of the car and start writing away in his notebook, his eyes following Henry's retreating figure.

Henry slept late the next morning and felt all the better for it. He promised himself another quiet day to recover fully before getting down to the serious business of copying the documents, securing a solicitor and hawking them round. When he pulled back the curtains he immediately noticed the Renault parked in the same spot it had been the day before. The man inside looked as if he was staring up at Henry's window. As soon as Henry spotted him, the man lowered his head, clearly trying not to appear too conspicuous.

Henry moved away from the window. What was going on? Was the man from the social security spying on him? A few years earlier he had done a bit of moonlighting and signed up for his social security cheque. Perhaps they had finally caught up with him … But then again, they couldn't prove anything after so long. Perhaps the man wasn't a social security inspector. Perhaps he was a Government official … Good god! They might be after the documents. Somehow or other they had found out that he had them … If that was the case there'd be more than one of them. They always travelled about in pairs. But this man was seemingly alone. Maybe he wasn't a government official, Maybe he had been employed by them … In that case – he could be a hired assassin waiting to strike! Some of the most vicious killers looked like funny little men …

Henry's door buzzer went. He almost jumped out of his skin. He crept toward the window and peeped out. There was no-one in the Renault. The man had come to get him … The buzzer sounded again. Henry didn't know what to do. There was no escape, unless he was prepared to jump out of a third floor window. He was surprised how frightened he felt. Yet there was no alternative – he had to face what was coming to him. At the third press of the buzzer Henry opened the door.

'Henry Alan Drake?' The man stood in the doorway.

'I don't use the Alan bit, although that is my middle name.' Henry held on to the door to stop his hands from shaking.

'May I come in? This won't take long.' The man forcefully stepped in without giving Henry a chance to say anything. He didn't appear to be carrying anything, although his bulky raincoat could've hidden a gun with a silencer quite easily. From out of his top jacket pocket he took a small notebook. 'You are Henry Alan Drake, formerly of 3 Rutland Mansions in South Kensington?'

'Yes …' Then Henry's nerve completely went. He went over to the bed and pulled out the folder of documents. He held them out to the man. 'I believe these are what you came for. Take them and please leave me in peace. I promise I won't say anything to anyone. Please don't hurt me, I've just come out of hospital …'

The man looked puzzled and simply continued with his questions. 'Was your mother Catherine Jane Drake?'

'Yes …' Henry was still holding the folder.

'And did she reside at 35 Rydhurst Avenue in Ealing from 1984 to 1999?'

'Yes! Who are you?'

'I'm sorry, sir, I should've introduced myself. Eric Diggins, PI.'

'Eric Digginspi …?'

'No, PI as in private investigator.'

'What do you want? You haven't come for these?' He held the folder up again.

'I don't know what you are showing me, sir. Birth certificate, perhaps? I've already got a copy.' The man gave a momentary smile, which highlighted a couple of yellowing teeth.

Henry put the folder down. Either this man hadn't actually come for the documents or he was playing a very shrewd and cunning game. 'You've been following me, haven't you?'

'You noticed …?' He looked briefly hurt. 'I had to make sure that it *was* you. We can't afford to approach the wrong people in our job.'

'So why did you approach me?' Henry was still not totally relaxed.

'Have you any means of identification?'

'What for?'

'To prove you really are Henry Alan Drake. Just a mere formality. Just for the records, you understand.' He smiled again.

'What records? What the fuck is this all about?'

The man winced visibly. 'I don't think that kind of language is necessary, sir. I'm only doing my job.'

Henry felt like exploding with a dozen further expletives, but wasn't that confident. The man was still an enigma and could turn nasty at any moment. Rather than enter into some shouting match, Henry took the easy way out. He got hold of his passport, driving licence and an American Express card. 'Is that sufficient proof of who I am?'

'That will do nicely – as they say in the ads.' The man actually grinned, revealing more yellowing teeth. A cursory glance at the passport and cards satisfied him.

'So – why are you here?' asked Henry. 'Why have you been looking for me?'

'To be honest, sir, I don't know.'

'What …?'

'My instructions were to find you. Not all of my clients give reasons why they want someone found. Sometimes it's better not to know, if you know what I mean?'

'No, I don't know what you mean. Who are your clients?'

'Ah, that I can help you with. In fact I've got a little card here that I've been instructed to give to you.' The man searched in his pockets and produced a grubby business card, which he handed over to Henry.

'*Agbert, Buller and Cayzer, Solicitors*', stated the card, with an address in Mayfair.

'This means nothing to me.' Henry wracked his brain but couldn't connect it with anything. 'What am I supposed to do with it?'

'They would like to see you. If you give them a ring, an appointment will be made. That's all I can tell you. My part of the contract has been carried out. The rest is up to you. Thank you for being so helpful and understanding. But a little advice from a seasoned hand. In my experience, you don't have to swear to get your point across. Good, simple language will get there just as well.' With a final yellowing smile, the man bowed his head and walked out of the flat.

Henry was left stood there in a daze. Was he finally going mad? He looked again out of the window. The Renault had gone. If he wasn't holding that card he might have believed that he had dreamt it all.

54

The chauffeur-driven car turned onto the motorway and gradually increased its speed. Henry, who was sat in the back, couldn't quite work out the route they were taking. Instead of going into the centre of London, the car was heading due south, in the opposite direction.

Henry shuffled uneasily for a few minutes before addressing the driver. 'Excuse me … This isn't the way to Mayfair?'

'It certainly isn't.' The driver's head didn't move.

'We're *not* going to Mayfair?'

'Going in the wrong direction if we were.'

Henry didn't like the sound of this. 'Where *are* we going, then?'

'We'll be there in about an hour, traffic permitting. As long as some idiot doesn't prang into another. Accidents always hold you up. No consideration for other road-users … Out of the way, you old bastard!' The driver tooted his horn at a car that was going very slowly and holding up the flow in the fast lane.

'I was under the impression that I was being taken to Mayfair. Nobody mentioned anything about a longer journey.'

'Can't help you there, guv. My instructions were to pick you up and take you to Montcasse Manor. Been there before, have you?'

'I've never heard of it …' Henry was confused again.

'Really? Not a bad place. Took the missus and kids there for the day once. Not a touch on Alton Towers, but the family enjoyed it.'

'Why am I being taken there?'

'If you don't know, I can't tell you!' the driver laughed. 'Thought you might have won one of them competitions. You know, free day out at Montcasse Manor by chauffeur-driven limousine. I do quite a lot of those.'

'I don't remember entering any competitions …' Henry sat back in the seat, trying to figure out what was going on.

'Then it must be your lucky day, guv. The funfair's okay, and the actual grounds are quite nice. Didn't care much for the house. Lot of old furniture and things. Never been one for history. But there's something for everyone. I'm sure you'll have a good day.'

'Will I?' Henry gazed out of the window as concrete gave way to countryside. He no longer had the strength to question or argue anymore. If it wasn't one thing it was another. His life had been shunted about in so many different directions lately that he just didn't know where he was. He had rung the solicitors as requested, and they in turn had told him that a car would come and pick him up. He had demanded a proper explanation, but they had stubbornly refused to discuss anything over the phone, and said that it was in his own interest to go along with them. So here he was in this limousine being taken for another mysterious ride.

The sign publicising 'MONTCASSE MANOR – Open to the Public' came into view as the car crossed through some ornate gates that opened onto a long driveway. Henry was beginning to like the look of this – until he saw something that made his stomach churn uneasily.

Above them a helicopter circled. To the left another helicopter stood on its landing pad. What disturbed Henry was not just the sight of the helicopters, but the fact that the one on the ground had a large 'M' monogrammed on its side – the same 'M' he had seen on the one he had been forced into when he had been abducted by those women. The distinctive yellow and red colour scheme convinced Henry that it was the *very* helicopter they had flown in. 'Have they always been there?' he asked the driver.

'Was when we last came here. Took the eldest up for one of their trips. Nice little experience. You should try it.'

'I have ...' Henry felt panic setting in. The whole ruse was a carefully planned set-up. This place was at the centre of the operation and he was being lured into its net. The nightmare had returned.

'That's the funfair over there. Don't go on the ghost train, it's crap. The house itself is just round the corner. I've been told to take you to the family entrance, where the public aren't allowed. Champagne with the aristocracy, eh!'

'Or death in the wine cellar ...' Henry saw that there were quite a lot of people milling about, having picnics, riding ponies. The perfect place in which to get lost, in which to disappear and never be seen again. Was this where they were going to finish the job? When he had got knocked over by that car, had it *not* been an accident? It was all starting to add up ...

'There we go.' The car pulled up at a side entrance that was cordoned off. The driver got out and opened the door for Henry to get out. 'You're to go in there and ask for a Mr Montcasse.'

'Are you going to wait for me – to take me back to London?'

'Sorry, guv. Got instructions to return. Got a wedding this afternoon in Richmond.'

'How am I supposed to get back then?' Henry's fears were growing by the second.

'Perhaps other arrangements have been made. Anyway, have a nice day.' The driver got back in the car, not wanting to prolong the conversation.

'I believe they're going to kill me!' Henry uttered dramatically.

'Don't touch their hot dogs,' the driver whispered conspiratorially, 'or it *will* be the death of you! See ya.' He then quickly drove off, laughing to himself.

Henry watched the rear of the car disappear round the corner. He wondered if he should make a bolt for it. Save himself before it was too late. Get lost in the crowd before being mercilessly obliterated from life.

'Mr Drake?' A dark, deep voice bellowed behind him.

'Yes ...' Henry automatically twisted round, to come face to face with a ghoulish-looking man in his seventies.

'This way please ...' The man walked toward the side entrance.

'Mr Montcasse?' Henry knew it was too late to run away now.

'I'm Tonks, the butler. Mr Montcasse will see you inside, sir. Follow me, please.' Tonks led Henry into the large hallway. 'If you'd wait a moment, sir, I will tell Mr Montcasse that you are here.' And he disappeared through one of the doorways.

Henry looked at the double staircase with all the portraits hung on the walls. One picture in particular caught his eye. There was something strangely familiar about the face that stared down at him. He read the small gold plaque at the bottom: '*Lord Randolph Montcasse*'.

The dark, deep voice made Henry jump. 'This way, sir. Mr Montcasse will see you now.'

'Would that be Lord Montcasse I'm seeing?'

'The Lord is dead, sir ... Through this door, please.' Tonks led him down a corridor and stopped outside one of the doors, which was slightly ajar. 'In here, sir.' And then he walked away, leaving Henry stood there.

Henry slowly pushed open the door and saw someone seated at a desk with his back to him. He gave the door a couple of taps.

'Come in, Mr Drake. So glad you were able to come.' Richard swung round in his chair and looked at Henry. 'Good god ... It's *you* ...' He couldn't disguise his surprise.

'You ...' Henry closed his eyes for a second to think. 'You were at that house – with those women. You had a rifle ... I thought you were going to kill me!'

'My dear man. *You're* Henry Drake ... Well, I never ...' Richard couldn't believe the coincidence.

'Are you going to kill me now? Is that why you tracked me down and brought me here?' Henry was too stunned to think clearly.

'Why should I *kill* you? Please, sit down.' Richard was starting to get confused.

'I ... I *know* about the Prime Minister ...'

'I see ...' Richard's manner became suddenly serious.

'And ... and he ordered you to find me and dispose of me. That's what this is all about, isn't it?'

Richard smiled and relaxed. 'That couldn't be further from the truth.'

'The truth. And what is it *this* time? What piece of bullshit are you going to try to confound me with?' Henry's tone had become aggressive.

'Bullshit, eh? It depends on how you look at it.' Richard tried not to get angry. 'Well, well, well ... You turning out to be *the* Henry ...'

'The Henry what? Stop playing games!'

'I feel you are in for a big surprise. So I'd sit down if I were you.'

'Surprise? I've had them all lately. I don't think anything you tell me will surprise me, after what I've been through.' Henry sat down grudgingly.

'I do ...' Richard smiled and made himself comfortable in his chair.

An hour later, Henry found himself unable to speak. Richard had been very businesslike and dispassionate about the whole thing. He had spent the entire time going over all the facts regarding Randolph's will; his own adoption; Randolph's brief affair with Henry's mother; and the new responsibilities that Henry had become heir to.

Henry had listened open-mouthed. And yes, as Richard had predicted, he *was* surprised. He certainly looked it. 'That's it in a nutshell,' Richard concluded. 'All the details and legalities will take some time. It'll also take a bit of getting used to. Any questions?'

'My father was a Lord ...' Henry said in a trance.

'And now you are. Lord Henry Montcasse.'

'Montcasse ...' Henry muttered.

'How does it feel?' Richard looked at him.

'Unreal.'

'Hard to believe?'

'Beyond my wildest imaginings.' Henry breathed deeply.

'I'm sorry about all the subterfuge beforehand.'

'I did wonder ... This really is all genuine?' Henry was still feeling stunned.

'Of course. The relevant papers are all here for you to look through. I'm here to answer all your questions and guide you into your new role as best as I can. Just take your time. I hope you will stay here tonight. After all, this is *your* home now.'

'I've rather usurped your place. I'm surprised you've taken it all so calmly and generously.'

'My place is in politics now. That's what I want to do. I want to make a difference. Even without any proof, I'm going to do my best to hound that man out of office. Thomas Lane has got to slip up sometime. I intend to be there when he does.'

'I believe I might be able to help you there.' Henry smiled. 'Is it a matter of some documents that were mislaid ...?'

It was Richard's turn to look stunned then.

55

It didn't take long to topple the Government.

From the moment Henry handed over the folder to Richard, events escalated at an alarmingly rapid pace. There was no time to lose, and Richard made absolutely sure that nothing could or would go wrong. He orchestrated the whole thing single-handedly, with such professional and Machiavellian expertise that even the media couldn't keep up with the sheer swiftness of mounting events.

Richard cleverly approached it from a political rather than a sensational angle. His machinations were conducted behind closed doors. The newspapers, in fact, were the last to find out. It all simmered furtively and then exploded like an assassin's bullet striking unexpectedly. One moment all was seemingly fine – the next, all hell had broken loose.

Richard's intention was not only to see justice done and ensure that Thomas Lane and the rest of the party were thrown out of office, he also wanted to ensure that his efforts didn't go unrewarded.

The leader of the Liberal Democrats was the first to know, since he had made no secret of the fact that he would shortly be stepping down as leader. It was on the cards that there would soon be a leadership contest, and Richard put himself forward as a front runner. He wanted the main prize, and he would happily go across to the Opposition and do a deal with them if the present leader didn't support him and persuade everyone else to vote for him. Richard had proved that the material in his possession would give their party a more than even chance of forming the next Government. There was no fight. Richard's natural charisma and qualities of straight talk and confident leadership made him the popular choice, and he soon emerged as the new leader of the Liberal Democrats. It was a calculated and cleverly-timed manoeuvre.

Next was the easy bit. A private and informal audience with the Prime Minister at Number Ten.

'Richard, welcome! Congratulations on the leadership.' Thomas was good at appearing interested and welcoming to someone he had never met before.

'Prime Minister …' Richard smiled, pleased that it was only the two of them.

'Nice to get to know the opposition before we start haranguing each other across the Chamber.' Thomas gave him a drink.

'I don't think it'll come to that.'

'Absolute cobblers, dear chap. You'll be up there with the rest of them trying to tear me apart and get everyone to notice you. That's what it's all about!' Thomas was in particularly good spirits since he'd heard that the American President had invited him over to Camp David for a short holiday break.

'Have you enjoyed being Prime Minister?' Richard looked him in the eye.

'Funny question. Of course I have. Never a dull moment. If you're ever lost for a good joke – you know who to come to!'

'I get all my jokes from Pete Darney ... You know him by any chance?'

Thomas's wide grin suddenly thinned. 'Darney? Don't think I do.'

'Used to be a comedian ... until he disappeared from the circuit ... Was last heard of running the country ...' Richard had plunged straight in.

'What's this all about, Richard?' Thomas kept cool.

'Let me tell you a funny story. You'll like this; straight up your street.' Richard held his hand out, gesturing for Thomas to sit down, which he did after topping up his own glass. 'There once was a Prime Minister who had the brains but not the personality to be an inspiring leader. There was also a comedian who had everyone in fits of laughter but didn't know how to do anything else. Because they looked similar to each other, they decided – with the help of a bit of plastic surgery – to swap places. The comedian, who now became the Prime Minister, succeeded in telling the biggest joke the country had ever heard ... What do you say to that?'

'Bollocks.' Thomas forced a smile.

'Is that all? No funny riposte or *bon mot*?'

'It doesn't deserve one. A bit surreal for my taste. Well, it's been nice meeting you, Richard. I wish you every success in leading your little party. We must have dinner sometime ...' Thomas stood up to bring the meeting to a conclusion.

'But I haven't quite finished the story.' Richard remained seated.

'I'm afraid I have a busy diary to fulfil. If it's three o'clock, it must be the Home Secretary for our daily agenda meeting.'

'Alex Brook, of course! He knows the story. In fact he helped to give it a bit of life. And then there's Charles Carter; we mustn't forget him. He helped to finance some of the icing on the cake.'

Thomas took a deep breath and gave Richard a determined look. 'You can't prove anything – not that there's anything to prove.'

'But I can, Prime Minister – or can I call you Pete?' Richard withdrew several sheets of paper from his inside pocket. 'These are photocopies, naturally. Just the tip of the iceberg ...' He passed them over to Thomas, who scrutinised them very carefully. Richard had chosen the bits that left no-one in any doubt.

'What do you want?'

'There is a choice.'

'A choice, he says? A gun, a capsule of cyanide, or the gas oven? Death by chocolate is a nice way to go – the only downside being that you need a bigger coffin to cater for all the weight you've put on.'

Richard smiled. 'Everyone will miss the humour.'

'There's always another joker standing in the wings ... So what is this choice?'

'You can either honourably resign, with the rest of your colleagues, particularly Alex Brook and Charles Carter, and call a General Election – which you will not take part in. Or ...'

'Or ...' Thomas had suddenly relaxed. As if a burden had been lifted.

'Or I make all the papers and photographs available to the press.'

'A mauling by the savages. Very nasty. The pen might be mightier than the sword, but only a newspaper can dispense the shit as well as wipe it away.'

'I'm sorry that either choice is not ideal.' Richard meant it. He couldn't help but like and admire Thomas for what he had done.

'I believe you are … and since I'm not a total prat, I know it's my job you're after.'

'Only if they agree to change the wallpaper in here.'

'Pretty ghastly, isn't it?' Thomas smiled and held out his hand. 'Well, Richard … thank you.'

'For what?'

'For being fair. For letting me make my exit with a little dignity. It's best to leave them laughing.'

'The documents will stay in my possession until such time as they become irrelevant.'

'You're not going to publish them?' Thomas was surprised.

'Not unless I have to. And just for your information, there are two other complete copies of the originals, which are all safely hidden, and should anything ever happen to me …'

'They'll suddenly appear as if by magic?'

'The power of politics makes ordinary people do extraordinary things.'

'And thereby lies a tale …'

Richard stood up. 'Shall we say one month? Give you a bit of time to make your preparations?'

'I'll be ready to take my curtain call …'

Thomas Lane – aka Pete Darney – kept his side of the bargain. At the end of the month he announced his resignation and called a General Election. A minor sexual scandal involving the Prime Minister himself, along with some financial misdemeanours by Alex and Charles, were cleverly fabricated as justifications. Alex and Charles had naturally collaborated with Thomas to come up with this believable scenario as to why the present Government was no longer fit to continue running the country. The real reason never surfaced, and Thomas's true identity remained a secret. There was shame but no recriminations.

The Liberal Democrats did indeed win the subsequent Election and consequently Richard became the new Prime Minister. Throughout the weeks and months of the campaign, Richard had never stopped seeing Delia. She had been the first person he had turned to after Henry had given him the documents. Since she had expended so much time and energy in getting them in the first place, he had felt it only right to offer them back to her, to use as originally planned. But Delia had believed that Richard would make far better use of them himself. The ends had been more important than the means. 'Get out there and kick arse!' she had instructed him after their first lovemaking session since that time before the siege.

'Only if I can kiss yours first …' he had said, dragging her back to bed.

'We're going to win, aren't we?' She had snuggled close to him.

'All thanks to you. Do you love Jeremy?'

'No. Let's not talk about him.'

'Would you leave him for me? Delia, it's a serious question.'

'Yes.'

'And if I become Prime Minister – will you marry me?'

'Even if you don't – but you will.' She had kissed him then, and omitted to mention that she and Jeremy had already agreed to a quick and amicable divorce.

It had always been Delia's dream to become the wife of the Prime Minister. This dream was fulfilled when she finally married Richard at a private ceremony held at Number Ten itself. It was the first time that a whole Cabinet had acted as honorary bridesmaids.

They lived happily ever after ...

But this is not the end of the story.

Not everyone involved in the proceedings – in small or large part – was afforded an outcome as happy as Richard and Delia. The one common factor running through the events guaranteed that their lives would never be quite the same again – whether the impact proved positive or negative. That inexplicable force that brings people together and shapes their destinies still had a few more surprises up its sleeve.

56

Thomas Lane never really left the public eye – instead he arrived in an even bigger way. He was nobody's fool. He didn't go and hide away at some private retreat to surface secretly when all the fuss was over. He did the opposite. He confronted his public head on, and made such a comic virtue of his sins and misdemeanours, on numerous television chat shows, that he became more of a *cause célèbre* than ever. The people loved his self-deprecating stories, which had them laughing with rather than at him, and before long he was hosting his own chat show. He became a star in his own right.

Despite Thomas's fall from grace, the American President insisted that he and Pamela still come to Camp David as agreed. They used the opportunity to spend a few days in Las Vegas, where Pamela got a quickie divorce from the real Thomas and then married the pretender in a drive-in wedding. The happy couple never looked back.

The real Thomas Lane, once the true Prime Minister, had changed his name to Sidney Carton. It was a far, far better thing he did, than he had ever done before. He became a political guru of the internet, setting up own website, which was accessed by major political figures from around the world. It developed into the most powerful political chat room on the web, dispensing advice and solutions on how to manage people and run countries. He used his brilliant mind to make such revolutionary advances in the political world that his name eventually went down in the history books as one of the great political philosophers of all time.

Alex Brook and Charles Carter also left the political scene. Despite their reputations having been slightly tarnished, they managed to survive and turn their attentions to industry, where they both made a lot of money for the least effort.

Simon Dodson and Matthew Croome both became disillusioned with their careers and decided to call it a day as far as politics were concerned. Simon, after Melissa had left him, opened a couple of successful Westminster restaurants, which were patronised mainly by Parliamentary personnel bored with eating in-house. Matthew, on the other hand, left London completely and became a lecturer in political history at Lancaster University.

Jeremy Hayward was the only one who stuck to politics and continued to play an important part in his party's future. As a leading member of the Opposition, he never lost an opportunity to give Richard a hard time. It wasn't simply because he had lost Delia to him, but because he passionately believed in his party and its policies, and was determined to try to help them regain their lost power and popularity. Jeremy's efforts eventually bore fruit when his party won the next General Election five years later – and Jeremy became the new Prime Minister.

Jack Nightingale, a bit of a lost soul since his divorce from Stella, had had enough playing policeman and soldier in organisations where no-one really knew what they were doing. He took the plunge and became self-employed doing what he knew best. He saw a gap in the market and went into the security business – but with a difference. He trained and hired out bodyguards and minders for the well-heeled and those in the entertainment world. It was at a special function at Montcasse Manor, where he and his team were responsible for security, that he had literally bumped into Melissa, one of the guests. Neither recognised the other from their brief contact during the siege, but the attraction was mutual. Melissa found Jack's natural, earthy smell an instant turn-on. Jack found her ample and voluptuous body, coupled with the sensuous look she gave him, very desirable. They didn't waste any time getting to know each other better. Jack's persistent flatulence didn't bother Melissa in the least. She could also fart with the best of them. It was a match made in heaven. Oddly enough they never discussed the past or what they might have been through, so the fact that their lives had previously touched never surfaced. What was more important was that they had found each other. The past was the past. It was the future that mattered; a future that would give them three children.

Stella's deep wish to have children was also granted. She had a boy and a girl, each from a different father, and even though both men wanted to marry her, she had firmly made up her mind to stay single and bring up her children on her own. She didn't want to tie herself down to any one man in particular; and anyway, she had built up a successful independent television production company that specialised in female issues and concerns. She didn't need a man to complicate things or to tell her what to do. She was more than happy having complete control. She often thought of Jack and what might have been if he hadn't missed their anniversary celebration. Those babies might have been his. When her children got older, she strictly banned them from having whoopee cushions – it was too painful a memory.

Scott gave up the television business. He felt he had better things to do with his life than waste his energies chasing silly news stories. The disastrous incident at the house, coupled with discovering his true sexual identity, had served to transform him. Scott had never been so happy, and his subsequent civil ceremony to Rory, performed by a gay vicar, completed that euphoria. They combined their assets and opened a wine bar in Tunbridge Wells, which proved an outstanding success. The town witnessed so many coming out parties that it superseded Brighton as the gay capital of the south.

Rory made several attempts to try to find his real father and to discover who he really was. He enlisted the services of the British Red Cross and the Salvation Army to see if they could come up with anything. One of them did, but the findings were so controversial that an immediate stop was put on the search. Rory decided to dig a little deeper himself, and discovered a close and important link to the Royal family. But that's another story …

Archie went back to The Dog and Duck, courted and then married his Beryl, and together they went and managed a little pub in Newquay in Cornwall. Archie became renowned for being able to handle himself with difficult customers. Many young thugs felt the force of his fists. However, it was one hardened delinquent who finally got the better of Archie by fatally stabbing him in the heart after a disagreement. Beryl never got over the loss.

Terry was granted the promotion and transfer he had been after for years – to become a Chief Inspector with the London Transport Police. This was in memory of his father, who had been murdered by a couple of young crack addicts while driving a night bus. Terry's personal mission was to make sure that no-one else would get away with that kind of crime. *'There are no bad passengers, only those that are misguided. Set them off at the right stop so that they will alight at their true destination'* – another maxim of his father's that guided Terry in his new job.

Kieran and Barry kept in contact with each other as occasional drinking buddies. It was during one of their drunken evenings together that Kieran persuaded Barry to join up with him as a mercenary. They were flown, with six others, to one of the troubled African states to try to quash some local terrorist activity. They survived many skirmishes during that venture. What they didn't survive was a bomb planted on the plane that was going to take them back to England.

Of all the people involved, the one whose life changed most radically was Henry Drake – now Lord Henry Montcasse. But there was still something missing in his life. Something that meant more to him than the title, the house and the wealth all put together.

57

Serena, having got over her initial disillusionment at life with Matthew in the weeks following her return, settled back into a steady, boring routine. She was surprised how easily the memory of Henry gradually faded away. Absence made the heart grow forgetful – and, after all, Matthew had always been a considerate, attentive and dutiful husband who had never hurt or lied to her. They discussed starting a family, and this was to have been the next step in their relationship – until the scandal of the Prime Minister's resignation, followed by the collapse of the Government, changed all their priorities.

Matthew, whose recent promotion had promised an assured future, was personally devastated by the turn of events. The rug had been whipped from under his very feet, and he landed with a heavy bump. He found it difficult to come to terms with the loss of his position and livelihood. In self-pitying desperation he turned to Serena for comfort. She took him in her arms and gave him solace. For the first time, he really needed her support, and for the first time, Serena had something to fully occupy her.

Unfortunately the sympathy and consolation that she lavished upon her husband soon went sour. Matthew had taken his downfall badly, and instead of facing the situation and doing something about it, he turned bitter and sulked all the time. It didn't help when he was overlooked for a post in the new Opposition party's Shadow Cabinet. He was deemed part of the old regime and thrown on the scrapheap. He wasn't strong or determined like Jeremy, so he didn't fight back. He no longer listened to Serena's sensible advice, or cared about anyone else. She found it an uphill battle trying to appease and inspire him.

It was at this time that Henry decided to hold his first formal party as Lord of Montcasse Manor. The same party where Melissa would meet Jack. Henry had organised it on the pretext of wanting to celebrate his emergence as the new Lord – but the whole thing was really a calculated ploy to see Serena again for the first time since the siege.

With Richard's help, an impressive guest list was drawn up, comprising luminaries of the social and entertainment world. Henry added a few popular personalities that he wanted to meet, and as a postscript told Richard that it would be fun, as Delia was naturally coming anyway, to include Melissa and Serena. Richard had turned out to be a tower of strength and a genuine friend in helping Henry over the transition from a nobody to a Lord. They shared many confidences with each other, but the one thing Henry kept close to his heart was his real feelings toward Serena. The outside world had yet to learn of the new Lord's identity, and Henry made Richard promise not to let on, and to ensure that Delia said nothing to Serena and Melissa about who he really was. He wanted to surprise them – and that he certainly did.

Henry wasn't content simply to greet Serena and Melissa as a customary welcoming host. No, he wanted to take them unawares – as a sort of private joke, reflecting how they themselves had originally taken him unawares. Henry thus persuaded Richard and Delia to help him plan his separate private scenario away from the hubbub of arriving guests. He would mingle with them later, but first he wanted to act out his little prank and give them a good laugh. It would also hopefully furnish him with an ideal opportunity to talk to Serena alone.

In one of the small bedrooms, one that was generally used as a kind of storage area, Henry got Richard to tie him up in the same way Melissa had at the house when he was held prisoner. For one reason or another he had kept the combat clothes that Serena had given him, and so he wore these as an added reminder.

'Is that all right?' Richard tied the final knot as Henry lay on the bed.

'Melissa did them tighter, but that'll do for effect, thanks.'

'You quite sure you want to go through with this?' Richard smiled.

'It's just to show that there are no hard feelings. Why be conventional? Isn't it true that most hereditary peers possess a touch of madness?'

'Well, your father – our father – certainly came up with a few eccentric ideas in his time.'

'I wish I'd met him …' Henry shuffled himself to get comfortable.

'You would've got on. Right, all set?'

'As ready as I'll ever be. Turn the main light off, leaving just this lamp on. Oh, and please close the curtains.'

Richard did as requested. 'By the way, why did you bring that up?' He pointed to the empty vase that Henry had put on the bedside table.

'A little personal joke that they might appreciate.'

'So the plan is that Delia, giving whatever excuse, is to bring Melissa and Serena – but nobody else – up here as soon as they arrive?'

'I've given Delia an outline of roughly what to say. She's been very understanding.'

'She thinks the whole thing's a hoot. I've married someone with a very strange sense of humour.'

'Wasn't it Thomas Lane who said that appreciating humour was akin to appreciating life, and that those without a sense of it lived life like zombies?'

'He's been a hard act to follow … Okay then, I'll go and tell Delia. I hope it produces the right effect.' Richard still thought it was an odd ritual to go through, but it seemed to be harmless, and Delia had entered into the whole spirit of it.

Henry watched Richard exit and lay there starting to feel nervous. It had taken him months to finally pluck up the courage to see Serena again. He could've phoned, he could've written, he could've stood outside her Bloomsbury house and waited until she came out alone. He could've done all these things – but he just hadn't had the nerve. She was married, probably very happily, and he didn't think he had the right to barge into her life for his own selfish reasons. Any rejection would've crushed him, so he had felt it better to stay away and try to forget her. Yet he hadn't been able to, and until he had satisfied his feelings by just seeing her one final time, he wouldn't be able to rest.

'Darling, it's been ages. How are you?' Delia kissed Serena on both cheeks and gave Matthew, who had come with her, a quick peck.

'Delia, you look blooming.' Serena could see how happy she was.

'Can't complain. And Matthew, how's life treating you?' Delia asked, although she knew the answer already.

'Bloody awful,' he grunted. 'To think that—'

He was about to start whinging when Serena interrupted. 'We might be going up to Lancaster. They've asked Matthew to come as Senior Lecturer in Politics. Haven't they dear?' It sounded like a death sentence.

'Bloody hinterland ... What I should be doing is—'

Serena cut across him. 'Delia, is Melissa here?'

'Somebody mention my name?' It was Melissa, on her own, who had crept up behind them.

They all kissed each other warmly. 'Now ...' Delia lowered her voice. 'Before we all get too sloshed to know where we are, there's an old friend I'd like to reintroduce you to ... Matthew, I'm afraid this is a girls only thing. Would you excuse us?' She dragged Serena and Melissa away before Matthew had time to say anything. He grabbed a glass of wine off a passing waiter and went in search of someone to moan to.

'Simon not with you?' Serena asked Melissa as Delia led them up the main staircase.

'I thought everyone knew. We've split up ... Well, I've left him ... I'll tell you all about it another time.'

'I'm sorry, I didn't know ...' Serena had been completely out of touch with everything and was far behind all the gossip.

'One of those things. How's Matthew? He looked pretty pissed off to me.' Melissa recognised Serena's martyred expression.

'He's taken his loss of position pretty badly ...'

'I can see that. Might you really be going to Lancaster?' Melissa crumpled her face, which said it all.

'There haven't been any other offers ...' Serena tried her best to smile.

'So, Delia, *where* are you taking us? A private little orgy with a pride of young men, all very *proud* to see us, by any chance?' Melissa saw Serena wince, but ignored her.

'It's rather odd, really,' Delia whispered conspiratorially as she took them down one corridor and up another small staircase. 'Not that either of us will ever forget, but our little encounter in that house in Perdsea has unexpectedly brought up some unfinished business ... something that we forgot ... well *someone*, really ...'

'Delia, what are you talking about?' Melissa was annoyed because she couldn't guess.

'You'll see. You'd better prepare yourselves,' Delia said in as serious a tone as she could muster, while approaching the door behind which Henry lay. 'We only discovered him this evening. The poor thing's been like that for *months*. How he got here is *such* a mystery ...' Delia carefully opened the door, squeezing every ounce of anticipation out of them.

Henry lay on his side so that they couldn't immediately see his face. Delia's false cough made him slowly turn round to face them. 'Thank god! You're here at last! Could someone please pass me that vase. I'm *dying* to go …'

For a moment Melissa and Serena stood frozen to the spot. Then Melissa, having caught the twinkly look in Delia's eyes, suddenly burst out laughing. '*Henry*, you crafty bugger! Delia – you set us up!'

'Hello, Melissa. Just a little trip down memory lane …' Henry smiled, pleased that Melissa had taken it like a good sport. 'Hello, Serena. A lot of water's gone under the bridge …' was the best he could bring himself to say at that point.

Serena continued to stare in icy amazement. 'Henry …' she mumbled, and an avalanche of forgotten feelings uncontrollably bubbled to the surface, before she suddenly burst into tears and ran out of the room.

'Serena … It was only a little joke …' Henry called after her, but it was too late.

'What's the matter with her?' Melissa turned to Delia.

'She's never been the same since we left that house. I believe Matthew's been difficult. Poor dear, I think she's heading for a nervous breakdown.'

'So would I be if I was heading for Lancaster. There's no social circle there at all,' Melissa said in all seriousness.

'I'm sorry. It was only meant as a bit of fun …' Henry was cursing the fact that he had ever thought of it. The whole thing had backfired terribly.

'Bloody good wheeze as far as I'm concerned.' Melissa chuckled out loud.

'I'd better go and see if she's all right.' Delia was at the door.

'I'll come with you.' Melissa followed her out.

Henry was left feeling so utterly dejected and depressed that if he'd had the means, he would've killed himself right there and then. The only problem was – being tied up rather constricted his movements. In all the concern about Serena's behaviour, Delia and Melissa had completely forgotten about Henry. It was not until two hours later, when people were beginning to wonder if they would ever get to see the new Lord, that Henry was eventually released. But it was too late. Serena hadn't stopped. She had gone straight back home on her own.

58

The helicopter made a wide circle over the whole campus, flying round several times until the pilot was happy it was safe to land.

Below, amid the throng of students criss-crossing on their way to lectures and tutorials, a lone female figure was heading toward the playing field. The grey concrete jungle of the university felt like a penal colony to her. The last couple of months had been sheer purgatory, so the urgent message for her to meet the helicopter had come as a welcome diversion.

Delia had been in constant communication with Serena since she and Matthew had moved up to Lancaster. Matthew had stoically got into the swing of things, leaving Serena alone and bored. As his income had dropped considerably, he didn't think they could afford to have a family yet. Chance would have been a fine thing, since their sexual activities were practically nonexistent. Serena felt trapped and unhappy, and for the first time had confided in Delia totally her feelings about Matthew; about Lancaster; about having children; and even about Henry, whom she had been unable to get out of her mind since that disastrous confrontation at Montcasse Manor. Delia had done as much as it had been possible to do over the phone to try to keep her spirits up. It wasn't until she had felt that Serena had reached a very low ebb that she had arranged to meet her at the campus. Nobody was to know – not even Matthew – because of the security that surrounded any visit the Prime Minister's wife might make.

Serena walked to the middle of the field and watched as the helicopter began its decent.

'There she is …!' an excited voice piped up from the back of the helicopter.

'Yes, Tom, I can see. Now, you know exactly what you have to do? It's very important.'

'I won't let you down, promise.' Tom Montcasse was thrilled to have been allowed to come on this trip. Not only that, but he had been given a duty to perform, which really delighted him. Henry had agreed to let Tom stay on at the Manor, and treated him like the brother he never had.

'I'm touching down,' the pilot alerted them.

Serena stood about 50 metres away, her long hair blown about by the downdraught from the helicopter, as it gently landed.

With the blades still rotating, Serena saw a hand emerge from the open door and beckon her to approach. She couldn't see who it was, so bending low she headed for the opening.

Two pairs of hands were waiting to help her in. She grabbed hold of one, which belonged to Tom. She was about to take the other – when she saw whose it was. 'Henry …'

'Get in Serena …' Henry held out his arms.

Serena froze again. 'What's going on? Where's Delia?'

'Just get in, please.'

'No … I can't …' Serena held back.

'Okay, Tom, remember what I told you.' Henry turned to Tom, and together they forcefully grabbed Serena and pulled her into the helicopter. 'Okay, take her away,' he shouted to the pilot as he closed the door.

'This is madness! What are you doing?' Serena felt the helicopter take off.

'What I should've done long ago. I love you, Serena. I have from the beginning.'

'What …?' She was completely thrown.

'If you care nothing for me, then say so now, and we'll take you back down again. I mean it.'

'He really does!' Tom decided to join in. 'Please stay and live happily ever after!'

'Well, Serena …?' Henry looked her in the eyes.

'Can we talk about it?' her tone softened.

'For how long?' he asked.

'Thirty … 40 years …?' she smiled.

'Sounds fair enough.' Henry took her hand.

'Yippee!' Tom threw his arms up in the air, and as a result of his excitement, suddenly farted. 'Sorry, I blew off,' he giggled.

'I think that's where we all came in …' Henry laughed.

About The Author

Evgeny Gridneff was born in London and lived with his parents and grandparents in a council flat on the White City Estate in Shepherds Bush. His mother and father were both Russian variety artistes and circus performers. His early years were spent touring with them in numerous circuses and variety theatres in England, living in caravans and theatrical digs and being educated in a different school each week – attending over 100 in total. Between the ages of 8 and 9 he shared a large bus with six chimpanzees when his parents toured around Europe with a chimpanzee act. The chimps became his surrogate brothers and sisters. He had no formal schooling during this period, and most of his reading matter came from *The Dandy*, *The Beano* and *The Beezer*, which his grandmother sent him from England.

As a teenager Evgeny ran at an athletics event at the White City Stadium and was the sixth fastest young quarter-miler in London. In his formative years he also spent time at Wormwood Scrubs (outside, not in).

Over the years he has done many different things and tackled various jobs to pay the rent, including:

- a cartoonist exhibiting in West End subways;
- a carpet seller in Shepherd's Bush Market;
- a salesperson at Burtons;
- a teaboy in an electronics factory;
- a graphic and photographic designer;
- a cleaner in St James's Palace;
- an extra in British and Dutch TV;
- a bottle operative at the Heineken factory in Amsterdam;
- a labourer, painter and wallpaper-stripper in house renovation;
- a travel agent clerk and postboy;
- a teacher and lecturer;
- a stage manager in a Soho strip joint;
- an accounts clerk;
- a cleaner with a domestics agency;
- a book factory operative; and
- a ceiling art restorer at Carlton House Terrace.

Later Evgeny trained at the Central School of Speech and Drama and then spent eight years in the theatre as a stage manager/actor working for both the Royal Shakespeare Company and the National Theatre. After that he worked for many years at the BBC as a script editor and drama producer on several popular and award-winning TV series, including *Tenko*, *Blott on the Landscape*, *Star Cops*, *To Serve Them All My Days* and *The House of Eliott*.

He now spends his time writing, working with photographs and drawing cartoons. *A Stink in the Tale* is his first novel.

ALSO AVAILABLE FROM TELOS PUBLISHING

<u>CRIME</u>

PRISCILLA MASTERS
WINDING UP THE SERPENT
CATCH THE FALLEN SPARROW
A WREATH FOR MY SISTER
AND NONE SHALL SLEEP
EMBROIDERING SHROUDS
SCARING CROWS

MIKE RIPLEY
JUST ANOTHER ANGEL
ANGEL TOUCH
ANGEL HUNT
ANGEL ON THE INSIDE
ANGEL CONFIDENTIAL
ANGEL CITY
ANGELS IN ARMS
FAMILY OF ANGELS
BOOTLEGGED ANGEL
THAT ANGEL LOOK
LIGHTS, CAMERA, ANGEL
ANGEL UNDERGROUND

HANK JANSON
TORMENT
WOMEN HATE TILL DEATH
SOME LOOK BETTER DEAD
SKIRTS BRING ME SORROW
WHEN DAMES GET TOUGH
ACCUSED
KILLER
FRAILS CAN BE SO TOUGH
BROADS DON'T SCARE EASY
KILL HER IF YOU CAN
LILIES FOR MY LOVELY
BLONDE ON THE SPOT
THIS WOMAN IS DEATH
THE LADY HAS A SCAR

ANDREW PUCKETT
BLOODHOUND
SHADOWS BEHIND A SCREEN
DESOLATION POINT

ANDREW HOOK
THE IMMORTALISTS
CHURCH OF WIRE

TONY RICHARDS
THE DESERT KEEPS ITS DEAD

OTHER CRIME
THE LONG, BIG KISS GOODBYE
by SCOTT MONTGOMERY

NON-FICTION
THE TRIALS OF HANK JANSON
by STEVE HOLLAND

TELOS PUBLISHING
Email: orders@telos.co.uk
Web: www.telos.co.uk

To order copies of any Telos books, please visit our website where there are full
details of all titles and facilities for worldwide credit card online ordering, as well as
occasional special offers.